1770

Through the Fire

Fiona Cawdron

Cover art image credit: **Beti Bup Design Group**

Imprint: Independently published

ISBN: 9798386634896 — Paperback

ISBN: — Hardback

For all those who have walked through their own personal fires,
who have faced life's trials and tribulations
and come out the other side.
No one goes down life's path without some scars.
If you have overcome, I applaud you.
For those still striving, may you find courage in Ally's story to
persevere and find beauty in the journey along the way.

In 1770, Alison Singleton had a lot to look forward to. That summer would be her first season in London's high society. The allure of dancing by candlelight in gilded ballrooms hid the stark reality that most women of her age would become trapped in an early marriage. When news came from the colonies that her father had to remain at his military post in Virginia, her mother decided to join him in the New World.

Ally had an adventurous spirit. She saw this as the perfect opportunity to escape the trappings of class in England and explore America. Little did she know what awaited her on the other side of the Atlantic. Between the British Army, the colonists, and the Native Americans, tensions were rising.

Act I

England

News

"Ally, be a dear and pour the tea."

I barely heard my mother.

"Hmmm...?"

My charcoal stick glided across the page. I thought a light shading under the chin and a smudge along the neckline should suffice. I liked how the angle looked. Mama's low-cut, square bodice was of a similar design to yesterday's, but today she had on a lace fichu. The material had been secured with an ornate brooch. If I was going to add that kind of detail, my drawing was going to take considerably longer.

"Alison!"

The sharpness of Mama's tone broke my concentration. I might have been eighteen and ready to attend my first season of ballroom dances with eligible bachelors, but Mama still thought of me as a young girl.

"Can't you ring for Agnes to do it?" I asked as I continued to sketch on my paper. I forgot about her dress for the moment and focused on getting the delicate lines around her eyes just right.

Those gentle blue eyes glanced my way with a look of disappointment.

"Agnes is waiting for the post. Although, with all this rain, it will be a miracle if it makes it here before noon," she sighed.

Mama gazed out the high arched window, looking across the vast gardens toward the gates of the estate. Drops of water ran in trickles down the outside of the glass, while the warmth of her breath caused a cloudy fog on the inside.

I didn't need to be a mind reader to know why Mama was so on edge. We'd been waiting on news from America for over a week. My beloved Papa had recently been stationed there. He was in charge of a military garrison sent to protect the settlers. Over the past few years, they'd been trickling into the colonies in greater numbers.

Shortly after he arrived, he sent us a letter to let us know the passage across the Atlantic had been uneventful. We were eager to learn more.

I must admit I was intrigued to know what his new life was like. My guess was that he had been busy in his new role. Perhaps he hadn't had the opportunity to write anything of substance. Papa could talk for hours about the subjects he was interested in.

I missed him terribly.

It wasn't the same wandering around our gardens without him. When he was at home, we took long daily walks. During them, he would point out interesting facts to me. Once, as we passed the hives set up at the back of our property, he mentioned that the worker bees were female. I was fascinated to learn that a single bee produced only half a teaspoon of honey in its lifetime. Since then, I'd become more conscious of how much I spread on my morning toast.

Papa's passion for life was infectious, and I relished every moment we spent together when he was here. I liked that his ardent spirit for life had rubbed off on me. For I was no dormouse to laze away the day and was always looking for some adventure or task to occupy me. My father often joked that I was more like a son to him than a daughter. I could tell he loved my curiosity.

An ornate oval teapot sat steaming on the wooden table to my left. I eyed it with annoyance for interrupting me from my task at hand. I got to my feet, putting the portrait on the chaise. I tugged on the stays of my bodice to make it more comfortable. This dress seemed to squeeze the life out of me. A bit like being trapped inside on a rainy day, I thought.

I poured the tea. As I set the fine china cup brimming with the dark brew alongside Mama, I noticed her hand shaking. Compassion welled up inside me.

"I'm sure we shall soon hear from Papa."

She almost smiled.

"Let me see your drawing, my dear."

As I placed it in front of her, she murmured, "You have real talent. I wish I were as creative as you."

I don't think she realized, but I'd managed to catch the sadness that never left her eyes of late. Secretly, I was pleased with her praise, but I wish I'd caught a smile on her lips.

From outside the window, a sudden movement caught my eye. A horse and its owner were trotting beside the bright yellow spring daffodils that lined the drive.

"Mama, a rider."

She shrieked when I announced the arrival of the post. She flew downstairs with the grace that might have come from someone many years her junior. It was comical to see her unbridled enthusiasm. I followed her downstairs, rushing along in her wake. We made our way through the large front doors to the portico. Mama couldn't keep still. She paced back and forth, willing the man to quicken his pace.

Agnes was redundant, as no sooner had the rider come to a stop than Mama was right beside him, clamoring for the mail. She paid no attention to her hair, now damp from the rain, that clung in wispy strands to her nape.

"You'll be happy to get this, my lady, no doubt," he said as he took the letter from his leather satchel.

A quick nod was all that was afforded him.

Agnes paid the man his coin as he tightened his coat about him. After a friendly wave, he set back off in the English drizzle.

"Let's read it by the fire, Ally," Mama squealed.

Back upstairs, some semblance of normality had returned. Mama patted the water drips on her face with her handkerchief as the fire's comforting warmth calmed us both.

She was hesitant to open the much-anticipated letter.

"Do you want me to read it to you?"

She thrust the letter into my outstretched hand and played with her fingers nervously.

Breaking the red wax seal, I wondered if this letter would contain the news my mother desired.

I skimmed the text to ensure I would not be surprised by anything I encountered. Within the first few lines, I could tell all was well.

For the next few minutes, tales of daring rescues and determined survival entertained our ears. His stories made it sound more heroic than I surmised. I had heard about the many fatalities that occurred in America due to disease and other hardships. It was not an easy life. As I neared the end of the letter, my heart sank. It would be a very long time before my father returned to us. It wouldn't be the simple transfer of leadership to another colonel that had been expected.

As I glanced up, I saw a determined look settle upon my mother's face. She was a devoted wife and loved her husband. Papa's career had tried and tested her patience before. Their constant separation caused her more anxiety each time. This was to be my father's final commission. Six months at most was what his superiors had told him. It had already been longer than that.

"Ally, you're not going to be happy with me."

"Why do you say that, Mama?" I asked.

"Well, we've been busy preparing for your debut into high society, and now I'm afraid I am going to ruin it for you."

She couldn't look at me. Her hands were clasped tightly in her lap.

"I can't abide here," she said. "It's doing me in, constantly waiting to hear from your father. I must join him in America. From what he's mentioned in his letter, his appointment won't end anytime soon. If I don't sail before winter, I may have to wait another year. I'm sorry if that isn't what you wanted to hear. The timing couldn't be worse, could it? I know you were looking forward to going to London and attending the balls for the start of the season."

Mama was right. My entrance into my first season was what most girls my age longed for. There was no other choice—that was what young ladies did in England. Yet deep down, I knew I wasn't ready to be tied down like a mare in the stables. That's the image that came to mind when I thought of marriage. I had only just finished my formal education. I knew plenty of facts but little about how life operated in the real world. What I lacked was experience. Did I want to go through a season and stay in England without my mother? As it was, it already felt as though I was waiting in limbo until something better came along. Would that be living with a tolerable husband in a tolerable house? Then, once again, I would be waiting for something else to happen. Children, perhaps? The idea wasn't appealing in the least—not the children part—but being stuck in one place with one circle of friends and relatives. The monotony of the endless years ahead of me appeared as restricting to me as the corset wrapped around my ribcage. My heart yearned for something more. Up until this point in time, I had been unable to voice these concerns to my mother.

But America? Young women didn't go to America unless they wanted colonial life. Still, the prospect of such an adventure thrilled me. The new world offered new opportunities. I likened it to a sweet treat being offered at afternoon tea. At first, only one slice of cake was offered, but then another equally delicious, different morsel was displayed. Choice—that's what I wanted. It was a heady mix when previously you only had one option.

Mama looked up at me, and another thought occurred to her.

"Ally, you could still have your season. I can make arrangements for your Aunt Mary to chaperone you. She is already in London and has seen your two cousins well suited. Although how can I miss my only daughter's coming out into polite society?"

She was torn. I could see that. Her hasty decision to leave now would rob us of a special time we should've shared together.

I took her hands in mine. My mind had reached a conclusion.

"Mama, when I have my season, I want you there with me, not Aunt Mary. There is still plenty of time. I don't mind waiting a year or so. Having the chance to visit Papa and see another part of the world is terribly exciting."

She smiled at me. "Really?"

I nodded.

She clapped her hands together in delight. "When have you not been up for a challenge, my darling girl?"

I smiled. That was probably the first time my inquisitive nature had pleased her.

She said, "It's such a waste not to use at least some of those new gowns." She looked thoughtful once more. "Why don't I talk to Lord Addington and find out the best time for sailing? You never know. You may be able to attend a couple of balls and see what all the fuss is about. London is on the way to Southampton, after all."

Mama was being kind. I must admit I was intrigued by the prospect. Being able to sample the grandeur of the most highly prized social event of the year without having to sell my soul was tempting. The mention of our friend and neighbor was also a good idea. As he was the owner of the largest shipping company in England, he'd know the sailing conditions on the ocean at this time of year.

My thoughts returned to London and how my friends would be spending their summer. Many of them had gotten themselves worked up about gaining a match in their first season. Their own mothers often contributed to this. To not receive an offer of marriage was seen as a failure. That seemed like way too much pressure to put on oneself. Others would hold out for titles or wealth, but none of that had ever appealed to me. Most of those marriages would end up where they could hardly stand the sight of each other. Couples lived separate lives in different estates. I wanted a home filled with love and affection, and I didn't think that sort of thing could be forced. What did it matter if I waited? Why were men not encouraged to marry as soon as they came of age? They had the freedom to choose when they wanted to settle down. I suppose they had their careers to think about, but it was unfair that the same standard didn't apply to women.

Going to America would be a chance to experience more than crowded ballrooms and a hasty courtship. The more I thought about it, the more I liked the idea of accompanying my mother, but a niggle of doubt still plagued my mind. It was a big decision. I wondered if I would even like it over there. Our tea had long since gone cold, but Mama didn't seem to care anymore.

Changes

Life until this point, had been a peaceful easy existence. Growing up on our country estate was idyllic. Not only did I have the luxury of private tutors who schooled me in any number of fascinating topics, I also had a working estate on which to escape. Getting out in nature allowed me to understand these heady topics with a healthy dose of reality. Still, despite all this, I felt something was lacking. I had yet to experience any place beyond my own isolated world. The furthest I'd traveled south was to the Salisbury Plain in Wiltshire. Here I was able to visit Stonehenge. Its prehistoric monuments towered over me as a girl and posed many questions to my enquiring young mind. However, it was always my home that felt like a comforting blanket. Somewhere I was safe, someplace I could always come back to.

Our home, North Hill Estate, was gifted to Mama for her dowry upon her mother's death. My grandmother, Lady Catherine, had outlived her husband, the Earl of Cambridge, by thirty-four years. Being blessed with only two daughters and no other male relatives, the Earl had placed his daughters in a unique position. They were more fortunate than most because they had their choice of suitors. Mama's elder sister, Mary, couldn't abide the country, so she wisely inherited the well-appointed townhouse in London. My mother was thrilled to reside at the country estate once she married my father. Although she held the title of Lady, she preferred to be known as the wife of a colonel. For her, Papa's service meant more than the privilege of her class. I loved the way she chose her own path rather than accepting what society dictated, and I felt the same way. Life was to be lived, not endured.

Mama was frantically ordering the household staff around like a sergeant major readying for battle. All that needed doing was packing a few trunks for a month-long sea voyage. But that was Mama. She worried over the smallest things.

To say I wasn't nervous about our venture would have been a lie. The unknown was scary. I would be secure if I stayed here. On the other hand, the realization that I would not be with the two most influential people in my life made my choice easy.

Mama fluffed about my room removing dresses from a large chest at the end of my bed. She laid the garments in two piles, one to go and one to stay.

"To be honest, Mama, the more I think about it, the more excited I become."

I was caught up in the act of action itself.

"I'm glad to hear that," she said, stopping her sorting for a moment. "This will undoubtedly be your biggest adventure yet."

She smiled.

My whole world had been turned around. Suddenly, I was heading in a new direction.

I sat on the floor in the middle of my room, deciding what I would take with me. The patterned rug was littered with what I thought were sensible choices. My drawing supplies, for sure. Choosing between books from our library was a problem. Looking through them, I limited myself to two: *Lord Callister's Poetry* and a book entitled *The Naturalist's Look at England*. At least I could remind myself of home if I missed it too much. Whereas poetry would soothe my creative side.

Looking at the pile of elegant dresses Mama had picked, I wondered if any of them would be suitable. The skirts were adorned with lace and fancy stitching. They were beautiful, but how practical would they be on the dusty ground of Virginia? I was a girl who liked knowing what she was getting herself in for. Even with the little I knew about our destination, I doubted there was any use for hooped petticoats. These cumbersome additions were a hindrance used to impress others. I couldn't see how they would serve any purpose in the New World.

Agnes entered my room carrying a note. Her long black skirt swished as she tried to dodge the assortment of items strewn across my floor.

"This arrived for you, Miss Ally. It's from the Addingtons."

My best friend in the whole world was Margaret Addington, or Maggie, as everyone called her.

"Thank you, Agnes. Is their driver still here?" I wondered if Maggie was waiting for my reply.

"No, Miss, he headed back straight away. The weather is still pretty miserable."

I nodded.

The dark skies outside had made the servants light the candles early, even though it was only mid-afternoon. Their reflection shone off the glossy surface of the oak furniture.

When I had written and told Maggie of our news of traveling to America a couple of days ago, she'd been devastated. We'd grown up together and now we'd be separated by an ocean. I had wanted her to hear it from me in person, as I knew Mama had already drafted a note to her father, and I didn't want her to hear it secondhand. Rhett, her older brother, had just returned from the colonies himself. Rhett had been my childhood crush. When I thought about him, my heart beat a little faster. When we were younger, I tried not to let him see how much he meant to me. He was eight years my senior and would often look at me like an annoying gnat that needed to be swatted away. Even so, the three of us had formed a strong bond. Having no siblings of my own, they were like family to me. When I wasn't at home, you could always find me on the Addington's estate, which was next to ours.

Maggie had constantly teased me about her brother. She'd known how I felt about him almost as long as I had known myself. It was impossible to hide anything from her. Neither of us had seen him in nearly three years. While in America, he was promoted to captain. I wondered what had prompted his return home now. It was bittersweet for Maggie as she was getting one of us back, only to lose the other.

I opened the damp paper and read its contents. Several of the words were smudged, but I could still read them.

Ally,

I hope you are free tonight to join us for dinner and that the wet weather will not put you off. Don't know why I wrote that. It would take a team of wild horses to drag you away from what I am about to tell you. It's been ever so hard to correspond by way of letter this past week with all these goings on. If I see one more rainy day, I shall scream. You know I would. Rhett will be here tonight as his recent return and promotion is cause for a special celebratory dinner. Mother said it would not be the same if you were not here with us. I quite agree. Aren't you interested in seeing him? Ha, I know you are. Besides, we have much to discuss, as you well know. Come as soon as you are able.

Love Maggie

My heart raced. Rhett would be there! I wondered how he'd view me now that I was not such a gangly young girl. I had filled out in all the right places. Would he even notice? I would make sure he did.

Agnes was busy picking up the discarded clothes by my bed, folding them with care to return them back to the chest.

"Agnes, no time for that now. I have to get ready for dinner at the Addington's manor. What time is it?"

"Two o'clock, Miss."

"Good. If we hurry, I can be there by four."

Mama chided me, "I suppose you want me to clean up this mess?"

I looked up, ashamed, not wanting to cause her any stress.

She waved her arms around, indicating the ruinous state of my bed chamber.

The smile lines around her mouth told me she was playing with me.

"Go," she said. "Enjoy yourself. I know you have been itching to get over and see Maggie."

"Rhett will be there, too," I added.

"Will he now? I better tell Fred to get the chaise ready then. I've had enough packing for one day anyway."

Winking at Agnes, she closed the travel trunk with a flourish.

Ours was an older chaise with a black buggy set over aging wooden wheels. It was designed for a single horse, which had the advantage of being quite agile, although it couldn't carry more than two passengers.

"I'll leave you two so you can get ready."

She kissed me on the top of my head.

"Oh," she said. "Might I suggest the blue silk?"

She picked up one of the dresses meant for London and laid it on my bed.

"But Mama, that is one of my best ball gowns. Won't I be a little overdressed?"

"Nonsense. If the Addingtons can't see you looking your best, then who can? You have plenty of other dresses with which to impress the gentlemen in London. Now make haste. You're wasting precious time."

Perhaps she was right. The idea of dressing up for Rhett held enormous appeal.

I sat in front of my wooden dresser, looking at my reflection in the mirror.

"What can you do with my hair, Agnes? Make me look like a real lady."

15

She giggled, "You are a real lady already, Miss, but I have some tricks up my sleeve. Are you trying to impress a certain someone?"

She knew me too well. Agnes had been with our family since I was born, and I probably depended on her too much. This was a fact I realized would not continue for much longer. She glided the silver hairbrush in slow strokes, smoothing my naturally wavy long blonde hair.

I felt guilty. "Agnes, I never asked you how you feel about us leaving?"

The hair brush stopped, and she looked at me. A sad expression lingered on her features.

"I will miss you all, that's for certain. It won't be the same working for someone else."

What! My hand darted to my throat. "Surely you will wait here with the rest of the staff for our return."

"When would that be, Miss? A house without family means a house without staff."

Mother hadn't mentioned any of this.

A thought occurred to me, "What about the grounds and the horses? You can't just ignore those things."

"I believe she has asked the Addingtons to take care of that."

I turned to face her, still in shock.

"Where will you go? I might not see you again."

Tears started running unchecked down my cheeks.

"Don't worry, Miss Ally, when you come back, I'll hear of it and come knocking on your door again. I should imagine most of the staff will. Your mother has been good to us. Now stop this crying. You're starting me off, and you don't want your red eyes to be your most dominant feature tonight, do you? She handed me a hanky and patted her own eyes with her apron.

"We're a right pair, aren't we, Miss?"

My mood was as damp as the grey skies outside.

She added, "Come on. Before you go, I'll show you a few simple hairstyles so you won't feel helpless without me in America."

"I don't have time for that, Agnes," I complained.

"We've got weeks yet, remember," she answered, soothing my jagged emotions.

She smiled at me as she fixed my hair expertly and fastened it with pins. It was a work of art.

She was right. There was no use being down in the dumps. I would see her when I got back. Still, I felt terrible that her life would change so much. But that was how life was for the servants. Nothing stayed the same for long. Change need not be bad. I hoped this would give Agnes and the rest of the staff a fresh start.

After getting dressed, I headed down the stairs.

My mother smiled. "We can talk about your evening tomorrow. I think I'll retire to bed early tonight. All this decision-making has quite worn me out."

She stifled a yawn.

"You look lovely, by the way."

I had to admit that the bright blue silk did bring out a similar colored hue in my eyes.

She held out my plain woolen cape, which seemed out of place over such a fancy dress.

"You still need to keep warm," she reminded me. "We don't want you catching a chill."

I decided not to ask my mother about the staffing arrangements. There would be plenty of time for that later. I would make sure Agnes received the highest recommendation so she'd be assured of a good position. Besides, Mother had already admitted she was weary. The last thing she needed was for me to question her about it now. I knew she would be as devastated as me to see them all leave.

Normally, I'd walk the quarter-mile down the lane to Maggie's home. That would never be possible in this dress. As it was, I had to hold my skirts up and dodge the puddles to get onto my ride. My shoes were covered in tiny white fabric rosettes - an entirely unsuitable outfit for traveling down a muddy country lane. I felt like an imposter to be dressed this way. It didn't feel like the real me at all, but rather like a singer at an opera, dressed to delight an audience.

The covered buggy rocked gently on the cobblestones as I rode down our driveway with Fred, our stable hand.

"You're looking right fancy tonight, Miss Ally," he said. "Special night, is it?"

"You could say that, Fred." I smiled at him. His weathered, wrinkled hands steadied the buggy with care.

I asked, "Are you fine to stay and wait for me until after dinner tonight? I would hate to think you had to come back in the dark to collect me."

"Don't worry yourself about it, Miss. I don't mind waiting in the least. You know as well as I that the Addingtons have the best cook around these parts. Madame DuPont always gives me a good feed, and besides, she tells the most fascinating stories about her homeland. That's not to say Miss Finch isn't good at her meals."

His reference to our housekeeper was amusing. I'd always suspected there was more to their relationship than they let on.

He changed the subject.

"Would you look at that?" Fred exclaimed. "Makes you feel like everything is going to be all right in the world, doesn't it, Miss?"

A magnificent sunset lit the surrounding fields. For the briefest moment, the grey skies had parted and nature had put on a spectacular display. Tinges of orange, red and pink blended together, stretching across the sky.

"Yes, it does, Fred. Yes, it does."

Dinner

It didn't take long before the entranceway to the Addington's estate came into view. Well-trimmed trees lined either side of the long drive, if you could call it a drive. It was more like a road. Whereas our home was modest, the Addington's was one of the finest estates in the county.

As children, Rhett, Maggie and I raced the length of this path many times. We were always left panting by the end of it. Thinking of that memory made me smile.

As we rounded the bend, a three-storied mansion came into view. Its simplistic rectangular design was anything but plain. Each floor facing the vast courtyard had nine windows. The tan-colored stone stood in contrast to the rambling ivy that covered it. In front of the house was a large lake. To my delight, several of the resident swans had fluffy, grey goslings following close behind. We crossed a small bridge. The clatter of the wheels changed as they rode over pebbles on the other side, announcing our arrival.

"Here we are, then," Fred said as he stopped the carriage in front of Addington House.

Maggie was there waiting for me. She waved enthusiastically. For a moment, I thought I saw her big brown eyes blinking away tears.

As soon as I'd stepped down from the carriage, I was enveloped in a tight hug. I was thrilled to see her as well.

"It has been far too long," she said.

"I know."

In fact, it had been a little over a week, yet so much had happened. It felt like a lot longer.

"Oh, my God, Agnes has outdone herself. You look amazing."

She took my hand and twirled me around like a spinning top.

Several strands of my hair had come unstuck due to Maggie's enthusiasm, but I paid it no mind.

"My, my, what are you wearing?" she said.

She opened my cloak to inspect my new dress.

"Do you like it?" I asked. "It's new."

"Like it, I love it. Your mama has good taste, and that bust line - Ooh la la!"

I chuckled.

"I feel positively naughty," I admitted.

Maggie was as close as I would ever come to having a sister. We shared everything.

There was one thing I was dying to know. Maggie was a year older than me and had been to London last season, where she'd set her heart upon a gentleman, Charles Alistair McKenzie. Recently he'd come to visit her at home, but because of the awful weather, I hadn't had the opportunity to visit or ask her about it. It wasn't something Maggie could have shared in her notes with me, as my mother would often want to hear what she'd written.

My curiosity got the better of me.

"What news of Charles?"

"Oh, look at what I've done," she said, noticing my hair.

"Don't worry about that—what of your news?"

She looked coy, but immediately a wide smile beamed across her face.

"I'm so hopeful, Ally. We had a lovely time in the parlor. Mother even allowed us some private time, and Charles and I shared our first kiss."

I stood there with my mouth agape. At this moment, Rhett decided to come striding out of the entranceway. This was not how I wanted him to see me, looking like a disheveled carp coming up for air.

"Aren't you a sight?" he teased.

I couldn't tell if his comment was meant to be a compliment or not. He did his best to tuck the stray pieces of hair behind my ear, brushing my neck ever so slightly as he did so. I shivered at his touch.

"You have turned into quite the stunner, Miss Singleton. It's good to see you again."

I blushed at his words.

"You, too." I echoed.

"You think me stunning. I'm taken aback at your boldness, my lady," he grinned.

"Oh, Rhett, leave her be," Maggie said. "You can't tease Ally like you used to."

"Why ever not? It was a pastime I was quite fond of."

Large raindrops started to fall on the ground, peppering us relentlessly.

"Let's go inside," he suggested.

He was right, in any case. I did think him stunning. In his long blue velvet tailored jacket, he cut a fine figure. His dark hair was thick and wavy. It was tied at the back with a matching blue ribbon. On some men, mid-length hair looked silly, but not on him. He was handsome. His eyes were a deep chocolate brown. His mouth, I thought, was his most attractive feature. Many times I had imagined kissing his lips. None of these things had changed since I last saw him. Now, a certain self-assuredness radiated from him. As I looked at his broad back, I couldn't help but admire the man he'd become. He had a muscular presence about him. Perhaps it was the hard toil of working in America. Usually, the gentry's only excuse for exercise was taking their horses out for the occasional gallop or to go off hunting. With Rhett, though, there was no pretense. I watched him walk ahead and thought it was a shame he'd come back home. Being in the regiment stationed in Jamestown would've given us time to spend together. Now that was no longer a possibility. I sighed inwardly at that lost opportunity.

The Addington's home was just as impressive inside as out. The foyer was the size of several rooms. A wide staircase, covered in a fine burgundy carpet, branched off in two directions. It was the perfect complement to the dark stained wood that dominated the interior. Various tables held all manner of oddities that Lord Addington had collected from exotic ports. There were ornate vases set alongside the bust of a roman senator and a colorful stuffed parrot from who knew where. The bird's bright feathers were in sharp contrast to the rest of the house. I was reminded of Montague House, the British Museum in London. Everything in this house was a wonder.

Rhett took my cloak, and his eyes swept over me with appreciation.

He smiled.

"I feel like I need to whisk you off to London. I think the season has started already."

I bowed my head, embarrassed.

"Don't be an arse, Rhett." Maggie came to my defense. "You know Ally won't have a proper season this year. The least she can do is wear these lovely gowns her mama got for her. We are celebrating your return. Can't she get dressed up for that?"

This time it was his turn to be embarrassed.

"Of course, I meant no disrespect, Ally," he apologized. "It came out all wrong. I was only trying to say you look wonderful. Forgive me?"

He took my hand and looked at me so forlornly that my heart melted instantly.

I couldn't resist teasing him, "You're forgiven. I'm glad I was able to make you tongue-tied. My dress had the desired effect after all."

The three of us burst into laughter.

Maggie grabbed my arm and pulled me in the direction of the kitchen. "I have it from a good source that Madame DuPont is making her special hot chocolate. Come on."

I gave Rhett a sidelong glance. What a shame I couldn't get to talk to him straight away, but Madame's lovely refreshment was waiting.

"I'll be in the drawing room," he said, "having something a bit stronger, but you girls go ahead. I know how much you enjoy that little treat."

This was true. Madame DuPont's hot chocolate was a highlight of our childhood. Still was, if I was honest, although she didn't make it quite so often these days. The drink was something she'd learned to make in France. Remembering its rich, silky texture had me salivating.

"How long has Madame been back?"

I knew she'd just returned from visiting her relations in Paris.

"Three days. Poor thing, we've asked her to do this fancy dinner with little to no warning. As soon as she learned you might be coming, she asked me to bring you to her."

We danced down the stone stairs to the basement kitchen. An assortment of delicious smells teased my senses as we stepped across the threshold of Madame DuPont's domain. A large table dominated the middle of the room. Several dishes were already laid out on the oak surface. They remained a mystery, though, hidden under cloches. The large clay domes never gave any clue as to what lay under them. Madame was most secretive when it came to what she was preparing for dinner. Mrs. Addington was the only one to know the full extent of tonight's feast. For the rest of us, it would be a delightful surprise.

The kitchen staff bustled around, following the cook's directions. Madame's back was to us. She was beating an egg yolk in a pot hanging from an iron bracket over the hearth. The bricks behind it were blackened with soot, demonstrating their use over the years. Her sizeable arm wobbled as she whisked the mixture with a fork. She traded her fork for a spoon and tasted the drink. After sipping and pausing for a moment to savor the taste, she was satisfied. She took the pot off the fire, turned around and put her marvelous creation on the table. It was then she saw us.

"*Ma chère. Te volià.*"

Madame threw her arms wide, inviting us in for a hug. We ran over and were engulfed within her embrace. She felt like a comfortable pillow, all squishy and soft. Chocolate smears adorned her apron, and when I finally pulled away, she tut-tutted.

"*Dans ma hâte, regarded ce qua j'ai fait. Vous ave du chocolate sur vote belle robe.*"

She couldn't believe some of the chocolate had marked my dress.

"Hurry, get me a cloth. We must get this out before it stains."

One of the kitchen girls brought over a damp rag and handed it to Madame DuPont.

"Let's get you cleaned up."

Madame rubbed the side of my bust vigorously. Maggie and I looked at each other and laughed.

"It is no laughing matter, Miss Ally. If we don't get this out now, your dress could be ruined."

Her accent was adorable. Madame DuPont had been a part of the Addington household for as long as I could remember. Even though most English gentry had little regard for the French, the Addingtons preferred good food over prejudice.

"Don't worry yourself, Madame. Look, it's coming out already."

She wagged her finger at me.

"You know very well that if you want some of my hot chocolate, you must speak to me in French."

I took a deep breath and tried to remember the nuances of the language.

"*Comment aurais-je pu oublier notre petit jeu?*"

I reminded her that I had not forgotten our little game. Whenever Maggie and I wanted anything from her kitchen, which was often, we needed to speak in her native tongue. At first, we had no clue what she was saying. Over the years, she taught us conversational French. It seemed to give her a sense of pride that she could impart her history to us. In some ways, we were like her adopted daughters.

She smiled at us and pulled two mugs toward her.

"*Et combine aimeriez-vous , Miss Maggie?*"

"I'll have a whole cupful, please."

Madame DuPont was having none of it and remained stationary. The pot was poised above the mugs.

"Oh, right."

Maggie corrected herself.

"*Je vail prendre une tasse entière, s'il vous plaît.*"

Madame poured the thick, steaming liquid to just below the brim.

"Careful, it is still hot. Take small sips."

She cautioned us as though we were still children. Perhaps we would never be grown up in her eyes.

Our favorite beverage was as good as it ever was, with a faint hint of cinnamon hitting our tastebuds. We closed our eyes in appreciation.

"*Bien, oui?*"

"*Oui, oui,*" we agreed in unison.

Madame DuPont started speaking excitedly about her recent trip, waving her hands around as she talked.

"*Laissez-moi vous raconteur mon dernier voyage à Versailles. Vous saves, je suis allé rendre visite ...*"

Maggie and I looked at each other unable to keep up with her recount.

Madame sighed, seeing our confusion.

'I suppose I need to tell you the story in English. My enthusiasm gets the better of me sometimes."

We nodded. Happy that we could enjoy our hot chocolate without having to decipher her every word.

"Well, you know I went to visit my sister in Paris. While I was there, guess who got married in Versailles?"

She paused for the briefest of moments before continuing.

"Prince Louis XVI and Marie - Antoinette."

She clapped her hands in delight.

Maggie interrupted, "Aren't they younger than us?"

"*Oui,* he's fifteen, and she is only a year younger."

Maggie wrinkled her nose up at me, and I grinned.

"There were over five thousand guests, and a crowd of two hundred thousand watched a fireworks display in their honor."

That was impressive, I thought. French royalty certainly did things in an extravagant manner.

"But that's not all. There were so many people watching the spectacle, over a hundred people were trampled to death in the crowd."

Our eyes went wide.

"That's awful," Maggie said. "Who would want that happening at their wedding?"

Madame DuPont looked serious.

"It doesn't bode well for their future, does it? Something like that is a bad omen."

I hadn't realized Madame was superstitious.

"You didn't go, did you?" I asked, concerned that she could've been hurt.

"*Non, non.* I heard about it from my nephew. He went. The young ones are interested in seeing that sort of thing. I'm too old for a long carriage ride." She patted her backside. "Even though there is plenty of padding here, my old bones don't like the jostling."

As we drained the last drops of our drink, a contented feeling settled in our stomachs.

"You two youngsters better let me get on with my job. This dinner isn't going to make itself, you know."

Madame DuPont was always the one to say who came and went in her kitchen. We were just the grateful recipients.

"*Au revoir et merci pour le chocolat,*" I said.

She blew us a kiss and went on to instruct her helpers with their tasks.

Heading back upstairs, we joined the rest of the family.

The rich oak fireplace in the middle of the drawing room gave off a delightful warmth. It felt wonderfully familiar. Many hours and fond memories had been garnered here over the years with the Addingtons. A large ship's wheel held center stage on one of the walls, proudly displayed like a treasured painting. A gold-framed map of the trade routes hung on another wall, leaving no doubt about the origin of the family's fortune.

Sybil Addington rose from her chair and greeted me with a kiss on the cheek. "How wonderful to see you again, Ally. Maggie has been beside herself waiting for you to arrive."

"Thank you for having me over to be part of your celebrations," I replied.

She gave a little sniff.

"I see you two have already been down to see Madame DuPont. I hope you haven't spoilt your dinner."

"Oh, mother," Maggie groaned. "A little drink before dinner won't hurt any."

"I suppose you're right, my dear."

Sybil was much like my Mama. Age had not taken her beauty. She had a tender heart and treated everyone she met with kindness.

Rhett handed me a glass filled with a small amount of amber liquid. I sniffed it warily. It smelled potent.

"How about another drink then? It's whiskey. Made from grains of rye and wheat. I brought some back with me. I thought you might like to try a taste of America."

His cheeky grin told me all I needed to know. I knew not to trust that look or the drink.

"You knock it back in one go. It's what everyone is drinking there."

I took a small sip and spluttered, much to Maggie's amusement.

Rhett said, "Ally, you'll find America is very much like that drink. Strong, rough and hard to swallow. Maggie tells me you are to set sail for there at the end of next month."

"That's the plan. I have many questions about it all," I replied.

"Well, that's a wonderful excuse for you to sit next to me at dinner. Although I warn you, the tale of it might not be to your liking."

"Rhett, do not scare the poor girl," Sybil said. "She is to visit her dear papa." She turned to me. "It's such a shame you'll be leaving London before the end of the season. Will you have a chance to attend some of the balls?"

"I'll do my best," I said.

"Fabulous, Maggie will be glad of the company. Won't you, dear?"

"I will, Mama, but whatever will I do without Ally when she's in America?"

Although I didn't say it, I was sure her suitor, Charles, would fill that void for her. I had to get more details about their relationship once we were alone.

Her father, Lord Addington, made his way from the adjoining study.

"Damn it. That's the second trade run we've lost in a matter of weeks," he mumbled. "Losses like this hurt our reputation."

Rhett said, "The weather across the Atlantic is terrible at the moment. To lose ship, crew and cargo is heartbreaking, but our reputation is hurt least of all."

Lord Addington replied, "It doesn't change the outcome, though, does it? People still expect goods to arrive and trade to continue despite the weather. And they blame me. Anyway, enough of my troubles."

He looked at me, "Welcome, Ally, my dear. How wonderful of you to join us now that we have Rhett home. We're all together once again."

"Like old times," I laughed.

"Indeed. We have to make the most of it before you head off. I'm glad your mother listened to me and decided to wait a little longer before sailing. It should be a much more pleasant experience for you both by summer."

I was glad she had taken his advice. To learn that ships had already been lost at sea this year was concerning to hear.

We sat there in the glow of the fire, reliving older, simpler times. As children, Rhett, Maggie and I had no responsibilities. We lived from one moment to the next with the joyous fervor of youth. Why should that change? Was it because we were being cared for then with no more thought for the morrow? Now that we were older, we had started caring for others.

The maid rang the dinner bell, announcing it was time for us to make our way into the dining room. Before we could get to our feet, Lord Addington said, "Just a moment. I have something I'd like to discuss before we eat."

Maggie looked at me with a smile, but I didn't understand why. She was bursting with eagerness, sitting forward on her seat.

Her father turned to her, saying, "It will come as no surprise to you, Maggie, that I have had an offer of marriage from Charles McKenzie."

I gasped. I looked at Maggie again. Her dainty feet were bouncing up and down in excitement.

Lord Addington continued, saying, "I assume this is what you want. I won't accept until I have your nod of approval. After all, I'm a modern father. Your happiness means more to me than anything."

He gave his only daughter a wink.

Maggie leaped to her feet and rushed to her father's side, throwing herself on his lap.

"Oh Papa, I love him so. Yes, yes. A thousand times, yes."

Tears of joy streaked down her cheeks.

"Well, that's that, then. We've another reason to celebrate tonight. Rhett is home, and my little girl is all grown up and about to start a family of her own. I couldn't be more proud of both of you. Charles is a good man from a good family."

He stroked her hair gently.

I looked at Rhett, and he returned my gaze.

It seemed our childhood memories would now be just that, memories to be cherished, not lived. Those days were gone.

Sybil Addington was beside herself.

"My darling daughter, engaged. I can hardly wait to start making arrangements. Don't keep that poor boy waiting a moment longer, Henry. Send him a note at once," she chided her husband.

"Settle down, Sybil. He has waited a week already. Another day will make no difference. Let's eat. I'm starving."

I glanced at Maggie, and we grinned at each other, considering her father's robust shape and the straining buttons on his waistcoat. Starving wasn't a word I would use when describing her papa.

Before heading in for dinner, Rhett lingered by the fireplace. I went over to him.

"What do you think of the news?" I asked.

"Things must change, Ally. We can't be children forever," he said. "What about you?"

"I am happy for her. She seems smitten," I replied.

"Hmm, that's the problem. With Maggie, it's all about the feeling. I hope she isn't taking this commitment lightly. Charles is the first man to show her any attention. She may be caught up in the fantasy of marriage, rather than the man himself."

"Can you help what you feel?" I asked.

"I guess not, but you should temper it with reason, too."

"Always the sensible one." I gave him a playful shove.

"Someone has to be with you two ladies," he smiled as we walked into the dining room together.

The meal was delightful. We started with a perfectly delicious hot soup. Ideal, considering the now howling gale outside.

A plate of poached quail in a white wine sauce was accompanied by lightly braised asparagus spears. The delicate white flesh of the fowl was tender and juicy. After that came venison pie. Its rich gravy gave off the most fantastic aroma. Sybil touted that Rhett had garnered the meat himself with a single shot in the backwoods. Finally, an astonishing array of sweet pastries, jellies, fruits and sugared nuts were brought out. All this delicious fare was topped off with bottomless glasses of the most exquisite red wine.

Mama always taught me that too much wine was not a good look on a lady. So I only sipped at it.

After we had eaten, I turned to Mrs. Addington, "I'll have to get up at the crack of dawn and walk halfway across the county to aid my digestion, after eating all this. Mrs. DuPont has outdone herself yet again."

I patted my midriff with appreciation. To my surprise, Rhett had not shared my enthusiasm and had hardly touched his dinner—a fact that hadn't gone unnoticed by his mother either.

"Rhett, are you feeling poorly?"

"Not at all, Mother. The meal is a bit rich for my tastes."

"What sort of food did you eat in America?" I asked.

"Pretty much whatever you can hunt. They have deer and bison, and the farms provide corn and beans. I'm not going to sugarcoat it, Ally. America is different from England. Do you think you are ready for such a drastic change?"

"I have no idea," I replied. "You became accustomed to it, though, didn't you?"

Perhaps it was unwise of me to respond in such a manner, but I took offense at the hint that I might not be able to handle whatever lay on the other side of the Atlantic.

Lord Addington tactfully changed the subject. "Rhett, did you know Lord Elmore has his stallion in the fourth race at the Derby next weekend? Perhaps we should make a day of it and all go together. I'd like to see if he can beat Sir William's horse. It hasn't been beaten in six races. Putting money on a horse like that is almost certain coin."

Rhett replied, "If the track has firmed up by then, Sir William's mare may do well. I've heard she likes hard ground, but I wouldn't be putting any money on her if the weather doesn't clear."

"Trust you to know all the details, my boy."

Sybil Addington chided her menfolk, "Why on earth are we talking about horse races when we could discuss Maggie's wedding? Surely that is the more exciting topic."

"For some," Rhett mumbled under his breath.

"What was that, dear?" his mother asked.

"Nothing of importance."

His father motioned to Rhett. "Come and leave the women to their plans. I'm expecting some spices to arrive from Persia next week. I want your help with ideas for their distribution.

For the next hour, we sat in the drawing room and talked through the details of Maggie's upcoming nuptials. I stifled a yawn. It had been a long and eventful day.

I stood, ready to take my leave, saying, "Thank you for a wonderful meal, Mrs. Addington, but it's getting late, and I should be getting home."

"Nonsense, Ally, dear. Haven't you heard the weather outside? The rain is coming down in sheets."

Maggie took my hand, saying, "Oh, Ally. You don't want to get wet. Won't you stay the night with me? It'll be fun."

I said, "I suppose I could send Fred back with a message."

"Yes, yes," Maggie replied. She clapped her hands, and her dark hair bounced around her heart-shaped face. At last, we'd get some time to discuss the many things in our hearts.

"Indeed, you must stay," Sybil said. "Your mother would not want you out in this tempest."

I had to agree with her.

Poor Fred, he'd waited here for naught. At least he didn't have too far to return.

It had been a lovely evening. I'd have liked to ask Rhett more about his time abroad, but to my dismay, while I was drafting the note to my mother, he retired to bed early.

"You'll have to excuse Rhett," Sybil said. "I feel his time in America has changed him from the carefree young man he once was before going to America."

"I suppose our experiences do change us," I said. "Those experiences help us grow, form our opinions and make us better equipped to face future challenges in life. I have a feeling America will do the same for me."

"Mmmm... that's a mature way to look at it, my dear."

Maggie got up from her plush velvet seat and grabbed my arm.

"Come on, let's go to my room where we can talk."

She said this without adding what I knew she meant—in private.

Maggie's room was grand. Mine overlooked the stables on our estate. Hers had a balcony above the inner courtyard, where an abundance of roses bloomed in the summertime. When the windows were open, the sweet smell wafted up from the bushes below. Her maid had turned down the bed and lit a fire. A lamp glowed on her dresser, reflecting light off the mirror. I settled on her bed and ran my fingers over the delicate embroidered flowers on the coverlet.

"Can you believe it, Ally, me a married woman. I'll get to look after my own household and do whatever I like."

She danced around the room, stopping by one of the windows and wrapped the floor-length velvet drapes around her like a mock gown.

"I'll sleep till noon and busy myself with charity events with the other married ladies from the parish. We'll dine with society couples and spend our evenings playing cards or some such thing.

Maggie plonked herself in front of the mirror and began brushing out her thick, dark, curly hair.

"You make it sound most pleasant," I chuckled.

She eyed me with suspicion. "You mock me, I think. Is that not the kind of life you want?"

She answered her own question.

"No. You always were more adventurous than me. Is that why you have decided on this hair-brained idea of going to America? You're practically giving up your first season. You can't get that back, you know."

She looked at me in the reflection of the mirror.

I sighed.

"I'm not ready for a season, Maggie. There seems to be an awful lot of expectation on young women. If you don't find a match, you keep returning until the deed is done. Once you're married, everything changes. Pretty soon, there will be children, and where will the adventures come from then? You won't be sleeping in till noon, that's for sure." I reminded her.

"That's what maids are for, silly," she said, poking her tongue out at me. "Besides, you'll have adventures with your husband."

She gave me a wicked grin. She pulled her cotton bed cap over her hair and tied it under her chin.

"I wonder if I shall still wear one of these once I am married. This seems ridiculous when trying to entice your husband to lie with you."

"If that was the only thing you had on, I'm sure he wouldn't complain."

We both burst into a fit of giggles at the prospect.

Once our laughter had abated, Maggie continued, "Perhaps you're just waiting for *you-know-who* in the next wing to get up the nerve to start showing some interest."

Did she have a point? Possibly. Either way, I didn't want to feel like an eighteen-year-old girl trapped in an older woman's body till the day I died. I wanted to live a little, and if America gave me a chance to do that, I was willing to take that risk.

"It's not forever, Mags. You know me, I'm a free spirit. I can't stand being stuck here like some decorative bird in a cage.

"Now, enough about me. Tell me all about that kiss."

I grinned with delight.

Be Prepared

I walked down the wide staircase to the breakfast room. Sunlight dappled the carpet through large windows by the entrance, promising to deliver a fine day.

Maggie had kept me up half the night with the recount of her darling Charles. Talk of marriage and children had become all too real. Was I a little jealous? I smiled at the thought. Not even remotely.

"You're looking very pleased with yourself this morning, Miss Singleton," Rhett said as I set foot in the parlor.

Apart from the servants, he was the only one awake at this hour.

A blush rose to my cheeks as I gazed at his lips. Get a grip, girl, I chided myself. There were important things to discuss.

"I was hoping we could spend some time together today," he said.

"I'd like that," I replied as I took a hot buttered roll from the breakfast counter.

He smiled. "Be careful what you wish for."

"Look, Rhett, I hope you didn't think I was rude when we talked about America at dinner. I'm determined to do my best there and—"

"Not at all, Ally. It's just that even your best may not be good enough."

I stared at him and could see he was deadly serious.

"That is why I want to spend today outside these walls, preparing you, as it were."

That sounded ominous, I thought.

"You'll need to change out of that pretty day dress and put on riding breeches."

The prospect of getting out in the country with Rhett appealed to my sense of adventure. I could hardly contain myself. With all the wet weather lately, it seemed an age since I'd been on a horse.

"I can't remember when we all last went riding together," I mused.

Rhett was blunt. "Maggie won't be coming, Ally."

The disappointment must have shown on my face as he said, "Maggie isn't going to America, and this won't be a trot in the park. Now, get going. Who knows when that sister of mine will be up."

When had he got so bossy, I wondered. Like an obedient schoolgirl, I hurried to my room and opened the chest at the bottom of my bed. Maggie's house was like a second home to me, as mine was for her. I had stashed a variety of spare clothes here for occasions such as this. As I changed, Maggie's sleeping form lay prone on her stomach, buried between two plump pillows. There was no point waking her as she always slept late. Anyway, I would probably be back before she arose.

Mud squished beneath my boots. The smell of the stables filled the air. For some, it was a pungent smell but for me it meant freedom. I wandered over to the horse I usually rode, a gentle grey mare that had seen many adventures with me. I caressed her nose fondly, and she nuzzled into my palm.

"Not that one today. You can use my stallion," Rhett said.

"Oh, I couldn't possibly," I gasped.

Rhett's horse was far too big for me and was as feisty as its owner. Even though I had grown up riding, I doubted I would be able to control him.

"Nonsense, you'll be fine. Be firm with him and show him who's boss. You can do that, can't you? Besides, we'll be racing, and I want to give you a chance to beat me."

Rhett knew me too well to pass up a challenge like that.

Did he just wink at me?

Right, I thought to myself. I had a point to prove.

Blaze, the magnificent chestnut beast, was restless beneath me. He stamped his hooves. He knew I didn't belong on his back. With my thighs pressed tightly on his flanks, I took a firm grasp of the reins. There was no side-saddle today. I hated to think how sore I would be tomorrow.

Rhett had chosen a quick black gelding called Midnight. From how the horse cleared its nostrils, I could tell it was just as eager for the ride as I was.

No sooner had we left the stables than Rhett held his hand aloft and then dropped it, signaling the race was on. Hooves dug at the gravel path. Sudden, raw power surged beneath me. I crouched low and followed Rhett's lead. He charged off down the causeway. The ground was muddy on either side.

Clods of dirt flew from beneath Midnight as we left the main path. Blaze had an uncanny sense of the competition and quickly overtook the gelding. I did well to hold on.

When we were younger, we'd often race our horses along here. Rhett usually won, but today he seemed content to follow behind. It was almost as if he was spurring my horse on to go faster. Trees whipped past on the side of the path. The wind grabbed at my hair, causing any loose strands to fly behind me.

As we galloped beyond the family chapel, I stopped having fun and started to get frightened. I crouched low in the stirrups and leaned forward. The hair on the back of the horse's mane flicked up, catching my cheek as I held myself close, trying to become one with Blaze. Sweat broke out on my stallion's neck. If I fell at this pace, I could break my back. The image of my mangled body lying in the grass tried to force its way into my mind, but I couldn't let it blur my thinking.

We were heading for the woods, and it would be foolish to continue at this speed. The air raced past my face. As the fields came to an end, I pulled back on the reins to slacken the pace, thinking I had won the contest. Rhett spooked my horse from behind, making it take off again through the woods. Branches flew past me. A thin twig caught the side of my face, scraping my cheek. It took all my skill to duck and weave through the trees. It was difficult not to slide sideways as we dodged the thick trunks to avoid the low-hanging branches. My gloved fingers clenched the reins.

Rhett gave me no quarter. He was still following far too closely, chasing me, scaring Blaze.

I dared not take my eyes off where I needed to go.

"Rhett, fall back," I yelled.

Didn't he hear me? What the hell was he thinking? Angry tears started to stream down my face, and I knew I couldn't hold on much longer.

I spotted a clearing over the creek to the left. I swung Blaze in that direction. We would have to make a significant jump to clear the water. As I wasn't experienced with this horse, I was unsure whether he'd pull up short of the stream and send me flying over his head. If there's one thing a horse understands, it's conviction. I set my heels against its flanks, driving it on. Blaze leaped across the creek. His hooves dug into the far bank, dragging us into the clearing.

I pulled up and glared at Rhett, who had stopped on the other side of the brook. He was content not to make the jump. To me, that was a wise idea, as I was fuming. I would've wrung his neck if he had been within striking distance.

"What was that about?" I bellowed. I didn't recognize my own voice. I was shaking with so much anger that it was hard to breathe.

"What you're feeling now is how you might feel if you had outrun a native."

"But why would I need to?"

"If you were alone, he might try to claim you as his own," he replied.

The thought of someone forcibly taking me was horrifying. It was something I'd never considered before. It was shocking to think anyone could do that to me.

"You did well on that jump," he said, sensing my mood had dropped. He was trying to raise my spirits. Besides, it was a small consolation considering I'd almost been flung off.

I felt drained and slid off the horse and crumpled in a heap on the ground, not caring if I got mud on my clothes. They were speckled with it anyway.

He waded through the creek and knelt beside me.

"I didn't mean to scare you, Ally. I want you to know the things you may face in America. The natives are a real threat and can't be trusted."

I was still angry with him. "I'm not sure *you* can be trusted."

He didn't even bother replying to that statement.

"It's their country, Ally. If you're going there, you need to be aware you're the outsider."

"Perhaps they don't trust us for a reason," I said.

Rhett nodded, conceding my point. "Some of them work with the English. They trade furs and help us with tracking, but their way of life differs from ours. They have many tribes. Sometimes they even fight among themselves."

"Did you ever get chased like that? I asked.

"No, but I don't have blue eyes like the sky and golden hair like the sun. Many of them would never have seen a woman as beautiful as you."

How did he always know what to say that could turn my feelings around? Damn him! I tried not to smile, but I was pretty sure I was blushing.

"Give me your hands," he said.

I was unsure what he meant, but I did as he said. He grabbed my wrists, holding them tight.

"If someone grabs your hands," he said. "Twist this way, rotating your hands toward their thumbs, and you'll break their hold."

I did as he said. As I moved my hands, he tightened his grip, squeezing hard, but he was right. I was able to twist free.

Rhett pushed me back, surprising me. I flopped onto my back in the grass as he said, "If someone is laying on top of you, pinning you down—"

To my horror, he lay on top of me, pinning my arms above my head. I could feel his breath fanning my face. It was the closest I'd ever been with a man. For the briefest of moments, time stood still.

"—get your knee free and kick him as hard as you can in the groin."

"You mean like this." I wriggled. I was about to do as he suggested when he shifted his weight. His hand pressed against my thigh, preventing me from raising my leg. Although he meant to protect himself, it felt nice to feel his hand there.

"That didn't work at all," I said.

"I was expecting it, that's why. If you take them by surprise, it'll work."

At that moment, he seemed to notice the intimate position he was in. His cheeks went red. He rolled over on the grass and looked up at the sky.

"You're impossible," I said, lying next to him. I felt a turmoil of emotions. On one hand, I despised him for treating me so harshly. On the other, I understood his concern. He liked me. Could he love me? What was holding him back? Why couldn't he tell me how he felt?

"I'm sorry, Ally. We aren't kids anymore, and that was inappropriate. My God, if our parents had seen us, they would want us to be wed."

"Is that what you're afraid of?" I asked, prodding him further. "Would that be so bad?"

"I—I don't know," he stammered. "I'm still figuring out the

direction I want to take with my career. Until that's sorted, I'm not in a position to pursue a relationship with anyone. And you. You're going to America."

I stared at him, but he refused to meet my gaze.

"I can't possibly prepare you for everything," he said. "Are you sure you won't stay here with us?"

He started picking at the long grass without thinking.

I wish he'd said *with me*.

"I've thought about staying behind, but this is an opportunity too good to miss."

He nodded.

"Does your father even know that you and your mother plan to go over? You'll be there before he can get word back to you."

"We sent a letter via the last ship that set sail," I said. "That was all we could do."

The ground was damp beneath me. I could feel it starting to seep into my clothes.

"Ally, it's dangerous. Just getting to America is dangerous. People die on the open ocean all the time."

"I could have died falling from this dumb horse," I argued.

"Fair point," he agreed.

"Rhett, I want to live a little before I settle down. Get to experience things I wouldn't otherwise do. Why do men have all the fun and women have to fit in with their plans? You know I'm not like Maggie in that regard."

He said, "I can see you've made up your mind about this. You've always wanted everything life had to offer. It would be a crime to hinder your enthusiastic spirit. And I feel you won't be satisfied until you've had your fill of adventures."

He stood up. He helped me stand by offering his hand. I wiped a wayward strand of hair from my face.

Rhett smirked.

"What now?" I said, still feeling unsettled by our conversation.

"You have dirt on your face," he replied, pointing at my left cheek.

I gave it a rub.

He actually laughed. "You've made it worse. Come over by the creek."

He led me down to the water's edge, and we knelt in the grass. He dipped his fingers in the cool water and washed the dirt away.

His touch was gentle as he focused on the task at hand. I watched him. It was as if nothing else in the world mattered at that moment. I liked that. If he did something, he did it right. A frown appeared on his brow.

"You've scratched your cheek."

His fingers traced the tender spot, making me wince.

"I didn't intend for you to hurt yourself."

I bit back an angry retort, wanting to see where this intimate moment would lead. Our eyes locked together. With faces only inches apart, his eyes wandered to my slightly parted lips. Did he want to kiss me? It seemed so. I leaned closer. I could actually sense the struggle deep within him. His heart was telling him one thing, and his damned logical head was telling him something different. It was telling him all the reasons it wasn't a good idea to start something here and now. My mind was telling me no such thing. Maybe I should just take the initiative. I could imagine his lips on mine. Moving together, the sweet taste of him in my mouth. What if he rejected me? That was a scenario I wasn't ready to accept. It appeared we had both been thinking too much about it, for he shook his head and stood up. The moment was lost.

"Come, I want to show you how to track an animal."

My heart sank at what could've been.

He took Blaze by the reins and led him back over the water.

I was disappointed. Was I just imagining that he was showing interest in me? It seemed he didn't want to act on his feelings. Was it because he thought I might not return? Was it because he didn't want to leave me feeling conflicted about the journey? I'd always been there in the background, silently waiting for him. Only now, I was the one leaving. Perhaps he hadn't been prepared for that. Maybe I wasn't either.

The Hunt

In the days that followed, it was as though I was living in two worlds: one with Rhett, where I was in survival mode, and the other I was accustomed to in high society.

Rhett had spent a great deal of time with me lately, and I loved every minute of it. Even if there were no more romantic moments, just being in his company was enough. He'd taught me about covering my tracks, hiding techniques and living off the land. He had also shown me how to make traps to catch rabbits. I enjoyed these male-centered activities, apart from the gutting of the animals, which I still balked at.

We came to an unspoken understanding. Neither of us was willing to bring up the moment we'd shared by the creek. We could have—we should have kissed. He knew that I knew what he wanted to do that day. Just as he knew that I wanted him to take me, but he didn't act on his desire. He must have realized my mind was made up and I was going to America regardless. Rhett was a gentleman and wouldn't take advantage of me. Above all things, Rhett was rational. There would be no point in starting something that couldn't be finished. It was better to keep our feelings in check. That was easier said than done when spending so much time together.

One morning he rode up to the door of our estate. He had a rifle slung across his back. I was in the stables and had seen him arrive. I led Bella, my dappled mare, outside and hoisted myself onto the saddle. I gave her a neck pat, encouraging her toward Rhett.

"What are we hunting today?" I asked as if it was an everyday occurrence.

"Deer. And you're going to shoot it," he replied.

I took a gulp. Killing rabbits had been difficult enough. They were usually already dead by the time we got to the traps. A deer was a whole different beast altogether.

I put on a brave face, but inside I was nervous. We trotted to the back of the estate, which bordered a heavily wooded area. This forest was home to a herd of red deer.

"We'll ditch the horses and tie them here. Don't want them to get spooked by the gunshots. We need to be quiet in how we walk. Even a broken twig can scare off a hind."

He handed me the rifle and told me always to carry it pointing toward the ground.

"If it goes off accidentally, it won't hurt anyone. You'd be surprised at the number of self-inflicted gunshot wounds people have. Safety comes first."

As we walked deeper into the woods, he motioned for us to slow our steps. Sure enough, in the clearing to our right stood an adult deer. It was feeding on a clump of grass and hadn't noticed us. We crouched behind a fallen tree trunk. I took the rifle and rested it carefully on the log. Rhett came up behind me and positioned the gun into my shoulder, whispering into my ear.

"Don't be surprised. The rifle will give a bit of a kick. Hold it steady, and go with the movement. Resist the temptation to raise the barrel above the target, when you take the shot. Line the bead up at the end of the barrel so it is pointing just behind the front legs. You want to hit just under her shoulders."

I would have preferred if Rhett had called the deer an '*it*.' Referring to the animal as '*her*' made it personal. I nodded. The deer was facing us head-on. I waited until it stepped into a better position. I was aware of how near Rhett was to me. His breath, so close to my skin, was doing all sorts of things to my body. It was useless getting distracted by him because that meant we'd be out hunting here longer. Could I really do this? Take this animal's life? Indeed, it would be eaten, but we had plenty of food, and we'd be leaving for London in a few days. Was it really necessary?

"I know what you are thinking, Ally. Do you have to do this? Every time I kill something, I ask myself the same thing. Sometimes the answer is easier than others. When it is my life over theirs, the answer is simple. In grey areas, it's harder. Think of it like this. There will be enough meat on that deer to feed both our households for the next two weeks. Does that make it any easier?"

I whispered back, "Nothing about this is easy."

"Wait until you have to look it in the eyes while it's dying."

"I thought you were trying to help," I hissed.

The deer raised its head, sensing us. As it did so, it moved into position.

"Take the shot, Ally," Rhett urged.

He moved away from me as I fired. I was surprised by how mechanical the process was. I pulled the trigger. The hammer lashed out and struck the flint. There was a spark of light and a puff of smoke, and I thought that was it. A fraction of a second later, there was an almighty bang. The butt of the gun slammed into my shoulder, none too gently. Smoke billowed around us, and the smell of gunpowder hung heavy in the air.

"By Jove, you've done it!" He gave me a slap on the back and barreled over the log toward the animal. I wasn't sure if I was excited about it or not. Decidedly not, I thought upon reflection. Putting the gun down, I stayed put. Rhett encouraged me over.

"Do I have to? Shooting the poor creature was hard enough."

"Get over here. That wasn't a clean shot. We need to put it out of its misery."

"No," I said as the realization of what I had done sunk in. Killing an innocent deer felt wrong. Rhett, though, was bubbling with enthusiasm.

"We have to gut and butcher it."

"You have to be kidding me."

"Come," he said.

I walked over to the fallen animal. There was fear and disbelief in its eyes. I'd seen plenty of stag heads adorned on the walls of estates, but their eyes always looked cloudy. They never seemed real. Our eyes met. She seemed to beg me to answer: why had I done this to her? For her, life was wonderful, and yet now it was over. Her eyes were so large and round and full of pity. I knelt down, wanting to comfort the dying animal, but it was repulsed by my presence. Its legs thrashed about as blood oozed from the hole in its side. I had done that.

Rhett pulled a knife from his trouser leg and offered it to me. I shook my head, unable to speak. I watched in horror as he slit the dying animal's throat.

"I don't think I'll be able to look at venison the same way again."

"If you're hungry enough, Ally, you will eat anything," he replied.

Rhett ran the knife down its stomach. A thin red line appeared before the contents of the deer's insides spilled onto the grass. Steam rose as the intestines flopped onto the cold ground. I turned and vomited up my breakfast. Taking a few deep breaths, I turned back again to see Rhett had rolled up his sleeves and was dismembering the doe's hind leg from its body. He could have said something about my weak disposition, but he could see I'd stepped beyond my limits.

Blood dripped from his fingers. I thought about how savage Rhett looked at that moment. He was preparing me for what lay ahead in America. Before today, I knew this was how people lived their lives every day in the country, but I didn't really understand the implications. Now, it felt visceral. Living on an estate, I was sheltered from the harsh reality of what it took to survive off the land.

London

A few weeks later, Mama and I made the trip to my Aunt's townhouse in London. Aunt Mary was the only one in attendance as her husband had gone to the continent on business. She didn't seem too upset by our imposition, though, eager to have her sister with her for a couple of weeks. While there, Rhett had tasked me with an assignment. It wasn't too arduous. He wanted me to walk for at least an hour a day. Most days, I did this already. In London, it was easy. There was so much to see and do. Rows upon rows of shops and wide streets sported some of London's finest homes. Beautiful women paraded around St. James's Park under their parasols. Sometimes Mama accompanied me, but for the most part, Agnes agreed to come. That way, my mother wouldn't be forced to introduce me to any prospective suitors. My maid was not considered an official chaperone. This suited me fine. Agnes was raised in London, so she showed me some of the poorer parts of town, further away from the city center. There were days when we would be gone for hours, so absorbed were we with our travels. The summer bloom of flowers with their lingering scents made for a delightful backdrop to our wanderings. In contrast, the streets stank, and for the most part, we avoided them.

Waste from the houses ran in channels down the center of the road. As often as we could, we made for the hills where we could breathe easier.

Rhett's words echoed in my head. "I want you to build up your strength and stamina. It will stand you in good stead on the ship."

He'd also shown me some simple exercises that, if any woman had seen, she would have wondered what I was up to. That is precisely what my mother had thought as she entered my room one morning.

The windows were open, letting in a gentle breeze that blew the thin fabric of the curtains. The furnishings in my bedroom had a decidedly French flair—white painted wood with ornately carved edges and gold trim. This furniture was much more delicate than at our home. Her taste was a bit like my aunt herself—a petite wisp of a woman with white powdered hair and the fashionable black dot on her cheek. Apparently, her fashion statement was all the rage in Paris. No doubt we'd be seeing this French influence in the ballrooms of London in the not-too-distant future. So far, Mama and I had not been persuaded to follow her look.

This morning I started with gentle stretches, building up to balance poses. I was wearing a petticoat and in the middle of a leg lunge when she opened the door, surprising me.

"What on Earth are you doing, Ally?"

"Strengthening my leg muscles, Mama."

"Why would you want to do that?" She looked shocked.

"I want to be fit for our voyage," I answered.

"Well, I suppose that's good, but it seems redundant, especially as we'll be cramped up on the boat all day."

I grinned as Mama was not one to put forth too much effort. She never joined Papa and me when we walked around the grounds at home.

"I came to remind you that you must be ready by nine o'clock for the Davenport's ball this evening. I thought you could wear the burgundy silk dress. What do you think?"

"Shouldn't I wear the pale pink one? Aren't bold colors more for the opera or the theatre?"

"Usually, that's true. This party is a more private affair. I want you to stand out and not be confused for a debutante. This way, everyone will remember you."

Being my first ball, I deferred to her judgment.

"Of course, Mama"

"I'll get Agnes to arrange your hair."

"I'd like to do that by myself," I said. "Agnes has been teaching me some hairstyles."

"Oh, that's wonderful. I have every confidence in you, my dear. Did you realize Maggie will be there? The Addingtons arrived in town this morning."

This was news to me. Tonight's festivities suddenly became a whole lot more interesting. I would finally meet Charles, and I was excited beyond belief that Maggie would be there. Sure, I had attended country balls before, but nothing as spectacular as one in London. By all accounts, they were magnificent. Everyone dressed in their finery, hopeful of being doted on by handsome young men while dancing the night away. I wondered if Maggie's parents would attend or if Rhett would act as her chaperone. If he did, would he ask me to dance?

Later, as I regarded my reflection in the gilded mirror, I couldn't help but admire my handiwork. There was something to be said for accomplishing things on your own instead of relying on others all the time.

I decided dressing for a ball was a bit like painting a work of art, only I was the canvas. My dress flowed over my skin, clinging to all the right places. It was a simple style but more daring than my other gowns. It had short bell sleeves and a low neckline with boning across the bust. Delicate silver beading swirled in a pattern reminiscent of leaves on a vine. My hair was held in a French braid adorned with jewels. I felt a sense of pride knowing I had created this image of myself. More important though, was that the woman looking back at me had a new depth to her. I could take care of myself.

That night, the ballroom was a sea of shimmering colors swirling in merriment. The dancing had already started by the time we arrived. It was everything Maggie had described to me and more. Candlelight reflected off the mirrors, making the room seem larger than it was. At a guess, there were easily over a hundred people already in attendance. And more carriages were arriving. Mama placed her hand on my arm. With her other hand, she fanned herself.

"It certainly is hot in here. I think Lady Davonport should have restricted the guest list. This room is too crowded."

I was nervous. I straightened my dress even though I didn't need to. Renowned composer John Alcock sat at the harpsichord playing a selection of his compositions. Waiters offered champagne in crystal-fluted glasses. My mother took one and drank it like it was water.

My eyes scanned the dance floor for anyone familiar. I spotted Maggie dancing with a handsome young man I assumed was Charles. She was beaming up into his eyes. He was looking at her like he had a treasure in his possession. I was happy that she had found someone suitable.

I decided that tonight I was going to enjoy myself. I would choose as many partners as possible. I didn't want to give the wrong impression. I would leave in a couple of weeks, and who knew when I would return? If ever, was a thought I pushed out of my mind. I wouldn't be afraid of what might be.

A warm hand touched my elbow. I turned to see Rhett standing there, looking resplendent in his formal military uniform. His jacket was bright red and adorned with polished brass buttons. It was the first time I'd seen him clean-shaven since he'd returned home. I wanted to reach out and touch his smooth cheek. If we were in private, I might have.

"Rhett, what a lovely surprise," Mama said.

"It's a delight to see the two of you here."

Mama fanned herself, asking, "And where's Maggie?"

Rhett pointed at a couple dancing by the harpsichord.

"Oh, she looks marvelous and so happy."

"That's her fiancee, Charles McKenzie."

"You must introduce us later."

56

"Of course."

Mama looked around for another glass of champagne. She spotted a waiter and stepped through the crowd toward him, muttering, "I won't be getting much of this in America."

Rhett whispered close to my ear, saying, "You look amazing, Ally."

I enjoyed the compliment.

"I didn't even need my maid."

"I should hope not. I was referring to your form, not your dress. I can tell you've been doing your exercises."

"Ugh, I'm not some filly on show."

"Isn't that why all the young ladies are here?"

"Not me. I just want to dance."

"Then allow me the honor of your first dance."

Mama returned to us, holding two glasses of champagne—one for each of us. Rhett turned to her while gesturing to me with his hand outstretched, saying, "May I?"

"You may," Mama replied. She looked quite content having both glasses to herself.

With that, Rhett whisked me onto the dance floor, not even waiting for a new song to begin.

I teased him. "Has anyone here caught your eye?"

"There are many beautiful women, but then you try to get to know them and..." His voice trailed off. "Most girls only tell you what they think you want to hear. It all seems like too much effort."

Rhett had never stepped away from a challenge before. I felt he wasn't being entirely honest with me. But I was glad to hear he wasn't interested in making a match.

"Don't you want an heir?" I asked as we danced across the polished wooden floor.

"There's plenty of time," he replied. "I don't understand why people rush these things. Being with someone your whole life is quite a commitment. Let Maggie give the family some heirs. It looks like it won't be long before that happens anyway."

Nice deflection, I thought.

Continuing the conversation, I added, "I never asked you what your promotion means. Where will you go from here?"

Rhett looked away for a moment, thinking about his answer.

"Father wants me to quit the army and take over the family shipping business, but I don't know that my heart is in it. After coming back from America, my priorities have changed. I don't want to go back to the colonies."

I asked him, "What will you do?"

"I'm thinking about politics. I've seen too many things—bad things. I've seen injustice there and even right here in England. That has made me think about our laws. They need to change. I can't do that in shipping or the regiment."

I was surprised. This was a side of Rhett I'd never seen. Like everyone else, I'd assumed he would continue his career in the army or go into shipping. From the look in his eyes, I could see he trusted me. Perhaps even more than his parents or sister. I doubted he had spoken this openly with them. It wasn't easy to know what to say in reply. Usually, the conversation while dancing revolved around pleasantries, not life-changing decisions.

"Have you spoken to your father?" I asked. I wasn't curious about Lord Addington's response, rather I wanted to know whether I needed to maintain Rhett's confidence.

"You're the only one I've told, Ally."

As the string quartet played, I struggled with how to respond.

"I think you're brave," I finally said. "It takes courage to do something that's not expected of you."

"I have time on my side. I'll help Father until an opportunity arises, but shipping is not where I'll stay."

I had no doubt Rhett would be competent at whatever he decided to do. The fact that he wanted his vocation to have meaning and not settle for one that was familiar spoke volumes.

"Do you know why I came here tonight?" he asked.

I held my breath. He wasn't about to declare his intentions now, was he?

"These private parties are a good opportunity to talk with influential people. A number of lords are here tonight."

I sighed. I should've known by now not to get my hopes up where Rhett was concerned. I changed the subject.

"Can you introduce me to Charles? I've been dying to meet him."

When the song finished, Rhett ushered me over to where Charles and Maggie stood before the refreshment table. She squealed with delight when she saw me approaching.

"Ally, this is Charles McKenzie," Rhett said.

"Pleased to meet you, at last, Miss Singleton. Although I feel I know you already. Maggie tells me all about your adventures together."

"I hope not." I winked wickedly at her.

Turning my attention back to Charles, I noticed the good-humored gleam in his eye. He didn't appear to be an overly serious man, which was good, considering Maggie's spirited character.

"I've been eager to make your acquaintance too, Mr. McKenzie, now that you've stolen my dear friend's heart."

Maggie batted my hand playfully. "Oh, Ally, you make it sound like Charles has swept me away. I gave my heart freely, you know."

"Of course you did, my dear," he patted her arm. "Let me add that your friendship seems more like sisters, so you'll be welcome at our home anytime after we are married."

I said, "Sir, that is very gracious of you. You've put my heart at ease, and I thank you for it." His kindness touched me.

Maggie said, "Unfortunately, Ally is leaving for the colony of Virginia in a few days, and I've no idea when I shall see her again."

Her mouth turned into a cute pout. This reminded me that leaving her behind would be difficult. Especially when she had played such a big part in my life.

She said, "Not having Ally at my wedding will be awful."

I laughed. "The wedding will still be wonderful, and you'll look stunning."

She took my hand, saying, "I will miss you dearly."

With her wedding being six months away, it was not possible for me to attend.

"Can't you wait until next summer? How will you be able to wish me luck, without touching my dress on the wedding day?"

She looked at me with pleading eyes.

Rhett said, "Maggie, you're putting Ally in a difficult position."

"It's fine, Rhett," I said, interrupting him. I turned to Maggie, adding, "It breaks my heart too."

I caught her hands in mine and fought to blink back tears. She sniffed. The candlelight caught the tears in the corners of my eyes, causing the room to blur. It was all I could do not to bawl.

Rhett sensed the emotion building between us.

"Come now, this is supposed to be a party, sister. Nobody has died. Let's have a dance."

He took Maggie by the elbow. Charles offered me his hand, and we joined them on the dance floor. The music spirited us away, making us forget for a time that our lives would soon be changed. In between sets, Charles and Rhett entertained us with stories.

After the late supper, the music started playing once more. The melody from the string quartet floated around the room.

"Boys," Maggie said, "You do realize that half the night has gone, and Ally is yet to dance with any other young man."

"And that's a problem?" Rhett asked, joking with her.

Charles laughed too, but Maggie was serious.

"Of course it is. It'll be daylight in a few hours. Stand to the side, Rhett. You can act as Ally's chaperone and introduce anyone who may be bold enough to come over and ask her for a dance. I fear we have monopolized her evening long enough."

Maggie always did have my best interests at heart. I looked at her. She gave me a shy smile. Did she have an ulterior motive? She must know it was too late for any last-minute tricks. I would not stay in England just because I met a man tonight. Besides, no one in the room compared to her brother.

It didn't take long for several fellows to come over. Soon my dance card was full. Rhett agreed to anyone that asked. I felt he gained a certain satisfaction in seeing me squirm, particularly with some of the older gentlemen. I crossed out the last dance just in case Rhett should ask for it. It would serve him right if I pretended to be clumsy and drew attention to him on the dance floor. I chided myself. That was spiteful and not something a young lady would do. I glared at him instead. He smiled back.

The dancing was pleasant enough, for no man of worth would come to a ball without knowing how to escort a woman across the floor. When it came to those with a title or the obscenely rich, the rules tended to be more relaxed. These men could afford to be more choosy and would only put forth an effort if it was worth their while.

Lord Morrish was on his second dance with me. He was both titled and rich. He'd been one of the most eligible bachelors for several seasons now. On a couple of occasions, he'd stood on my toes. I don't think he noticed. I did.

"You look radiant," he said. I was more interested in my aching feet than his advances.

At a guess, Lord Morrish was ten years my senior. I wondered why he had taken so long to choose a wife. Did he enjoy coming to these private balls year after year to see what was on offer before making up his mind? Somehow, I had the impression he was content with his bachelor lifestyle, which wouldn't change much after he wed. His piercing dark eyes and pitch-black hair framed a handsome face. He meant well and tried to be kind, but he was a little clumsy, which annoyed me.

"Thank you, my lord."

"You are easily the most beautiful woman at the ball tonight."

"I mean not to offend you, sir. Don't you think beauty is two-fold?

I see life as more than a dance."

"You think me fickle," he said. "I fear you have already judged me and found me wanting."

I smiled. He was quick-witted and intelligent.

"Why are you here, my dear?" he asked.

"I wanted to experience a ball. Perhaps meet some interesting people and dance till sunrise."

He smiled. "And there's nothing wrong with that. I have been doing that for several years. I find you interesting. Are you here with your mother?"

"Yes, my lord."

"Would you join me for a carriage ride tomorrow should I call on you?"

I lowered my head. "I am afraid we are preparing to leave for America next week. I wouldn't want you to get your hopes up."

He laughed loudly. Heads around the ballroom turned to stare in our direction.

"My, you're a bold one, Miss Singleton, and quite refreshing at that. Most young women are only too willing to do whatever it takes to snare a wealthy lord."

"It's an excellent thing then that I'm not like most women, isn't it?"

I smiled at him, enjoying his cat-and-mouse game.

"Indeed it is."

He returned me graciously to Mama, remarking what a charming daughter she had raised, and set off for his next potential conquest.

Maggie said, "Lord Morrish certainly looked like he was enjoying himself."

"He's pleasant enough. Used to getting his own way too often, though, I imagine."

Mama said, "He is a very influential man, Ally. You'd do well to stay on the good side of him."

"All is well, Mama. I think he found our conversation quite

refreshing for a change."

Charles came over with two glasses of champagne for us.

The more I thought about the two of them, the better suited I thought they were for each other. Charles had grown up in the country and was studying law. He wasn't bad to look at either and had a gentle nature. I could see why Maggie liked him. She would run rings around him, though, once they were married. It didn't seem like he minded her boundless enthusiasm.

As had been the case with most of the evening, my eyes darted around, looking for Rhett. I saw him dancing with a particularly beautiful older woman.

"Who is that?" I asked my friend Felicity, who had come to join our small group. My guess was she'd wanted to quiz me about Lord Morrish.

"That is the widow, Gwen Llewellyn. She was married for a year when her husband, who was in Parliament, died in a hunting accident. He was a lot older than her, but it still came as a shock. It looks like she is well and truly out of mourning now, doesn't it?"

Apparently so. Their heads were close together, and they were both enjoying a deep conversation. I didn't know quite how to feel about that. I had no claim over Rhett, and I was leaving soon. What future could there be for us? Even though I was telling myself to be logical, I couldn't help but wish I was in his arms at that moment.

"This is the last dance, ladies. Ally, we should leave before the rush," Mama said.

Reluctantly I said my goodbyes and helped her to our carriage.

I'd had a chance to sample a London ball. Although I enjoyed it, I didn't see the sense of going to another. I imagined that one was very much the same as the next. Same people, different clothes. My sights were set on what lay ahead of me. I couldn't find meaning on the dance floor in London. I needed a purpose in life. The only reason to go to another ball would be to spend more time with Maggie, but I could do that during the day when she wasn't in the arms of Charles. There were other forms of entertainment to enjoy each night, like listening to the orchestra playing Bach's *Fantasia* or one of Mozart's symphonies.

Mama had promised to take me to the pleasure gardens in Hyde Park. These were sections of the park where peacocks were on display alongside flower gardens overflowing with roses in bloom. Gentry went there to see and be seen.

Where would everyone be when I returned?

Would my friends be the same? I doubted it. I knew I wouldn't be. As I climbed into the carriage, I glanced back at the entranceway. Rhett was standing there by the marble pillars. His silhouette was unmistakable. Neither of us waved. We simply accepted that we were parting ways.

Departure

The bell rang from downstairs. Curious, I rushed to close my trunk, wanting to see who was calling on us as we finished packing.

Mama and I were due to set sail on the *Heart of Oak*, commissioned in 1762, bound for new shores. I had to keep reminding myself that I would soon see Papa. He would have received news about our plans by now. Would he be happy that we were sailing to America? I hoped so.

Today we were to leave our world behind and ride by carriage from London to Southampton.

Lord Addington had secured us a cabin on one of his ships. We'd waited an additional two weeks before departing. Our ship was intended for carrying goods rather than passengers and needed to be filled before leaving. For me, the moment had come all too soon. I'd been enjoying my daily walks around Hyde Park with my friends.

Last weekend, I said my tearful goodbyes to Maggie. We had a picnic. The day was glorious, with blue skies and cheerful birds masking our sorrow at parting. I hadn't seen or heard from Rhett since the ball. Maggie mentioned he'd been in Southhampton already. It was hard to imagine I wouldn't see him before I left. Perhaps I'd see him at the docks. There was much to thank him for. He hadn't needed to spend time with me, preparing me for my travels, but he had. I'd made a gift for him. It was a sketch of our time together fishing by the stream. I wanted to give it to him in person as a memento, but I felt shy handing it to his father in his absence. I decided I would send it to him along with a note. Our time together recently had been special—at least, I thought so.

Standing at the top of the staircase, I heard rather than saw Rhett.

"Good day, Mrs. Singleton."

My heart skipped a beat as he greeted my mother at the door.

"Why Rhett, what a surprise, we were just about to leave for Southampton," Mama replied.

"I'm glad I caught you then. I want to accompany your carriage to the port and see your family safely on board. That is if you don't mind. My father wanted to ensure all the arrangements were to your satisfaction. Besides, I have some business there."

I wondered if this was his idea or his father's.

I sauntered rather than rushed down the stairs, determined to be ladylike.

"We should like that very much," my mother said. "It is very kind of your father to think of us. Ally mentioned you were in Southampton recently. Surely you didn't return to accompany us."

Rhett reddened from the implication, "I don't mind. This time of year, it's a beautiful ride."

"I could join you on horseback," I said, perhaps assuming too much.

My mother wasn't impressed. "Ally, a lady would ride such a distance in a carriage."

"Oh, Mama. It will be fun. Like old times back on the estate."

Mama paused, which was as good as a yes. I clapped my hands with excitement, signaling that the question was settled, for me at least.

Rhett addressed my mother, seeing the concern on her face and anticipating her protest. "It's no bother, Mrs. Singleton. We have four or five good mares in the stables. I'm sure I can find one that's suitable."

Mama sighed. "We're to leave within the hour. Can you arrange it before then?"

"It's no problem, ma'am."

"I want to make Basingstoke by nightfall.'

"We will," I said, excited to spend time with Rhett. Even though I loved my mother, being cooped up with her on a carriage ride was daunting. We would have plenty of each other's company crossing the Atlantic.

"This will be good for Ally," Rhett said. "Riding is therapeutic before a long sea voyage."

Rhett winked at me, knowing full well that I preferred to be outside on the back of a horse than stuck inside a carriage.

It was a fine day for a ride, and there were few other travelers on the road. The sun shone, seeping into my bones. A light breeze blew wisps of my hair over my face, but I didn't care. Rhett and I rode behind the carriage. We were far enough away that the dust and dirt didn't bother us. My horse was a gentle mare that was content to trot along. The relaxing motion soothed my mind.

"Is there anything I should know about the crossing?" I asked.

Rhett had hardly spoken since we set off. He seemed content to enjoy the fresh air outside of London.

"The sea should be calm at this time of year. Make sure your mother goes on deck as often as she can. The fresh air will do wonders for her. If it gets rough, stay indoors."

"Is it that dangerous?"

"I've seen storms that swept sailors overboard. The waves can come out of nowhere. One moment, you're standing there, swaying with the rocking of the ship. The next, you're being washed across the deck as a rogue wave sweeps over the bow."

"Mama said the outlook was for fine weather during our passage."

"That's what they tell all the passengers. The outlook is always fine. Don't worry, the captain will let you know if there's any danger."

"Ah," I said, nodding in time with the rise and fall of my saddle.

"Look to be helpful, Ally. Being useful on such a long journey will help the days pass quicker."

"I'll try."

"How long do you intend to stay in America?"

My mother and I had talked about this at length. Depending on how we found this new life, she was prepared to stay there with my father for years. In my mind, I hadn't decided one way or another whether I'd stay. I thought it was best to make that kind of decision once I knew what I was committing myself to. For me, this felt more like an adventure than a permanent state of affairs.

I echoed these thoughts to Rhett.

He said, "I'll give you and your mother a return note so that if you want to come home, you can. All you have to do is arrange passage at the dock in Virginia."

I thanked him. It was good to know that option was available.

"Rhett, do you think I'll like it over there? From your account, you couldn't wait to get back here."

"I think it'll be a novelty for you," he replied. "You've had a sheltered upbringing in the English countryside, so it'll be new and exciting. Pretty soon, you'll get used to the harsh reality of day-to-day life there. If you're staying at the fort, I think you'll tire of it quickly."

"What a low opinion you must have of me to say so."

He laughed.

"Not at all, Ally. The drudgery of army life saps the heart and soul out of people, let alone someone as lively as you. I know that's the reason I didn't want to stay. I felt like I wasn't contributing very much over there. You're too creative to get stuck in that system. After all, you have everything you could ever want right here, yet you feel the need to explore the unknown."

By *here*, was he referring to my home and friends or himself?

"Perhaps you're right," I said. "But I think within all of us is a desire to know what lies beyond our own little world."

"Not for Maggie, it seems."

"She has her own things to look forward to, and I don't begrudge her for that. I wonder if Papa will let me do much exploring. I don't just want to see the inside of the fort."

"You'll need a companion if you want to travel outside the fort. I don't think your father will want any of his men doing that job. In my regiment, they had natives that acted as scouts. They're trustworthy, but he's not going to let you go too far, even with them."

That wasn't what I wanted to hear. "What are the natives like?"

"They have strong moral and family values. You've got to realize they've lived in the Americas for thousands of years, so they have a vast knowledge of plants, animals and natural medicines."

"And they don't mind Europeans coming to their country?" I asked.

"At first, they did. There were many skirmishes and plenty of killings on both sides. Now that the tobacco trade is established, it has lured more of our land owners and slaves there. Farmers, too, are eager to try and make a living. That, along with the army, has meant that the natives are pretty much outnumbered. There would be severe consequences for any of them that attempted to try and do anything silly."

"I can't imagine they're happy about what is essentially an invasion."

"It's a big country, Ally. There's plenty of room if everyone shares."

I said, "It seems like a land divided, what with the Spanish, French and English all staking their claim. You know what it's been like in Europe. Will America be a land in a constant state of conflict as well? What do you think will happen?"

"That's the problem," he said. "All these nations want ownership of the New World. I've no idea how it'll play out, but I don't want to be in the middle of it when it does."

"Do you think I'm walking into something bad?"

"I hope not. Maybe it's just the pessimist in me coming out. Look, if people never took risks when doing things, we'd never progress. Who knows what the future will hold."

Rhett had given me a lot to think about. Whichever way I looked at it, I was still excited about the prospect of going to the colonies.

The ride south dragged on but in a good way. Farmers worked in the fields, rolling hay into bails. Cows leaned through wooden fences, trying to eat the long grass growing by the roadside. Birds darted through the trees, chasing insects.

We talked idly, joking about the good times when we were growing up. Some children came running up to us as we passed through one of the villages, offering us apples for a farthing. I tossed them some coins, and they threw us an apple each. On biting into mine, I spotted a worm and spat it out. I patted my mare's neck, leaned forward and fed her the rest of the apple. Rhett thought it was hilarious.

By the time we arrived at the inn, dusk had settled. While Rhett saw to our carriage, we followed the innkeeper's wife to our room. It was a humble abode with two single beds, each covered by an orange and green bedspread. Anywhere would be good to lay my head tonight. My limbs complained from the long ride, but I wasn't going to moan to Mama about it. I covered my mouth as I yawned. The basin in the corner of the room was a welcome sight.

Mama said, "Why don't you get cleaned up first? You look like you've been dragged through the hedgerows. I'll find the brush so we can do your hair. I know I put it in here somewhere."

She rustled around in her overnight bag.

I peered closely at my reflection through the black spots that marked the mirror above the basin. Surely my reflection was worse than reality.

The cool water was a welcome relief on my skin and seemed to wash away the efforts of the journey.

I patted my skin with one of the towels. They were scratchier than those I was used to, but I should not expect the same home comforts from now on. Everything was going to be different. In all probability, our living conditions on the ship would be even worse than these.

"You know, Ally, if I had thought about it, I would've left a couple of days ago, and we could have spent a few days in Southampton before we sailed."

"Why is that, Mama?"

I sat down at my mother's feet, and she began to brush my hair. Long soothing strokes relaxed me.

"The spa gardens are there. The spring water they discovered is very good for you. Apparently, they've also made a road by the beach. The outlook is supposed to be very pretty. It would've been nice to relax a little before our trip. I'm such a ninny not to have thought of it before."

I answered, "Perhaps we shall have time to stroll along the beach before we set sail."

A knock at the door made Mama jump.

"Yes," she said.

Rhett's voice came from the other side. "I'll meet you, ladies, down in the dining room when you're ready. I'll have a drink at the bar so take your time. There's no rush.

"All right," my mother replied. "We'll be down shortly."

We heard his footsteps disappear downstairs.

"Such a nice young man. You've been spending a lot of time together lately, haven't you?"

"Yes, we have," I answered.

She probed further, "Do you think there could be more than just friendship between you two?"

"I've always liked him, Mama, but the timing has never been right. He has come home just as I'm leaving."

She was quiet for a moment. "Yes, that's a shame."

"He did say that he will give us a return note so that if we want to come back at any time, we can."

"By the sounds of it, somebody might not be content for you to stay in America."

I had thought the same thing but had been unwilling to get my hopes up. All I knew was that, for whatever reason, Rhett was reluctant to act in any romantic way toward me. He'd spoken of his career and desire to get into politics, but I couldn't help but feel there was more to his decision. I knew I couldn't force him to like me in that regard.

"You two should write to one another while you're away. Sometimes men can express their feelings better when you aren't right in front of them. Your father courted me with his pen first."

I made a face. I did not want to think about how my father courted my mother.

Mama continued, "He was away an awful lot. Maybe that's why I get so excited about receiving his letters. Although nowadays there are far fewer words of love."

She sighed.

"Mama, you know Papa adores you. After all these years, it's plain to see."

"Yes, I know. I'm a hopeless romantic at heart. A woman always desires to be courted even after they're married."

She tied my hair into a simple knot at the back of my head and made ready herself.

Downstairs we had a quiet dinner of lamb stew and potatoes in the lounge area. Mama excused herself and retired early.

Rhett again voiced his concerns about the native people in the colonies. He felt they were being taken advantage of. The settlers and the troops seemed to crowd them out of the supposed New World.

The immigrants also had their troubles with the English. They felt the army representing the King was too demanding of the migrants trying to build new lives for themselves. They were keen to escape the tyranny of a greedy monarchy.

"Believe me, Ally, America is a powder keg about to explode.

There's so much going on below the surface. You'll need to keep your wits about you as people have their own agendas. Inside the Williamsburg Fort should be safe. If trouble arises in the town, you should get yourself back to England as tensions will only continue to smolder."

He handed me the slip of paper for the return passage. After our conversation, I was sure the only reason he'd done so was to ensure our safety.

The following day passed in a blur. Before I knew it, we'd arrived at the dock.

It was a hive of activity. Even the sea birds were in a hurry, squawking loudly. The smell of fish from vendors on the wharf was pungent. That, along with the stench from an incoming tide, made me feel sick to the stomach.

Rhett laughed, seeing my reaction to the smells.

"Already, you are turning your nose up at this venture, Ally."

Laborers rolled large barrels up the planks of the ship closest to us. The name *Heart of Oak* was plastered across the stern. There was no going back now. I felt conflicted. A sense of excitement filled me, but also a tinge of regret. I was looking forward to this adventure. To step outside the norm was thrilling. To see new cultures was something few people would ever experience. It would be easy to stay here, but I couldn't. Part of me thought it was lousy timing. Rhett was starting to see me as someone other than his sister's best friend. I was sure of it. But if I hadn't been going to America, we wouldn't have spent so much time together.

As we stepped onto the deck, I was in awe. Three masts towered above us. Hundreds of ropes stretched from the deck to various parts of the masts. A couple of sailors dangled precariously over the horizontal yards that held the sails, mending a tear in the fabric. I watched as another team of sailors raced up a rope ladder like monkeys at the Hyde Park Zoo. Their black boots were a contrast to the white sails. Thick ropes held the coarse linen in neat bundles until it was time to depart. Heavy pulleys secured the ropes.

Rhett ordered our belongings on board and ensured we were comfortable with our cabin.

It was small but manageable, with two single bunks and a washstand. I was pleased to see it had a desk in the corner. However, our trunks took up almost a quarter of the space. A door led to a common area where the captain entertained during meals.

My mother asked, "Rhett, is there a larger cabin onboard? We can hardly swing a cat in here."

"Yes, there is," he joked. "But that would mean you'd have to take command of the ship."

I laughed at the thought.

"I can get your trunks put into the hold. You should keep anything you want to use on the journey in your room. Once at sea, the crew will have little time to retrieve your things. Here, I have a couple of other items for your passage."

He opened a linen cloth that had been placed on our bedding.

"How wonderful," Mama exclaimed.

She loved gifts of any description.

Rhett handed Mama a bag of semi-dried rose hips.

She peered inside, sniffed and raised her eyebrows.

"Believe me, you'll come to appreciate them in the weeks ahead. Scurvy can be a real problem on long voyages, and fresh produce will soon run out. There are sweet biscuits, dried fruit, candied ginger and nuts. These are things you won't get on the ship, and they'll make your trip more bearable."

"Mmm, delicious," I said.

"Make sure you lock your door at night and whenever you leave your cabin. The sailors are usually decent, hardworking men. A few have been known to have light fingers, but the captain is onto them. Finally, here are two bottles of good-quality rum for the end of your journey. It's customary to show your appreciation to the crew when you arrive. They are the ship's strength and soul. Choose someone who has impressed you and give them this small token."

Mama took his hand. "Rhett, what would we do without you and your family? You've all been so kind. I wouldn't have known about any of this. We're indebted to you."

"Not at all," Rhett replied. "Look, the ship is not set for departure until later this afternoon when the tide is right. Let's get you a decent meal before you go. Ship meals aren't fancy."

From the look on her face, I think that surprised Mama a little. Perhaps she hadn't thought about our journey's details, focusing only on seeing Father at the other end.

"Can we go to the beach?" I asked. "Mama says it is quite the talk around London."

He smiled, "Yes, so I've heard. I believe they've built bathing houses and other shops there. Perhaps we shall find an establishment where we can eat and enjoy the view."

Mama was delighted, "Rhett, when you come down on business, you should afford some time to sample the town. Being focused solely on work is good for no one."

I could see my mother working her magic, longing to see us together, which was embarrassing given I was about to leave.

We strolled along the boardwalk, amazed at the number of people enjoying the summer sunshine. Our parasols gave some relief from the sun, but already I could feel a trickle of sweat run down the side of my face. Mama was busy fanning herself with her spare hand. I wondered how a colonial summer compared.

Two men in bathing robes walked through the gentle waves. A crowd had gathered around them to watch their antics. The bathers laughed as the waves repeatedly greeted them, spraying them with water and wetting the hem of their garments. Their wet clothes clung to their bare legs.

"It's scandalous," Mama said.

"I don't know, Mama, it looks quite fun. Imagine how cool and refreshing the water must be."

Rhett teased my mother, "I wouldn't mind going in myself if I had the proper attire. Perhaps you're right, Mrs. Singleton. Next time I'm down this way, I should take a dip.

My mother was horrified, "But they have bare feet."

I replied, "Well, you wouldn't want to ruin a perfectly good pair of shoes, would you?"

It was as if the sight was too much for her. She turned away and started looking for somewhere to eat. Rhett and I looked at each other and grinned. We didn't want to make my mother uncomfortable, so we followed her lead. We found a cute little tea house and sat at an indoor table. The large window afforded us a view of the beach. Thankfully for Mama, it was away from the bathers.

While we enjoyed a delicious meal of smoked fish, Mama quizzed Rhett about his future.

"You said you have business here in Southampton, Rhett. Does that mean you are partnering with your father in his company?"

The serving woman brought over our tea in small delicate cups. He picked up the cup and took a sip before explaining himself.

"I don't mind helping my father out. He has a lot on his plate right now, with business expanding across the Atlantic. Shipping is not a passion of mine. I'm rather more interested in people than things."

Mama's blank-eyed expression demanded further clarification.

"I feel working conditions and laws could be better for all. The government's taxes on the goods we send to America are excessive and, in my opinion, unreasonable. The colonists see no benefit from the money raised in their own country, making it a tough life for them."

Mama said, "That may be so, but someone has to pay for the army over there."

Rhett laughed. "The army over there? The one I was in? Why are they there? What war are they fighting?"

Mama replied, "Isn't the Stamp Tax being used for our soldiers? Doesn't the Crown protect the colonies from the French and the natives? I don't see why people get upset over paying tax."

Rhett replied, "There are no armed garrisons in Liverpool or Southampton. Why should there be one in Boston?"

I knew precisely why Rhett said Boston and not Virginia. He was trying to avoid implicating my father. I felt conflicted by this discussion as Papa was one of the army's senior officers. I knew that's why my mother felt so strongly about this issue.

Rhett must have been able to sense her passion. He didn't want an argument but rather to promote discussion.

He said, "Some taxes were repealed, but new ones have been brought forward. There seems to be a consensus that the colonies should make their own laws and government, but the King resists change."

Mama asked, "What about the natives?"

"Truth be told, the natives get on remarkably well with the settlers. There are always a few bad apples, but the tribes don't fight us. For the most part, they're only interested in trading. As long as the settlers respect their customs, they live peacefully with us. The British seem to be there more to keep the French out, but the French keep themselves to the Mississippi."

"Well," Mama said. "That's comforting to hear. I did read in the papers about an altercation in Boston where soldiers were forced to defend themselves from some of the colonists. Is that sort of thing common?"

Rhett scratched the stubble on his chin. "Like every case, there are two sides to the story. I wouldn't believe everything that you read back here. It started from a dispute about payment on an invoice and escalated from there. If people think they aren't given a fair go, their emotions tend to get heightened at the slightest grievance. It's easy for situations to get out of control. As long as you're not drawn into any conflict, you should be safe enough... What will you do there, Ally?"

Although I understood Rhett's need to pivot to something else, I wished it wasn't me.

"I—I haven't given it a great deal of thought. I guess life will unfold before me."

"Be sure to weigh up your options so you can make sound decisions, and don't get caught up on fleeting feelings," he warned. He sounded like Papa.

"No need to worry, Rhett. You've prepared me well."

Even though I bristled at his admonition, I felt happy that he cared enough to say something.

"Speaking of which," he said, "we better start heading back."

Mama left the inn ahead of us, walking briskly back to the dock, giving us some privacy. When we reached the pier, Mama said her goodbyes and headed up the gangway to join the captain by the wheelhouse.

I fiddled in my pocket for the drawing and placed it in Rhett's palm.

"What's this?" he asked, unfolding it.

"Us," I said with tears welling up in my eyes.

As he looked at the sketch, sadness descended on his face.

"I will treasure this," he whispered. "I hope to see you again soon."

He held my hands, and we both stared down at our fingers. A sudden wave of emotion overcame me. I threw my arms around him and pressed my lips to his neck. I loved the smell of him.

"If I come back, it will be because of you."

"I could take that a couple of ways, Ally."

Rhett didn't let me go but pressed himself closer to me. He placed his hand on the back of my neck, holding me tightly.

"Take it whatever way you like, Rhett," I replied, enjoying the feeling of his body against me.

Tears ran down my cheeks. Not for the first time, I wondered if it was too late to pull out of this crazy venture. I'd always been so confident, but now I doubted my decision. Did I really want to go to America? Was I simply following my mother? As I stood there before him, everything within me said, *stay*. The problem was that I needed to find myself. I wasn't Maggie. She might be content to settle down. If I stayed with Rhett, I'd always wonder what could have been on the other side of the Atlantic. Perhaps it was a sense of adventure. Maybe it was a longing for the unknown, but I needed something more than Rhett could give me right now. Even though I hated to admit it, I wasn't content to become his shadow. If we were to be together, I had to be his equal. At this point, I felt incomplete. I knew I needed to grow as a person.

It seemed like we were standing there forever, but I couldn't pull myself away from him.

He leaned back and looked into my eyes, saying, "You are making my collar all wet, sweetheart. The ship will sail without you if you don't let me go."

"Would that be so bad?" I asked, losing my resolve and feeling a moment of weakness.

"Not for me." He wiped my tears away with his thumb. I desperately wanted to stay with him, but I knew it wouldn't be right. I would be less than I could be. I needed to be strong for both of us.

Even so, I wanted him to kiss me, to assure me that there was a future for us somewhere down the line. If there were a moment when he could show me, it would be now.

Sailors pushed past us on the dock, looking on with amusement. The ship strained at the ropes holding it in place against the pier, longing to set sail.

But Rhett didn't move. He stayed still. I wondered if the attraction had been all one-sided. Did he have the slightest regard for me at all in that way? The way a woman yearns for the sight of her man, longs for the sound of his voice and, perchance, his touch.

Reluctantly, I withdrew from his embrace.

"Will you write to me?" I asked, still clinging to hope.

"Of course. I want to know about your adventures and how you hate it over there and can't wait to get back to me."

I smiled, noticing how he said *"back to him,"* not back to high society, not the estate, not my friends and family, not England itself.

Gosh, I was a fool to read something into every word, but that is what comes from pinning your hopes on one person. I needed to grow up. Maybe I was already starting to.

I took a mental image of this strong, confident, handsome man before me, committing it to memory. I wanted to remember the look in his eyes as the sun broke through the clouds. The *Heart of Oak* might be sailing to America, but I was sailing into the unknown.

The Heart of Oak

At Sea

There was so much to see as we made our way from the harbor's calm waters into the deeper channel of the estuary. I leaned on the railing, watching the ship glide effortlessly toward the ocean. The wind had picked up nicely, and we sped along. The ropes pulled tight as the sails stretched out above us.

A young gentleman walked up next to us and said, "It's quite a view, isn't it?"

He had deep-set eyes that seemed to catch every movement on the distant hills.

"Indeed it is," Mama replied.

We sailed out of the river mouth.

White cliffs and sandy beaches made a stunning contrast to the vivid blue water. Colorful wildflowers dotted the landscape, and I thought what a pretty picture it made.

The young man seemed to read my thoughts. "Not only is it picturesque, but it's also teeming with wildlife."

"Really?" I asked. I was excited at the prospect of learning more.

Mama brought us back to reality with the formalities.

"Nice to meet you. I'm Mrs. Singleton, and this is my daughter, Ally."

"Oh," he stammered. "I get so excited about these things that I forget my manners. My name is Albert Miller."

He tipped his cap in our direction. His fine wispy hair was blown in all directions by the breeze.

"Recently, I made a field trip to the Isle of Wight and collected quite a few specimens," he said, pointing to the island we were passing.

"Interesting." Mama made it sound anything but as she moved off to the side. I, however, wanted to know more.

"Mr. Miller, what sort of things did you discover?" I asked.

His face lit up at having a captive audience.

"When you look at a piece of land, you first think of how beautiful it is. The plants and flowers capture our attention immediately, but if you step closer, you'll discover a whole community of creatures living there."

I had often paid attention to such things on my walks with Papa. We'd spot a myriad of insects that buzzed and burrowed their way through the woods.

He continued, "Would you believe I found a green bush cricket over two inches long?"

Mr. Miller fiddled in his pocket, and I half expected him to fish the said creature out. Instead, he produced a small pocketbook and turned the page to show me a most remarkable drawing. He ran his finger over it reverently.

"Do you see these wings?" He pointed to the detailed, intricate patterns. "They rub them together, making a grating sound that can be heard for miles."

He stopped and listened as if to hear them from the ship. I strained my ears. Out on the edge of the wind, I did indeed hear insects calling.

I remarked, "Your drawing is exceptional. I see you have taken the pains to label it."

He replied, "For me, it is a joy to do so. In fact, I hope to be able to draw many plants and animals in America. My father said, and I quote, *'England is too small for you, lad. Take an escapade across the ocean and see what you can find.'* And so, here I am."

I smiled at the imitation of his father's low voice.

I had never thought about drawing something other than for the sake of capturing its beauty. He was using his drawings to capture knowledge as though it were written in a letter or a book.

"Mr. Miller, I want to see some of your other drawings. I've dabbled with art, but only for enjoyment."

"I don't class my drawings as art. More science-based illustrations would be the term."

"Science?" I said, only vaguely familiar with the word.

"It's from the Latin, *scindere*. It means to distinguish between similar things, to separate one thing from another."

"Oh," I replied.

He flicked through the pages of his book, showing me the birds he'd drawn, sitting on nests or soaring in flight. "Whereas the captain might speak of seabirds following us on our journey, I would talk of frigates and gannets, shearwaters and terns. Most people only see birds. I see wonders of nature."

"Well, your sketches are beautiful," I said. "You're an artist, even if you don't think so."

He blushed, embarrassed at the compliment.

He continued, "If you're interested, I'd be happy to tell you more about them. Who am I to deter an enquiring mind?"

He gave me a shy smile, and suddenly, the long sea voyage was shaping up to be not so long after all.

Albert Miller had a remarkable intellect. He could recall the most obscure facts about any given creature.

One day as we sat on the deck looking out across the vast blue ocean, he confided in me. "Most of my youth was either spent outdoors collecting specimens or in the libraries learning; it was a good job my parents were so accommodating. They enjoyed exploring almost as much as I did, although they didn't always like the things I brought home."

"Oh, like what sort of things?" I asked.

"One summer day, shortly after my fifteenth birthday, I brought home this."

He turned his notebook to a page where he'd drawn what looked like a snake. He held his finger over its title so that I couldn't see its name.

"My mother had a fit and wanted me to get rid of it immediately. She didn't like any type of reptile. I explained that this was not a snake, but a legless lizard called a slow worm. They're marvelous creatures and wouldn't hurt a fly."

He laughed at himself.

"Well, that's not true. They are probably partial to a fly, should they be able to catch one. But they are a great asset in any garden, for they love eating slugs and snails. No matter how much I tried to reason with my mother that it posed no threat, she would have none of it. She insisted that I remove it miles away."

"And did you?" I wanted to know.

"Hardly. I made my sketch and then let it loose in our garden. Cook was quite impressed with the number of bug-less cabbages we had that year. I knew better."

He tapped the side of his pointed nose with a knowing look.

I laughed, "Your friend here had a grand old time eating the caterpillar larvae in your garden that summer, didn't he?"

"And my mother was none the wiser. That's the great thing about creatures. They go about their business, and we don't really appreciate their impact on our environment. They're just existing, but if at any point the balance gets upset, too much of one thing, not enough of another, we'd soon come to respect them a whole lot more."

A commotion at the bow drew our attention away from our conversation. My mother beckoned me over.

"Ally, come see. I've never seen anything like it."

We hurried to the front of the ship and peered over the edge. A spectacular sight greeted me.

Grey shapes darted in front of us. Their smooth skin glided effortlessly through the water.

"Ah, a pod of *Delphinidae,*" Albert muttered.

"They swim so fast," Mama exclaimed in awe.

Albert answered her, "They are using the wave from the bow of the ship to propel themselves forward."

"How clever of them," said my mother.

The dolphins were graceful. They hardly made a splash as they entered the water, time and time again.

"Fascinating creatures," Albert continued. "They have a decent life span, too. Anywhere from 20-50 years. Perhaps you'd like to draw them, Miss Singleton, in my notebook. I've brought a new journal for this trip, and I think it only fitting that you should draw our first creature on this endeavor."

"Really?" I asked, surprised at his request.

"Of course," he said. "Besides, my stomach is already a little queasy, so I'm not sure I'm up to the task. I have every confidence in you."

That made one of us, I thought. Never before had I attempted to draw something that was moving at such speed. The boat's movement would also make sketching a challenge. I hated to think I might lose Mr. Miller's notebook overboard should I try to rest it on the railing. Looking down, I noticed several holes near the floor of the deck. Ropes wove in and out of them. If I looked carefully, I could see the dolphins through the holes. There was nothing else to do. I lay down on the deck, taking charcoal out of my apron pocket. The strangest sensation came over me as I lay prone on the deck, moving with the rise and fall of the ship. When standing, you couldn't feel anywhere near the same movement as when you were lying down. Peering out at sea and watching the dolphins frolic,

I could almost imagine myself moving among the waves with them.

The form of their bodies started to take shape on the paper in front of me. They had rounded, beak-like snouts and bulbous foreheads. Their small but intelligent-looking eyes, in line with their mouth, made their appearance one of the cutest things I'd ever seen. Everyone was mesmerized by these majestic creatures, so I had plenty of time to work on my sketch unhindered.

When finished, I dusted off my gown and tapped Mr. Miller on his arm. I held out my drawing for him to inspect.

"By golly, you've done a grand job of it," he exclaimed, looking at the image in front of him. "That was no easy task. You've captured the way the dolphins jump through the waves. All I have to do now is write some facts down. Do you think your mother might permit me to use your talent once we get to Virginia?"

My mother turned, "Not without a chaperone, Mr. Miller."

"Of course, of course," he replied. Like the notion had only just occurred to him.

At first, sailing was a novelty. I would watch the sailors go about their routines while working on the ship. Everyone had a job to do, and Captain Barton ruled sternly, keeping the crew busy from morn to eve. There was always something that needed mending or fixing, even if it was sewing new sails together in preparation should they need them. I had come to appreciate that these men viewed working on the ship with a certain sense of pride. They loved the challenge of being at sea. The sailors were ingenious and self-sufficient. Nothing was thrown away. A broken hinge could be used to repair a stay, while torn sails could be repurposed beneath the hull as hammocks and room dividers.

As time went on, however, the intrigue of ship life wore off. Mama and I settled into our own routines. It was a new experience to keep our quarters clean and orderly. We had a small rope draped across our room. When there was a breeze and we could open the porthole, we hung our washed clothes to dry. It meant the space in our room was significantly diminished, so we tended to spend more time up on deck. Mama likened it to living in the laundry room back home, although that room was much larger than our cabin. My appreciation for our household staff increased dramatically. There was a certain satisfaction in completing mundane chores. However, once they were finished, I couldn't wait to find Mr. Miller and see what he was up to.

Each day was predictable. All guests were to be up by 7:30 and seated for breakfast by 8 o'clock. The decks had already been cleaned and swabbed by then. Breakfast consisted of a thick type of ground oatmeal or burgoo, as the sailors called it. The tasteless gray goop filled our stomachs. Thankfully, the Captain allowed us to sprinkle a liberal teaspoon of dark brown sugar on it, which melted like a film on top, making it more palatable.

Every day the endless expanse of the sea stretched out before us. The seabirds that had hung around at the beginning had finally stopped appearing. Mr. Miller said the gulls were the last to leave us. The water took on a dark, murky depth that told us we were far from land.

The weather was fine, with a stiff breeze making the sails puff and bloom. I loved feeling the wind on my face and hearing the creek of the ropes holding the sails. It reminded me of riding fast on my horse. Thankfully, neither Mama nor I succumbed to seasickness. The sea was calm.

After our morning walk, I would write to Maggie. I was determined she'd have an account of my journey. I wanted to make her feel like she'd been right there with me. Maggie would enjoy hearing about the details. I knew she would show her letters to Rhett. Although he might find them boring, having made the crossing himself, I suspected he would see how happy and excited I was about the voyage. Perhaps that would make up for my sudden departure. Writing to him was more difficult. As time passed, I tried to convince myself that our moment on the dock meant something special, but I couldn't quite commit those feelings on paper. It made it all too real. I would wait until he made the first move. I didn't want to appear foolish, and I didn't want him to think I couldn't control my emotions. Rhett was not one to look favorably on that type of gushing.

Some mornings were spent pleasantly copying Mr. Miller's drawings. He said I was a competent apprentice.

"Have you ever wondered how birds fly?" he asked one day as I sat there duplicating the details on the feathers of a Northern Wheatear.

"With their wings, I suppose," I answered. I was not used to such in-depth conversations while trying to draw.

"If you compare the same-size bones in birds to a squirrel, you'll find that bird's bones are much lighter. It's not just their wings that allow them to fly. Their bodies take to the air easier. Isn't that interesting?"

"I've never given it much thought," I replied.

"How did this come to be? These are the sort of mysteries I seek to uncover. The *why* behind things. Nature is a puzzle. Have you ever played with a dissected map?"

"Oh, I have," I said. "My friend Maggie has several. One of Europe and another of Wales. Her father liked to tease us, scattering the pieces on the study table. I loved the way no two pieces are the same, and they fit together like keys in a lock. They can be quite the puzzle, slowly revealing their image."

"How did you figure out how to put the map together?" he asked.

"Not from any knowledge of European countries," I replied. "We started on the corners and worked around the edges, matching up the pieces by shape and color."

"That's what science does," he said. "Naturalists like myself put pieces together so that we may understand the whole picture. We may not have it all figured out yet, but one day, who knows, the things I discover in America might fit into a bigger puzzle that explains life as a whole."

His enthusiasm was to be admired.

Mama sat next to us, working on a delicate needlepoint as a gift for Father. She smirked as she looked over in our direction. "Is it time for lunch yet, dear?"

Mama must have thought I needed rescuing. Lunch in our cabin comprised of cheese and hard biscuits washed down with tea.

We appreciated Rhett's supply of goodies but would have to ration them to ensure they lasted. Having our own stash gave us a sense of freedom in the close confines of our quarters.

During the afternoons, we headed outside again. I would watch the sailors work. I met one fellow who was kind and friendly. Like all the sailors, he was a bit rough around the edges. One day, he called me over.

"Girlie, can you come over here and give me a hand?"

"Sure," I replied, almost cutting him off with my enthusiasm as he continued.

"My old fingers don't work like they used to."

His stiff fingers struggled to tie knots in the thick rope. I remembered what Rhett had said about keeping busy and was keen to learn and be helpful.

Tommy had been working on the ships for over twenty years and had plenty of yarns to pass the time away in the afternoons.

As we sat there coiling the ropes, he said, "I had a daughter."

"Had?" I replied, perplexed. He was cheerful, so I wasn't ready for what came next.

"She and her mother died of the pox."

"Oh, Tommy. I'm so sorry."

"It was long ago, so I'm used to the loss. No use being sad about it now. I'm glad she and her mother were a part of my life, and I have many good memories here."

He patted his muscular chest.

Years of manual labor had given him an impressive physique despite his age. His skin was brown and wrinkled from working outdoors, but those around his eyes and mouth were smile lines.

He continued, "This motley crew is my family now."

He gazed about him fondly.

Tommy would tell me about the comings and goings on the boat. Some days I would read to him from my little book of poetry. He had a copy of the Book of Psalms that I read to him on Sundays. It belonged to his wife. I don't know that he cared for the Scriptures so much as the sentiment of the verses she loved.

He chewed tobacco, which I found to be a filthy habit. He kept it hidden under the rim of his hat.

"You wouldn't have any tobacco, would you?" he asked one day.

"Me?" I said, pointing at myself to remind him I was a lady, not a sailor.

"Ah, worth asking," he said.

"I tell you what, Tommy, I have a bottle of rum for you when we dock, but no tobacco."

He grinned, showing his yellow, stained teeth. With that, he took off his hat, tore a small piece out of the lining and chewed on it.

"What are you doing?" I asked, astonished by what I was seeing.

"Eating my hat," he replied as though it were perfectly normal.

"That's a figure of speech," I said, laughing at him. "You're not supposed to take it literally."

He laughed in reply. "Where do you think that saying came from, Lass?"

"Are you serious?" I asked.

"We spit wads of tobacco when they lose their taste. This ain't no different. Shame not to chew that cotton after it's soaked up all that flavor over the years."

"You're a wild one, Tommy," I said.

Mama enjoyed being at sea. Each day, she'd converse with passengers from the other cabins. There was a newlywed couple trying their luck in the new country and a businessman keen to discover trade in the colonies.

Dr. Taylor was the ship's surgeon. He was often busy below decks treating patients or in his cabin treating the crew.

Our cabins were located beneath the wheelhouse and opened onto the quarter deck. We weren't supposed to go below deck. Tommy told me more than a dozen families were in the cramped conditions down there. They had to fend for themselves, being given a food ration every day. I didn't like the class distinction. I knew it was necessary with such limited space, but it didn't seem kind and reminded me of what Rhett said back at the inn. Like him, I was starting to see that such distinctions caused hurt to people.

Each evening, when we went in for dinner at 4 o'clock, the lower classes were allowed to come topside. We would often hear the children running around, glad to be outside. After dinner, I would return on deck, and Mama would retire early. By then, the families had gone, and the crew would play dice or cards—those who weren't rostered on to work, that is. It was a four-hour rotation as the chores never stopped. Most of us would join in for a sing-along after dark. The atmosphere was carefree, The crew downed their beer rations with glee.

One evening, as the sun set over the ocean, the doctor came and sat by me. He was a middle-aged, balding gentleman with a cheery countenance. A cool breeze blew. The sky was radiant with reds, yellows, and pinks stretching along the horizon.

"It doesn't bother you being around all the foul-mouthed fellows here, Miss Singleton?"

The sailors swore a lot. I was not offended as long as it was not directed at me.

"They do no harm. It is good to see them relaxing. It is such hard work on the ship," I answered.

"Indeed it is. Below deck is no picnic either. Those families sacrifice a lot to start a new life in a foreign land."

I was curious. "You spend most of your time down there. What are you treating?"

"Quite a few children don't do well with the rocking of the boat and get sick. Adults seem to fare better. If we don't keep fluids up in the young ones, they can dehydrate. Being on deck helps, but they don't get much sunshine."

The weather hadn't even been that bad. I had noticed the ship's movements were more pronounced when lying down at night. It had taken some time, but I'd gotten used to the gentle sway.

I was reminded of the candied ginger we had in our cabin.

"Perhaps I could come down with you tomorrow," I suggested.

"Well, if you can put up with this lot, I don't see any harm in it," he smiled.

"Will you be onboard this ship for the return voyage?"

"No. One voyage a year is more than enough for me. When I get to the settlement, I'll swap with Dr. Johnson. He'll return to England. He's already been in the colonies for two years."

"What about your family back home? That's a long time to be away."

"I'm a single man, Miss Singleton. The time my profession demands of me doesn't lend itself to family life. Although I could be persuaded to take a wife in America if the opportunity presented itself."

He looked at me with an appreciative glance.

That is not what I meant. I hope I hadn't given him the wrong idea. I had only wanted to go below deck to see if I could help the travelers, not to spend time in his company.

"Dr. Taylor, it is my wish to be helpful to the families. I have some candied ginger. I thought the children suffering from seasickness could use some."

In saying this, I wanted to make my intentions clear. He glanced red-faced over to a group of sailors shrieking with delight at having their numbers come up on the throw of their dice.

"Certainly. I'll see you tomorrow after breakfast, then."

He raised his mug in my direction and joined the crew in their activities.

Dolphins off the bow

Below Deck

There was a strange calmness to the sea the next day. The wind dropped. Our sails drooped as we floated along with the current.

As I headed below deck with Dr. Taylor, the first thing that hit me was the rancid smell of ammonia. It was overpowering. I pulled my handkerchief out of my apron and held it over my nose.

Dr. Taylor smiled at me. "You'll get used to it after a while."

The hold had been sectioned off, using sheets stretched across ropes hanging from the ceiling. This offered a semblance of privacy for the families down below. Most of the hold was dedicated to cargo, leaving them little room to live.

Blank looks and hushed whispers greeted us on the orlop deck where the ropes and chains were stored. Grimy faces stared at me from behind crates. Small hands touched my ankles as I stood next to the doctor.

I smiled at the wide eyes glued to me.

"How is Leo doing this fine morning?" the doctor asked as he ruffled the matted red hair of a lad lying prone on a thin mattress.

The boy's face was white. He had dark rings around his eyes. His mother wiped his cheeks with a damp rag.

"Not much has changed from yesterday, doctor. He can't seem to keep anything down."

The doctor pressed his ear to the boy's chest. "Try to give him small amounts of fluids regularly and get him up on deck this afternoon even if he doesn't feel like it. My nurse here has something he can suck on, but sit him up until he's finished."

For a moment, I wondered who he was talking about. I didn't know there were any nurses on board. Then I realized he was referring to me. Had he given me that distinction to seem professional? The people here might not take too kindly to having a passenger from above deck come below to satisfy her curiosity. I put a piece of the crystallized ginger in the mother's hand.

"Thank you kindly, Miss," she whispered.

I helped her sit Leo up. He eyed my offering warily.

"It tastes sweet and will make you feel better."

Hands came from all directions. This woman had several other children, and they, too, wanted some ginger. I reached into my pocket to accommodate them all.

"Is your husband with you?" I asked. I saw no sign of one.

"He had an accident on the docks. It's just the children and me now. My brother lives in Virginia and owns a store in Jamestown. The shipping company gave us passage as Joe died on the job. I have no family in England. I thought a new start might be good for us all."

I was shocked to hear how she discussed the loss of her husband as though it were routine. Her entire life had been upended. And now she and her children were rotting in the hold of a sailing ship.

"I'm sorry to hear about your husband, and I hope Leo feels better soon."

"Thank you, Miss. Just getting anything into him at the moment is a relief."

Her son was happy sucking on the ginger.

I nodded and followed Dr. Taylor.

The next stop was an infected finger of an older man, which had swollen to double its size.

The doctor took a knife from his bag, a bottle of rum and a wooden peg.

"Here, bite down on this, Bill," he said, shoving the peg in the man's mouth.

"Aw, Doc, I thought the rum was for me mouth." He winked at me.

"Afraid not, old boy. The rum is to clean the knife; otherwise, you'll get another infection."

"Waste of good rum, that is," Bill replied.

"Miss Singleton, could you grab a bandage from my bag and stand by while I drain the wound?"

The doctor made an incision near the tip of Bill's finger and held it over a small bowl while he squeezed gently. A copious amount of pus and blood oozed out.

For me, this was way worse than gutting fish. I wished I'd stayed above deck with Tommy. Instead of looking at the man's finger, I focused on his clenched jaw. Sweat beaded on his face.

Once the doctor was finished, he poured rum on the wound and patted it dry.

"Bind the finger from the tip to the base, not too tightly, mind. And tie it off."

"Yes, doctor," I replied, affording him respect.

Bill grimaced as I wrapped the bandage around his finger. "That hurt like the devil, doc."

"Let's see how it's doing in a couple of days," the doctor said, putting his equipment back in his black bag. "If you're lucky, I won't have to take the finger off."

At first, I thought he was joking, but from the look on his face, it was a real possibility. I'd always known that simple acts like a cut or a graze could result in an infection. I'd never considered how quickly it could spread and how brutal the remedy had to be. Amputating even a finger would change this man's life forever.

I was horrified by the conditions in the hold. The horses in our stables back on the estate fared better than these families. My heart went out to folks like the mother of poor Leo. I couldn't help but wonder if their isolation below deck contributed to the maladies they were suffering.

The morning went by quickly. By noon, I was thankful for the fresh-smelling air back on the quarter deck.

"Is that what you were expecting, Miss Singleton?" the doctor asked.

"I had no idea what life was like down there," I replied. "It's just awful. There must be something more that can be done for them."

"It's a hard life," he said. "There aren't many options this far from land."

"But couldn't they have more portholes? They need good air."

"In bad weather, a loose hatch can swamp the hold," he replied.

"What about proper cabins or decent bedding?"

"Who's going to pay for them?" the doctor asked.

"But there must be more we can do."

"At least the Addington Line allows them on deck once a day," the doctor said. "Not every shipping company does that."

For me, this was a shocking realization. I couldn't imagine being allowed to come out for only an hour a day as a respite from those conditions.

I looked about and wondered why my life had been favored. I could lean over the railing and watch the dolphins frolic in the ocean. I could feel the sun's warmth on my skin whenever I liked. I could come and go as I pleased. I could walk the deck freely and have access to all manner of things the passengers down below couldn't. The harsh reality was that the family I was born into and our wealth were the only differences between us and them. Money allowed me to lead the type of life I did. It didn't seem fair.

"It's not pleasant down there." Dr. Taylor's remarks broke my deep musings. "It's likely to put you off your lunch. Thanks for your help today. The children responded well to you. Something about a lady speaking kindly to them can do wonders."

I didn't know about that. I felt powerless.

"Even so, doctor, it would be nice to do more for them. Leo seems to be languishing down there."

"I must admit I wish I could do more too, but I have limited resources on board the ship. Did you know this is my third trip over to the colonies?"

I shook my head.

"On my last journey, I was treating a native who had come into town to trade. He had one of the worse coughs I'd ever seen. Sickness had settled in his chest, and you could hear his lungs filling up with fluid. I'd tried everything I could to help the man but to no avail. He begged me to find some cedar bark."

"Bark?" I said. I was curious about where this conversation was heading. Why would someone want bark? Berries or even leaves, I could understand, but not bark.

The doctor said, "As I was out of options, I couldn't see the harm in using it. I'd read before that chewing willow bark could help with fevers and pain. A chaplain around a hundred years ago had stumbled upon this fact accidentally. So, I thought maybe the cedar bark could help with this man's respiratory problems. The Royal Society in London has been much more open lately in accepting the use of plant derivatives to treat ailments."

I was fascinated. "So the natives have been using natural remedies to heal themselves? "

"Yes, exactly, for thousands of years. They've been gathering their knowledge of plants for a long time. They'd seen how trees use their bark to ward off insects, fungi and mold. The same things that help the tree survive can have healing properties in humans."

"That is quite remarkable."

"Isn't it? They've even figured out the correct dose. If you use too much willow bark, you can get stomach cramps and bleeding. That's one of the reasons I keep going back to the colonies. I'm not too proud to know that there is much I can learn from the natives. What I wouldn't give to garner that type of knowledge. Using their remedies combined with what we know in the medical field would be invaluable to us in England. It's easy for us to judge the natives as uncivilized, but there is much we can learn from them. If you get the chance to visit a village, do so. You'll be amazed."

You could tell why Dr. Taylor had become a physician from the passion he had for helping people.

"That's one of the reasons I came with my mother," I said. "I want to experience America. I can't imagine you'd get a more authentic encounter than visiting a native village. So, don't keep me in suspense. What happened to the man? Does your story have a good ending?"

He laughed.

"Well, I wouldn't have told you if it didn't, but yes, he made a full recovery. That was a few days before I was due to return to England. Since then, I've been reading up on the subject. There is nothing like getting knowledge firsthand from the people who use it in their daily lives. The difficulty is that they're so remote. The natives can be suspicious of our motives, and I'd need to visit their villages and gain their trust to learn more."

"Perhaps you will get your chance this trip," I said.

"Yes, maybe, although when you are a doctor, you can't just take off into the wilderness. There are always a lot of folks in town who need help, which poses a bit of a problem."

I could see his dilemma.

"You could arrange for some local people to visit you instead."

"That could work, if I could persuade them. It's certainly worth considering, Miss Singleton."

He smiled.

Dark billowing clouds gathered on the horizon. The wind had picked up, but it was erratic, blowing the flags around in different directions.

Tommy was working with a block and tackle to tighten a rope. Up above the deck, sailors climbed along the yards, gathering in the main sails on the three masts.

"Have you seen this, Miss?" Tommy asked, pointing out across the ocean. "A bad storm is coming our way."

I followed his gaze.

"Should hit us tomorrow. We are shoring everything up in preparation. You best hunker down in your cabin and take care of your Mama."

"It seems we are heading straight for it, Tommy."

"We can't outrun it, so best to confront it straight on. The strongest part of the ship is the bow. We are fully laden, so that will help keep us stable. Don't worry too much, Miss. The crew will do the best they can. During storms, we have thirty-minute shifts, giving the men a bit of a break if it gets rough."

"You aren't worried?" I asked, eager to gauge the seriousness of the situation.

"Oh, aye, Miss Ally. You've got to have respect for the sea. Been through a fair few storms in my time. This one looks like a doozy."

"How far are we from land?"

"Far enough that it won't matter if the ship goes down—if that's what you are worried about."

I gulped. He must have realized how it sounded.

"Look, Captain Barton is the best there is. He'll do everything in his power to make sure that doesn't happen. Odds are it won't be bad enough to sink us, but it could get rough, so stay put, you hear. Make sure you've got everything you need before it hits. You don't want to be wandering around even in your cabin."

I nodded.

"Be sure to tie down your belongings. The ship will heave and roll, but don't worry. She won't go under."

A lump welled up in my throat. Before we departed, Rhett's father, Lord Addington, mentioned he'd just lost two ships so far this year. Would ours be the third? I wanted to believe Tommy.

"It'll be challenging, Miss. Hold onto the straps on the side of the hull in your cabin, and you'll be fine."

My thoughts immediately went to Leo and the other poor souls below.

Tempest

After dinner, the Captain echoed Tommy's words and ordered all passengers indoors until further notice. At least the families had been able to get up on deck one last time before the storm hit. Rations would be given to everyone as they weren't anticipating any cooking for several days. The galley was frantically making preparations and distributing dry food.

On my way to the cabin, I stopped by Albert Miller's open door. He had a large trunk open and was sorting through several books.

I asked him, "Do you have everything you need?"

He could be a bit forgetful at times, his mind preoccupied with his more important ideas. I wanted to make sure he had the essentials covered before the storm hit.

"Yes, yes, I think so. Just getting some reading material together. By the sounds of it, we may be stuck in our cabins for quite a while."

I was certain I wouldn't be sitting back, doing any reading while the storm raged on. That was where we were different. Mr. Miller used every spare minute to further his studies. I suppose it wasn't a bad idea to take your mind off things with no one else to talk to.

He asked me, "Would you like a book to read?"

It would have been rude to refuse.

"Certainly. What do you suggest?"

"Here's one I think you will find interesting."

He handed me a book called, *"The Natural History of Carolina, Florida and the Bahama Islands: Containing the Figures of Birds, Beasts, Fishes, Serpents, Insects and Plants."*

"Mark Catesby was a British naturalist. He was one of the first to create an illustrated survey of plants and animals that inhabit America. It was published around 25 years ago. His unique approach displayed the animals and plants together as they are in nature.

"Thank you." I patted the cover. "I'll be sure to take good care of it."

On opening the book, I saw a well-drawn bird in the midst of a bush covered with purple berries.

He smiled, "That's one of my favorites."

"I'll look forward to talking to you about it later then. Take care, Mr. Miller."

Already the ship was starting to sway with the swell of the ocean. I stumbled rather than walked back to my cabin.

Mama and I secured as much as we could.

We went to sleep with a deep sense of apprehension, unsure what the night would bring.

We didn't have to wait long before we were woken by loud peals of thunder.

The noise of the wind howling outside drowned out the creaking of the hull.

As the ship pitched and rolled, I climbed down from my bunk, wanting to be next to Mama. I hooked my arm through the ladder's rung and held on so I wouldn't be flung to the floor.

Even with the window shut, the storm howling outside sent a draft through the cabin. The desk drawer fell to the floor with a loud bang, making me jump. It spilled my letters in a mess, the ink bottle having broken in the process. As I made my way down the ladder, my feet touched the floor, and immediately, my legs buckled under me.

"Leave them," my mother admonished. "Letters can always be rewritten. It is not worth hurting yourself."

She scooted over against the wall and hung on to the straps as I eased myself down next to her. Mama gripped me about the waist with one arm as I held my own arms around her middle.

Lightning crackled through the clouds, splitting the darkness. I snuggled next to Mama, just like when I was a child. The night seemed to go on forever. I could hear the comforting sound of her heartbeat against my ear.

We held each other through the night and prayed for daybreak.

The shaking of the vessel was so violent that Mama and I feared the ship would be torn apart at any moment.

I lost track of how many days we were caught in the grip of the storm. I worried we would never get to say goodbye to Father. That thought was more than my poor mother could bear. Our eyes were puffy. Our pillows were wet from our tears. We told each other how much we loved each other, afraid that these words would be the final ones we would utter.

From the first day, any thought of food vanished from our minds. We tried eating some cheese and biscuits to immediately find them spewed up over the side of the bed. I crawled on my knees with a rag to clean up the mess. I was thrown against the side of the bunk that was bolted to the floor. This was a fact I hadn't paid any attention to, but now I knew why all the furniture was held in this manner. Any loose possessions would roll around the cabin, traveling whichever way the ship was leaning.

Our beds became our life raft carrying everything we thought we would need while the sea of various objects swirled around us - a mess of clothing, travel bags and pillows were strewn on the floor. Our toilet bucket had tipped over, but when survival was your only option, it didn't seem that important.

There was no need for conversation. The panicked look in our eyes told us how we felt. There was at least some comfort in being able to cling to each other. My head pressed against my mother's breast like a babe.

Exhausted, we managed to drift in and out of sleep. Each time we woke, we hoped the storm had ended. It got to the point I could have died and not cared. Although, in reality, that wouldn't have been pleasant. I tried not to think about it. The sea was powerful, and we had the nerve to try and cross it on pieces of wood that were joined together. How naive were we? Any one journey could be safe or tragic. Was it luck or fate or neither of these things that played a part in our outcome? I had plenty of time to think in a situation like this. If I never did another ocean crossing, it would be too soon. Would I risk this again for the chance to get back to England? How did sailors do it? They risked their lives every day, never knowing when their time was up. I suppose that could be said about any activity in life, but why risk it time and time again? All these thoughts kept swirling around my head like the turbulent waves below us.

By the second or third day, we'd run out of water. I told Mama I would venture to the galley to refill our waterskin. By this time, she was in no state to argue with me.

The benches in the dining room had been lashed against the far wall. Water sloshed around my feet. On reaching the hallway, I found myself pressing both arms against either wall to stay upright. I staggered down the corridor, watching as the deck pitched and heaved beneath me. At points, I had to step off the walls to continue on. I opened the fresh water barrel and had to time refilling my waterskin to avoid being drenched by the sloshing waves within.

A door banged at the top of the ladder leading out onto the deck. Rain lashed the opening. With the waterskin over my shoulder, I crept up the stairs, wanting to secure the door.

Waves crashed over the bow of the ship, sending up a wall of spray.

Water washed across the deck as the ship rolled. To my horror, there were sailors climbing on the rigging, working with the sails. The captain was yelling at them to cut loose a sail that had broken its line. The heavy canvas cracked back and forth like a whip.

I watched in astonishment as a sailor was swept across the deck in front of me. For a moment, he disappeared beneath a wall of water. I feared he'd been dragged overboard, but he was secured by a safety line. His limp body lay draped over the gunwale. Several other sailors ran to his aid as another wave swamped the deck.

A familiar figure staggered toward me, struggling against the sway of the ship.

"Back to your cabin, lass," Tommy yelled over the howling wind.

He reached out and shut the door, securing it with a bolt.

Being below deck, it was easy to become absorbed in our own misery and forget the crew was risking their lives to keep us afloat. I shivered with the cold and made my way back to the cabin and collapsed next to Mama.

One morning, we woke, and the ocean was still.

Mama and I looked at each other. The woman staring back at me hardly resembled my mother. Her face was grey and gaunt. Only her eyes mirrored the soul I knew.

Our strength had gone. At first, we ate a small amount, our stomachs complaining of its return to normality. Eventually, we started feeling better.

"My God, Ally. Is it over?" Mama cried out.

I stepped off the bed and tiptoed between the scattered items. Our room was a mess, and it stank. As I unlatched the porthole, I could see the flat expanse of the sea before me. I breathed in the fresh air, thankful to be alive for a little longer. The breeze from outside was a welcome respite but not as great as the sense that danger had passed.

The sky was blue. The sun was radiant and warm.

I turned and smiled at Mama.

"We made it," I gasped.

Suddenly we were laughing like schoolgirls as sheer relief washed over us.

"I've never been so happy to see the sky, Ally. I don't want to go through anything like that ever again."

I couldn't have agreed more.

We looked about our room, resigning ourselves to the fact that we would have to sort it out before we ventured outside. Later we stepped out into the dining room to see what carnage the storm had caused.

Cook was already getting the utensils out for a meal on the large table.

"Captain says you're to stay here and make sure everyone is all right. I'll have some food on the table in a jiffy."

"Where's Simon?" I asked him. The boy who usually set the table was nowhere to be seen.

The cook shook his head and hurried off. That was an ominous sign.

Most of the other passengers were also beginning to emerge from their cabins. Robert and Emily Pembroke, the newlyweds, took their places at the table. He hung his head on his elbows. She stared straight ahead, not even taking us in. Louis Montgomery, the businessman, came out weeping hysterically.

"My arm, my arm," he moaned, clutching his forearm across his chest, but there didn't seem to be any obvious deformity or swelling. It was strange that we hadn't heard any sound from his cabin until he came out in public.

"Take some deep breaths and sit down here," my mother said, trying to comfort him.

"It hurts too bad," he sobbed.

My friend, Albert Miller, had not yet come out. Where was Doctor Taylor?

"Mama, you wait here while I go and find the doctor for Mr. Montgomery."

She encouraged him not to move his arm but to cradle it as best he could on the table.

I was unprepared for the row of bodies I witnessed when I made my way onto the deck.

Corpses wrapped in white sheets lined the walkway. Ropes bound their chest, arms, waist and legs. Some of the bodies were only half the height of the others, which broke my heart. A child's tartan cap lay on the wet deck. One by one, the crew loaded the bodies onto a plank and lifted the end. With that, the dead slid to a watery grave. Each time a body splashed, my chest heaved with grief. I watched as they disappeared beneath the waves.

The captain looked solemn. He stroked the thick grey stubble on his face. He saw me approaching.

"Miss Singleton, this isn't the place for you. I haven't given permission for the passengers to be on deck yet."

"Sorry, Captain, but I'm looking for Dr. Taylor. Mr. Montgomery has hurt his arm."

"Yes, I could hear him from up here. In my experience, those with serious injuries make less noise. As you can see, we have far weightier matters to deal with. The doctor is treating the passengers below. Once he has finished there, I'll tell him about Mr. Montgomery. Try and calm him best you can. Use some whisky if needed."

He stared straight ahead.

"How many," I whispered.

"Eighteen souls. Ten were crew."

Where was Tommy? I was anxious. I looked around the deck for him. As much as I wanted to question the captain about him, I couldn't. I could see the anguish in his eyes. For him, the crew was like family.

"Is there anything I can do?" I asked.

"Cook could use a hand," he said, dismissing me. He was finding something for me to do other than watching the dead being buried. "Tell the others not to come out yet."

"Yes, sir."

"Don't tell them why."

"Understood, captain."

With that, I turned and headed back.

"Oh, Miss Singleton," he added as an afterthought. "Thank you."

Back in the dining room, I relayed the captain's message that the doctor was treating passengers below deck.

"That's damn inconsiderate," Mr. Montgomery complained. "My pain is almost unbearable. He should be looking after first-class passengers, not steerage"

"And yet you are doing admirably," Mama said, turning away from him and raising an eyebrow at me. I understood her gesture. When I first met Mr. Montgomery, he seemed pleasant enough, but when he was pressed on matters, he tended to be overbearing. When he had an opinion, rather than listening to others, he tended to take the matter too far. He didn't temper his thoughts with reason. Dr. Taylor was anything but inconsiderate.

I let Mama know I'd be helping out in the kitchen. She waved me off. I was quite happy to leave him to her care.

When I entered the galley, the cook had a fire burning in the steel oven. He was lowering a concoction of dough-like mixture into the copper steamer. The smoke from the wood fire wafted up the chimney. You could tell Abe was glad to be cooking again.

"Food won't be ready for a little while yet, Miss," he sniffed.

"The captain sent me to give you a hand."

"Oh, did he now?"

That seemed to undo him. He wiped tears from his eyes, turning away, ashamed to let me see. It was then I realized Simon must have been among the dead I'd seen committed to the ocean. From the look on my face, Cook must have known I knew. He remained composed.

"I think everyone needs a good, hot feed, so I'm making pea soup and plum duff for afters. And I don't even think it's Sunday."

We had tasted Cook's weekly treat a couple of times before, and it was easily the best-tasting item on the ship.

"Well, that sounds delicious. What do you want me to do?"

"I've still got potatoes left, so let's get some of those peeled and chopped. Put them into this pot along with some onions. Do you know how to peel a potato?"

He looked skeptical.

"I've never actually done it, but I have skinned rabbits."

"Close enough," he said with a grin.

Cook was a big man with tattoos on both arms. I'd never seen him clean-shaven. His real name was Abraham or Abe, but most people affectionately called him Cook. He was head and shoulders above me, but he moved around the kitchen with speed and efficiency.

Somehow, I managed not to mess anything up under his watchful eye, and soon I was stirring two enormous pots of pea soup.

He spooned a little into a bowl and tasted it.

"Pretty good, Miss. Needs some salt, though. You always got to taste it before you serve. Why don't you dish these bowls up and take them into the dining room. You can start eating straight away. No need to wait for the captain or the doctor. They told me they'll eat later."

I followed his directions but came back straight away. I didn't feel I could leave him shorthanded. I could always eat afterward. He seemed surprised that I'd returned but he kept washing bowls in the sink.

"The crew have collected people's dishes from downstairs. A right state those folks were in. The captain is letting those passengers have their meal on the deck today. There's a bit to clean up down there. I'm sure they'll be glad to see the sunlight."

I helped him ladle bowlfuls of the steaming green soup. The second-class passengers formed an orderly line. They were quiet and patient. I kept my eyes downcast, filling bowl after bowl. It was too hard to face the look of suffering in their eyes. Some felt the hurt more keenly than others, having lost loved ones. We ferried them through the kitchen and out onto the deck. The families were disheveled but thankful for the warmth and comfort of a hot meal. There was no sign of the bodies I'd seen earlier, but the image of them still haunted my mind.

Again I searched for Tommy. He was probably below helping scrub down.

I did see Bill, who grinned at me, flashing his toothless smile. He held up his finger to show me all was well.

I also spotted Leo's mother, surrounded by her three children clamoring for her attention. I didn't see Leo. When she looked up at me, I noticed her swollen red eyes. She glanced away, signaling to me it was too soon for consolation. No words were needed. Leo would never make it to America. I wondered if she considered this price too high to pay for her new life.

I sat down, weary not just from the storm but everything I had endured on this journey. Rhett was right. We hadn't even reached the new land yet, and already I was a changed woman. Far from my sheltered upbringing on the estate, the harsh reality of life had been thrust upon me. It gave me no warning. It threw its ugly face straight into mine. I stared out to sea. How much longer before we arrived? I wanted the remainder of this particular chapter in my life to be over with.

Abe thrust a bowl in front of my nose.

"Here, get something in your belly, lass. By the way, the doc looked at that fella's arm."

"Mr. Montgomery?"

He nodded. "Seems it was just a mild sprain." He grinned. "Carried on like a proper blockhead, he did. Used almost half a bottle of me best rum while the doc poked at him. Now he's snoring like a sailor in his cabin."

"We should all be so lucky."

"Right, you are. I'd best be getting back."

I savored the calming broth, sipping it and relishing the warm, smooth flow down my throat. At that moment, there was nothing I wanted more. Somehow, amidst all the heartache, I was at peace. Mama and I had survived the storm. The sun shone down on me. I closed my eyes. Warmth seeped into my skin, and I delighted in the rare feeling of a full stomach.

It felt good to be alive.

Life was simple—food, warmth and love. Anything else was a bonus.

A sudden shriek shook me from my lethargy. It was Mama's voice. I hurried into the dining room. There was a commotion around Mr. Miller's door. I rushed over to Mama, who was beside herself.

"I was taking him some soup because he hadn't come out," she said, stammering. "I—I found him like that."

I looked through the doorway and saw poor Mr. Miller curled up with a large bloody wound on his head. I was shocked. He'd crumpled on contact with the timber joists in his cabin. He must have been trying to stand and been thrown about as we crashed through the waves. My heart sank. From what I could tell, he'd been dead for days. I couldn't believe it. Tears ran unhindered down my face, and sobs racked my body.

Dr. Taylor pulled a bedsheet over him, saying, "Poor fellow broke his neck." He looked at me, "It would have been quick."

Death is harsh, horrible, and brutal beyond anything I'd ever imagined. For all the distinctions we place on class in society, everyone is equal in death. Those above and below deck fared the same. None of it was fair. He'd been so excited about his venture in America, and now death had stolen not only his life but his future.

Mr. Miller's books on botany lay strewn on the floor along with his collection equipment. I felt terrible. He had so much zest for his studies. The world would be a poorer place without him. I took a deep breath and wiped my face with the back of my hand. Nothing could be done, but out of respect, I picked up his books and stacked them back on a shelf. I could at least show I cared by tidying up the things he valued. I went and fetched the book he'd lent me. I could never look at it again without sorrow for his loss.

I closed the door to Mr. Miller's cabin. Mama looked pale. She was shaking. That surprised me.

"You sit down, Mama. Let me get you some hot tea. I think you're in shock."

I helped her to the dining table and placed a mug in her hands. It was only then that I noticed the tremor in my own fingers. Mama wasn't the only one struggling with Mr. Miller's sudden demise. At that moment, I realized how precious our chats on deck had been. I'd never again have him pointing out the subtleties of the natural world. He had been a gentle soul. He deserved better.

I went and got the metal teapot from the galley and poured a drink for my mother, encouraging her to take little sips.

She said, "Poor Mr. Miller. His parents will be heartbroken when they learn of this. I should have shown a little more support for his interests."

She took a shaky breath.

"Your father will think me a silly woman for coming once he hears the state of things on the *Heart of Oak*."

I comforted her, saying, "Mama, he will think no such thing. He'll be grateful we are there with him. Safe and sound."

I put my arms around her and felt her breathing return to normal.

The captain walked in. He looked like he'd aged several years since the storm began. His shoulders were stooped. His face was haggard. He milled around as if looking for something. For the past few days, he probably hadn't had much sleep.

"Do you want something to eat?" I asked.

"Aye, that would be grand. It's been a while."

He slumped down onto the bench seat, and I went to the galley to get his meal.

Upon returning, I asked him, "Have you seen Tommy?" I was reluctant to bother the captain, but I worried my only other real friend here had died.

"He's not well, Miss," he said between slurps of soup. "He broke his leg."

"Where is he?"

"In the doctor's cabin waiting for treatment."

What did that mean? My heart ached. This day was not getting any better. I hoped Tommy's injury was something that could be treated easily.

Aftermath

I knocked on Dr. Taylor's door.

"Come."

Inside, the doctor was vigorously washing his hands in the basin.

Tommy was lying on a table. A sheet had been stretched out over the wood. Blood dripped onto the floor.

His leg looked awful. The bone below his knee was protruding through the skin. Blood had seeped from the exposed marrow, staining the white fragments. The broken tip was jagged, reminding me of a tree branch that had snapped in a storm. What a hideous sight! I wanted to turn away and run, but I couldn't abandon him. I didn't know if I had the stomach to be of any use, but Tommy was my friend. We had formed an unlikely bond, one that I was determined to strengthen in whatever way I could.

Two crewmates stood on either side of him. I knew Lenny and Dave worked with Tommy on similar shifts. Lenny supported his head while Dave poured a generous amount of rum into Tommy's mouth. Most of it dribbled down the side of his neck.

Once the bottle was drained, the doctor cut away Tommy's trouser leg.

Dr. Taylor said, "You came at the right time, Miss Singleton."

Tommy groaned. If he hadn't moved, I would have thought he was dead. The shock must have shown on my face as the doctor said, "I need your help. Can you help me?"

I nodded, unable to say anything.

He rummaged through his equipment bag, saying, "There is no way to fix a broken bone like this. If he doesn't lose the leg, gangrene will set in, and he'll lose his life.

"First, I'll need these instruments boiled in the galley. When you take them out of the pot, use tongs to avoid touching them with your hands. Put this blade in the fire under the stove. It needs to be red hot to cauterize the arteries. Please leave it in the coals until I tell you. Understood?"

"Yes."

Tommy was in a great deal of pain. He barely seemed coherent. I'm not sure whether he knew what was about to happen. The other crewmates in the room did. They braced, ready to hold Tommy down.

Dr. Taylor said, "I've given him some Valerian root. It's a sedative and works well with alcohol. I'm doing as much as possible for him, considering the circumstances."

Tommy moaned. His hands went limp. His eyes rolled back. It seemed the pain had overwhelmed him, which was merciful given what was to come.

"Can you handle these?" the doctor asked, laying his instruments on a towel.

"Yes," I said.

The array of equipment needed was overwhelming. I recognized a filing rasp. I'd seen the stable boys using them on horse hooves, but I had no idea why the doctor needed one. There was a bone saw, pliers, clamps and a knife. These were butcher's tools. They all had curved metal at the end of their wooden handles, allowing them to be hung up like kitchen implements. The cauterizing iron was heavier than I expected.

I took the instruments and rushed into the galley. Cook looked at me with knowing eyes. He didn't say anything. He already had a pot of boiling water on the stove. I placed the iron in the coals and the remaining instruments in the pot. Steam wafted around the wooden handles.

Mama was in the dining room. We exchanged a glance through the open door, but neither of us said anything.

"When the time comes, use this," Cook said, handing me a wooden pole. As all of the instruments had hooked ends, I realized what he meant. I could use the pole to carry all of them back to the doctor without touching them.

"Thanks, Abe," I said. The look in his eyes was one of dread. He'd seen this before. That much was apparent. The worry lines on his brow told the story that some didn't survive this.

"I'm ready," the doctor yelled down the hallway. "Tell me you're ready."

"Ready," I called out.

"Bring them in."

I did as the doctor instructed, leaving the iron in the fire. The two men tightened their grip on Tommy's shoulders as the doctor got to work. I stood in the doorway, holding the pole in front of me as he took each implement in turn. He worked quickly and efficiently.

After tying a tourniquet around Tommy's upper right thigh, he peeled back a flap of skin that covered two-thirds of Tommy's lower leg. I was perplexed. I was not prepared for the amount of blood that ran onto the floor and didn't understand why the doctor would leave a loose sheet of skin hanging down beside the table.

Sweat formed on the doctor's brow. He mumbled to himself, "Arteries. I've got to find those arteries."

I watched in utter horror as he separated the muscles and tendons from the two bones. He applied clamps to the arteries and took a deep breath.

"Got them," he said, wiping his brow with the back of his bloodied hand. He turned to me and said, "Now, woman. I need the iron now."

I rushed down the hallway and into the galley. Smoke wafted from the glowing end of the iron as I pulled it from the coals. Even the wooden handle was hot. I tapped the metal against the rim of the oven, knocking the ash loose, and ran back and stood in the doorway. The tip of the iron glowed in a soft red hue.

"Once I cut each artery," the doctor said, "I need you to put the iron on the tip until I say so."

There was a real possibility Tommy could bleed out if this weren't done correctly. I nodded. As awful as this was, I knew it was the only way to save his life. Although the physiology was similar, this was much worse than dealing with the animals Rhett caught. Back then, we were taking life. Now, we were saving one.

"Ready?" he said. I wanted to say no. I'm not sure anyone could ever be ready to cauterize an artery. I nodded again.

He cut the first artery, and I pushed the iron against the bloody pulp. Steam billowed into the air. The smell of burning flesh lashed at my nostrils.

"Again," he said, cutting the other artery. I turned the iron around and pressed the other side against the exposed flesh. In truth, I wanted to run. I wanted to hide. I never wanted to see such a gruesome sight again. With both arteries severed, he released the clamps.

The next step was even more brutal. The doctor sawed through the bone. The severed leg fell to the wooden floor. Next, he filed the end of the bone on Tommy's leg. Watching the rasp drawn back and forth and seeing shavings of bone fall to the floor was heartbreaking. I was no longer needed, but I couldn't pull myself away. I had to stay there for Tommy.

Finally, Dr. Taylor arranged the skin flap over the exposed stump of flesh and bone. I expected him to stitch the skin in place as though he were working with an animal hide, but he didn't. He placed a cloth bandage over the whole area, using a sticky tar to hold it in place. Within fifteen minutes, the grisly task was finished.

He whispered to himself. "Done. I'm done."

It was only then that I realized what a toll this process had taken on the doctor. One of the crew wrapped Tommy's severed leg in a sheet. Blood quickly soaked through the cotton.

Another began wiping up the blood on the cabin floor with a mop. I stood back from the door, pushing my shoulders against the opposite cabin. I didn't know what to do. I was still holding the smoldering iron. Someone took it from me. I wasn't sure who.

"We need to get Tommy back to his quarters," the doctor said.

"You can put him in Mr. Miller's old cabin," the captain replied as he came up beside me.

I turned, looking at the next cabin. By now, Mr. Miller must have joined those other poor souls at the bottom of the ocean.

The doctor looked weary. He was covered in blood. His eyes looked soulless. I doubt he'd had much sleep. It would only be through sheer exhaustion that he would slumber tonight.

The crewmates helped carry Tommy into the next cabin. As for me, I stood there staring at the leg wrapped in the blood-soaked sheet. I knew what had to be done. I felt I owed it to Tommy to be the one to commit this part of his body to the sea. I picked up the still-warm leg and proceeded onto the deck with it. I was careful to avoid stares from the passengers, going to an area restricted to crew only.

A few of them knew what I was doing. As I threw it overboard, I wondered what would be next for Tommy. His whole life had been spent working on ships at sea. Without his leg, an already challenging job would be seemingly impossible. As the bundle sank beneath the waves, bile rose in my throat. I couldn't help myself. I leaned over the railing and vomited until my stomach was empty. The sailors looked at me with pity. One of them brought over a wooden bowl, offering me some water to clean my face and hands.

Time was a blur. I wasn't sure if it was minutes or hours that had passed, but Mama came to find me. I was sitting on one of the barrels by the central mast. I felt empty in every regard. Mama rested her hand on my shoulder, comforting me.

"I'm so proud of you, Ally. I understand how difficult that was for you. I couldn't have done that."

During the operation, the other passengers had gone up to the main deck, but Mama had stayed in the dining room and had seen me rushing between the galley and the doctor's office. The door had been open. I wasn't sure how much she'd seen. I wondered if she'd been waiting for me to return to her. I wanted to distance myself from those cabins for a while. I'd witnessed too much sorrow down there and wasn't ready to go back yet.

Mama took my hands in hers, saying, "No young woman should have to go through what you did today— yet you've come out of it stronger."

"It was hard, Mama. It was so hard."

Tears ran unchecked down my cheeks.

"I know," she said. "Life is not just about the good times. We have to deal with challenging times, too. The fact that we're alive means that death and loss are also a part of our existence. For you can't have one without the other. Today, we looked tragedy in the face."

I squeezed her fingers. "I—I feel numb. I don't know what to think."

"This will pass," she said. "Life has a way of sweeping us on. We'll be carried to new shores. Like this ship being driven on the sea."

"I guess," I replied.

"We all have to deal with heartache. We never want to. We're never ready. But we must be strong."

"How can I be strong?"

"You already are." She paused before adding, "I haven't told you this, Ally, but I lost two babies before you were born."

I stared at her in shock.

She continued, "Each time, your father and I were so happy to find out I was pregnant, only for the child to be stillborn. We went to doctors around the country, wanting to find out what the problem was with me. They had no answers.

"When I realized I was expecting a third baby, I was afraid history would repeat itself. Your father insisted I have complete bed rest, but that gave me too much time to think about all that could go wrong.

"Seeing our friends have children was tough. I'd given up hope. I thought your father and I would only have each other. Every time I felt you move inside me, instead of being glad, it filled me with dread. I was sure I would never be a mother. Slowly, time went on, yet I couldn't believe I might experience the delight of bringing forth a new life. It was only when you were born that I allowed joy to fill my soul. You were perfect."

I wiped my face as Mama recounted her story.

"There are highs and lows in every life, Ally. Today was a low, but there will be highs again, perhaps not tomorrow or the day after, but they will come."

She smiled at me as only a mother could.

"No one likes the lows, but I'd rather experience this life with all its highs and lows than not experience it at all. We don't get a choice in being born, but I figure life is a gift to be cherished. We don't have to like all of it, but there is always something to be thankful for."

"And I'm thankful for you, Mama." I hugged her. "Today was tough, but as you said, not every day will be like this. A weight has pressed down on my soul this day. Hopefully, tomorrow it will be a little lighter."

She replied, "And it is all right if it isn't, but keep going, and someday it will be."

A rainbow stretched out overhead. With the storm now passed, the day seemed to promise better things to come.

Mama stood and reached out her hand to me. "Come. I think Cook has some plum duff on the table. You better get some before the captain and the doc eat it all."

I didn't feel hungry, but Mama was right. I needed to eat.

The horror of the day seemed to fade as I descended the stairs into the dining room. Abe's big brown eyes held a compassionate look as he handed me a tray laden with soup and a plate full of plum duff and whipped butter. The smell was amazing.

The captain and Dr. Taylor were downing rum from small glasses.

"It's been a hard day," Abe remarked. "But we're here. We've made it to the other side of that damn storm."

"Have a seat, Miss Singleton."

The captain raised his glass in my direction.

"Your help today was invaluable."

"She'd make a fine nurse," the doctor echoed.

"Never again," I said.

Mama lathered the plum duff with butter for me. I watched as it seeped into the doughy mixture.

The captain smiled. "You know what works well with plum duff?"

I shook my head, thinking he was suggesting a sweet accompaniment.

"Rum!" He poured me a glass and slid it down the table in my direction. I smiled. There were good things in this world. A friendly gesture was one of them.

I poured the rum over my plum duff.

"That's damn good," I said, coughing as I swallowed a mouthful. I wasn't used to such strong liquor, but I enjoyed the warmth in my throat.

The doctor and the captain roared with laughter. It was absurd. After all that had happened, we were laughing together. So many lives had been lost. So much pain had been endured. Perhaps this was the only way to address the anguish. Life holds hope for the living. Maybe hope is what we needed to carry on. Or maybe we just needed more rum.

Tommy

For the next few days, Tommy drifted in and out of consciousness. When he was awake, I would spoon-feed him. The doctor seemed happy with his progress, and his stump was free from infection. As the days went on, Tommy lost his zest for life. Even the Psalms I read failed to spark any life in his dull eyes. A kind of depression seized his soul, which was understandable given the pain he'd endured and the loss of his leg. He complained about spasms extending below his knee, which was impossible, but he felt them all the same.

One of the crew fashioned a pair of wooden crutches for him. The doctor gave me the task of getting Tommy up and moving again. No easy feat when he'd lay there staring at where his leg used to be. Being kind to him didn't seem to help. I even arranged for his mates to visit and offered to have him carried on deck for some fresh air, but he refused. Often, I'd sit with him in silence, sketching in my book, just wanting him to know I was there. Rather than working on getting out of bed, he became more subdued.

One morning, after various attempts to get any acknowledgment from him, I lost my temper.

"Tommy McBride, do you think I've spent all this time over the past week caring for you like a newborn babe just for you to lie there in self-pity? For God's sake, get your derriere out of that bed now!"

That got his attention.

He looked me square in the eye.

"I can still feel it, you know. It feels like my leg's there even though I know it isn't."

Finally, I had a response. This is good, I thought.

"Many a ship has been lost in a storm at sea, but we survived. You and the crew should be proud of what you accomplished in that tempest. Tommy, you have to go on. You still have much to give and a full life to live."

"What good is a sailor with one leg?" he asked. "The sea is all I've known."

I tried to sound cheerful. "I know the future is scary. It scares me too, but you are far from useless. New adventures await you in America."

"Who is going to employ me in the colonies?" he asked.

I hadn't been prepared for that question, but as soon as I heard it, I knew the answer.

"Me," I replied.

I stood by the door, so he had to sit up and turn to see me.

"I don't want your pity, Missy."

"Tommy, this could be good for both of us. Once we arrive, Mama will be preoccupied with Papa. I don't even know what I'll do in Williamsburg, but I do know I need someone I can trust. My father will restrict my movements if I'm on my own. I need a friend, and I know you would look out for me."

"So you are trying to buy my friendship?" he sounded offended.

"I was hoping I already had your friendship," I replied. "What I want is your service."

"I don't see how much help I could be to you?"

Right then, I knew I had him. "How would you feel if I was your daughter and I walked around the settlement on my own?"

A frown settled on his weathered features.

I added, "You aren't going to be able to accompany me if you are stuck in this bed."

I put the crutches under my arms and hopped about the cabin, saying, "See, there's nothing to it."

He laughed at how ridiculous I looked in my long skirt as I bounced around with one boot held high behind me. Then I held the crutches out to him.

"Your turn."

He took the crutches from me and examined them.

I said, "Look, you have two choices. Work for me or spend the rest of your days begging down by the docks."

Reluctantly, he swung around and positioned the crutches under his armpits. Testing their strength, he rose with trepidation and rocked forward toward the door.

"Come on," I said. "Let's go on the deck and get some fresh air. It's a beautiful day to be out at sea."

"I have missed it," he agreed reluctantly. "I'd like to feel the ocean breeze on my cheeks again."

Over the next few days, Tommy got used to his new sea legs. We took turns around the deck. It took a lot of effort for him to feel confident again. The doc said once the stump healed, he could switch to a strap-on peg. That would free up his arms. Tommy liked the sound of that.

I continued to help Abe in the kitchen and learned how resourceful you needed to be in a ship's galley. Each evening, after my chores were finished, I worked on a drawing of my kitchen mentor. Since our journey was nearing its end, I gave it to him. I thought I had captured his enthusiastic grin perfectly, although he swore his mouth wasn't so big. Tears welled up in his eyes. He wiped them away, thanking me.

"That's real nice of you, Ma'am," he stammered. "You'll do all right in the New World. You're not like some of those hoity-toity ones who expect everything to be done for them. You care about people. That will take you a long way."

I didn't have the heart to tell him I was one of those hoity-toity people a few months ago. Had I changed that much on the high seas? Perhaps I had.

"Thanks to you, Abe, I'll be able to cook my own dinners. Next time you pull into port, be sure to look me up for a meal in Williamsburg."

"Right you are. It will be good to see how Tommy's doing as well."

He gave me a bear hug.

I was thankful for the relationships I'd developed while on board. If I'd kept to myself, I would've missed out on the beautiful connections I had made.

I'd rewritten the stack of letters for Rhett and Maggie. I gave them to the captain to take back on his return voyage. I knew they'd be surprised and proud to hear about the things I'd been doing. I left off the worst parts of the story, so they wouldn't worry.

White sandy beaches stretched along the shore. Lush forests reached inland. There was no sign of civilization, but that excited rather than worried me. I was sure we'd happen upon it soon. I could hardly wait to get on dry land again. I made sure to spend the final afternoons of our voyage with Mama. She enjoyed the sunshine on deck, watching as the American coastline passed us by. We'd made it. We'd crossed the Atlantic. We'd reached the New World. Was I prepared for all that lay ahead? Probably not, but I was willing to learn.

Act II

New World

Arrival

The following morning I awoke to the sound of gulls squawking overhead. Boots pounded on the deck above me. I was confused by all the commotion. As I peered out of our porthole, I was surprised to see waves breaking on rocks not more than fifty yards away. Scattered islands formed a line into the entrance of the bay.

A stiff wind had hastened our arrival at the entrance of the river. Mama and I stood on deck as our vessel limped toward Jamestown.

The crew were busy, tying down the main sails, while the passengers were getting what glimpses they could of this foreign land. Some families from below deck were already carrying their meager possessions in their arms. Leaning over the railing, they were keen to catch every detail of their new home.

I don't know what I expected or what vision of America I held in my head, but initially, I was disappointed. Even though settlers had been here for over 150 years, there seemed to be very little going on. Unfamiliar landscapes continued on behind muddy and swampy banks.

"The port is around the next bend, Missy," Tommy stated. "There'll be more action going on there."

"I should hope so," Mama said as she swatted away a huge horsefly.

She'd gotten used to the idea of Tommy being around.

When I first put forward the idea of him being my companion, she hadn't liked it. His time in the empty cabin near our quarters had meant that he was allowed to eat with us. Those meal times made for some memorable moments, and the above-deck passengers had come to look on Tommy fondly, albeit at arm's length.

I think the captain was relieved that Tommy could be helpful again in some capacity, for he was now free to hire an able-bodied deckhand in Jamestown.

"Tommy, who should I give our rum to?" I asked.

He looked a bit affronted.

"You aren't technically part of the crew anymore," I reminded him.

He mumbled under his breath before saying, "What about Lenny and Dave."

Those two had been a big help to Tommy.

"Sounds good. Can you organize that?"

He wandered off on his crutches, looking for his friends.

"Do you think Father will be here to greet us?" I asked Mama.

"I'm sure he will do his best, dear."

As we rounded the bend, we got our first sight of the Jamestown wharf.

An ocean-going ship was already docked at the port, but there was room on the long wharf for our ship to come alongside. The crew tied off behind a fishing vessel and lowered a plank to the pier.

Jamestown was a hive of activity. Goods were being loaded and unloaded. Fish was sold from wooden carts. Furs were bundled into crates, ready to be shipped back across the Atlantic. Merchants traded with settlers. The presence of soldiers was surprising as, in England, they tended to keep to forts. There were even slaves with skin as black as night.

My eyes were drawn to the natives. They were extraordinary and nothing like anything I'd ever seen in England. Their skin was beautifully tanned, while their dresses were colorful and ornate. The men were shirtless. Some wore loincloths, and others skin leggings. They kept their hair long in plaits, although a few of them had partially shaved the side of their heads. Many of them were wearing bone jewelry. The women wore modest buffalo-hide dresses with fringed sleeves. Their outfits were adorned with intricate beading. Some of them carried young children on their backs. They were oblivious to yet another ship arriving as they bartered foodstuffs and furs.

This was not the bustling city I had thought it would be. It was like a very poor cousin to a port town in England. There were no brick buildings but rather crude structures made of wood. The only indication to tell one from the other was the white-painted signs that were displayed above the main door.

Tommy patted me on my shoulder, "I've arranged with the captain to get the crew to help unload your belongings."

Our eyes were busy scanning the commotion for one particular figure.

It didn't take me long to spot him. Papa was dressed in full military uniform and looked resplendent in his bright red jacket. A handful of soldiers surrounded him with muskets resting over their shoulders. A cart and a team of four horses stood off to the side.

My mother yelled over the call of gulls, "George. George!"

She waved frantically to get his attention.

He raised his hand in a much more subdued manner than her. Papa held her gaze with an affectionate smile. I blew him a big kiss which he caught and placed near his heart. We had done this ever since I could remember, whenever he came home from a particularly long stint away.

It was good to see him again.

Nearly a year had passed since I'd set eyes on Papa. He looked thinner. His uniform sagged on his frame. He'd aged a lot in that short space of time. I noticed he was clean-shaven. The lines on his face had deepened, and his eyes portrayed a weariness I'd not seen before.

Perhaps having his family around him would remedy that.

Mama could not contain her joy. Much to my father's embarrassment, she embraced him. The soldiers looking on were amused at this unusual display of affection toward their commander. Next, he drew me into his embrace, and I felt comfort in the familiar smell of his pipe, which permeated his uniform. Sudden tears started running down my cheeks.

"There, there. It's all right now." He kissed my hair. "Let's have a look at you. Is it possible you have become even more beautiful?"

I smiled and answered, "Only a bath will restore me to my former glory."

He laughed, saying, "In that case, we'll get these trunks loaded and sent off immediately. I expected a lot of luggage, but you girls have outdone yourselves."

It seemed nothing could dampen his mood at the moment. In reaction to his comment, I looked around and noticed we had somehow acquired more belongings than when we started.

"There has been a mistake," I said. "I don't think all this belongs to us?"

Tommy said, "Oh, that will be me, Miss Ally."

He bowed, leaning forward on his crutches and introducing himself to my father. "Tommy McBride, sir."

I said, "Tommy is my aide."

My father didn't look convinced by a middle-aged man on crutches. Tommy didn't seem to notice or care.

"Captain asked me," he said in his typical broken English. "He said I had to clear out Mr. Miller's cabin as he had another passenger booked on the return voyage. I collected Mr. Miller's valuables and locked them in the captain's cabin to give to his family. He said all this other stuff had to go as they already had a full load. It's mostly books, and I thought you might like them, Miss Ally."

"Well," I said. "I can only hope that's what Mr. Miller would have wanted. If his family wants them back, we can arrange to do that at some other time. Could you let Captain Barton know that before we leave, Tommy?"

"Sure thing Miss Ally. I'll get the lads to tell him."

He relayed the message to one of the crew who was nearby.

My Father enquired, "What happened to Mr. Miller?"

The image of poor Mr. Miller lying broken on the cabin floor came flooding back. I didn't know how to begin to describe the loss of such a unique mind. I stammered. Tommy came to my rescue.

"We had a right doozy of a storm, sir. Lasted for four days. The waves hit fifty feet in height. We lost crew and passengers. I was washed across the deck and fell into the hold. My leg got caught in the ladder's rungs and snapped like a branch."

My Father looked horrified.

"It was awful, dear," my mother said. "I've never been so scared."

Papa said, "The Atlantic can be treacherous. I'd hoped you would have a mild crossing, but there are no guarantees. It seems you're all ready for a few home comforts. The barracks outside Williamsburg are nothing fancy, but it's better than being cramped up on that ship. I'm glad we've had clear weather for the last few days. Otherwise, the roads would be a quagmire and damned near impossible to get through. Let's get going."

With the trunks loaded, we climbed onto the cart and sat up front next to the driver. Tommy sat on the rear of the wooden deck. My father climbed onto his horse and signaled his men to move out.

Our journey was painfully slow. There were no paved streets here in America. The wagon rolled over the dusty main road. As we left the bustling commercial center, a smattering of houses heralded the more civil lifestyle of Jamestown. Rock walls enclosed functional gardens laden with all manner of vegetables. Pretty flowers were a luxury and a waste of space here, it seemed.

I wish I'd worn my breeches so I could have marched alongside like the soldiers. Instead, I felt every bump in the road as we rolled along. As we departed the outskirts of town, we increased our elevation, and the stench of the docks was soon behind us. The trip gave me plenty of time to look at the country around me. Geese flew in a V-formation overhead. Songbirds could be heard from the woods. The fall colors in the trees were magnificent. Red, yellow and orange leaves swayed in the gentle breeze. Some, having fallen onto our path, were being squashed in the dirt by the hooves of our horses. Now and again, a squirrel could be seen scurrying among the trees as we disturbed their quiet foraging. I took a deep breath feeling glad I could experience the wonder of another way of life.

After a time, I hopped down and ran up to my father, who was leading our small convoy. I needed to stretch my legs.

"Bit slow going for you, Biscuit?" he said, looking down at me. He winked.

It seemed ages since I'd heard my childhood nickname spoken from his lips.

It brought a smile to my face. I remembered the biscuits he used to sneak for us from our cook's pantry as we were about to go wandering around our estate. We would arrive back shortly before dusk, and Mama would wonder why we weren't hungry for supper.

"Oh, I'd love a biscuit," I said.

"I'm afraid the biscuits over here are more like scones. And not the fluffy ones Miss Finch used to make, either. I wouldn't even feed them to the pigs."

He sighed.

"Speaking of home, how's Fred coping with Pepper?"

Papa's favorite speckled horse lived up to its name. He was feisty and strong-spirited. My father was the only one that appeared to have the stallion's respect. One of Fred's jobs was to ride him. On more than one occasion, our groomsman had been chucked off the back of that animal.

"There's only one master for that horse, Papa. But of late, it's become apparent that even he's given up hope for your return. He lets Fred take him for a gallop with no complaints."

"Well, that's good to hear, for Fred's sake. That horse isn't the only one that wishes I was back home."

I felt I had to confide in Papa.

"You do realize that our horses are now being looked after at the Addingtons. Fred and the other household staff have gone on to other positions."

"No, I didn't know. That's a damn shame. Fred was one of the best stable hands I've ever had."

I echoed his sentiments when I thought of my maid, Agnes.

He turned his head over his shoulder to look at his wife before fixing his gaze back on the trail in front of us.

"Well, what's done is done. I can't blame your Mama for wanting us to be together. She must be serious about staying here if she's shut up our home." Another thought occurred to him. "I would've told her not to be so hasty if I knew what she was thinking."

"I wanted to come too, Papa. Why should you get to have all the adventures without us?"

He chuckled.

"It's not that I'm not glad to have you here. I can't tell you how good it is to see you again, but this is no place for the likes of you two. To think I could have lost you on the voyage over scares me. I'll have to be on watch now, ensuring you're all right. As if I don't have enough happening at the moment."

He seemed lost in thought. Rather than looking down at me from his horse, his eyes were straight ahead. It was the first time I'd felt like a burden to my father.

"Rhett has been preparing me a little," I said. "I can fish, make traps, hunt, and even gut rabbits. I can cook, too. I learned that on the ship."

A couple of the soldiers gave each other sidelong glances. Some even snickered under their breath. I left out the part about helping amputate Tommy's leg, as there was no need to worry my father completely. I'd like to see those soldiers cauterize a bleeding artery.

Papa responded, "Well, good on you, Biscuit, but that doesn't ease my mind any. Tonight we will house you and your mother in my quarters.

Then tomorrow, we'll get you some decent lodgings in Williamsburg. I can't have you staying at the barracks. We'll visit each other when we can, but the fort is no place for women."

He looked at the soldiers surrounding him.

"I'm only going to say this once, and you can get the word out." He directed his speech toward his men. "My wife and daughter are mine. You treat them like you would treat me. If I hear even an inkling that this is not the case, you will have to answer to me. Is that clear?"

"Sir," they said in unison.

It was evident that my father commanded respect here. He turned back to me.

"Thank you for accompanying your mother here, Ally. That had to be a tough choice to make. You left your friends in England, and I know you were about to come out for your season."

"Mama needed me," I said. "And I'm glad I came. I got to attend a ball in London before we left, but I'm in no hurry to settle down. I feel like the whole world is out there waiting to be explored, and I haven't seen any of it yet."

"Well, I'm glad I get to keep my little girl for a bit longer," he chuckled. "Sing us a song, would you, my dear? It will help pass the time, and the lads here will appreciate it."

It was such a joyous fine day. I was happy to fulfill my father's request. He always seemed to know what each moment required.

A robust sweet melody escaped from my lips from an old song, *The Oak and the Ash.*

O fain would I be in the North Country,
Where the lads and lasses are making hay;
There should I see what is pleasant to me,
A mischief light on them enticed me away
Oh, the oak and the ash and the bonnie ivy tree,
They flourish at home in my own country.

How long had these men been here in America? Some might have brought families, but I doubted it. Most of them would be separated from them. I could only imagine how the soldiers must feel, being so far away from their loved ones. We were lucky in that we could visit Papa. Most other people didn't get that luxury. Songs of home stirred the spirit in this foreign land. A few of the men cleared their throats, and a couple of the younger men hastily wiped at their eyes. In a situation like this, raw emotion bubbled underneath even the most hardened of men.

Williamsburg

It was odd being on land after so long at sea. Even as I was lying in the cot that night, it felt like I was still swaying on the ocean.

Father had a modest cabin on the east side of the Fort with an office, bedroom and guest room overlooking the yard.

Tommy bunked with the soldiers in the barracks, which was no doubt a novelty for them. He enjoyed being around men with whom he could have a yarn. He'd retell his adventures, washed down with copious amounts of beer and cider. Like the sailors on the ship, drinking kept the men's spirits up. From the guest room, I could hear them laughing and yelling into the night. In the next room, there were squeals and giggles. It seemed I wouldn't sleep much on my first night in America.

The following morning, Mama and Papa were coy while eating their eggs and beans for breakfast. It was heartening to see their love rekindled.

Papa informed us that we would travel the short distance to Williamsburg later that day. Since our belongings were already loaded on the wagon, he wanted to make haste and get us settled into our new lodgings beyond the fort.

"Why can't we stay with you?" Mama asked.

"This isn't England, Joyce. The King's commission doesn't guarantee loyalty. It should, but it doesn't. Having you and Ally here would be a distraction—for the men and for me."

He gave her hand a squeeze.

"You're better off in Williamsburg, where you can mix with the gentry and attend church. It also gives me an excuse to go into town more often."

Reluctantly, Mama agreed.

I looked at Papa, "Did you hear about the settlers in Boston? Rhett told us about the trouble up there."

My father didn't look pleased with me raising this topic.

"Our garrisons are here to keep the peace," he said as though he were defending what had happened. I meant no offense, but my father was quite passionate.

"Rhett should have told you both sides of the story." He looked down at his mug, breaking eye contact with me. "It was a mob—a riot. They should have never harassed our soldiers. Our troops are here to support the Crown."

To my surprise, Mama said, "I heard they were upset with Lord Hillsborough."

"That's no excuse for violence."

"I agree," I said, wanting to show my father I was being thoughtful and not taking sides without understanding what had happened, but I was curious.

"It was the 29th Regiment," my father said. "A mob began swearing and harassing one of the sentries. Extra soldiers came to help. The civilians began throwing stones and clumps of ice at the troops. A shot rang out. No one is sure who fired first, but then the soldiers started to fire on the crowd."

"How many people were killed?" Mama asked.

"Three, with eight others wounded. I think more died a couple of days later."

"It sounds awful," I said.

"I knew the captain there at the time," Father said. "An Irishman named Thomas Preston. He's a good man. They tried him for murder, but it wasn't his fault—his soldiers fired before he could take command."

"What happened to him?" Mama asked.

"He was acquitted and sent back to England."

"But that wasn't the end of it," I said, knowing from Rhett that the shooting continued to cause rumblings throughout the colonies.

"They're calling it the Boston Massacre," Papa said. "I call it stoking the fire. The whole mess should have been left as it was, but too many so-called patriots are using it to stir up trouble."

He got up from the table and opened a drawer, pulling out a folded sheet of paper. He handed it to Mama, saying, "They printed this propaganda piece called *The Bloody Massacre Perpetrated in King Street*. It is a one-sided representation that makes our soldiers out to be the instigators. This has been circulating through the thirteen colonies. It has inflamed tensions in Jamestown and Williamsburg."

The picture showed what appeared to be an officer giving orders to a line of British soldiers. They fired into the crowd. I noted that the British faces were sharp and angular compared to the colonist's softer, more innocent features.

Papa pointed at the drawing, pushing his finger against it as it lay on the table.

"Look at this! It's not honest. They make us out like we were lined up in a battle formation. And these colonists here—they're dressed as gentlemen. They weren't. They were laborers."

My father was red in the face. Mama fell silent. I didn't know what to say.

"It's a distortion of the truth," he said. "That's what riles me!"

As much as I loved my Papa, I felt I had to say something more. People had died needlessly. He was convinced the tragedy was being used to cause more trouble. I could see he was worried about something similar happening in Virginia.

In a soft voice, I asked, "What caused it? Why were they there in the first place?"

"They just were," my father said. "They'd been harassing the soldiers all day. Truth be told, they'd been harassing them for weeks."

"But why?" I asked. "Nobody does that without reason."

"They weren't being heard," my father said, surprising me with his honesty.

"Shouldn't they be heard?" I asked, remembering Rhett's comment about the colonist's concerns being repeatedly ignored.

My father hesitated. I don't think he'd considered the motivations leading up to the riot. His pause told me he was uncomfortable with this discussion.

Mama said, "All this must be causing you a great deal of stress, dear."

He nodded. Papa took the drawing off the table with less vigor than he'd shoved it down. "They shouldn't have been there. Neither side should have been there that day."

I said, "They should have been talking to the governor, not the soldiers."

"Yes, yes," he said, pointing at me. "Precisely. We're soldiers, not politicians."

"And Williamsburg?" Mama asked.

"It's a good town," Papa said, wanting to soothe our concerns after such a heated debate. "You'll like it there. It's charming. As it's the capital of Virginia, it receives the finest trade from both the north and the south. The markets are well stocked. There's civility and class. You'll have access to butchers and bakers. I'm told the garden parties are the talk of the thirteen colonies."

Mama looked pleased. I had expected something a little more

exciting than garden parties. I was disappointed that I wouldn't have more time at the fort. I wanted to see for myself the life Papa was now living, but he had determined it was not to be. When he came to visit us, I'd have to make biscuits and quiz him instead. How often would he make the journey to town? At the very least, I hoped to see him weekly.

Papa had already made inquiries for us in Williamsburg. He'd found a boarding house with two spare bedrooms. When it came to Tommy's lodgings, he suggested a saloon room in the local tavern. He wrote Tommy a letter of introduction and sealed it with wax. I wasn't sure having Tommy live in the tavern was wise. I would have to keep him busy during the day, or he would quickly become accustomed to never leaving that accursed place.

Papa welcomed the idea of having Tommy accompany us. With all the uncertainty, it meant he didn't need to assign a soldier to our care. Tommy's jovial nature and no-nonsense wit would serve us well.

The following day, the plan was for Tommy to drive the wagon into town. That proved to be more of a challenge than expected.

"Damn and blast this stupid leg," Tommy muttered. He rocked forward on his crutches and leaned against the wagon wheel. With one hand, he pushed the crutches into the back of the deck behind the seat. I went to help him up, but he waved me away.

"I'm not sure this will work," Papa said as he stood on the side of the dirt track.

"I'll be able to get up there in a minute, sir," Tommy replied. He held the wheel and hopped up, getting his good leg on one of the spokes. Even so, he couldn't reach the high spring seat with his arms to pull himself up.

"If I could get a push, I might make it," he said, sounding defeated.

My Father was frustrated. "You have to be able to do this on your own. Otherwise, how do you expect to manage at the other end? The ladies won't be able to help you down."

Papa turned to the officer beside him, saying, "Lieutenant Browning, go and find Sunny, will you? We're going to need his help."

"I can do it, sir," Tommy insisted, but he was stuck standing on that one sideways spoke of the front wheel.

"It's fine," my father said, tapping him on the arm and pointing at the rear of the wagon. "Let's get you on the flatbed instead."

Reluctantly, Tommy climbed down. I grabbed his crutches, but he wouldn't let me help him. Pride won out, and he hobbled away from me. Tommy leaned forward over the back of the wooden flatbed and did a push-up, swinging himself around as he did so.

"There," he said, triumphant as he sat facing back toward the fort. It was a small win, but Tommy's ego was still intact.

My parents stood beside the horses talking as Tommy and I chatted at the back of the wagon. After about ten minutes, the lieutenant returned.

"What the devil took you so long?" my father asked.

"Sorry, sir, I found him down by the river."

Standing next to the lieutenant was a native scout. He looked about my age. He held a line full of fish and beamed at my father.

"For your dinner, chief," he said, displaying his still glistening catch.

I could see why he was called Sunny. He had a large sun tattoo on the left side of his chest. A black spiral with alternating long and short rays adorned his hairless torso. His smile almost reached both ears. His countenance was welcoming. It made me feel warm, like on a summer's day. He was well-built with muscular, solid shoulders and striking facial features. His almond-shaped eyes were framed by long dark lashes. They would be the envy of many young girls back home. His long, straight black hair was tied back in a simple ponytail.

"Looks good, Sunny," my father replied as the lieutenant took the fish from him. "I have an important job for you. I need you to escort my wife and daughter to Williamsburg. Drive them and their companion to Mrs. Tinsdale's boarding house. Once there, wait while they settle in. You can see Father Cawley about staying in one of the church rooms. Report back here every third day with any useful information, including meetings with the townsfolk. You'll act as our relay, carrying messages back and forth. We'll give it two weeks and review it after that."

My mother sighed. "You mean we won't get to see each other for at least two weeks?"

"I don't like it any more than you, dear, but I don't want to inflame things in Williamsburg. At the moment, the army needs to stay well clear of the town. Hopefully, after you have settled in, tempers will have simmered down. We'll see what the situation looks like. You can come and visit me then."

Sunny climbed up and took the horses' reins.

I gave Papa a long hug. He leaned back and said, "Mrs. Tinsdale is an army widow from a well-to-do family. After her husband died, she wanted to stay in Williamsburg. Your mother will get on quite well with her. Mrs. Tinsdale has many connections in town and will help with anything you need."

"We'll be all right," I said, climbing up next to Sunny. "Don't worry, Papa, we have managed quite well on our own over the past several months."

Mama gave Papa a kiss and a hug. They spoke tenderly, but I couldn't overhear what was being said. He then helped her climb up beside me.

Heading out of the compound, Papa laughed, "Oh, and Ally, don't chew Sunny's ear off."

Sunny looked horrified and put his hand over the ear I was facing. He was taking Papa literally.

I laughed and said to Sunny, "It is just an expression, meaning I talk a lot."

When he didn't look like he was feeling relieved, I added, "So your ears don't get sore from me talking. We also say, don't talk your ears off."

This seemed to make him relax, and once again, he showed me his radiant smile.

I hoped we could be friends. It would be nice to have someone my age to converse with, although that could prove harder than it seemed.

During the journey, I noted Sunny's English was remarkable. He spoke well, considering it was not his native tongue.

"Sunny, how did you come to speak English?"

"Missionaries used to come to our village. They wanted to convert us."

"Did they?"

He seemed reluctant to reply. He might've been worried about offending me, but I didn't care.

"We learned the language. We used it to trade with the English."

I noted that he didn't mention anything about his beliefs.

"Do you believe in God?"

"I believe in *Ahone*."

I'd never heard anyone talk of any other god before. I wanted to ask him about what the missionaries taught him, but it seemed clear he had no interest in our Jesus.

"We are thankful for all *Ahone* provides. All of life is intertwined. The physical and the spiritual are bound together."

I had a lot to learn about Native Americans, and I was glad someone like Sunny could talk to me about it.

"Why did your family want you to come and work for the English Army?"

"My father was one of the twenty-eight chiefs from the *Pamunkey* Tribe. His forefathers before him realized the foreigners from across the sea were here to stay. Many of our people were wiped out by attacks and disease. Colonists kept coming in increasing numbers. We found it was easier to trade and help the English than be wiped out altogether. I'm the third son of the chief and was sent to the English fort to learn your customs and to see what was happening in your colonies. My brothers are responsible for the tribe. I am free."

I was intrigued. "So why are you here with us? Surely, you've learned English ways by now. You could be anywhere?"

"For now, I am content. We share one land. The safety of my people depends on the safety of all people. I don't work for your father, even though he likes to think so."

I looked over at my mother sitting next to me. She had been content to listen to our conversation so far. I was sure Sunny's comment would get a reaction from her, but she smiled at me as if to say, let him think what he wants.

Something told me, though, that Sunny was no man's servant. He helped my father because it benefited him and his tribe.

He continued, "Since I'm neither army nor settler, I can come and go between both places and track and trade with all."

"You must not like us for coming and upsetting your peaceful existence," I said. If ever I felt like an outsider, it was now.

"Many tribes have come and gone from these lands. It has never been peaceful. You're just another tribe. A big greedy one, but you are a tribe. If our people are to survive, we must learn to work together with you."

Sunny taught me a valuable lesson on the way to Williamsburg today. My respect for the native tribes rose significantly. If this was their outlook, the future didn't seem so bleak.

We approached a large wooden bridge, which stood over a sizable creek. Beyond that lay the entrance to the town. The main street was straight and long. A mixture of houses and various establishments lined each side of the road.

"Once we cross this bridge," Sunny said, "Mrs. Tinsdale's is the first house on the other side."

We pulled up outside a two-storied, white-painted building. The home had pretty blue shutters that framed the windows. It was quaint. A large porch surrounded the bottom floor, where an assortment of furniture sat. Swing and rocking chairs seemed to say come and stay a while.

Mama said, "Now this is more like it, Ally. What do you think?"

"It looks lovely," I replied.

Already we'd attracted a number of stares from the residents gathered around the blacksmith's shop opposite the house. I guess newcomers would always be a novelty, especially a well-dressed lady and her daughter, a rough-looking one-legged man and a native. I waved, and they returned the gesture.

Lace curtains gave a tell-tale twitch before a silver-haired lady stepped through the front door. She walked gracefully toward us, a smile on her face.

"You must be the Singleton ladies," she said, extending her hand.

"Rose Tinsdale. Happy to have you come to stay. Usually, it's only business gents we get around these parts. It will be lovely to have some female company for a change."

Mrs. Tinsdale was a petite woman with delicate features. Her striking amber-colored eyes looked toward our belongings.

"You can have your things brought up the stairs to the two back bedrooms at the end of the hall.

She eyed Tommy doubtfully.

Mama replied, "Thank you for making your home available. It is charming, by the way."

"Think nothing of it, dear lady." She hooked her arm through my mother's. "As a former army wife, I know a few home comforts go a long way when visiting your husband. Now come inside. I have some tea and cakes freshly made."

Mama looked back at me. I wondered how much Father had told Mrs. Tinsdale of our plans and the length of our stay. Was he perhaps going to try and persuade Mama not to stay too long in America?

"I'll help Sunny with our bags," I said to Tommy.

Not wanting him to feel useless, I added, "Why don't you have a little look around this end of town?"

"Right you are, Miss," Tommy replied, hopping off the wagon.

Bless his heart. He was trying his best to fit into his new role. Hopefully, I'd be an easier taskmaster than his captain. I smiled at the thought.

"You're strong for a white woman," Sunny said as we lugged a trunk upstairs. We were trying not to scuff the woodwork in the process.

All those exercises back in England had come in handy. Although it wasn't for escaping the natives but to help get our belongings up to our new lodgings. Once the trucks were sorted, I put my hands on my hips and drew in some deep breaths. Sunny looked like he hadn't even broken a sweat.

"I'll wait outside, Miss Ally."

I looked around my room. It was warm and inviting. The late morning sun beamed through the large windows on the back wall, making the dark patterned carpet look faded in some parts. I had an excellent view of the surrounding countryside with its rolling hills and idyllic landscape. There was even a tiny balcony where I could sit outside. My eyes were drawn to the large four-poster bed which dominated the room. There was even a bath in one corner. I almost cried out for joy. I chided myself. I must put any thoughts of my own comforts aside and get Tommy settled first. Once I stepped into the luxury of that bath, I wouldn't be coming out for a very long time.

Mama was happy enough to have Mrs. Tinsdale's company for the afternoon and put up little resistance to my idea of exploring the town.

"You must take some cakes for yourself and your acquaintances, dear," Mrs. Tinsdale said kindly. She handed me a linen-wrapped bundle of goodies. "You've worked up an appetite getting those trunks up the stairs."

I thanked her. Living here was not going to be burdensome in the least.

We caught up with Tommy. It was no surprise to see him chatting with some of the locals. He'd be an excellent source of information on the comings and goings of the town. You couldn't help but be drawn to his friendly personality.

On the short walk down the road to the tavern, I handed out the food bounty. Tommy inhaled his cake in seconds. Rather than hobbling along on his crutches, taking the occasional bite, he'd decided to stuff it all in his mouth. The pound cake crumbs on his beard were the only clue that he had devoured two pieces with haste. Sunny was polite but looked at the treat with apprehension.

"You haven't had cake before, Sunny?" I asked, surprised.

"I'm not used to this sort of food," he replied. "I love honey, but we don't use sugar when we cook. To me, it's strange to mix with flour."

He sniffed it and nibbled a corner, wrinkling his brow. "It doesn't seem to have much substance. It melts on your tongue almost as soon as you put it in your mouth."

"Exactly," I said, relishing the taste with delight.

He handed me his share. "If you like it so much, you should have mine."

I wasn't saying no to more cake when I hadn't had any in weeks.

We eventually stood in front of the most popular place in town: the tavern. The large establishment was a detached brick building consisting of two floors.

Sunny hesitated. It seemed he had no desire to step inside. I paused, curious as to whether he would say anything.

"I've seen many men drink that bad water. It's not wise for a man to lose his senses. It makes him weak in body and mind."

Tommy raised his eyebrows. He didn't agree. "Plenty goes on in there, lad, that doesn't involve drinking. Most taverns in a town like this use the upper rooms for meetings and business. Sometimes even a makeshift courtroom, if needed."

I fingered Papa's letter in my purse, hopeful we would be able to secure Tommy a place to stay. Most of the tavern's regular clientele were probably working since it was midweek, and it was too early for the lunch trade. Usually, only men frequented taverns, so I wouldn't have enjoyed entering, even if Tommy was with me. I was confident it would be quiet.

It was a dark and musty place that smelt of wet wood and tobacco. Several tables and chairs were scattered around the room. On each side of the large fireplace were worn, comfy-looking couches. Behind the bar, a buxom middle-aged woman was wiping glasses. She looked surprised to see new customers.

"What can I do for you folks?" She looked us up and down. "Millie's the name. I haven't seen you in these parts before, have I?"

Determined to keep this as professional as possible, I replied, "Very pleased to meet you. I'm Ally, and this is my friend Tommy. We've recently arrived from England and have come to stay for a while."

"Well, you two make a right pair, I must say," Millie replied, unsure of our relationship.

Tommy held out his large calloused hand and shook Millie's petite one.

I continued, "Tommy is to assist me in town. I have a letter here from my father requesting lodgings for him."

I held out the letter. Millie took it and read its contents.

"You're Colonel Singleton's daughter. This is starting to make more sense now. It says here that you and your mother are staying with Mrs. Tinsdale. Well, it's always good to have new folks in town. We could use a breath of fresh air around here. Something tells me you'll be just that."

She winked in our direction. "I have a room that Tommy can use. Come round the back, and I'll show you."

Millie smiled, showing a couple of missing teeth.

This was good news. I could tell Tommy thought so as well. He was grinning like the cat that had caught the proverbial mouse.

Tommy's rucksack jostled on his back as he followed along on his crutches.

Millie showed us a small room with a single bed and washstand. It wasn't much bigger than our cabin on the ship, although it had a few homely touches. There was a small table and chair in one corner and an animal skin rug on the floor. A window had a view of the side street. The morning sun warmed the bedroom. A colorful patchwork quilt covered the bed. The room even had its own fireplace.

"Oh, this is grand, ain't it, Miss Ally?" Tommy sounded impressed.

I was glad Tommy was pleased. However, I doubted how quiet it would be during the evenings. Although thinking about it, the ship was hardly a place of solitude. Tommy had probably become accustomed to noisy interruptions.

"And the rental of the room includes meals?" I asked.

"Yes, Miss. A hearty breakfast at nine o'clock and a dinner meal at seven," Millie said.

She mentioned a sum I thought was more than fair and would hardly make a dent in my monthly allowance. Within a few minutes, it was all settled.

Millie added, "If you need anything else, Tommy, just let me know. You'll find we're a friendly bunch for the most part. Just don't take the side of the Crown, and you'll fit right in. Some of our patrons can get a bit passionate about that topic. Best you steer well clear of it."

Tommy answered, "Don't worry, Miss Millie. I stick to my own business—although I do like a yarn and have plenty of stories to share.

"I bet you do, Tommy. We'll have to chat over a drink, but that'll have to wait. I've got the lunch crowd coming in shortly. They don't wait for anyone, if you get my drift."

She bustled away, leaving us to ourselves.

I said, "I leave you to settle in, Tommy. Do you need anything else?"

"Nah, Miss Ally. Captain paid me my due. I might wander a bit later on and get the lay of the land. Are you all right on your own with Sunny? We've only just met the lad."

I nodded and smiled, "I trust father's judgment."

Besides, I had come to my own conclusions about Sunny. He would do nothing to jeopardize the peace between my father and his tribe. In the little time I had known him, I knew he was honorable.

"Sunny can see me back to my lodgings. Don't worry, Tommy. You won't lose me on the first day."

I arranged to meet Tommy at the doctor's office the following day to check up on his leg. I hoped it would be healed enough for Dr. Taylor to attach the peg leg. It would give Tommy more stability and increase his mobility and independence.

Sunny had waited patiently outside until I returned.

As I walked out, he said, "Once we get back to your boarding house, I'd like to get the horses unhitched and take them over to the blacksmith's yard. One of them has a loose shoe."

I looked in my purse, saying, "I might need to talk to Mama about blacksmith fees. Do you have any money on you?"

"No," he replied. "But they have an account for the army."

I was surprised Sunny wasn't carrying any money, so I asked, "Sunny, does my father pay you?"

"No, Miss Ally. I get food and shelter. I do not need money. The great god *Ahone* and the land provide all I need."

This concept was foreign to me. Even though many of the male friends I knew had inherited money from their relations, they'd been working toward careers so they could provide for their own futures. Not striving to have an adequate source of funds was seen as a weakness somehow.

"What if you need money for something? What do you do?"

"What would I need to buy?"

"I don't know, a new axe or a horse, for example."

"We can trade pelts for things that can't be found on the land. But in reality, there is very little we can't resource ourselves. Wild horses roam these parts. We catch and tame them. Men use money because they have forgotten how to harness the land. They specialize in one skill to exist. We utilize many skills and work together to achieve the same goals."

I could see his logic.

We walked along the main road back toward Mrs. Tinsdale's boarding house.

Sunny asked me, "Why did you bring so many things on your journey? Are you planning to stay for many moons?"

"Yes, we do have rather a lot of possessions, but not all of it is ours. One of the passengers on the ship died in a terrible storm. The captain gave us his belongings, mainly books from England, I believe."

Sunny pondered out loud, "The sea must have been fierce to kill a man."

I replied, "Not just one man, Sunny. Many men, some women and children, too. Tommy broke his leg in that storm. Many lives changed during those days."

I hadn't thought of it like that before. Tommy wouldn't even be in Williamsburg if it wasn't for that storm. He'd be sailing back to England by now. One incident changed the course of his life forever.

"It was a terrifying experience. I thought the ship was going to be destroyed, and we'd all perish."

I shuddered from the memory of it.

Sunny brought me back from those painful thoughts.

"I should like to see books from your country."

"I'd be happy to show you them, Sunny."

It would be fun to teach Sunny about my home, and hopefully, he could teach me about his customs and culture. We were the same and yet completely different. Our beliefs and ways of living were mysterious to each other.

"Did you know someone from my tribe once traveled to England and met with your King? She'd been captured in a war with the English and married a white farmer. She believed in your God and died in England from a sickness. After many years, her son returned, met his relatives, and became a tobacco farmer. Her name was *Matoaka*, but they nicknamed her *Pocahontas*."

It was interesting to hear about ethnically mixed marriages. I'd heard of her story. Marriage could be complicated at the best of times without having so many differences thrown in. I wondered if many of them occurred here. I should wait until I'd known Sunny more than a day before asking him. I smiled.

He said, "I might not get to travel across the great sea, but at least I can learn about the differences in our countries from your books."

"Let's set aside the first part of the day to do some reading," I suggested. "Tommy doesn't have breakfast till nine, so we won't need to

156

collect him until after that. I can get us food from Mrs. Tinsdale's, and we can picnic by the river."

"What is this picnic you speak of?" Sunny sounded intrigued.

One step at a time, Ally, I reminded myself.

We returned to the blacksmith's shop, which had a large stable area behind it. We arranged to leave the carriage and the horses there. The town was small enough for us to navigate on foot. I looked with envy at some of the riding horses.

"Is it possible to hire a horse?" I inquired.

"You ride, Miss Ally?" Sunny interrupted.

"Yes, Sunny. I've been riding since I was a little girl."

The blacksmith replied, "We don't see many women riding here, Miss, but I can certainly rent one out to you."

I could already sense Father's disapproval of me gallivanting through the countryside on horseback. I didn't want to be cooped up in this small town when there was a whole new country to explore. Besides, I now had the perfect guide, a much better one than a one-legged elderly sailor. All at once, the world before me had opened up with endless possibilities.

New Life

Steam rose from my bath in a fragrant mist. A few sprigs of lavender floated on the surface of the water. This was a luxury, even here in civilized Williamsburg. Our host warned us that once a month, we could look forward to such a treat. I wiggled my toes in satisfaction. Had anything ever felt so good?

Mrs. Tinsdale's guesthouse was a godsend. The woman was a kind soul who'd found a new purpose in life after her husband died. He'd left her with a rather sizable inheritance, and she had channeled some of it into her new business. She delighted in looking after her guests, and this little slice of heaven was in stark contrast to the rest of the town. Father had known exactly what we needed after the long voyage.

It had been a week since we'd arrived in Williamsburg, and I was enjoying myself immensely. I fell asleep each evening on a full-sized mattress with beautiful, sweet-smelling linen. My room at the back of the house faced away from the town. The creek snaked its way behind the rear yard, giving me the most scenic backdrop imaginable. It was like nature's canvas was laid out before me. I would wake to the sound of bird song, something I hadn't realized I'd missed at sea. Mama was equally pleased with her lodgings in the room across from mine. Most of the other guests only stayed a night or two. Long-term tenants were few and far between.

Louis Montgomery, from the *Heart of Oak*, was also staying with us. He had secured a position collecting taxes on behalf of the Crown. The previous collector had recently given up the post and decided instead to try farming. Apparently, dealing with irate settlers didn't seem to bother Mr. Montgomery, especially when he could afford the comforts of a home like Mrs. Tindale's.

When he came home from work, he would sit down and recount the day's events. He'd complain bitterly if he couldn't catch up with some poor farmer to exact taxes from them and then crow like a rooster when he did. All the while, he'd be filling his mouth with sweet treats before dinner. I was less than impressed. The power of his position did little for his weak disposition. He enjoyed the perceived strength his post gave him.

Since we arrived in Williamsburg, I'd seen firsthand the emotion and frustration of some of the townsfolk. Whenever people met together, there was little else on their minds. The tavern, the general store and even church on Sundays were all places where the hot topic of unreasonable taxes was being discussed. Papa was right: the army and the government were seen as one and rarely seen as favorable.

As I floated there in the bath thinking about these things, I closed my eyes and took a deep breath. I exhaled slowly, calming my nerves. It was hard not to get caught up in the dramas of this town. The settlers were diligent workers that found it difficult to get ahead in their new land. It would only take a harsh winter or a crop failure to see them brought to their knees.

The water in my bath was starting to lose its heat. My skin had long since gone wrinkly. Reluctantly, I reached for my towel.

I was meeting Sunny soon. I'd gotten into the habit of wearing breaches around him as it was far more comfortable, not to mention practical. We'd done a little exploring together—nothing too far away and always within sight of the town. He'd become my chaperone by default, even though he wasn't a relative or family friend. Mama hadn't said anything about the arrangement because Papa trusted him. I loved the freedom this gave me.

I rummaged in Mr. Miller's chest for another one of his books to read with Sunny. The young botanist's journal had been on top. That particular notebook had stared at me for days. The leather cover was soft and supple. Untying the ribbon that bound it, I'd turned to the first page, where I'd sketched the dolphins frolicking in the waves. Albert Miller had already added his notations about them in his distinct cursive writing. This was something he would never do again. He should've been the one to have gone through his belongings on arrival. I felt like I was somehow invading his privacy. The top layer within the chest had a huge hooded winter coat, gloves and a couple of pairs of breeches. I had tried them on previously, and although they were a little long, I could adjust them. They would be too small for Tommy. Sunny had refused them, saying his skins were much more comfortable than the scratchy English material.

Sunny had a basic grasp of reading but struggled with more complex language. He enjoyed it when I read factual books to him. Those with vivid descriptions and pictures were his favorite. Today I thought I would mix it up a bit, so I picked *Travels into Several Remote Nations of the World* by Jonathan Swift. I would have to explain to Sunny that *Gulliver's Travels* wasn't factual.

When I opened that book, there was an inscription on the inside from Albert's father that read: *To my only son, May your adventures take you on a lifelong journey of discovery. Each step takes you closer to your goal, hopes and dreams. Your loving Papa.*

Life was cruel. It could lead you into a false sense of security and then, in an instant, be gone forever. Mr. Miller's dreams would never become a reality now. Or could they?

An idea formed in my mind. Mr. Miller had wanted to document the plant and animal life here in America. I wouldn't be able to travel extensively to do that, but I could cover this small part of Virginia.

Diagrams were easy enough to draw, particularly as I'd been practicing them with Albert during our journey. Sunny and his people could help me, already having a vast knowledge of the local flora and fauna. I also remembered that Dr. Taylor had wanted an understanding of the plant life here for medicinal uses. Suddenly it felt like I had a specific purpose. Jonathan Swift would have to wait. I was thrilled to know Sunny and I would have our own adventures.

Looking out the window, he was already waiting outside. I tied my still-damp hair up and raced downstairs to grab some bread and hard-boiled eggs from the breakfast bar. I wrapped them in a linen cloth and put them in my bag.

Sunny greeted me with his usual wide grin. I had become enamored with his effervescent personality. His innocent and enthusiastic nature was not something I had witnessed before. Everything seemed amazing or sacred to him. It was always refreshing to be in his company.

This morning we ventured a little further down the riverbank than usual.

"What are we reading today?" he asked excitedly.

"We're not reading," I said. "We're drawing and writing."

He looked at the bag hanging over my shoulder. The sketchbook lay to one side. I reached in and held up my sharpened charcoal sticks with a smile.

"We have a project," I announced, handing him one of the boiled eggs. "It's going to be a team effort. I need your help, Sunny. You know how you're interested in England? Well, the people in England would like to learn about your country, too. So we'll document the plants and animals that live here."

"Miss Ally, I'm good at many things, but to draw as they do in your picture books is too hard for Sunny."

It was the first time I'd seen him look dejected.

"Don't worry. I will draw them. All I need you to do is explain their names and what they are used for. You'll be excellent at doing that. You and your family have lived here for hundreds of years. You know the history behind these plants and animals and how they interact."

"This is true, but I should take you to my village. The women there know all the local plants." He was sounding excited about the idea now. "I need to leave before the next new moon for our annual celebration of the Earth's creation. It's a three-day feast with dancing. It is here that I will be recognized as a man. I will have my hair shaved and finally be like my brothers."

I could see how important this was to Sunny. I felt honored to be invited, but I wondered what his family would think about bringing a young white woman along, not to mention what my father would say.

We sat in the meadow, and I sketched wildflowers. Leaves were beginning to fall from the trees so I made charcoal rubbings. It was impossible to capture their brilliant colors, but I noted them in the margins. Their shapes were stunning. Sunny told me about the birds and animals that would frequent these woods, so I included those details with the descriptions of the plants.

I didn't meet Tommy until after eleven. He was behind the bar, stacking glasses when I walked in. Sunny, as always, had refused to come inside.

"What time do you call this then, Miss Ally?" Tommy asked. "It seems to be getting later and later each day. Should I be worried?"

He enjoyed teasing me.

"You look like you're keeping busy anyway, Tommy. Has Millie put you to work?"

"Oh, aye."

Dr. Taylor had been able to fit Tommy with his new artificial leg, which meant he could do a whole host of extra tasks now. This had improved Tommy's demeanor. He was pretty much back to his usual jovial self.

At that moment, Millie appeared from the back carrying an armful of bottles. "Oh, Miss, I'm sorry. I didn't mean to take Tommy away from yah. It gets a bit much sometimes doing this all on me own. He's so handy."

"Not to worry, Millie. Tommy looks happy to be helping you out."

I don't know if I've ever seen a sailor blush, but that was definitely pink creeping up the sides of Tommy's neck. He busied himself rearranging the glasses on the counter.

Another idea sowed its seed in my mind.

"You know what, Millie? How would you like Tommy's help on a more permanent basis?"

She sounded excited. "That would be grand, Miss Ally. The locals have taken a shine to him. They love his tales."

Hmm, not just the locals, I thought, by the looks of it.

Tommy was a charming character, if not a bit rough around the edges, but he was a caring man, and Millie enjoyed his company. As it was, I think I'd overestimated his mobility, even with his new wooden leg. Though I would have liked to have him accompany me around town and out into the country, it wasn't practical. Perhaps he'd found the home he was looking for here with Millie.

"Tommy, I have a new project I'm working on with Sunny, which requires my time, hence the late hour. I think it would be best if you continued helping Millie in the tavern. What do you say?"

"Seems like you women folk have figured it all out anyway," he replied.

"You're happy with that, then?" I asked, wanting to make sure this change wasn't too much for him.

"As long as I'm busy, Miss, I don't mind what I do. It's idle hands that will drive a fella mad. What about your folks, though? How do they feel about you spending so much time with a native? I wouldn't want to be agreeing to something they're against."

"I'll talk to them, don't worry. As you said, I think they'll be happy to see I've found something useful to do."

Millie addressed Tommy, saying, "If you're working for me, I'll cover your lodgings and wage. You should see the number of customers he draws in. He'll pay for himself and then some."

Tommy laughed. True to her word, a group of men entered the tavern at that moment. They walked up to Tommy and patted him on the shoulder like long-lost buddies. Then another group arrived and another.

"Looks like the lunch rush has arrived early." Millie winked at me.

I made a hasty retreat.

Outside Sunny looked surprised.

"Where's Tommy?" he asked.

"He's got a better offer," I said. "He'll be working in the tavern from now on."

"Oh," Sunny said.

As Tommy was technically my chaperone, I wondered if Sunny felt uncomfortable being alone with me. That Tommy was barely ever with us out in the woods wasn't a concern for me. I understood it wasn't practical for him to explore the countryside on a wooden leg. For Sunny, though, it was probably a worry. My father had charged him with ensuring my safety. A change in circumstances like this would warrant an update.

I said, "Do you think we could go visit my father?"

Sonny looked toward the forest and said, "I'm due to report back to him, but he's a man who doesn't like surprises. Us turning up unannounced may not be a good idea."

"How about a fishing trip then? We could head up the river and detour to the fort on the way back. That way, it won't be obvious."

He smiled. "You're clever and a little tricky, Miss Ally. I think that could work. You usually get what you want, don't you?"

I grinned back at him, "Most of the time, Sunny."

We made a brief stop at the local store to pick up some cheese, pickles and an assortment of cured meats for lunch. The lemon drops on the counter looked enticing. I wondered if Sunny had ever tried sweets. I got the clerk to add two small bags to my order. Father had a sweet tooth like me. It would be good to spoil him for once.

The day was perfect. The water rippled as we glided on its still surface. The air was so fresh out here. Sunny let me paddle the canoe.

And after some instruction, I felt I'd grasped the basics. If only Maggie and Rhett could see me now. I'd been too busy to think of home, although it was always at the back of my mind. Lately though, other things had taken priority.

My old life seemed miles away. And it was. I decided I should write and tell them all about my new quest. If I was to get my letters on the next ship, I must ask Father when it was due to sail.

We ventured up past the fort. Sunny put his net out, and it flowed downstream.

The river was abundant with blue catfish, but we didn't catch one for ages. I sat at the far end of the canoe and drew a rough sketch of Sunny repairing the net.

"Are you ever going to catch something?" I asked, jokingly as the afternoon wore on.

"You might want to put your book away," he said, grinning as he cast the net beneath the shade of an overhanging tree. The canoe rocked. I grabbed at the sides as he hauled the net in. It could hardly contain the fish flapping around.

Sunny emptied his catch into the bottom of the canoe. Fish frantically flapped about my legs. Sunny was in fits of laughter as I lifted my feet, squealing as I tried to avoid the wet, wriggling creatures.

To my surprise, he began throwing them back in the water.

"What are you doing?" I asked, still not game to put my feet down. Several of them were still flipping around the bottom of the boat.

"You should never take more than you will use. The Earth needs to refill what we take from it. Otherwise, it'll not only be the fish that die."

He ran a length of twine through the gills of the remaining fish, linking them together.

"Can you hold one up?" I asked, pulling my sketch pad back out. Sunny was patient as I sat there drawing not only the catfish with its distinct whiskers but also his hands and arms. Most of the detail could be filled in once we got back home.

Laden with our bounty, we made our way back down the river to the fort.

We had only seen a few other boats on the river—two traders heading inland to barter with the natives and another fishing canoe. Sunny knew the man and his son were from a peaceful neighboring tribe. He explained that raiding parties have war paint and feathers in their hair. He assured me we were safe on the river as no one could sneak up on us unannounced.

"Have many white people been taken by natives?" I asked.

I almost dreaded his reply.

"Two weeks ago was the latest. A settler on his farm was attacked, and the army found his body and that of his pregnant wife. The raiders stole his horses and burnt the buildings."

I had difficulty believing the natives would do such a thing without provocation.

"Were they provoked?" I asked.

"Sometimes the Europeans, or *Wasicu*, as we call them, take liberties. Like venturing onto sacred grounds and disturbing our ancestors or hunting on our lands and taking too much. Other times people in the tribes get frustrated and angry that their way of life seems to be changing from the old ways. They want to remind those people they are the custodians of this land."

I said, "It seems we need to be educated into knowing how to respect your ways."

"That is happening more with the *Wasicu* and native tribes mixing, but there are still people on both sides who won't listen to reason. Then they do the wrong thing, which increases tensions further."

I guess there will always be people like that, but did that justify taking someone's life and their future? That brought me back to reality. I had to keep reminding myself that although our little trip was idyllic, it could be only a moment away from disaster.

As we drifted down the river, we filled our bellies with the goodies from the general store. Afterward, I held out the bag of sweets to Sunny. He eyed them with suspicion.

I popped one into my mouth, and immediately it was filled with lemony goodness—just the right amount of sweetness with a sour pop.

I closed my eyes in pure delight. That was enough for Sunny to grab a handful and fill his mouth with them. Immediately his eyes squinted shut, and his mouth, although full, puckered from the tartness.

"You are only supposed to suck on one at a time," I chuckled.

I guess both of us were on a learning adventure.

We made our way to the shore and pulled the canoe onto the bank. I helped Sunny clean and gut the fish.

"You're full of surprises, Miss Ally. I have never seen a lady from your country do this before."

"It's not my favorite thing to do," I assured him. "Do the women in your village do this too?"

"Both men and women fish. They clean their catch before bringing them back to dry or cook. The men hunt, and the women gather. Meat can be heavy to load on and off horses."

It seemed now was an excellent time to raise the topic of how his family might view me coming to visit their village. I wanted to ask him before bringing the matter up with my father. If I was allowed to go, this was going to have to work for both sides. I was desperate to learn about their native way of life and document their culture in my sketchbook. They had survived thousands of years using only the resources from the land and working together. To me, that was impressive.

"Sunny, you said you have to leave soon for your village. I know you invited me, and I'd like to come, but what will your family think of me? Has anyone from our community ever been to these events before?"

"You would be my guest," he said, not answering my question. "That is good enough for them. My entrance into manhood takes three days, and after, there is a great feast and much dancing. I will be reborn. The new men are the honored guests, and whatever they ask for, within reason, will be granted."

I would have felt more comfortable if he'd answered my question directly, but I felt I couldn't push the point further.

168

"How long will it take to travel to your village?"

"We can take the horses and be there in three days."

The thought of a three-day horse trek was daunting. As much as I loved riding horses, being stuck on one for days could be torture. Even so, it would be worth it for the experience of visiting a Native American village.

"What do you think my father will make of the idea, Sunny?"

"You are his most prized possession, Miss Ally. He will not like the journey unless I can convince him there is no danger."

"Can you do that?"

"Life is full of risks—like that water moccasin sunning itself on the rock over there."

I turned behind me and saw a snake curled up about thirty feet away. I hadn't noticed it when we arrived. I made a mental note to be more observant in the future.

Sunny said, "We can only be vigilant and prepare for what we can. I'll give your father a detailed plan of our trip and what is involved. He knows me to be reliable, so we will see. Let me suggest it to him."

I had no idea about the details, so maybe that was best. After all, Papa was a logical man.

We tied our fish together. Sunny strung half of them over his shoulder, giving me the other half to do the same. This was the vision my Father had of me as we made our way into the Fort. He was surprised to see me.

"Ally, you should have told me you were coming," he chided gently.

"We were out fishing and caught more than we needed. We thought we'd drop some in for you."

"Thank you," Papa said, holding me at arm's length and wrinkling his nose. "You smell of fish, but these will be nice for dinner."

"I'll get them to the cook," Sunny said, taking my fish from me and walking off toward the mess hall.

Papa smiled at me and said, "I see you're making yourself right at home here. How are you getting along at Mrs. Tinsdale's? Do you and your mother have everything you need? "

I nodded.

"Mama and I love it there, and we have settled in nicely."

"You aren't leading Sunny on a merry little dance now, are you? Getting him to do your bidding?"

He already knew the answer to that as Sunny reported back to him about everything. Instead, I told him how Tommy was now working at the tavern. He wouldn't have heard that news yet.

"You can't have Sunny indefinitely, my girl. I need him around here, not just in town, you know. He's not your personal guide."

My smile faded. I'd become used to Sunny's company, and I didn't want that to change anytime soon.

My father noticed my expression. He said, "I guess he can remain there for now. It's more important for me to know the state of things in Williamsburg at the moment. Some of our officers went into town a couple of days ago for supplies and were taunted. It will only take one soldier to react to see the whole damn thing blow up like in Boston. Sunny tells me rumblings are happening whenever people meet. I don't think they are taking too kindly to the new tax collector."

"Mr. Montgomery?" I said. "He lives with us at Mrs. Tinsdale's house."

"Does he now? I hear he is a no-nonsense sort of fellow. Anyway, I've purposefully kept my men out of town unless it is essential for them to be there, but this isn't a long-term solution. I've contemplated having you and your mother join me here, but you'd both be miserable. Instead, your poor old Papa has to be sad without you."

I felt sorry for him. None of this was of his own making. It was interesting to see how my father viewed Sunny. I'd only thought of Sunny as a friend, but for Papa, he was a shadow in the town. He was able to be his eyes and ears without anyone realizing it.

"I've brought you a surprise," I said.

His face lit up as I handed him the second bag of lemon drops.

"Mmm," he said as we walked back to his quarters. "Ah, the simple pleasures. Thank you, Biscuit."

I laughed at his use of my nickname. It was cute when I was younger. Now, it was a little embarrassing but still fun. I was glad Sunny wasn't there, as I'm sure he would've teased me about it.

"You'll like my new project, Papa," I said as we entered his quarters.

"What has that pretty little head of yours got planned now," he sighed as he set about starting a fire in the hearth.

"Do you remember Tommy telling you about Mr. Miller?"

He nodded, "The man that died at sea? The one who had all those books? They made my horses' lives a misery getting them back here."

I teased him. "Papa, don't forget we were also pulled along by those horses. Are you sorry about us as well?"

"All right, good point. Go on, what's got you so excited then?"

"Well, Albert Miller was an amazing young man interested in documenting the plants and animals in this country. Onboard the ship, he showed me how to do labeled drawings. Here, look."

I pulled out my sketchbook and showed Papa what I had drawn so far. He lingered on the likeness of a hawk I'd sketched while sitting in a meadow on the edge of town. His finger touched the paper, tracing its delicate feathers.

"Careful," I admonished, noticing the soot on his fingers. He took out a handkerchief from his pocket and wiped them clean. A smile lit up his face as he looked at the sketches I'd done of the Virginia forest and my leaf rubbings. He took the time to read the notes I'd written beside them.

"These are good, Ally. I knew you loved art. These are quite remarkable. What will you do with them?"

He started turning the pages himself, discovering my other illustrations.

"Mr. Miller wanted his work to be remembered. I felt awful about what happened to him, so I thought I could do the drawings and put them in a book. Then I'd send it to his father to have published. We could include our names with a backstory about how this venture came about."

He looked at me with pride. "It's a noble idea. I like the thought that my daughter could have her work published."

He paused for a moment. I wasn't sure what he would say next, but he seemed to understand my desire to get out into the countryside.

"You won't find the diversity of birds and animals you're looking for around Williamsburg. You may need to go further afield."

Here was the crux of the issue. Would he be able to see that his daughter was grown up enough to take on this challenge?

I said, "I'd need some help from Sunny and possibly his tribe. They know this country better than anyone."

There—the idea was out now. We looked at each other. I was determined I would not be the first to look away.

"You want to go to his village?" Papa asked. "Let me think about it. You know I'm not one to rush into things. It is not a *no*, but it isn't a *yes*, either. Don't get your hopes up and fill Sunny's head with all your wild ideas. He works for me, you know."

Too late, I thought.

I smiled.

Aster flower can be blue, pink, purple, white or yellow

Rumblings

It rained for the next two days, and I didn't hear from Sunny. Perhaps he did not feel it was proper to visit Mrs. Tinsdale's home. The downtime allowed me to add to my anthology of drawings and catch up on my letter writing. I was also working on a gift for Sunny. Even if I wasn't permitted to travel to his village, I wanted to give him something to remember about this important time in his life—his ascension to manhood. He'd been a godsend to me, enabling me to move about the countryside freely. His character was so friendly and unassuming that it felt like it was no effort to be with him. I gazed at his portrait with an artist's critical eye. The eyes were always the hardest to capture. Done correctly, it was like looking into someone's soul. I hadn't quite nailed it yet.

Mama had been envious of my trip to the fort, but I think in her heart, she preferred the home comforts offered here in Williamsburg. She certainly wouldn't get in a canoe and head upriver to see Papa, so her options were limited.

"I'm glad we came to America, Ally. Even though we can't see your father daily, knowing he is near is a blessing. Rose tells me she is expecting her son to visit today."

This was the first time I'd heard that Mrs. Tinsdale had a son.

That night at dinner, we got to meet him. Nathan Tinsdale was a strong man who looked like he hadn't seen the barber's razor in a long time.

As we sat around the table, his mother said, "You will have to excuse Nathan's appearance. He's been trapping in the wilderness for beaver over the summer."

"Mother, you should have told me we had such pleasant company, and I would have made more of an effort."

He tucked into his soup with abandon. Great globules were sticking to his beard.

His mother admonished him to slow down. "Nathan, you'd think you never had a decent meal."

"None as good as yours, Mother, that's for sure." He chewed another mouthful of fresh bread.

Louis Montgomery was at the far end of the table. I hadn't seen much of him since our voyage. Now that he was working for the Crown, he wore upper-class clothing and looked rather formal. There was a bruise beneath his right eye, which he'd tried to hide under some powder. I desperately wanted to ask him about it, but it would be impolite.

"Mr. Tinsdale," he said, putting down his spoon between bites. "How do you find the wilderness?"

"Call me Nathan. Mr. Tinsdale makes me sound like my father." He wiped his face with his napkin and rested it on the table. "Well, there's not much out there, and it can get pretty lonely, but if you don't mind your own company, it's grand. The stars shine like jewels at night, and you can hear every critter in the forest. It's nice to come home and get spoilt, though."

He smiled at his mother.

"Don't you fear the natives traveling on your own?" Montgomery asked.

"Most of them are harmless. They go about their own business. As long as you don't cross them, you're all right. By the sounds of the grumblings around here since I've been back and that shiner under your eye, you've got more to worry about than me."

Montgomery shuffled self-consciously in his seat.

"Violence won't solve these people's problems," Montgomery said. "I'm just doing my job. But I must admit the army seems to turn a blind eye to assault. Where are they anyway these days? When you need them, they're nowhere to be found."

Mama said, "After what happened in Boston, the army has had pause for thought before rushing into civil affairs."

Montgomery didn't look impressed. Having finished the meal, he got up and retrieved something from his bag. It was wrapped in a piece of cloth.

"I bought this today from a trader out of Jamestown. He managed to get it from an officer up north. Perhaps you'll tell me if I got a good deal, Nathan?"

He unwrapped the cloth. To my horror, a pistol lay there. The wooden handle was polished and ornate, while the barrel looked worn. A fresh piece of flint sat in the hammer, ready to be cocked.

I wasn't the only one to be shocked.

Mrs. Tinsdale's voice trembled. "Mr. Montgomery, that's not something that should be at the dining table."

"I mean no offense, ma'am. Rest assured, it's not loaded. For me, it's insurance, you might say. Who knows what may happen? I need to be prepared to defend myself, and after today I feel I have every right to."

I was horrified that Montgomery was willing to escalate to more violence. It was as if our community were like pawns in a chess game. Each responded to the move that was previously made. The more I thought about it, Rhett was right. If America was to be one country, the solution needed to come from higher up. Our rule makers weren't here to see the impact of their decisions. They were sitting in their comfortable offices back in Westminster, deciding how people should live. Mr. Montgomery was as much a fish out of water here trying to enforce these rules as someone from the Houses of Parliament would be.

"It's all right, Mama. Mr. Montgomery does have a point," Nathan said. "It's a fine-looking weapon. Do you know how to use it?"

"I've never needed to, until now. Are you able to show me?"

"Not around here, that's for sure. Word would soon get out if we started practicing behind the creek. We'd need to go further afield out of earshot."

"You can be sure about that," his mother said sternly. "What would my lodgers think hearing gunfire right on the doorstep? I'm sorry, ladies, that we're even having this conversation. It's not fitting at all."

My mother replied, "It's not uncommon for a man to want protection of this sort. Heaven knows I've been around enough guns in my own home. What's dangerous is if a man doesn't know how to use a gun properly or is easily overcome by his emotions."

Montgomery was defiant. "Strength makes bullies back down."

But who was bullying whom, I thought?

Mama was having none of it. "Remember, whatever you do will have consequences. Anger makes a lousy master."

Montgomery's face reddened.

"It's not like I'm going to be carrying it around with me looking for a fight," he said. "I'll probably keep it upstairs in my room, just in case. Your local lawman isn't much help. I've heard he's rounding up a couple of horse thieves down south. I haven't seen hide nor hair of him."

"Just make a complaint when they get back," Mama said. "Maybe a stern word will settle things down. No need to inflame things further."

I was quite impressed with Mama. I hoped Mr. Montgomery would heed her logic. She spoke from a place of wisdom, having been married to an army officer for thirty years. Between them, they had seen the need for moderation rather than anger to solve conflicts.

"Best you put that pistol upstairs," Mrs. Tinsdale suggested. "Then we can retire to the sitting room. It's been such a dreary few days. We could perhaps have some music to lighten the mood."

Although I understood her intent, it was as if a distraction would solve everything. That might only work for an evening.

Mrs. Tinsdale's piano sat gleaming in the corner. I'd been so busy that I hadn't even had time to ask her if I could play.

"Ally, you'd love to play something, wouldn't you?" Mama suggested.

Quite frankly, I wasn't in the mood. A cheery ditty or a sing-along didn't seem appealing, but I decided I would be nice for my mother's sake. Nathan must have sensed my reluctance to play the piano. He whipped out a harmonica from his trouser pocket and started a lively tune. Mama and Mrs. Tinsdale clapped along. Even Mr. Montgomery was tapping his feet in time to the music. Nathan played well. I stood beside the piano, glad he had taken the lead and spared me from an unrehearsed performance. I guess he must have had plenty of time to practice on his trips.

"Do you remember this one, Nathan?" his mother asked, sitting down on the piano stool. Her hands glided effortlessly over the keys. The next thing I knew, I was whisked about the room by Nathan, narrowly missing pieces of furniture as we danced.

"A pretty young woman shouldn't be so serious," he said.

"The room's a blur," I muttered, so taken off guard was I.

"As life should be," he chuckled.

I just went with his lead, suddenly stopping when the music ended. Everyone applauded.

"That was excellent," Mama exclaimed.

"Nathan was quite the dancer when he was in the military," his mother said. "We used to host dances when his father was alive." Her voice trailed away.

I found a seat on the opposite side of the room from Nathan. He certainly was full of surprises.

"You were in the military?" Montgomery asked.

"There wasn't any other option growing up in this household, but when my father died, I decided life had more to offer."

"How long do you intend to stay before heading out this time?" his mother asked.

"I could be persuaded to stick around for a while," he replied, looking straight at me.

He was mistaken if he thought he could sweep me off my feet so quickly next time.

The following day was Sunday, and the household left together mid-morning for church.

I noticed Nathan had shaved his beard and tied his hair in a ponytail.

He was handsome under all that hair, but there was more to a man than the outside appearance. These features would fade for all of us, and I wondered why we put so much importance on them. Perhaps there first had to be an initial attraction.

As we walked to church, he said, "I hope I didn't offend you last night with all my frivolity. Being on my own for so long, I forget about manners and polite society."

"I was taken aback," I answered honestly.

"How can I make things right?" he asked.

"Be yourself, and don't make any allowances on my account."

"Fair enough. I hope we can be friends."

"So do I," I answered.

The old parish church was built in 1678 from brick. Its bell tower was made from wood and seemed to have been added on top of the building as an afterthought. A stunning circular window over the entrance allowed the hall to be flooded with light. The pews were made from oak and lacked cushions, which I thought was an ingenious way to prevent people from falling asleep during the sermon.

Before the service began, Mr. Montgomery could be seen in a heated discussion outside the double doors with two families that owed the Crown money. Nathan had to escort Mr. Montgomery to the front of the church to separate them. As the two of them walked up the aisle, many whisperings and pointed looks were directed their way.

The clergyman preached a sermon about the love of God, but I knew it would take more than a few words from the preacher to dull the suspicion and discontent in this town. Tommy was nowhere to be seen in church, which didn't surprise me. He wasn't a religious man and was probably helping Millie in the tavern's kitchen. They had to prepare for the Sunday dinner rush.

A small handful of townsfolk opted to stay in the church for tea after the service, although most preferred to clear out to the tavern instead. Mr. Montgomery, Mrs. Tinsdale, Mama and I stayed with the Abbotts who ran the General Store. Dr. Taylor was also there. Nathan remained behind with us as well, although I felt he would've been much more comfortable at the tavern. He squirmed in his suit as if it were trying to eat him alive. He caught me looking at him.

"What's brought a smile to your lovely face, Miss Singleton?" he asked.

I teased him, saying, "I was observing how much enjoyment you were having being dressed up this morning."

"My discontent is obvious, isn't it?" he replied. "Next week, I'll go hunting, although that will break my mother's heart. What keeps you busy during the week?"

"I'm working on a project documenting the local flora and fauna of the area," I replied.

"Well, I may be able to help you out there. I've seen my fair share of critters on my travels."

"I'm working with my friend, Sunny," I said. "He's a local native boy who is assisting me."

"I bet he is."

Nathan seemed far from impressed.

I said, "Sunny has lived his whole life deeply immersed in this land and has some wonderful insights."

He replied, "Remember, we are from two different cultures with different beliefs and values. Much of what they believe is doused in superstition and fantasy. I would not put my trust in what they say."

I was undeterred. "You don't find their way of life fascinating?"

"Oh, they work well enough together out of necessity, but let's be honest, they haven't developed high society. They're primitive."

I felt my cheeks go flush with anger. How could he be so dismissive? This conversation was going nowhere. It seemed Nathan had already made up his mind about the Native American people.

"How do you think we'll integrate together in the future?" I asked.

"It's not going to be easy for them to adapt, that's for sure."

"So they will have to adapt to us?" I asked. "Not us to them?"

"All living things have to adapt or die, Miss Singleton."

That was the truth, but it was way out of context in this case.

I said, "So you're saying they can't have a future here unless they change to our ways?"

"I think that's a bit too black and white. All I'm saying is they aren't going to have an easy time of it."

And whose fault would that be? I wondered as I sipped my tea.

"I must admit conversation with you is very stimulating," he remarked.

Thankfully, at that moment, Dr. Taylor came over and introduced himself. He recounted our eventful Atlantic crossing, somehow making me sound like a saint.

"Seems Miss Singleton has many talents," Nathan said.

Why did it sound so lewd when Nathan offered me a compliment?

Our walk home was pleasant enough until we rounded the bend in the road. A group of men had congregated in front of Mrs. Tinsdale's house. They seemed upset. Shouts and taunts were directed toward Mr. Montgomery as he walked along with us. From the slur in their speech, it was obvious these men had come from the tavern. A few beverages had given them the courage to taunt their antagonist.

"Oh my," Mama said.

"Quick," Nathan said to Montgomery. "Go around the back and get the ladies inside. I'll buy you some time and try to reason with them."

I spotted Sunny at the side of the house, beckoning us to the back door. Where had he come from? Mrs. Tinsdale hurried up the rear stairs and turned the key frantically in the lock. We rushed inside. Mr. Montgomery ran down the wooden corridor to the front door. He struggled to slide a heavy oak sideboard in front of the main entrance. Sunny joined him, pushing it with his shoulder.

"What about Nathan?" his mother asked as the yelling outside grew louder.

Sunny peered through the curtains, saying, "He's in the garden talking to the Jones boys. I think he can take care of himself."

The crowd was getting larger. A horse-drawn cart pulled up with several more farmhands onboard.

Sunny whispered to me, "I'm going to have to get your father. This situation is getting out of control. Come with me, and we'll go together. That way, I know you'll be safe."

"I can't leave my mother."

Sunny was desperate. "I can't fit both of you on my horse."

I was adamant. "If something happened to her, I would never forgive myself."

He shuffled back and forth, itching to get going.

"I don't like this, but I don't have time to argue. The sooner I leave, the sooner I'll be back. Lock the door after me."

I nodded.

"Oh," he added, taking me to one side. "It might be a good idea to lock yourselves in your room."

"Why?"

"They're after him, not you. The more distance between you and them, the better."

With that, Sunny made for the back door.

Montgomery sneered. "Where's that Indian going? Trust him to run off when things get hard."

"Mr. Montgomery, hold your tongue, sir," I said. "He's gone to fetch my father. Clearly, we need help."

Out in the garden, someone knocked over the stone statue of a woman. The head broke off as it fell onto the cobblestone path.

"What was that?" Mrs. Tinsdale asked.

I went over to the window to investigate.

"It looks like your statue has been broken," I answered.

"Oh, dear." Rose Tinsdale sat down on the armchair.

Montgomery said, "Those fellows have gone too far this time!"

He started heading upstairs. Mama and I looked at one another.

"What are you going to do?" she asked.

"Show them who's in charge here," he said as he stormed off.

Mrs. Tinsdale said, "I don't want any trouble. Nathan is out there on his own. Broken things I can deal with. An injured son, I can't."

Montgomery had already reached his room at the top of the stairs. We hurried after him. Pleasantries be damned, we stormed into the room behind him. My mother stood between Montgomery and the window with her arms outstretched.

"You should wait until my husband gets here. Don't do anything foolish."

Montgomery fiddled with the lock on his desk drawer.

"The foolish thing would be to do nothing. Now out of my way, woman."

The windows in his room were open. The thin curtains fluttered toward us in the breeze. We had a much better view from up here and could hear the men's voices from down below.

"We want to talk to him, that's all," the eldest Jones boy argued. "That coward has hidden behind the skirts of the women folk in there."

Nathan replied, "Eddie, be reasonable, man. Who'd come out here to talk to you when you've got half the farmers from around the county

184

here, and everyone's riled up?"

"You're here, aren't ya."

"Yeah, but you didn't give me a black eye yesterday. Harassing Montgomery in front of the church this morning didn't help."

"There are two sides to every story, Nate. I bet he gave you his one-eyed version of it. He was the one who started getting physical yesterday. He shoved Steve here in the chest because we were getting in his face, or so he says. That's why I laid one on him. He can't go throwing his weight around and pushing people like that."

"So giving him a shiner was your solution then?"

"You got that right. My Pa is at home working day and night to get the next crop planted so we can have the money to pay his stupid taxes. And most of it will go to pay for Montgomery to live in luxury. Why should he live on our dime when we're struggling?"

Nathan said, "Maybe you should be on the farm helping your father instead of coming here stirring up trouble."

"Hell, Nate, we just want to catch a break. We don't even have the last shipment's pay from the dock master yet, but somehow Montgomery wants us to pay the tax. We got mouths to feed. Ain't that right, boys?"

The crowd behind him cheered in unison.

"Then don't pay the tax," Nathan said. "What can he do?"

"Oh, that's where he gets nasty. He says he'll lock up all the landowners until they front up with what's owed. How are we supposed to earn a living like that?"

By this time, Montgomery had his pistol out and was brandishing it about in the bedroom. We were just as likely to get shot ourselves, so cavalier was his attitude with his weapon.

"Ally, I think we should go to your room and wait. Rose, come with us, dear."

She shook her head.

"I can't. I need to know what is happening outside."

"As you wish. Be careful then," Mama pointed toward

185

Montgomery, who had his head out the window. We left and hurried to the back of the house but not before we heard the shout from outside.

'Look, there's that weasel! And he's got himself a gun. Watch out, boys! There's no telling what he might do."

Montgomery shouted, "And it's loaded too, so you might as well take off back home. I'll not be harassed by the likes of you."

Raised voices could still be heard outside. Among them, I could hear Nathan calling for calm.

Mama ushered me along the corridor and into my room.

"Ally, do you think your father will come in time?"

"I hope so, Mama. I really do."

I locked the door behind us.

Tension

A gunshot rang out.

Who had fired? Was Montgomery trying to disperse the crowd, or did one of the mob have a gun? Being at the back of the house had its disadvantages. We couldn't see what was happening. There was yelling and shouting. Glass shattered downstairs.

Dear God, was that Nathan trying to get into the house or someone else?

I dared not open the bedroom door to find out. Instead, I opened the French doors to my balcony and listened. There was a lot of swearing and cursing.

The fort was a little over a mile away. With Sunny riding as fast as he could, he'd be there and back within a few minutes. It would take my father longer to organize his men. What a mess! No matter how I looked at this situation, I couldn't see a good outcome.

"Ally, what should we do?"

Like me, Mama was rattled and had too many questions and no answers. As more and more time passed, the tension became unbearable. Not knowing what was happening was torment. I had no idea how much danger we were in.

"We're trapped," I said. "We can't wait forever. I'll go into the hallway and see what's happening."

Mama grabbed my arm. "We could wait a little longer. Your father should be here soon."

Or not, I thought. Feet pounded on the roof. Someone was running overhead.

Mama and I looked at each other, horrified.

The next moment, Sunny's face appeared upside down in front of the French doors. I'm not sure where he climbed up, but he had avoided the mob. He performed a forward roll, landing on his feet in the doorway. At any other time, I would have been impressed. Right now, I was relieved.

"Sunny, thank goodness you're back," Mama said. "Did you see what happened? We heard gunfire."

"Mrs. Singleton," he said as he caught his breath. "Montgomery fired a warning shot over the crowd, but all it seems to have done is provoke them further."

As if to prove Sunny's point, another window smashed downstairs.

"I think it's best if we stay here," he said, "away from the action, at least until the colonel arrives."

"I think you're right," Mama replied. "It would be folly to go downstairs. At least in here, we have some protection."

I looked at Sunny, "How did you get past them?"

"I have my ways, Miss Ally. I've been avoiding danger my whole life." He smiled. Did nothing upset this man?

"Well, it looks like we're right in the middle of it now," my mother remarked.

"Shall I go to the front room and see what's going on?" Sunny offered.

Mama nodded. "Try to get Mrs. Tinsdale to come back here. I don't like her in the room with that man. They're after him, and she can't do anything for her son anyway. Nathan can take care of himself."

"I'll see what I can do."

No sooner had Sunny left than a second shot was fired. That was followed by pounding on the front door. I was nervous. What if the crowd managed to get inside and Sunny was in Montgomery's room when they charged in? Would he try and protect that damn fool? That would put him in danger. I was not fond of that idea at all.

After what seemed like a long time, Sunny returned with Mrs. Tinsdale in tow. Except it was not the same lady we'd left earlier. Her skin was an awful shade of grey. One side of her face looked like a wax figure that had melted. Her mouth hung at an unnatural angle. Spit had run out her mouth and down her neck.

Sunny held his arm around her waist. He'd draped her other arm over his neck and held it tightly by her wrist. He dragged her through the doorway, her feet trailed behind on the floor, and her head lolled to the side.

At first, I thought she'd been shot, but there wasn't any blood.

"Oh my," Mama exclaimed. "Come. Lie her on the bed. Whatever has happened to poor Rose?"

Sunny laid her gently on the coverlet, taking care to lift her legs and lay them flat.

"I found her like this on the floor behind Montgomery. I don't even think he realized she'd fallen. He was still yelling at the crowd."

We were stunned.

The sound of wood splintering caused my heart to race. That had to be the mob. I hadn't heard my father arrive yet. Raised voices could be heard below us as some of the men entered the house. They sounded angry. The prospect of gaining their quarry drove them on. Sunny ran over to the door and locked it. Heavy footsteps pounded up the stairs. I felt conflicted.

On the one hand, I hoped they would leave once they had Montgomery in their possession. On the other, I worried about what they would do to him. We were helpless. Nothing could be done until my father came with reinforcements.

Mama wiped Rose Tinsdale's face with a damp cloth. "Poor thing. Thank god, she's still breathing."

We watched her chest rise and fall. At least that was something positive.

"What do you think happened?" I asked.

"It could be the shock," my mother said. "Who knows? Once that gang of youths goes, we'll get the doctor to take a look at her."

Montgomery yelled from the front room. "Where are you taking me? Let go!"

A sickening thud shook the wall. After that, there was no more shouting.

Sunny stood behind the door with the water jug ready to strike anyone that might try and come through. Mama and I knelt on the floor, barely aware we were both clutching the surrounding curtains of the four-posted bed. This was a vain attempt to put any object between us and imminent danger, even if the fabric was flimsy. To our relief, the men appeared satisfied to have their captive in hand. We could hear them retreating downstairs.

I'd been holding my breath. I let out a long sigh. Leaning against the wall, I closed my eyes and heard the unmistakable sound of horses galloping toward us along the road.

"They're here," Sunny said. Just hearing those words from his lips brought reassurance. I felt my muscles relax.

Mama sniffed, "I don't think I've ever been so happy to hear the army's approach."

Neither had I.

I ran to the French doors and saw my father leading about thirty armed men across the bridge into town. Only a few of them were in full military uniform. This was a sure sign he'd considered time a more important factor than appearance. It was frustrating to see them disappear in front of the house. Sunny joined me on the balcony.

"I wish I could see what is happening," I said.

A fresh concern entered my mind. My father was now in the middle of all this.

"Perhaps it is better you can't," my mother answered.

"There haven't been any more shots fired," Sunny added. "That's a good sign."

Yes, it was.

"It'll be all right," Sunny took my hands. "Your father knows what he's doing."

That was true, yet I couldn't help my mind racing to the worst possible scenario.

Sunny squeezed my fingers gently, getting me to look at him. "We just need to be patient for a little longer."

I appealed to him, "You couldn't go back on the roof, could you?"

He shook his head. "I'm not leaving you again. Once was hard enough. Besides, your father would never forgive me."

"And neither would I," Mama was quick to reply.

Footsteps in the corridor drew our attention to the bedroom door. The doorknob rattled as it turned. Sunny went back over and picked up the jug once more.

Through the door, Montgomery's voice could be heard. "Open up. It's me. The colonel bade me to come find you. Those lunatics have run off. He's trying to track them down."

"You're sure it's safe?" Sunny asked.

"Of course, boy. Now unlock the door," he demanded. "I'm somewhat responsible for those ladies in there, you know. I need to find out if they're well."

"Do you still have your pistol?"

Sunny didn't seem impressed with Montgomery's attitude. I wasn't sure how much I trusted him either.

191

Montgomery bellowed from the other side of the door, "I don't know what that has to do with anything, but no, I don't. It was stolen from me. One of those boys probably has a nice little keepsake now. If you don't hurry up, Indian, I'll report to Colonel Singleton that his little spy has hampered my efforts in rescuing the women folk here."

That was about as far from the truth as possible.

Sunny looked at Mama, and she nodded. I respected him for checking with my mother first. He unlocked the door, and Montgomery entered with a flourish. His waistcoat was torn, and his shirt had been ripped several times. Scratches marked his face and hands.

Looking toward the bed, he swore. "Bloody hell, what happened to Mrs. Tinsdale? I get waylaid for a moment and then find this!"

I'd taken about as much as I could from this man. "Sunny found her in your room, but you were too concerned with what was going on outside to notice her."

"Ally!" my mother reprimanded me.

"It's true, Mama."

"Or that's what he told you." Montgomery pointed the finger at Sunny.

"I have no reason to lie."

I hated how Sunny had to defend himself.

"The point now is: why are you letting this poor woman suffer any longer?" Montgomery seemed to enjoy throwing his weight around. "We need the doctor. Make haste, and help me carry her downstairs."

"I don't think that's a good idea," Sunny said.

"You wouldn't, would you? What are you going to do? Use some of your witch doctor tomfooleries to make her better?"

"Enough," my mother said. "Anyone in their right mind can see that Rose is too delicate to be moved. If you want to be helpful, find the doctor."

Montgomery wasn't about to argue with my mother.

"Fine. Have it your way, but I'd take her to the doctor right now. If anything happens to her..."

His veiled threat was worrying. I bit my tongue. I felt outraged at the suggestion that we were doing something wrong when he'd caused this. There was no guarantee that moving Mrs. Tinsdale wouldn't make her condition worse. She needed to rest.

Sunny stood there with clenched fists. Thinking it was a good idea to remove him from the situation, I asked him if he could find out what had happened to Nathan.

We waited ages for Dr. Taylor to arrive.

"What could be taking him so long?" I asked.

"I don't know, dear. Perhaps you should go and look for him, too. Did we put too much faith in Mr. Montgomery?"

Mama looked down at her friend lying there. She had not moved at all. Her eyes were still closed. I wasn't sure the doctor would be able to do anything to help her. Mama held her hand.

Finally, I heard someone approaching. The doctor entered the room. "Sorry I was held up," he said by way of explanation. "I had to treat a bad cut. It needed at least a dozen stitches."

His shirt was indeed splattered in blood.

"Thank goodness you're here now," my mother said. "I've been worried sick. I haven't a clue how to help her."

The doctor looked at the patient. "I didn't realize it was this bad." He shook his head. "I should have gotten more details from Montgomery."

"Don't blame yourself, doctor," I said. "Didn't he convey the urgency of the situation?"

"He just said she was in bed upstairs and to come as soon as I could."

"Maybe we should have brought her down to you?" Mama looked defeated. "We were debating that fact."

"No, rest assured you did the right thing, ladies. I need to give her a detailed examination." He got his instruments out of the bag.

Mama said, "I hate leaving her, but I should try to find my husband. I feel he'll want us to return to the fort with him. Will you let us know how she does?"

"Of course, That won't be a problem. I'll get word to you one way or another. How are you doing? It has been quite a shock."

Mama waved her hand dismissively. "A good hot cup of tea should sort me out."

"I can give you something stronger than tea if you wish?"

She thought about it for a moment and then shook her head. "Take care of her, doctor. That, most of all, will put my heart at rest."

He nodded, and we left him to his duties.

Outside, Sunny was talking to my father. He and several of the soldiers were over by the water trough with the horses.

As soon as Papa saw us, he came over.

He pulled us into his embrace. "You're all right now. Both of you."

The comfort from his hug was exactly what I needed.

Mama said, "Just when I was starting to enjoy it here, this happened. What are we to do?"

"We'll figure all that out later," Papa said. "You're shaking, my dear. Are you sure you're fine?"

"I'm feeling a bit worn out, that's all," Mama insisted.

He looked at his wife until he was satisfied she was well. He'd come to a decision.

"I'm going to take you both back to the fort now. Sunny told me about Mrs. Tinsdale. As soon as she's out of your room, Ally, I'll have the soldiers gather your belongings."

"Have they found Mrs. Tinsdale's son yet? Nathan tried reasoning with the mob, but we haven't seen or heard from him for a while."

"Sunny found him behind the blacksmith's shop. He took a blow to the head, but he's fine. He's waiting there until Dr. Taylor can check him out."

I said, "I should go and see him."

194

"I can have one of my men do that. My priority now is keeping you and your mother safe."

"Papa, I'm not a little girl anymore. I don't need to be coddled. I want to help."

He looked at me, "You'll always be my little girl and no amount of you telling me any different will change that."

In a softer tone, he added, "However, I understand how you feel, Biscuit. So I'm willing to compromise to an extent. Keep Sunny close. If you need anything, talk to Captain Johnson. He'll be leading the inquiries and interviewing the townsfolk."

"Absolutely." I gave him another quick hug.

As an afterthought, he added, "Oh, and where's Montgomery gone? He was supposed to return to me. I need to talk to him about his role in this palaver. He's been a bit elusive, playing the victim, but I have my doubts."

"I don't know. He's probably off sulking somewhere."

I watched Papa help my mother onto a horse. Today was full of surprises. I hadn't realized she was capable of riding. I'd never seen the slightest desire for her to do so back home. She preferred carriages.

As he waved goodbye, he said, "Your friend Tommy has been asking about you. I see him heading this way right now."

Tommy was hobbling over as fast as he could.

"Miss Ally, you know how to scare an old man half to death. I didn't know what was going on inside that house. Are you all right, lass?"

I smiled at his concern. "All is well, Tommy. Sunny has been looking after us."

"Well, thank the Lord for that. It was scary there for a while."

"It was," I admitted. "Look, Tommy, I must make sure Mrs. Tinsdale's son is all right. I'll stop by the tavern on the way back to the fort, and we can talk further. How does that sound?"

"That would be grand. Millie would like to see you, I'm sure. I'll go back and tell her you're fine. She's been worried, too."

I patted his arm. "Thanks for being concerned. It means a lot."

He cleared his throat, obviously embarrassed. "Ain't nothing after what you did for me."

I could see he meant it.

My attention went back to Nathan. Sunny and I hurried across the road toward him. He was sitting on the dirt, leaning against the side of the barn with his head in his hands. He looked up and groaned as we approached. As he pulled his hand away from the back of his head, it was covered in blood. He looked at the house.

"Where's my mother?"

He made an effort to get up. Staggering forward, he bumped into me and vomited all over my dress.

Sunny was about to say something, but I held up my hand.

"Sit down, Nathan," I said. "You're in no fit state to be wandering about. The doctor will be here shortly."

Sunny helped him sit back down.

"Sorry about your dress, Ally," Nathan mumbled.

"It's all right. It can't be helped."

I didn't have the heart to tell him the doctor was already with his mother.

"I wanted to thank you for trying to talk to the boys. We heard most of what was said from upstairs. Things would have been much worse if it wasn't for you."

He gave a weak smile. "Feels pretty bad to me."

"I mean it. That took some guts."

"Thanks. I've known most of those lads since they were young. If they were going to listen to anybody, I reckon it was me. I didn't count on Montgomery firing his damn pistol, however. That got them mad. I don't know who hit me, but if I find out..."

Dr. Taylor hurried over.

"That's his vomit, I take it?" he asked, looking at me and pointing at the sick dripping from my dress.

"Yes," Sunny said. "He tried to get up but was swaying all over the place."

"Looks like he may have a concussion."

Dr. Taylor inspected the back of Nathan's head and pulled a bandage from his bag. "I don't have time to clean this now. I'll do it back at my place. Miss Singleton, can you wrap this bandage around his head? Keep him still while I check on the others."

Dr. Taylor ordered some soldiers to bring two stretchers from his surgery.

Montgomery walked over to us.

Sunny said, "Colonel Singleton has said I'm to escort you and his daughter back to the fort."

"No one is escorting anyone," Montgomery bristled. "I'll go with you because I don't fancy staying here tonight on my own. The Carter, Edward, and Jones boys could be holding a grudge and come back."

"How's my mother?" Nathan asked. "I clean forgot to ask the doc when he was here. Not thinking straight, I guess."

I finished wrapping the dressing around his head.

Montgomery said, "I'm afraid she is a bit worse for wear."

"What do you mean? What happened to her?"

"The boy took her into Miss Singleton's room," he replied, pointing at Sunny. "She's had some sort of fit. I thought they should take her to the doctor immediately, but he didn't want to move her. In the end, it took Dr. Taylor quite a while to get to her. If anything should happen to her, we know who to blame."

"That's not true," I blurted out.

Nathan said, "Why am I only hearing about this now?"

He turned and looked at us, his face flush with anger.

"Calm down," I said, placing my hand on his chest as he tried to stand up again. He eyeballed Sunny.

I said, "Mr. Montgomery has a way of distorting the facts to suit himself. It wasn't Sunny's fault. Your mother was too fragile to move. It

197

could've caused more damage. I didn't tell you initially because you were in such bad shape yourself. Besides, I don't know what the doctor discovered after he examined her. He'll be able to give you a better explanation than me."

Sunny leaned down and whispered to me that he'd go and get the horses.

Wise move, I thought. There was no point arguing with someone when they were in this state. Even if he hadn't been knocked over the head, I doubted I'd have been able to reason with Nathan. His emotions were high, and he was looking for someone to blame.

After Sunny left, Nathan said, "You would take his side, wouldn't you?"

I sighed, "There are no sides. We were trying to do what was best for your mother. Don't go making trouble when there is none."

Nathan was angry. "Well, once the lawman returns, I'm going to get to the bottom of this."

"My father is making inquiries. He's the one you should be talking to."

"Is that so, Ally? Don't you know the army can be biased toward those that help them?"

I was mad. I'd tried to be reasonable, but he was determined to find fault.

"Are you accusing my father now?"

"I've been around the military long enough to know what goes on. If I want to lead my own investigation, I will."

I shook my head in frustration and glared at Montgomery. I couldn't believe he'd put this idea in Nathan's head.

Mrs. Tinsdale was brought out on the stretcher. Papa's men brought the other one over for Nathan.

I asked, "Can I do anything to help, doctor?"

"Not much can be done, I'm afraid. I'll need to monitor her. She has given everyone quite a fright."

He looked at me and gave me a reassuring pat on my shoulder. "Go and get cleaned up, lass. There isn't anything else you can do now."

I walked over to where Captain Johnson was organizing his men. His usually pristine uniform was dirty. He looked at me. My state was decidedly worse than his, but he was too polite to say anything.

"Two soldiers have volunteered to stay and will send news back to the fort," he said. "Some men will clean up the house and keep an eye out so no one returns to do any more harm. I suppose the perpetrators gave themselves a scare when they realized what they'd done. That's why they took off as soon as we turned up."

I said, "The army managed to come just in time. I shudder to think what might have happened if you had been delayed longer. The town doesn't have quite the same feel to it anymore. It's like a line has been crossed. Before, it was just heated words. Now it has boiled over into destructive actions."

"True enough," Johnson said. "It can go one of two ways now. Either the town will fall quiet, or these people will double down and things will escalate. I guess that's why your father wants you at the fort. We've already loaded up your belongings."

I turned to see the wagon drive back over the bridge. There went my only opportunity to get changed. I was sure Millie would have some spare clothes, and I really wanted to talk more with Tommy. Sunny strode over, holding the reins of two horses. By this time, Montgomery had come to join us. Sunny handed him one of the reins.

I said to the captain, "I'm going to swing by the tavern before I head back. I'll ask Tommy if he saw or heard anything of interest. Most of those fellows went there after church before they came here."

The captain said, "I'll get more details from the bystanders. A fair few people got a good look at the whole thing." He turned to Montgomery and added, "And I'll be needing a statement from you."

Montgomery was defiant. "I'll talk to the colonel about it when I get to the fort. I'm sure you can agree it's best if we get this young lady out of here safely."

I rolled my eyes.

"I'm pretty sure any danger has passed," the captain said.

Montgomery replied, "I'm going to swing by the treasury."

"You'll do no such thing," the captain said. From the tone of his voice, I could tell he'd had enough nonsense from Montgomery. He added, "The colonel was adamant. You'll remain with Sunny until you get to the fort."

"But—"

"That's final."

Montgomery was fuming. He climbed up on his horse. Sunny helped me onto the other one. The contrast between the two men was apparent. Sunny was content to jog along beside us as we rode through the town. From the scowl on his face, Montgomery clearly didn't appreciate being ordered around.

We stopped at the tavern, which was unusually quiet. Sunny waited outside with the horses.

"There she is," Tommy said when he saw me.

As I got closer, his eyes widened in surprise.

"How can you look worse than when I last saw you?"

I laughed, "I'm a bit of a mess, I know. I'm just glad we are on the other side of it. Did you hear anything over lunch? Was there any talk about what these people would do while they were here at the tavern?"

Tommy said, "The usual complaining about how the taxes are unfair."

Montgomery screwed up his face at that comment. He simmered with anger but didn't say anything. Tommy didn't appear to notice and stoked Montgomery's anger further, saying, "They think it's unreasonable to demand payment before they've been paid."

"The Crown will take its due," Montgomery said.

"Then the Crown will have their ire," Tommy replied.

Millie dragged me away from the argument. "Leave 'em to it. Let's get you cleaned up, Miss. Can't have you in this state."

She took me out the back, gave me some warm water to wash in and a change of clothes. Her dress was much lower on the bust than I usually wore, and I felt self-conscious.

Millie looked at me, "You wear it well, Miss, nothing to be embarrassed about. Shall I have your dress washed and sent to you?"

I looked at one of my favorite dresses. "No, Millie, get rid of it. It's pretty disgusting and reminds me of the awful situation we had to face."

"Aww, that's a shame. We don't get fabric like that over here," she sighed.

"You're welcome to it," I said. "I'll be staying at the fort anyway." I grinned, still struggling to adjust my bodice to some semblance of modesty. It was useless. My cleavage was on display for all to see. My father would have a fit. Tommy nearly had a heart attack when he saw me and looked everywhere except in my direction.

"I guess we can talk about what happened next time we meet," he said. "I'll be here if you need me."

I wasn't sure when I would be back in town again, so I hugged them both.

"Keep your ears open, Tommy. Listen for any goings-on that might lead to violence. My father will want to know who was involved."

"Aww, Miss Ally, you put me in a difficult spot. The boys come in here to relax. They ain't going to take too kindly to having me tell all their comings and goings. They'll pretty quickly figure out who's ratting on them. That won't be good for business."

"I'm not asking you to divulge everyone's secrets, Tommy. Only if they're planning something unlawful. Surely you agree with that?"

"Yeah, I guess."

"Hopefully, it won't be too long before we catch up again. Take care, my friend."

I waved from the door. As usual, Sunny was waiting for me outside. Mr. Montgomery was already back on his horse.

Sunny took one look at me and immediately pulled his shirt off.

"It was all that was available," I pleaded as he stared at my cleavage.

"Not a good dress for riding horses," he grinned. "The bouncing."

I tried not to laugh, but he was right, and I hardly wanted to give Mr. Montgomery an eyeful. We'd all had quite enough excitement for one day. I slipped Sunny's shirt over my head. The soft doeskin felt smooth on my skin. The tassels had feathers that swayed as I walked. I climbed up onto my horse feeling relieved that the danger had passed.

Mr. Montgomery was impatient. He was already trotting slowly back toward the edge of town. I didn't care. He was upset at the wrong people. Sunny and I hadn't done anything wrong.

As he walked beside my horse, Sunny asked, "Are you well?"

"I think so. This has been a shock."

I knew people were upset, but I felt their anger adversely affected the wrong person. Mrs. Tinsdale had borne the brunt of this. I hoped she'd be all right. It was good that we'd be staying with the army now."

Blame

As we rode over the bridge leading out of town, I found myself lost in thought. I hadn't liked the way Montgomery implied that Sunny was at fault for Mrs. Tinsdale's condition.

What would happen next?

I'm sure father would not let us return to Williamsburg.

Mrs. Tinsdale's home was no longer an option, and the tavern was out of the question. Removing Mr. Montgomery to the fort couldn't be a long-term solution either. I could see what father was trying to do by eliminating the source of conflict from the town, but these issues would have to be dealt with sooner or later.

With the sun on my face and the gentle sway of the horse beneath me, I longed for a simpler life where I could enjoy the beauty around me.

I sighed.

Sunny looked up at me as if concerned.

I said, "It's been a big day, that's all. I'm all right."

He nodded.

Mr. Montgomery was several horse lengths ahead of us, passing over another bridge. The sound of water running over the rocks was soothing.

I spoke softly to Sunny. "Thank you for your help today. I don't know what I would have done without you."

I realized at that moment it was true. Without Sunny, word would not have reached my father in time. It could have been a disaster.

"That was the fastest I've ever ridden, yet it still felt like it took forever to reach the fort."

I'd been thinking of the day from my own perspective. Sunny must have been beside himself, wondering what was happening while he was away.

We caught up to Mr. Montgomery. He turned in his saddle and broke his silence. "We could have died today."

"I'm sure it wouldn't have come to that," I replied.

"You don't know for sure."

"I do know that I don't want to speculate about it further. I hope Mrs. Tinsdale recovers."

"Well, some questions will be asked if she doesn't," he replied, peering past me at Sunny.

This was too much. I couldn't let Mr. Montgomery continue to blame Sunny for what had happened.

"Mr. Montgomery, who do you think it was that went and got the soldiers to rescue us?"

"It was the least he could do, considering he dragged us into the house in the first place."

My anger started to simmer. Sunny could see my hands tighten on the reins. Was there no reasoning with stubborn people and their pig-headed mindset? That's what really got us into all this mess in the first place.

"Give me strength," I muttered. I took a deep breath, "At the time, did you not think that going into the house was the most logical course of action?"

"I suppose so," he answered.

"It was you that inflamed the mob further when you fired your pistol. Until then, all they wanted to do was talk."

"Talk? You call a mob shouting and screaming at you talking?"

We were going around in circles. Perhaps he was redirecting the blame from himself.

"Mr. Montgomery, do you hold any responsibility for what happened today?"

He looked shocked.

I pointed out, "The mob wouldn't have come to Mrs. Tinsdale's if you hadn't argued with them at the church."

"You can't pin this on me," he said. "I'm doing my job. It's not my fault they got agitated about the situation. It's the law."

"Exactly, Sunny was doing his job as well. He acted on my father's behalf for our welfare."

"Hmm," was all I was afforded as a reply.

Sunny said, "Every man is accountable for his actions and the intentions behind them."

Mercifully the fort came into view. Mr. Montgomery spurred his horse on well ahead of us.

Sunny said, "I appreciate what you are trying to do, Miss Ally, but some men will find any excuse to look down on my kind."

"What do you mean, Sunny? That's no excuse. Whether it was you or anyone else doing what you did, I would say the same."

"You are different from the other pale skins," he said. "You see people's hearts, not the color of their skin. This is just one of many ways I am disrespected."

I hoped he was wrong, but even my father would question Sunny when we arrived at the fort. I hoped Papa would show no such prejudice. Sunny held the reins of my horse, leading it through the wooden gates.

Soldiers stood at their posts, scanning the woods for any threat.

"What are you wearing, Ally?" Papa said. He was waiting for us in the courtyard.

"I had no clothes," I replied. "Millie from the tavern gave me a dress, but it leaves little to the imagination."

As my father seemed offended by me wearing a native shirt, I lifted it over my head, revealing Millie's tight, low dress.

"Great horn spoon, girl, put it back on," he said, noticing the attention I was gaining from the soldiers. "Don't you know the men in the fort haven't seen such a sight in an age?" He laughed. "If you're not careful, I'll have another riot on my hands."

Sunny looked away, not wanting to attract the ire of my father.

Papa said, "Go and see your mother. She's quite upset over this whole business. Sunny, I want a debrief in an hour. Take the horses to the stables and settle them in."

With that, Father ushered Mr. Montgomery toward his office.

Mama was sitting at the table when I entered. She got up, and I ran over. Her arms enveloped me like a comforting blanket.

"We do get ourselves in some pickles, don't we love," she whispered into my ear.

"Not of our own making, Mama."

"I've been talking to your father, and he agrees we need to stay here."

Do I bring Mama into my confidence, requesting she petition Papa for me to go with Sunny to visit his village? Sunny said I should trust him to talk to Papa, so I'll stick to that. After today, my father may not need too much convincing.

"How are you holding up, my darling girl?"

"I'm a bit shaken," I said. "I have to admit Mrs. Tinsdale did not look in a good state. I wish we could find out how she's doing."

"Poor dear lady," Mama said. "She's had a rough time of it lately. To think we were snacking on biscuits after church only a couple of hours ago,"

I nodded.

"Your hair is a mess. Can I help you wash it?" she asked.

"That would be wonderful, thank you."

I removed Sunny's shirt to giggles from Mama when she saw the low-cut dress I was wearing.

"Fashions are quite different over here," she said.

I sat down in the kitchen. Mama had warm, clean water heating in a pot on the stove. She poured some into a wooden bucket and tested the temperature by flicking a few drops on her wrist.

"Lean forward over the basin," she said, gently taking my hair.

Water trickled over my nape and ran like a waterfall over my bent head. It reminded me of when I was a little girl. Mama would always wash my hair even though we had maids. As I got older, I outgrew my mother's panderings, much to her disappointment. For a brief moment, it was like being transported back in time.

Mama massaged my scalp with soapy hands, and I felt the tension drain from my body.

That a simple loving touch could do that was remarkable.

She patted my hair dry, giving it the sniff of approval.

"Thank goodness I kept a few belongings here. They haven't unloaded our things yet," she muttered as she took out a hairbrush.

Tenderly she stroked out the knots. It felt good to have clean hair again.

"Ally, I have been thinking..."

"Mmmm," I replied as the rhythmic motion of the brushing was almost hypnotic.

"I wouldn't be disappointed if you wanted to return to England."

That shook me out of my slumber.

"But Mama, we only just got here."

"And look at all that has happened in such a short time. I'm thinking of your future, dear. The prospects of a suitable marriage are non-existent here. You don't want to be an army wife, do you? I wouldn't recommend it at all. I love your father, but it is a hard life. The long nights away, not knowing the dangers they're facing—there certainly seems an excess of those in this country. I've thought long and hard about it, and I'm determined to stay with your Papa. He needs me, Ally. This situation has him so stressed. At least I can be a listening ear and offer him some comfort. I don't want to burden you, however. You have your own life to consider."

I know it took a lot for her to confess that.

"Rhett seems like a lovely man," she said, "and I know you like him. I saw the tender moment you had on the dock. It seems he's taken with you, too. All the letters you have written are not just to Maggie, are they?"

I looked at her face in the reflection of a mirror and smiled.

"This incident has shown me life is short, Ally, and you need to grab the opportunities you desire."

What a delightful thought life with Rhett would be. I could almost picture it. Summer down by the lake. Riding our horses together and parties with Maggie and her husband. In time, even children running around the estate. Best not to look too far ahead, I reminded myself. We were only starting to get to know each other again. Our letters would build on that.

Besides, I wasn't done with America yet. After working on the sketchbook and learning about the native flora and fauna from Sunny, I was determined to finish Albert Miller's book.

"I'll give it some thought, Mama. Coming into winter is not a good time to sail anyway. Let's review it after that."

The idea of another Atlantic crossing so soon didn't appeal either.

"Well," Mama said. "Be prepared that things back home may not be the same as when you left. After all, Rhett is an eligible bachelor, and more than a few ladies will have set their affections on him, I'm sure of it."

The thought that Rhett would meet someone and settle down made my insides churn. My correspondence so far had been factual. Should I express my feelings more? If he was interested in me, he had only to ask Maggie, who would tell him where my affections lay. But wasn't that up to me to make things clear?

Maybe Mama was right. This new world was so foreign to me that I felt I was floundering from one thing to the next. Familiarity was safe, but my experiences so far allowed me to learn more about myself and the world at large. Being here was a precious gift. I didn't see the negative experiences I had endured as obstacles but rather as opportunities to grow. I wasn't the same naive girl who left Southampton. Rhett had changed in America, and so had I. Would we both be better off for it?

A knock on the door brought a soldier with two plates of food. Steam wafted from a fresh stew. I could smell game meat. It was probably venison.

"The commander asked for these to be delivered to you. He'll be delayed for the rest of the evening. He sends his apologies."

Mama took the plates from him, setting them on the table.

"See what I mean, Ally? Life is unpredictable in the army."

After dinner, Mama excused herself and went to bed. It had been an exhausting day, after all. I read by candlelight for a few hours. I was ready to retire myself when Papa came through the door. He was weary. His shoulders were stooped. His boots shuffled on the wooden floorboards.

"Oh good, you're still up, Ally," he sighed.

He sat opposite me and took my hands in his.

"I'm sorry I couldn't have been here for you this evening. There have been a few new developments that you should know about." Papa ran his hand through his wispy grey hair. "Just when we thought things couldn't get worse, I received news that Mrs. Tinsdale has died."

"Oh no!" I whispered. Tears welled up in my eyes. I couldn't believe it, but I knew Papa wouldn't mislead me about something like this. My heart ached.

Before I could respond, Papa continued, "That's not all."

The way he said that gave me chills. He rose to his feet and paced around the dining table.

"It appears that the mob who started this have banded together, and no one is giving us any information. It forces my hand to station a permanent presence in the town. I'm not sure what will happen next, but I'll come down hard on any conflict. I have to. Unfortunately, they've brought this on themselves. It is not safe in Williamsburg. I can't guarantee the fort won't take some heat as a result of this either. I'm not expecting that because they'd be fools if they tried, but after the incident in Boston, I just don't know."

For a moment, there was silence between us.

"Father, I'm scared." I swallowed the lump in my throat, adding, "Montgomery has been stirring the pot. He put it in Nathan's mind that Sunny had something to do with his mother's failing health."

My father said, "Nathan's a good man."

"He is, but I fear that once his grief passes, he'll be furious that she died. He'll want someone to blame. He's already told me he's going to get the lawman involved."

A sob escaped me. I couldn't help it.

"It's no one's fault, Papa. All three of us agreed that moving her would be bad. Sunny only took her from the front room to get her away from Montgomery. That damn fool was firing his gun and provoking the crowd. That man didn't even realize she'd fainted."

He put his hands on my shoulders.

"There, there, Biscuit. Your mother told me what happened. You didn't do anything wrong. Not you. Not your mother. Not Sunny. It was an unfortunate accident brought on by the situation, no doubt."

I warned Papa, saying, "Nathan was already upset. He thought you'd protect Sunny if there were an investigation."

"Did he now? That lad is getting ahead of himself. I might need to watch him, too. I'm so tired of all this, Ally. Problems like this are popping up all over the country. I wouldn't say I like where it's heading. Mark my words, if we aren't careful, England may find the colonies torn apart. And whether they want to or not, the natives *will* find themselves in the middle of any conflict."

"You think it'll come to that, Papa?"

"I'm afraid so. It's not just the farmers that are up in arms. The landowners have also been hit hard by these taxes. If anyone is behind stirring up trouble with England, it's them, as they have more to lose."

"But surely they can afford to pay more," I said. "The farmers have basically nothing. Living from one crop to the next is the only way they survive."

"The rich don't see it that way, Ally. If anything, they want to hold on even tighter to their profits to increase their wealth. That old saying still holds true, the more men have, the more they want."

Rhett had said something similar. He'd cautioned me to come back home if there was any trouble.

"Why don't you retire from the army now, and we can all return to England."

Papa smiled at me.

"If only it were that easy. I would've done that long ago, but it doesn't quite work like that, Biscuit. I need a replacement. I've been trying my best to find one for the past several months, but no one wants to take up this position. And who can blame them? If I were in their shoes, I wouldn't want this commission either."

Now I saw why Rhett got out when he did.

"Don't you fret," he said. "I'll keep working on it. For a long time now, there's been talk of a division between us. England is too far away to care about the colonies and too caught up in her conquest of India. That doesn't bode well for Virginia. Already, prominent landowners like Washington are calling for boycotts against England. I'm concerned their anger and our neglect will spill over into unrest and more violence. Brother should not be set against brother. Perhaps some other young buck might want to take this commission and get the glory. I've no stomach for fighting our own people. In fact, I sympathize with the Americans—a new land demands new ways."

"What makes you think the Crown would be so heavy-handed?"

"The king does not tolerate insubordination. The British navy rules the waves. The British army is the greatest military force the world has ever seen. Unless the colonists can get someone to lead them, any opposition will be short-lived."

"Well, let's hope it doesn't come to that, and a peaceful solution can prevail."

"One can only hope, my girl."

He sat down next to me.

"Sunny told me his plan to take you to his village for their end-of-year celebrations. I can't say I'm entirely happy about that, but I can't keep you beside me forever. And I suspect you'll be safer away from Williamsburg. With these new allegations against Sunny, it's probably a good thing he's leaving."

My heart skipped a beat. Was he going to let me go?

"I have some conditions—"

Before he could finish, I wrapped my arms around his neck.

"Thank you, Papa," I cried.

"You haven't heard the conditions yet," he laughed.

I sat before him like an obedient puppy awaiting its master's command.

"I want at least two soldiers to go with you until you reach the border of their lands. I have the utmost faith in Sunny, but one man is no match for a hunting party. Once there, he has guaranteed me his people will escort you to their village."

I nodded.

"I'll send gifts to show our respect for their tribe. Their customs are sacred, Ally, and you must be on your guard not to offend them at any point. Do you understand?"

"Yes, Papa."

"Your presence there will represent me."

"Like Sunny representing his people here," I replied.

"Exactly. All eyes will be on you. If you're unsure of anything, ask. Seek permission before taking the initiative."

"All right," I agreed.

"The weather can be miserable when traveling during autumn, but it's only a couple of days up-river. The harvest celebration and the dedication of braves last less than a week. By then, I should've sorted out the mess in Williamsburg. At the moment, I feel safer with you out of here."

"When do we leave?" I asked.

"Tomorrow."

My eyes widened in shock.

Act III

Native America

Chepsin: Land

"Ready?"

Sunny leaned on my bedroom door with the biggest grin on his face. His arms were crossed over his chest as he watched me pack. I made sure I took my sketchbook and plenty of charcoal. Sunny had pulled off the impossible—convincing my father to let me go with him.

"How are you looking so relaxed?" I asked. "I've had next to no time to prepare."

He ignored my pleadings.

"I have a present for you," he said.

"What? When were we giving gifts?" I asked.

Already, I was in ambassador mode.

"Be calm. It's something you'll find necessary," he replied.

He handed me a set of neatly folded clothes.

"Oh! Thank you, Sunny."

I fingered the soft doeskin leggings and matching shirt.

"They're mine from last season. It appears I have outgrown them."

He flexed his bicep.

I laughed.

Sunny wrinkled up his nose, saying, "They're much easier to travel in than that dress you wore last night."

"Oh, I'd never wear that to your village," I said. "The only reason it's out is so Mama can send it back to Millie at the tavern."

As Millie's dress was sitting on the top of my bag, I tossed it playfully in his direction, saying, "Would you like to try it on?" He laughed, batting it onto a nearby chair.

Sunny seemed relaxed about me visiting his village, but I still wasn't settled. Our two worlds were entirely different. Even with Sunny by my side, I wondered if I'd feel isolated in the wilderness. I wanted to experience his culture, but I wasn't sure his tribe would feel the same way about me.

"Are you sure I will be welcomed by your people?"

Sunny replied, "I am sure. Nikkut and Attonce have three days' head start on us. They will tell my brother the daughter of the colonel is interested in visiting our village. Having a woman of standing from the *Wasicu* would be seen as an honor. If anything, they'll be disappointed if I turn up alone."

Sunny excused himself, saying he needed to finish preparing the canoe for our journey. I closed the door and kept packing. I was glad to have my sturdy walking boots. At least something I owned would be helpful.

I held up the clothing Sunny had given me. He was right. It would be a lot more comfortable than my riding gear from England. As I changed, I wondered what Mama would think of me in native clothing. I had to roll the pants around my ankles, but the top was a good fit. The pants were tight around the hips and bottom, but you wouldn't see that once I pulled the shirt over the top. I cinched a dress sash around my waist to hold up the trousers.

I stared in the mirror, smoothing the leather shirt down with my hands. What would Sunny's tribe think of me? I had no way of knowing what lay ahead. The only way to succeed on this journey was to take one step at a time. Otherwise, it would be too daunting. If I could prepare myself as much as possible, I would feel more confident. I told myself this was the adventure of a lifetime—now, I had to believe it.

There was a knock at the door.

"Are you done yet?" Sunny asked.

"Hold your horses," I said.

"We're taking the boats upriver. No horses," he replied.

At one time, this misunderstanding would have annoyed me. Lately, I'd come to see Sunny's literal take on the world as endearing. He took my bag from me.

My parents were waiting outside on the parade ground. Horses trotted past through the gates of the fort. A farmer offloaded hay for the stables. The hustle and bustle of military life continued.

Mama said, "You already look the part, Ally. I must admit Sunny's clothes will serve you much better than a dress."

We walked out from the fort under the watchful gaze of the sentries. Two canoes sat laden in the river. The sun shone sweetly in a cloudless sky. I felt nervous and excited in equal measure. In the past, the unknown would've scared me, but I was excited to experience life in a native village.

Papa kissed me on my forehead. "I've got something for you." He handed me a narrow wooden box with ornate gold trim. I opened it and saw a set of quills and an ink fountain. "I thought this would help you with your book," he said.

"It's wonderful. Thank you, Papa. It means a lot that you support my project."

"Always. Bye, Biscuit."

With all that he had going on, Papa still did little things to show he cared.

Another thought occurred to me. "Can you do me a favor and let Tommy know I'll be away for two weeks? I would hate him to worry about me."

"I'll see to it," my father said.

I hugged him and then turned to Mama, who embraced me as well.

She whispered in my ear, "Off on more adventures. This time without me."

That sudden realization sunk in.

"Ally, don't worry. Be yourself, and they will love you as we all do. How could they not, my gorgeous girl?"

She took off her wide-brimmed hat and tied it under my chin.

Tears flowed down both our cheeks. I didn't bother to wipe them away but let them fall freely.

"See you both soon. Love you," I said.

It was only as Sunny climbed into the canoe that I noticed he had a bow and a quiver of arrows. He placed them to one side but within easy reach. Around his waist was a large knife in a sheath. It looked like he was prepared for any eventuality. It was reassuring that the soldiers were armed as well. We were heading into the unknown, and humans were not the only danger in the wilderness. Sunny had told me about the bears he'd seen in the forest, and on some nights, I'd heard wolves calling to each other. I needed to be brave.

The canoe rocked slightly as I stepped into it. I took my seat behind Sunny. He pushed off with his paddle and began heading upstream. I turned, looked back and waved to my parents. Sunny worked the paddle, stroking against the current. He guided us up the river. I lost sight of my family as we rounded a bend.

Two soldiers followed in another canoe laden with provisions and gifts.

"Sunny, you may want to slow down and give the soldiers a chance to catch up."

"I want to get home as fast as possible," he said. "They'll keep up, especially if I give the paddle to you."

We both laughed. "How long since you've been home?"

"More than six moons. My last request was denied."

"By my father?"

He nodded, dipping his paddle in the water and drawing us along with a steady rhythm.

"I'm sorry. That must have been hard for you."

"I'll finally be able to meet the newest members of my family. My eldest brother had twin sons. They look the same. By now, they'll be sitting on their own and eating food."

He stared ahead wistfully.

"Sunny, do you have a special girl waiting for you?"

I was curious. I knew I was being forward. I didn't want to lead him on, but I did like him.

"When we're born, we're matched. Once we're older, we can choose who we'll be with if we want to change."

"Do you wish to change?" I held my breath.

"Yes."

He looked back at me and I looked away, pretending to be fascinated by the beauty of the countryside we were passing. As autumn was upon us, the leaves of the trees were golden yellows and reds, ready to fall. To my surprise, Sunny didn't elaborate. For the next few minutes, we continued up the river in silence. The foliage grew wilder, overtaking the river bank. The low-hanging branches were so thick with leaves I couldn't discern where the river ended and the bank started. Insects buzzed around us like they were angry because we were invading their space, but the river still managed to be peaceful. The reflection of the leaves on the water surrounded us with color.

Sunny continued, "Kinta is from a neighboring tribe. We have hunted together and are friends, but I don't have feelings for her. After we become men, we can take a wife. We can also have more than one wife for a period of time, like a contract. Once married, women can be with another man but only if the husband allows it."

I was horrified. "And the women have a say in all of this?"

"Of course. No one is forced to do anything they don't want to do. The man must have the woman's family to agree with the marriage."

I changed the subject.

"I didn't get to see what Papa had organized for gifts. Should we look at them before we arrive?"

Sunny replied, "I already had a peek. It's good. There are some items our women won't know what to do with, like sugar. You could teach them how to cook with it. We will probably trade the salt as we like our food plain, without, as you say, seasonings. But I didn't want to offend your Father by not taking it."

"Who will be meeting us before we get to your village?"

"My brother, Shiloh," Sunny said, lighting up as he mentioned his name. "He taught me everything growing up. I could never beat him at anything, even though I tried. My strength has improved, though. Maybe he's gotten lazy while I've been away. So there's hope."

He laughed. There it was, that massive grin of Sunny's that made me feel like everything was right in the world.

I said, "He sounds like a worthy leader. But I can't imagine anyone being better than you, Sunny."

I meant it. He looked embarrassed.

"Shiloh is second born. My oldest brother is Wynono. He's the chief. He'll be busy organizing the event."

"Can you tell me what exactly is involved in your initiation?" I asked.

He looked pleased with my interest.

"First, all the boys of age and ability go into the forest overnight.

Then we return and are painted white. Two days are devoted to dancing. On the third day, our mothers are painted black, and they mourn the death of their boys. They will prepare things suitable for our funerals."

My stunned silence prompted a further explanation.

"Then we run the gauntlet protected by the young Shaman. Afterward, there will be a great feast. We're still considered dead, though and do not eat. Finally, we're taken back into the forest for a few days, where we will stay under the guidance of the elders. When we return, we are reborn as men."

He sounded so proud. The only problem was that I was not expecting Sunny to be acting dead and missing for several days. I wouldn't be able to rely on him during this time. Quite frankly, that scared me. Did anyone else in the village speak English? If not, I needed a really quick lesson in essential words.

"You look worried?" Sunny said, turning to look at me as he paddled up the river.

I forced a smile.

"Sorry, Sunny. I thought your ceremony would be for a shorter period of time. I didn't think I'd be unable to talk to you for a week."

"I'll miss you too," he teased, splashing water at me with the paddle.

"What will I do then? Who will help me?" I asked.

"I will get Shiloh to help you and ensure you don't get into trouble. He won't be going into the forest with me."

This still didn't give me much certainty.

"Does he speak English?" I asked.

The air was suddenly filled with Sunny's laughter.

"Ally, thank you for reminding me I'm finally better at something than my brother."

Great, I thought. What could go wrong when communicating with a native that didn't speak much English? Our conversation came to an end.

Lost in my musings, I couldn't help but admire the beauty of nature around me.

Deer drank from the riverbank. Swallows flew low over the water, catching insects. The trees seemed painted with the boldness and variety of autumn colors they displayed. We passed a stream entering the river. Squirrels darted up the trees, gathering acorns for the winter. With no sign of human life in front of us, it felt as though we were the only people in the world. Glancing behind the canoe, I noticed the soldiers were nowhere to be seen.

"Sunny?"

"Hmm..."

"The soldiers. I can't see them. Do you want me to paddle for a bit? I don't mind."

"If you like," he said. "I'll try and spot them. They should be coming around that bend any moment. Here, wrap this cloth around your hand so you don't get blisters."

It didn't take long for beads of sweat to start trickling down my face. Paddling was hard work. Sunny had made it look easy.

"I see them," he said.

He waved, and they waved back. They had most of the goods in their canoe, so I imagine it was much harder to paddle than ours.

"How far are we going today?" I said, breathing deeply.

"Tired already?"

I poked my tongue out at him.

"Hey, a lady doesn't do that," he said.

"I don't feel much like a lady right now," I replied.

For the next hour, I felt every muscle in my arms. Alternating sides gave me some relief.

"Why didn't we take the horses?" I asked.

He replied, "The river is quicker. Tomorrow, Shiloh will bring horses for the final day as we need to go inland to reach the village."

If I was looking for sympathy, Sunny wasn't forthcoming.

"Here, stop for a bit and take some water."

He offered me the waterskin. Even warm water felt good on my throat. I gulped it down.

While I satisfied my thirst, he took up the paddle again. I didn't argue. I laid back, stretching out my weary limbs and fell into a peaceful slumber, leaning against the rear of the canoe. The warmth of the autumn sun was soothing.

Sometime later, shadows floated past my eyelids and woke me. The sun hung low in the sky, creating dusky shades. Sunny hummed a tune that gradually picked up pace and volume with his chanting.

Ly O Lay Ale Loya

Ly O Lay Ale Loya

Ly O Lay Ale Loya

Ly O Lay Ale Loya

Even though I didn't understand the meaning, the tune was haunting and powerful. He poured his soul into that song, which hung in the breeze. I felt like I was being transported not only across the land but also between cultures. I was going from one reality to another. It was utterly magical. There was a majestic rhythm to his chant.

"Did I wake you?"

From how he spoke, I got the impression he'd been chanting like this for a while without me realizing it.

"The singing helps me keep a good pace while paddling."

"For a moment there, I forgot where I was."

"You're in my world now."

My stomach growled.

He grinned. "Even in my world, we must eat. We'll stop and set up camp."

We pulled into the bank, bringing our canoe to rest near a clearing in the woods. The rough hide scraped against the pebbles as Sunny dragged the canoe up on shore. He offered me his hand as I stepped out onto the rocks. The soldiers arrived a few minutes later. They looked tired and didn't say much beyond the usual pleasantries. Sunny disappeared into the trees.

Above the banks of the river, there was a small grassy meadow. I arranged some bedding while the soldiers built a campfire. Then I boiled some water for tea.

"Thank you, Miss. One thing you can't do without is a good cup of tea. Ain't that right Will?"

"True enough," Will said. "I've been thinking about one all afternoon."

I said, "I'm sure you're looking forward to a canoe that's a lot lighter on your return. Is this the farthest you've been upriver?"

"Yes, Miss. Me and Johnny volunteered, didn't we? Anything beats being stuck around the fort all the time."

"Hush," Johnny said. "It ain't that bad."

"It's fine," I said, realizing they were worried the colonel's daughter might complain about them. "I would feel the same way. At least you are getting paid."

Will replied, "Join the army—see the world, they said. It's a different story once you're here."

We sipped our tea in silence until Sunny returned with two large turkeys slung over his shoulder.

"Now we're talking," Johnny said, excited at the prospect of fresh meat. "And here we were thinking it'd be old, stale bread for dinner."

Will slapped Sunny hard on the back, saying, "Sunny always comes through, don't you, my friend."

Sunny moved away from Will, putting some distance between them.

Will said, "Look, it's already plucked, gutted and everything."

Sunny said, "Better to leave any remains away from camp, so it doesn't attract bears."

The soldiers looked around nervously.

"Don't worry. I wouldn't have camped here if there were bear tracks nearby. But a bear can smell meat from miles away. We don't want their company for dinner."

"Yeah, I don't fancy being a bear's supper. Do you Will?"

He shook his head.

Sunny grabbed a couple of small branches that could take the weight of the birds and secured them in the ground, forming a small tripod on either side of the fire.

I scouted the area, noticing the abundance of insects that scurried around in the undergrowth as I disturbed their peace. A huge beetle caught my attention. It was green with black splotches on its shell. Large pincers on its head made it look particularly intimidating. I called Sunny over.

"Do you know what this is?" I asked, pointing to it.

"I see you are getting distracted already," he teased. "See the big horns on its head. We call it a horned beetle."

He picked it up. Its spiky legs wriggled furiously.

"If you look in that rotting log, you'll probably find large white grubs. These will eventually turn into those beetles."

"Really, that's amazing," I answered.

I used a stick to poke around and found several of the grubs. They were white with brown heads. A bluish tinge marked their rear. Getting a leaf, I picked one up. It twisted and curled in my palm. I brought it back near the fire and put it in my hat for safekeeping.

"Are you going to eat that?" Sunny asked.

"What? No," I replied, getting defensive. "I was going to draw it."

"They're good eating," Sunny said. "You should try one."

I shook my head at the thought. Sunny laughed.

"Oh, I can get some more for you if you like," I said.

"No," he replied. "They taste terrible."

I laughed and slapped him on the shoulder, saying, "But you were quite happy for me to eat one?"

He said, "Yes. We trick the kids in the village with these all the time, telling them how tasty they are."

"And they eat them?" I asked.

"Only once." He grinned. "Shiloh fooled me when I was five."

Sunny gathered the sticks he needed.

"Where's that beetle?" I asked, sitting by the fire with my bag.

"Right here," he said, and I saw it clinging to the side of his vest. It was caught in the fringe. He must have put it there while we were over by the log.

Sunny dropped the beetle at my feet, and I had to rush to retrieve it before it scampered off. While Will tended to the turkey, I grabbed my sketchpad and drew both of my newfound creatures.

The sun dipped behind the hills. A breeze blew, making it chilly. It was difficult but not impossible to sketch by the light of the fire. I was careful, as I wanted my drawings to be accurate. The delicious smell of roasting meat assaulted my senses and made my mouth water.

"Dinner's ready," Will announced proudly.

We were all hungry and looking forward to a good meal, but we had to wait for the two glistening carcasses to cool enough to eat, which was torture.

Sunny and I shared one while Will and Johnny ate the other. The two men each tore a drumstick from their turkey, blowing on their fingers and juggling the hot flesh between both hands. Sunny used his knife to slice shards of meat from the breast and then presented it to me on the end of the blade. It was the best turkey I had ever tasted. I didn't know if it was because I was hungry or if the campfire setting made it good; either way, it was delicious.

The stars were spectacular that evening. After we'd filled our bellies, the soldiers were soon snoring loudly.

"We leave at first light and will have breakfast on the move," Sunny said. "You had better get some sleep."

Something Rhett hadn't prepared me for was sleeping outside on the ground. Even our thin mattress on the ship was luxury compared to the itchy army blanket I lay upon. Facing the fire, my arms were warm enough, but my back was cold.

I tossed and turned for what seemed like an eternity. At night, the sounds of nature heightened my senses.

Sunny's voice startled me. "If you're still, you'll fall asleep quicker."

I hadn't realized he wasn't sleeping. "I can't get comfortable. Why are you still awake?"

He replied in hushed tones. "Someone has to keep watch, and Will and Johnny aren't much use."

He came over and sat close behind me.

I asked, "Do you think we are in danger here?"

"No, but I'm not taking any chances," he replied. "Relax."

He stroked my back in slow, deliberate movements. His touch was comforting, and soon I felt my eyes grow heavy.

The sun rose over the trees. The bustle of activity around the camp dragged me away from my precious sleep. Light peeked through dark threatening clouds. Today would hold many firsts for me, and I had to admit I was excited. Packing up my things, I could see Sunny was keen to get going.

Nothing seemed to dampen his spirits. He whistled while getting the canoe ready.

He said, "I'll start us off today. You still look half asleep."

A wide yawn was my only reply. I wondered how he could look so fresh when he'd slept less than me. Thankfully, the sun shone out from between the clouds, and we stayed dry on our river journey. Cheese and bread broke our fast. Mama had included some Haymaker's Punch in a leather waterskin. God bless her. The sweet, refreshing ginger drink was delicious.

"Shall I take over for you?" I offered once I'd finished breakfast.

He grinned. "No need. We're almost there. I could not have my brother see a woman paddling for me. I would never hear the end of it."

Shiloh

Sunny paddled into a tributary on our left. The waterway continued to narrow as we progressed. Still, it was wide enough to make crossing it a chore if you had to swim.

A large forest of trees lined the banks. A small makeshift jetty came into view. Several tall trees had been felled to make a clearing where four horses were tied together. There was no sign of their owner.

Like an animal aware of a predator, Sunny immediately scanned the area. The hairs on my neck bristled, and even Will and Johnny readied their weapons. Sunny shook his head and motioned for the men to stand down.

After securing the canoes to the jetty, we made our way over to the horses. All the while, Sunny examined the ground. Occasionally, he'd peer up into the trees.

I followed his gaze into the branches.

High above, I caught sight of movement. Sunny hadn't noticed, being in front of me. Through the leaves, I saw piercing eyes and a wide stripe of brilliant white running across a man's face. I took a quick breath.

Before I could breathe out, the man put his finger to his lips, indicating he wished me to be silent.

I felt mesmerized by his scrutiny. For a moment, we studied each other. He was dressed in a simple loincloth, but his presence was powerful, and I could not look away. The family resemblance to Sunny was undeniable. This had to be Shiloh. He had the same handsome solid features, but this man was mature, whereas Sunny had room to grow.

An impressive bear claw tattoo covered his shoulder and fanned out across one-half of his muscular chest. It was as if the animal had reached over his back and grabbed at his torso. Well-defined abdominal muscles narrowed down to strong hips and impressive thighs. I had no doubt this man was physically capable of anything.

As Sunny turned to face me, the man disappeared from the canopy above. I blinked, and suddenly Sunny was flat on the ground and pinned in a wrestling embrace.

The soldiers raised their muskets, readying themselves to fire. Sunny called out, "It's fine. All is good," as he wrestled with the man on the ground. He struggled in vain to free himself and then finally submitted, laughing. With a wide grin, the stranger helped Sunny to his feet. They embraced and leaned forward, touching foreheads. The affection between them was clear. The two men cradled each other's faces in their hands, whispering something between them.

I felt like an intruder in this intimate moment. They were oblivious to me. Sunny was so overwhelmed that tears streamed down his cheeks unashamedly. The two of them spoke in their language for several moments, then looked at me. I wish I knew what they'd been saying.

"Ally, this is Shiloh."

"Hello," I smiled and extended my hand.

He looked at my hand without smiling in reply.

"Welcome to our *chepsin*: our land," he replied coldly.

I nodded. I'd need to put forth considerable effort into building a friendship if we were going to be spending time together.

Sunny nudged Shiloh in the ribs. Something I imagined only he

232

could get away with. Sunny spoke to Shiloh in his native tongue, but this time he translated.

"I want you to be friends. You're two of the most important people to me."

Shiloh nodded, but I could see this was going to take some work.

We transferred our things from the canoes to the horses. Will and Johnny kept a watchful eye on Sunny's brother at all times.

Johnny turned to Sunny, saying, "We were under the impression there would be more men escorting the colonel's daughter back to your village."

Sunny replied, "You can rest assured that Shiloh and I are all that's needed. He'd have already scouted this area for any signs of danger."

With that, they said their goodbyes and returned back downriver to the fort.

Looking at the horses, it was apparent that the smallest one was meant for me. I felt a bit offended. Did the women in their tribe not ride often?

I glanced at Sunny, and he smiled. I would try not to complain for his sake. In the end, it didn't matter how I got to the village. That I was going in the first place was a miracle.

As we headed down the grassy track, it began to rain. I hoped my reception at Sunny's home would be a warmer one than I got from his brother.

Shiloh led the way with the pack horse following behind him. I was next in line while Sunny brought up the rear. We rode parallel to the river. The driving rain peppered our exposed skin like tiny stinging needles. Before long, I felt the cold seep into my bones. I started shaking uncontrollably. The others appeared oblivious to the conditions as we continued along the now muddy route.

The trail narrowed, and one of my horse's legs slipped. Immediately, I could tell she was in trouble. I hopped off and walked in front of her easing the burden of the weight on her leg.

Sunny called out to Shiloh that there was a problem.

When he turned around, he looked disappointed. He jumped off his horse and inspected the leg. I hope he didn't think it was somehow my fault. The track was making it impossible for the horses to go on, and mine was carrying the lightest weight. Shiloh looked up at the sky. His gaze then rested on me. Was that a hint of compassion on his face?

"We need to stop. It's too dangerous for the horses to go on. Let's find shelter."

I was surprised to hear Shiloh's English was almost as good as Sunny's. We led the horses deeper under the trees, where the branches were so thick that scarcely a drop of rain penetrated the forest floor.

Sunny said, "Come here, Ally. You're chilled."

He took off my hat and encircled me in his arms. His bare chest radiated heat through my wet clothes. Sunny started rubbing my arms in an effort to warm me up. Shiloh transferred the weight of the things my horse had been carrying onto the spare horse. It was now heavily laden.

"I'll get a blanket for you," Shiloh said.

Goosebumps rose on my arms. The wet doe skin clinging to my body didn't help. Shiloh returned and covered me with a blanket. Sunny wrapped his arms around me. Slowly, warmth seeped back into my bones. Up until this point, I didn't realize how cold I'd become.

Shiloh ran back to his horse and retrieved something from his saddlebag.

"My brother, Wynono, and his wife, Winema, sent a gift for you."

He handed me a fresh set of dry clothing. I reached out from under the blanket, accepting the gift. Unlike the clothing Sunny had given me, the beads on the long-sleeved top were colorful and set on strings attached to the bodice. There was also a pair of leggings and a fur cape. My teeth chattered as I stuttered, saying, "Thank you."

"Let's get you out of those wet clothes," Shiloh said, kneeling and undoing the laces on my boots. My stockings were dripping wet. I barely registered the prick of leaves and twigs underfoot. With trembling hands, I put down the dry clothes, unsure how to proceed.

Shiloh had no reservations. He reached under the blanket and pulled at my drenched leggings. At first, I felt embarrassed, but I understood his intent was to help. I felt the warmth of his hands on my bare legs. The heat felt so good. Sunny held the blanket as I crouched and pulled off my wet shirt. I struggled to get it over my head. I had to wriggle myself free of its clutches. There was no time for modesty.

Sunny held the blanket up around my neck, but it was loose and slipped off my shoulder. I would have felt more comfortable if it was tighter.

Sunny said, "We'll dry you off before you get dressed."

I wasn't too sure what he had in mind, but given how much I was shaking, I was in no position to argue. Shiloh and Sunny rubbed my entire body in the woven blanket until I started to get some feeling back in my skin. All my senses were heightened by their hands roaming over my naked body beneath the wool. If my father could see me now, he would never have agreed to this trip. The thought brought a wicked smile to my face. Although I would never admit it, I enjoyed the attention. The men were firm but gentle.

"Do you feel better now?" Shiloh asked.

"Yes," I replied. It was a relief to get out of those wet clothes.

"Let's get you dressed," he said.

I held my hands above my head, trusting Sunny not to drop the blanket. Shiloh pulled the top down over my shoulders, and I worked my body into it as the blanket fell away.

The knee-length doeskin tunic clung to my skin. It was made from the same material as Sunny's garments but fit so much better. It seemed to trap the warmth from my own body within it. He tied a fur cloak made of some sort of animal pelt around my shoulders. I was able to put the leggings on by myself.

"Now you look like a *crenepo*: woman," Shiloh said, complimenting me.

Sunny spread the blanket over the pine needles close to the trunk of the tree, forming a bed. The wind picked up. Rain swirled around us, with some of it reaching beneath the cover of the tree.

His brother said, "We will rest here until the storm stops."

"We need to stay warm," Sunny said, sitting on the blanket. I sat beside him, and he snuggled up against me. Shiloh surprised me by sitting down on the other side. He nudged up against me, wanting to get warm as well. For Sunny and Shiloh, this was natural. For me, it was an intrusion. I'd never been this close to one man, let alone two at once—and they were half-naked. Even when Rhett fell on top of me, we were both fully clothed. I wondered where I should put my hands. I fidgeted until Shiloh grabbed my hand and drew it over his shoulder. The cold and wet was starting to get to him. I did the same with Sunny, holding him close and imparting some warmth as I sat between the two brothers.

As the morning wore on, the rhythmic sound of the rain dripping from the branches lulled me to sleep. I rested my head on Sunny's shoulder and drifted off. I dreamed of hands and bodies entwined around mine. Before long, we were lying down, cuddling each other.

It was afternoon when I woke. Shiloh was gone. As I moved, Sunny's arms tightened around my waist from behind.

"Just a little while longer," he moaned, still feeling sleepy.

It did feel good to be held like that. When I finally sat up, I discovered my wet clothes strewn all over the ground. It was comical.

Shiloh was sitting on a rock, watching us.

"The rain has stopped. We should go," he said.

I got up and wrung out my old clothing.

"Give them to me," Shiloh said. He put them in the bag tied to his saddle.

When he returned, he held out a pair of moccasins. This man was prepared for everything.

"They work better than your boots," he added.

"Thank you. They are beautiful."

And they were. They were made from soft hide on the top and a more rigid upturned leather underneath, which cushioned my feet.

"Did you make these?" I asked, trying to make some conversation.

"I killed the animals," he said, smiling.

There it was. The same infectious grin as Sunny, although I had to work harder to get it from Shiloh.

"How is the horse's leg?" I asked.

Shiloh seemed pleased that I inquired about his animal.

"She's doing well, but I don't want to risk putting more weight on her," he answered.

Before setting off again, I realized it would be a good idea to relieve myself. I excused myself and walked further into the thicket. There was nothing worse than being on a horse and needing to go to the bathroom.

When I returned, the brothers were seated on their horses. Shiloh was at the front. My lame horse was tied to his. The pack horse carrying our belongings was tied behind Sunny's. I glanced from one to the other, waiting to be told who I would ride with. It was obvious I couldn't ride on the pack horse as there was no room. Would they make me walk? Surely not.

With a slight scowl, Sunny said, "You'll ride with Shiloh." It wasn't often that Sunny showed his displeasure.

Could my presence here have a negative impact on their brotherly bond? I didn't want that. My whole goal had been to blend into Sunny's culture without cause for offense. I especially didn't want to hurt his feelings.

"My horse is bigger," was the response from Shiloh.

That was logical, I supposed.

Shiloh held out his hand and easily pulled me up onto the back of his horse. I wasn't used to riding bareback, and I wondered how long I could endure it. I had to wrap my arms around Shiloh to stop from falling off. I squeezed my thighs together in another effort to maintain some balance on the animal's back.

The path by the river was a thin brown trail in the midst of long, spindly grass that swayed with the breeze. Looking across the plains, it seemed as if waves were washing over the tops of the grass, making ripples on the fields. After a while, a distance began to form between us and Sunny. The pack horse was slowing him down.

The longer we rode, the more uncomfortable I felt, but I wasn't going to complain. I was sure there'd be harder things to endure than riding a horse. The landscape changed as we ventured further. The river was our constant companion, but now it was heavily wooded. Trees towered over us. I wondered how long they had been watching over this land. I looked up at the branches as sunlight danced its way through the leaves. It was peaceful here.

It was hard to know what to talk about with Shiloh. I wasn't sure if he was interested in English things like Sunny had been. I was reluctant to ask too many questions about his home, so we rode on in silence.

"Water?" he asked after some time.

"Yes, thank you," I said.

He stopped the horse while we waited for Sunny and retrieved a water pouch. He offered it to me first.

"Why did you want to come to our village?"

There it was, straight to the point. Shiloh was a no-nonsense sort of man. I gulped down my mouthful and considered my reply.

"I respect your people and want to experience your way of life."

"And you respect my people because of your dealings with my brother?"

"Among other things, yes. But I've also heard about them from other people."

"Who are these other people?"

"A friend I knew in England who lived here and a doctor that has heard about your medicines."

"But they wouldn't have visited a Powhatan village, so how do you come to this respect?"

"I would have thought that was obvious. You've survived out here together for a long time. To do that, you must know many things. That alone demands respect."

I handed him back the water pouch. He took a long drink.

"There is to survive, and there is to live. You will see there's a difference."

He pointed to a ridge not far from us.

"Up there is where our ancestors lie. Buried in the earth is a sacred site. No man is to go there. For they have journeyed to be with all those who have gone before us. Their life goes on, and their spirit is free. So you see, they are forever more part of this land."

Was he speaking figuratively or literally?

I said, "In our country, once our family has died, we put up a memorial to say their name and how long they lived. Perhaps even something about their life."

He replied, "Our's are buried with their treasured possessions in mounds. It does not matter how long they lived but that they shared time with us. Their memory is continued by the stories we tell about them."

Our conversation was becoming very serious. I tried to bring us back to the here and now.

"Another reason I came with Sunny is that he's been helping me with a book I'm writing. Well, drawing, actually. We've been documenting the wildlife in these areas. He said that on this trip, we'd be able to find more plants and animals to sketch. My father, Colonel Singleton, agreed this would be a good idea."

"Your father has treated my brother with kindness, and from the look of all the gifts that my horse is carrying, we'll be indebted to him."

"Not at all," I tried to assure him. "These things are but a token to say thank you for letting me be a part of the celebrations with your people."

By now, Sunny had pulled up next to us.

"How are you doing, Ally?"

"My behind has been better. Can we stop for a bit so I can stretch my legs?"

"It will be dark soon," Shiloh said. "I should like to get to the village before then. It's too dangerous for the horses to travel at night."

I sighed, "Oh, of course. I understand."

"If you'd prefer, we can share the saddle?"

There was no way I could continue like I was, so I agreed. He dismounted and helped me down. I took the opportunity to rub my bottom and move my legs around before accepting his help back onto the horse. We left the river behind and headed inland.

I felt comfortable being cradled in Shiloh's arms. My hips were positioned in front of his, and he reached easily around my waist to loosely hold the reins of his horse.

We started to climb in elevation. Shiloh steadied his horse as it navigated the rocky trail. There were fewer trees now and more large boulders. It was as if the heavens had opened and rained down these giant rocks like hail. They littered the landscape, making it seem as though we were in another country altogether.

My back rested on Shiloh's chest. My groin pushed up against the front of the saddle.

Shiloh's legs were squeezed around my hips as he drove his horse forward. The gentle lope of the creature caused my pelvis to rock back and forth, pushing on the pommel. A restlessness gathered in the top of my legs.

"How are you enjoying the ride now?" he asked.

"It feels strange. There isn't much room on here, is there?"

"Unfortunately, no."

It wasn't that I was uncomfortable. The opposite was true. It was very pleasant. I found the ride pleasurable, and I didn't want to cause a fuss.

I shuffled my bottom closer to Shiloh to try and get more room and reduce the soft banging motion. He shifted his weight, wanting to be more centered on the animal. This gave me less room and pushed me against the horn of the saddle. Tension built with the rocking motion creating pressure against my loins, but it wasn't pain or discomfort I felt. It was a sense of warmth and excitement.

"We're only about an hour from the village."

"Oh," I said, finding it hard to concentrate.

Although Shiloh was a stranger, I felt at ease with him. He gave a little chuckle. I wondered if he knew what I was experiencing. I'd never felt anything like these sensations rising within me before. It was all I could do to hold on to the horn in front of me, pulling myself closer and harder with each step the horse took. All my focus was on the gentle rubbing sensation between my thighs. My breathing quickened, and even simple actions like swallowing seemed hard to do. Pleasant feelings blocked out all my other senses. I'd ridden plenty of horses before but never like this. I closed my eyes, no longer content to focus on the scenery around me. I was glad Shiloh was happy not to talk, for I would not have been able to respond.

We reached the summit and started going down the other side of the hill. Gravity shifted Shiloh's weight again, and his hips bumped into my behind. I leaned my head back on his chest, breathing heavily. It felt so damn good. I didn't want this feeling to stop. Wave after wave of delicious vibrations took over my body. I was building toward something. I didn't know what. All I knew was that I had to get there. Eventually, coming to the bottom of the valley, the horse took several quick steps in succession to secure its footing. The faster pace caused an intense feeling. Spasms coursed through every fiber of my being, taking me over the edge. I felt overwhelmed. Then as quickly as it had come, it was gone, leaving me throbbing. I was panting hard, taking short sharp gulps of air to try and regain some control.

Immediately, Shiloh shifted his weight to the back of the saddle and pulled me toward him, holding me tight.

For the next few moments, a great sense of contentment settled on me. It felt like I was being carried along gently upon a cloud. I opened my eyes. I saw that the sky was still overcast, but my skin felt flushed and clammy. I swallowed and tucked a stray piece of hair behind my ear.

He asked, "Was that your first time?"

That he knew what I had experienced left me so embarrassed. I was glad I was not facing him. It was such an intense moment for me. He didn't seem flustered at all by what I'd gone through. I was sure no

Englishman would be so gracious. For him, it was not in any way alarming or surprising.

"I don't think I shall ever look at horse riding the same way again," I managed to say.

He laughed.

Why had no one told me such a thing existed? I felt ignorant about my own body.

My God, had Sunny witnessed that? I felt horrified at the thought.

Looking over my shoulder, I could see Sunny rounding the bend at the bottom of the trail behind us. He gave me a friendly wave. He was being cautious, not wanting the pack horse to lose its footing. I waved back.

I let out the breath I'd been holding.

Shiloh said, "Don't worry. It will be our secret. There's no shame in feeling good, little one. Do not regret your time in the wilderness. Time is like a river. You cannot touch the same water twice because the flow that has passed will never happen again. Enjoy every moment of your life. I am glad you have experienced this."

His metaphor of a river was not lost on me. It'd been constantly in my sight for the past couple of days, flowing past me.

"I had no idea." I must have sounded very naive. "Is what I felt normal?"

"As normal as breathing. Although it takes a bit more effort to do. But wonderful all the same."

"Yes," I agreed. "Do men feel this?"

"It works differently," he said as our horse sauntered on along the path. "But I imagine the feeling is the same."

Why did I feel I could talk so freely with Shiloh? Perhaps there was some relief in being strangers as we could speak openly without the constraints of friendship or judgment.

"Did you feel that too?" I had to know.

Shiloh was blunt with me. "Men get pleasure when they're inside a woman. However, there are other ways to feel good. You do not know these things?"

It seemed to me that something that felt so wonderful should be taught. Perhaps it was talked about but only before marriage. Had I done something that I shouldn't have?

"How can I know? I'm not married," I replied.

"Even our unmarried women know this and experience these things before marriage."

"They do?" I asked, surprised by the notion. "It's not talked about in my culture. I didn't even know such pleasure existed."

"How then do you learn to please each other?" he asked. The idea of such ignorance seemed absurd to him.

"Over time, I suppose, only after you are married," I answered.

"Then you will learn much on this trip, little one, for our women are not shy."

"Neither are you," I chuckled.

At that point, I realized Sunny would not be the only one to go through a transformation. He was to become a man. I felt like I had just become a woman.

Vunamun:

See

I heard the village before I saw it. The delightful shrieks of children playing filled the air. A light smoky smell wafted toward us.

Sunny rode up alongside us with the other horse in tow.

"Ally, come onto my horse. You're my guest. We should ride in together."

"Of course," I replied.

Shiloh brought his horse to a halt on the edge of a meadow. I swung my leg over the pommel and slid to the ground. Sunny reached down and helped me up onto his horse. This time, though, I sat behind him. I wrapped my arms around his waist as we rode into the village.

Naked children ran up as soon as they saw us. They milled about the horse, touching our legs. Dozens of tiny eyes scrutinized me out of curiosity.

The women stopped their daily chores and shooed the children away, smiling at us as they did. The men glanced up, raised their hands in greeting, and returned to their duties. Like the men, the women wore leggings. Most had tunic tops, but not all were clothed from the waist up.

A few teenage boys around Sunny's age ran up to greet us, and I wondered if they would be going through the ceremony with him.

Shiloh brought the horses up in front of a large curved hut with a thick bark-like roof. Back in England, I'd seen pictures of teepees with leather hides stretched over wooden poles, but these huts were nothing like that. The walls were made from bundles of branches bound together to form a thicket. The bundles were stacked in the shape of a dome, insulating the inside from the cold. There were no windows, but there was an opening that formed a doorway. Smoke drifted from openings in the roof of these huts. Some of the buildings were oblong. They all had rounded curves. The sharp, square angles of European buildings were nowhere to be seen.

One of the nearby huts was only partially covered with branches, allowing me to see how the inner layer was made from animal hides stretched over a wooden frame. Several men sat outside that hut repairing the thicket. It must have been damaged in the storm that forced us to take shelter.

A native woman emerged from the hut and squealed excitedly when she saw Shiloh. She wore necklaces made of shells that jingled and jangled on her ample bosom. Her skin was bronzed like polished copper, and she had a tattoo of vine-like leaves snaking up from her wrist to her elbow. Sunlight gleamed off the long, dark, straight hair that flowed over her wide hips.

Shiloh dismounted his horse, and she jumped into his arms. She kissed him passionately on the lips. He returned her kiss, and she pulled him into the hut. The woman pulled on a piece of rope that dropped a reed mat over the entranceway. The two of them disappeared from sight.

"Who was that?" I asked, shocked.

Sunny chuckled.

"That is Shiloh's wife, Shako. We won't see them for a while."

"His wife?"

What had I done? I felt embarrassed by what had happened on Shiloh's horse. An intimate moment had transpired between us, but he was married. Shiloh had spoken so freely. I would have never guessed he was married. Sunny slid down off his horse and then turned to help me. He held out his hands, taking me by the hips and lowering me to the dirt.

"They've been together for two summers now," Sunny said. "Come, I want to find my older brother and introduce you."

I wasn't sure I was quite ready for another brother just yet.

Sunny said, "Since our father died, Wynono has been our chief."

"Do we need to present the gifts now?" I asked, trying to act normal but feeling lost. I wanted to do the right thing, but in this culture, I had no idea what was right and proper.

I mumbled, "Being here is a bit overwhelming."

"Ally, are you all right?" Sunny seemed concerned. I must have looked shocked. All the changes and differences were catching up to me.

"Look, I know it can take some getting used to. Our ways are freer than yours. Try not to be too worried. When I came to the fort, they did things differently there too, but you'll get used to our lifestyle."

Will I? I wondered.

"The women?" I stammered.

Sunny looked around as if nothing was amiss.

"Some of them are half-naked," I said. I clasped my hands to my chest, wanting to protect my modesty.

"It's beautiful, is it not?" he replied.

"Well, yes, but your people won't expect me to walk around like that, will they? I can't do it. It's too much."

Sunny reached out and took my hands gently. He held them while talking to me.

"As I told you before, you don't have to do anything you're

uncomfortable with. Winema had these clothes made for you to feel welcome."

I blushed. Shiloh had already made me feel way too comfortable and welcome, which was the real problem.

"Come, we'll take the horses to shelter. We'll present the gifts at dinner tonight."

Walking amongst the village, it was smaller than I had imagined. Around thirty or so oblong huts lay scattered amongst the farmed fields.

"These are temporary homes," Sunny said. "Since the land has yielded her crops, we'll move on to more fertile ground before winter sets in."

"Where will we stay tonight?" I asked.

"We can stay with Shiloh."

"No," I said a little too quickly.

Sunny raised his eyebrows at me.

"You didn't like my brother? It looked like you two were getting on fine."

"Hmm, I wouldn't say I didn't like him. I don't want to intrude on his family's privacy."

"It's fine, don't worry. I am his family, and they've been preparing for us."

Not even a day, and I was already regretting my choices. It was fine for Shiloh to be all *"live in the moment, little one,"* but I had to live with those choices and their consequences in the real world.

At the far end of the village, we came to Wynono's hut. Sunny made a distinctive whistle, and immediately a tall, lean man emerged. His bare torso was adorned with beads of bone and shell. Underneath, three jagged scars ran in a line across his chest down to his stomach. It begged a question, but it was not one I'd be willing to ask. Wrestling snakes adorned his upper arm and shoulder in a vivid blue dye. Even though he was not muscular like his brothers, his height gave him a commanding presence.

"Chebona!" He addressed Sunny affectionately. His long arms embraced him and then held him at arm's length. At first, I wasn't sure if this was a greeting, but from the way it was said, I quickly realized this was Sunny's native name. It would take some getting used to hearing Sunny being referred to as Chebona.

Wynono smiled. His attention turned to me.

"Welcome to my *yehawkan:* house."

He gestured wide with his arms encompassing the whole village.

"*Kenahor kenagh:* I thank you," I smiled.

Sunny introduced me, "This is Miss Ally Singleton, daughter of Colonel Singleton from the fort in Williamsburg."

Wynono clasped both my hands in his.

"Ally."

My name sounded foreign on his lips. He pronounced it as Ah-lee.

As if reading my mind, he said, "You should have a *Powhatan* name while you are here with us. For you, I choose *Takoda,* which means friend to everyone, as you are bringing our two worlds together."

"Takoda," I said. "I love it."

I looked at Sunny. It was the first time I hadn't felt like an outsider. His brother had put me at ease immediately, and for that, I was thankful.

Sunny took my hand and bowed his head slightly, saying, "It is nice to meet you, my dear Koda."

Already he'd given me a nickname.

Wynono said, "We are glad of Chebona's return from the English. And we welcome you to share our lifestyle in the spirit of *kenaanee:* friendship. You will be my guest tonight and meet my family."

"I am grateful," I replied.

He nodded.

Wynono took Sunny aside and spoke with him at length. It gave me a chance to look around the village. The fields had been harvested and all that remained were a few withered corn stalks or crinkly dead vine leaves. Plenty of labor had gone into securing the large amount of land they had planted in crops. The children headed indoors as the shadows crept across the ground. Families gathered inside their tents. A quietness descended on the village.

"How do you feel about a swim before we eat?" Sunny asked.

"What? Now?"

"It will be quiet at the bathing hole. Besides, I need to wash before I leave for the woods tomorrow. I stink." He raised his arm and sniffed, pulling a face.

I laughed. "Won't it be cold? Maybe you should wait until morning."

"It's coldest in the morning."

"Oh," I said. Given all that had happened during our journey here, I knew I was going to struggle with the cold in the wilderness. There was no sense in exposing myself to it any more than need be.

"We bathe naked," Sunny said, grinning. "If you want some privacy, now is the best time. Most people go there around noon."

"Ah," I said. "Well, I won't be bathing around noon. Wait a minute. You want me to go bathing *with you*?" I asked, feeling suspicious about his intentions.

"I won't look," he promised.

Still, the concept of bathing next to someone, with that someone being a naked man, was totally shocking to me. Yet I would have to bathe at some point. Did everyone bathe in front of everyone else? I should have asked more questions before coming here. This was about as far removed from bathing on the beach at Southampton as it could possibly be. If my mother thought those two men on the beach were scandalous in their bare feet, then what about this?

"If I agree, you have to do exactly as I say," I demanded.

"Of course, but we need to hurry. Wynono is expecting us for a meal."

Shiloh's hut was empty when we entered. Our belongings had been laid beside the makeshift beds, which were covered with furs. I rummaged through my bag and found two towels.

I grabbed a bar of lavender soap before I scurried after Sunny.

The sun had set. A bright moon had risen and cast a shimmering light on the water. Sunny was right. We were the only ones there. As soon as we got to the water's edge, he loosened his deerskin apron and ran into the river. I got a good view of his backside and let out a giggle.

He grinned at me, saying, "You looked."

After all I'd been through with Shiloh, I was feeling a little cheeky, so I replied, "Well, you didn't give me much warning, did you?"

"Did you like what you saw?"

"You've got a nice pair of hams."

"Pair of what?" he said, looking alarmed. He was already waist-deep in the water.

"Your butt cheeks," I said playfully. "Now turn around. I can't move as quick as you."

When I was satisfied he'd done as I requested, I removed my clothes. I stepped slowly down into the river. Damn, it was cold.

"Zounds," I exclaimed loudly as the water swirled around my thighs.

Sunny turned. I screamed, covering myself with my hands. I wrapped one arm across my chest and held the other in front of my groin.

"What's the matter? he laughed.

"It's cold—and you're looking."

"I thought something was wrong," he replied. "You look silly like that. Just get in. It's not that cold."

I waddled ungracefully until I reached deeper water. Then I crouched beneath the river with just my head and shoulders above the surface, more concerned about my vulnerable state than the frigid water. This was not the relaxing steaming-hot bath I'd been used to, but it was invigorating. Reeds swayed against my legs, tickling my skin. I took several large breaths, trying to adjust to the water's chilly temperature. Something brushed against my leg. That wasn't a weed. It was moving. I squealed in horror.

"Sunny, what creatures live in here? Something is wriggling around me."

"The river is home to fish, eels and lots of other animals like beavers."

How did the villagers think this was in any way pleasant? Clearly, they had never enjoyed the luxuries of a spa.

"You think this is a big joke, don't you?"

"Yes, it's pretty funny," he smirked. "But you'll find it will awaken every part of you. We believe the cold is good for your health."

I flicked water at him, not amused. Well, they had to tell themselves some such thing to get in here.

I scrubbed my arms with the lavender soap. It felt good to get clean. The water was still. Bats winged their way across the darkened sky. I sunk my head under the water and washed my hair.

"Do you want the soap?" I asked once I was done.

"I have leaves."

"What?"

"These bushes on the bank have leaves that act like soap when you rub them together. Come here. I'll show you."

He took a couple of leaves and rubbed them in his hands. A small amount of foam formed, and he spread it under his arms.

"See."

Nature was full of surprises. I wondered how the natives had discovered this.

As Sunny stood in the deep part of the river, he smeared the foam over his chest and arms. His muscles glistened in the moonlight, and my appreciation of the male form was renewed. He was lean and strong. His outdoor activities had left his body displaying all the right proportions. His chest, his biceps and forearms were as muscular as a stallion. Why was I even thinking like this?

"Sunny, do you want me to call you Chebona?" I asked.

He looked at me soberly.

"Do you want to?"

"Yes," I said, feeling it was more than a cultural pleasantry. Although he'd always be Sunny to me, I only now realized Sunny was his assumed name around Europeans. He'd grown up with Chebona.

"Would you like me to call you Koda?"

"Yes," I said. "I think so. I feel different here. I feel like a new person with a new name."

"Koda is a beautiful name."

I blushed.

It was strange talking so freely while naked in the darkness. By now, my body was used to the temperature of the river. I actually felt warm. With only my head and shoulders out of the water, they were all that felt cold.

"What does Chebona mean?" I asked. "Is it the same as Sunny?"

"Not quite," he said. "Would you like to guess?"

"Smiling One," I said.

"Close. Laughing."

"Well, it suits you perfectly. That's what I'll call you. Chebona—the laughing one."

He got up out of the river and walked to the tree where the towels were hanging.

Water dripped from his naked body. For the first time, I saw Chebona rather than Sunny. He was a man in every sense of the word, and he was not ashamed in the least. He dried himself with the towel rubbing every inch of his body. I shouldn't have looked because I expected privacy from him, but it was hard not to. In the background, laughter and chatter could be heard from the huts. It appeared the evenings didn't descend into quiet except when the natives were eating or sleeping.

What a day! I wouldn't be putting any of this in a letter to Maggie or Rhett. I thought about how I usually shared everything with them. Oh Lord, what would they think if they knew about my horse ride or bathing naked in the water? It was shocking, really. Yet somehow, in this setting, seeing Chebona like that was completely normal.

Smiling, Chebona held out his towel for me, beckoning me to approach the water's edge. From the way he held it, he was going to wrap me in it as I stepped up onto the bank.

"It's wet," I said. "I'll get my own towel."

"Okay, come and get it."

"Oh no, you don't. Turn around."

Chebona thought this was a great joke. He slung his towel over his shoulder, teasing me, wanting to see how I'd react. He set his hands on his hips and tightened his stomach muscles, knowing I'd been enjoying the view and challenging me to respond. In a lighthearted way, he was being defiant and playful. Seeing him standing there naked was both a delight and a shock.

"If you're not going to turn around," I said from within the water. "Put the towel over your head."

He laughed. "Do you know how stupid that will look?"

"Yes. I know. And that's precisely what I want. You promised you wouldn't look."

There were some distinctions of modesty that had to be upheld. Chebona might be comfortable naked in front of me, but I wasn't comfortable returning the favor. My towel hung on a branch beside him.

He put his towel over his head, covering his eyes, saying, "You're no fun."

I didn't reply. I'd had more than enough fun for one day with his brother on the horse. I stepped up out of the water, trusting him not to peek. Then I dried myself as quickly as possible and changed into my tunic and leggings. All the while, I kept an eye on him to make sure he kept his word.

Once I was dressed, I lifted his towel and kissed him on the cheek and said, "Thank you."

Tomorrow would be an important day for him. I wondered if, in the days to come, he would be the same old Sunny that I'd known before or if Chebona would be a new man.

We walked away from the river and headed toward Chief Wynono's hut for dinner.

Life in the Village

Dinner was a blur—emotionally and physically as there was smoke within the hut, and I was exhausted. I felt overwhelmed not only by the chief's hospitality but everything that had happened that day with Chebona and Shiloh. I smiled and talked, but in my heart, I just wanted to curl up in bed and go to sleep. I needed to reset my thinking before a new day came. Regardless of how I felt, I was determined to be kind and grateful for their friendliness. I made every effort to be cordial.

The meal was wonderful. We were made to feel like dignitaries being served a special *powcohiscora* or nut milk on arrival. Winema told me they remove the shells before grinding the sweet nuts, stirring in water to make the nutritious drink.

Wynono had two wives. Winema was his first wife. She was older and was clothed in a beautiful white doeskin dress. Her long dark hair was tied in a simple side plait that reached her waist. The other, Aponi, was close to my age and was heavily pregnant. She had a birthmark on the side of her neck. Sunny told me that they viewed such marks as a sign that the gods had touched her life.

All evening the baby within her had been active. From time to time, she would stop and hold her hand to the small of her back. It was obvious Aponi was in some discomfort. She bustled around the hut serving us. Her extended belly made it difficult for her to do the simplest of tasks. I offered to help, but she refused, saying we were the guests. Winema said that she expected Aponi to go into labor in the next few days. Sunny was excited that he would be here for the birth of another family member. Aponi was hoping for a boy as she already had two young daughters. They were older than the twins, walking and talking on their own. Not being used to young children, I was delighted that they wanted to come and sit on my lap.

Between them, they had six children, and I marveled at how wonderfully they all functioned together. Unless I'd been told, I wouldn't have known whose children were whose. These women had the same care and concern for all the children equally.

Winema's twin boys were delightful. They were the mirror image of each other. It was hard to tell them apart. Chebona played with them most of the evening. Lifting them up and spinning them around, much to their mother's horror.

I presented the gifts to the chief: seeds, sugar, flour, butter, metal cooking pots, tobacco, flint and twine. These were all useful items to a tribe that had to grow, gather or catch everything they needed. I also included some of my own jewelry and some hair ribbons. The wives fought over them playfully, much to the delight of Wynono. For him, his women were a sense of pride, and he liked them looking their best. For the older children, I had some playing cards, charcoal sticks, drawing paper and a bag of lemon drops which Chebona warned them against. He retold his experience in the boat, saying the English treats were torture.

The food was delicious. The roasted venison was cooked perfectly with squash, beans and *appone,* which was a bread made from corn.

After dinner, I tried in vain to teach the children some card games, but they seemed to want to make up their own rules and often cheated. Much laughter was had, and I vowed to keep practicing with them.

Even though I was tired, it was a wonderful evening.

It was only now that the enormity of what I had undertaken dawned on me. Just as Chebona had adopted European ways in Williamsburg, I needed to embrace the Native American culture in this village. I couldn't keep up the airs and graces of a European woman. In some regards, I had to be willing to let go of my old life.

Coming back into the darkened hut, the smoldering fire in the middle of the single room cast the outline of Shiloh and Shako's figures sleeping soundly. The coals glowed softly, sending a pleasant warmth through our lodgings. A flap had been opened in the roof to let the smoke out.

On my bed lay my clothes, neatly washed and folded. Shako must have spent the afternoon washing and drying them. Tomorrow I would make an effort to befriend her. Chebona's brother's wives might be my greatest allies here. I felt the silky fur of the pelts that were piled high to form my bed. They beckoned to me with the comfort they promised. There was one English custom I still wanted to indulge in. I crept over to my belongings and rummaged, as quietly as I could, until I found my nightdress. I wasn't ready to sleep in my clothes, and I certainly didn't want to sleep naked as was the manner of the tribe. By this time, Chebona had already lain down.

I slid into my soft fur skin bed, which was set beside his.

He whispered, "I enjoyed cuddling you this morning."

As he lay back on his bed, he turned down the furs, inviting me in.

I was tempted. But even though it would be warm and comfortable, I would be sending him a message that his feelings were being returned, and I couldn't do it. It was too soon. Too much had happened already today. Life was already complicated enough.

I shook my head and remained in my bed. His eyes mirrored his hurt.

It was best this way, I told myself. I reached out in the darkness and put my hand on his shoulder. From there, I could gently caress his hair. Within minutes, I heard the tempo of his breathing change as he fell asleep.

My first day in the village was a stark contrast to anything I had ever experienced. I reminded myself not to get anxious at the rate of change. This is what I came for—to see how the natives lived. I was the stranger here. I couldn't get upset because things were not the same as back home.

I changed into my shift beneath the fur skin. The familiar linen gave me a feeling of normality. After the cold of the storm and then bathing in the river, it felt wonderful to be in the warmth of the furs. With that, I fell asleep, embraced in their cocoon.

I woke to the sound of voices. Shiloh stood outside. He rolled up the cloth covering, tying it over the doorway. The morning sun settled on my arms.

A hand gently moved the hair away from my face.

"I will see you in a few days."

"What?"

Through bleary eyes, I saw Chebona kneeling in front of me. He said, "The initiation starts today. I need to leave."

"Right now?" I asked. Still unsure of my surroundings.

"Yes, the boys are all leaving together. We have already eaten, sleepyhead," he grinned.

"You could've woken me, you know," I said, feeling bad that I hadn't made more of an effort to fit into their routine.

"You looked so peaceful I didn't have the heart to wake you. Will you be all right?"

It was sweet of him to be thinking of my welfare when he had such a significant event waiting for him.

I nodded reluctantly.

He said, "You'll make some new friends. You already know Shiloh, Wynono and his family. They can introduce you to others. And then we shall have dancing."

He looked so excited.

"Go be a man then," I said, ruffling the hair on his head.

After he'd left, I looked around. No one else was here.

They're early risers, I guess. I stretched, glad to be able to move.

The bed of furs was so comfortable that I was hesitant to leave its warmth. As I looked around the hut's interior, everything looked simplistic. It was just the fire and the bedding. A few baskets lined the walls. One contained clothes. Another had a bow and some arrows, sticks and knives. I felt guilty at the number of possessions I'd brought just for my journey here.

"Ah, she is awake," Shiloh said. He walked into the hut carrying a bowl of steaming hot food. "For you: *ushuccohomen*. It is made from pounded corn."

The food looked like porridge. I spooned some of the thick gruel to my lips, blowing on it gently.

"Mmmm," I said. "Thank you."

It was tasteless, but I could see how it would fill empty tummies and keep them that way.

"Where's your wife? I'd like to thank her for cleaning my clothes."

"It is of no importance," he said. "She was happy to do it. She started her flow and is in the blood hut."

I swallowed my second mouthful with a gulp. That sounded awful. My eyes widened.

Shiloh was quite matter-of-fact in his description. "Every month, when a woman's blood starts, they go to a special hut, and I guess they talk about things and make crafts. I don't know for sure, as the men don't go there. The women stay until they have finished."

Did that mean I was here alone with Shiloh for the next few days? Give me strength.

"Other women come and help support the families when the wives have gone," he continued. "So you won't have to cook for me."

I tried not to laugh at the thought of me cooking Native American food over an open fire. I should be grateful for small mercies.

I asked, "You have no children of your own yet?"

A sad look swept over his face. "No, not yet. Although it hasn't been for lack of trying," he assured me. "Shako gets upset every time she isn't with child. She feels she has somehow failed me. I see her soul melt a little more each month."

I felt sorry for the two of them.

Shiloh said, "Women—when they have their flow—are powerful. They bleed but do not get weaker." He sounded proud of his wife. "Why do you wear your English clothes? They are not helpful." He looked at my white linen shift.

I said, "Last night in the river, I bathed and wanted to change into clean clothes. I agree your clothes are much better. I'll wear them today. This is a nightdress, for sleeping in."

"Why do you need to sleep in clothes? The furs keep you warm."

"I'm not comfortable sleeping naked," I said, looking at him and then looking away. "Is there somewhere I can wash my doeskin dress?"

"It doesn't need washing regularly, like your European clothes. The hide is cured, so dust and dirt don't stick to it like that material." He pointed to the dress that lay on my open trunk. "Every month, the women in the village wash our clothing. Because your other clothes were wet and muddy from laying all night on the ground, Shako washed them."

I hoped I hadn't offended her with my lack of diligence. I must remember that here, I didn't have a maid. I would hate to think Shako felt the need to wait on me.

I finished my breakfast.

He noticed my sketchbook among my belongings and pointed to it.

"Is that your drawing book?"

"Yes, it is. Would you like to see it?"

"I would."

I handed it to him, and he looked at the first picture. It felt like a lifetime ago that I'd drawn the dolphins. On the page, they came to life.

"I drew that when we'd just left England. These dolphins followed us for miles. They liked playing in the waves that the ship made."

Shiloh was fascinated.

"I've never seen these creatures."

"I hadn't either till I sailed here. Aren't they wonderful?"

He nodded. Page after page, he turned, studying the pictures with intense interest.

"I can't read your language."

"That's all right. Those words describe the different animals."

He flicked through the blank pages and came to the last page. It held the unfinished image of his brother.

"Huh, your drawing is so lifelike. It is interesting to me."

He paused, reflecting on the portrait.

"From now on, I need to treat my brother with more respect. In a few days, he'll be a man. I won't be able to mock him like I used to. He'll be my equal."

Shiloh sounded sad about this change, which seemed strange to me. I tried to cheer him up.

"Would you like me to draw you?"

He looked up. His smile showed me I had appealed to his ego.

"You'd do that?"

"Of course. I can do it now if you like."

"What do I need to do?"

"Sit over by the door. The light is good there."

I titled a page: *Life in the Village.* and set to work tracing his outline. I included details from inside the hut in the background. I wondered what the English gentry would make of this man with the tattoo of a bear claw reaching over his shoulder. His commanding form was apparent but capturing his powerful presence was no easy feat. He kept moving, but I felt too shy to tell him to sit still. To his credit, he stayed there for over an hour. At last, once I was satisfied with the drawing, I showed him.

"How did you do that?" he asked.

"Do what?"

"See my spirit."

I laughed, "You like it then?"

"I don't know. This is some kind of trickery. I should not be so easily seen."

"I think you look magnificent. You should be proud of the man you are."

He rubbed his neck, embarrassed. I found it fascinating to observe the differences between the two brothers with something as simple as a portrait. They were alike and yet entirely different.

"I am proud," he said. "Who will see this?"

"Hopefully, many people."

Shiloh puffed out his chest and took my empty bowl outside. Not knowing when he would return, I decided not to leave the security of my bed in case I needed to get dressed under the covers. As a distraction, I took my hairbrush and started brushing my hair. I didn't have a chance to do it before dinner last night, and sleeping on it had made it knotty.

I struggled to do the back of my hair, pulling out long strands with each brush.

As Shiloh returned, he noticed my struggle.

"Careful. You're too rough. Your hair will break. I will help you. Be still."

Shiloh took the hairbrush and sat behind me. He held my hair gently while working out the knots.

"Your hair is thick and has waves like the sea."

I laughed at his description.

He lifted it to his nose and inhaled. "It smells like flowers."

"I have special soap I can give to your wife. Her hair can smell like that, too. Better than the soap leaves."

"How do you know about the leaves?" he questioned.

"Chebona showed me."

"You bathed with Chebona?"

"It was either that or bathe with everyone else from the village. Most of whom I haven't even met yet."

Shiloh said, "You know he cares for you."

It was a statement. I nodded. How odd to be having this conversation with him as he stroked my hair.

I informed him, "I have a new name, Koda."

"It suits you, Koda, but you are, how do you say it, changing the question."

"Changing the subject," I said, correcting him.

He wanted to know my feelings for his brother. Feelings were complicated, I decided. Chebona liked me, but he was my friend. Could feelings grow from friendship? Then there was Rhett at home. There was friendship and attraction there, from my end at least. I still didn't know how he felt about me. Growing up, he had plenty of time to declare his feelings, yet he hadn't. Was I just his sister's best friend?

Shiloh stopped brushing my hair.

I turned around and faced him.

"Chebona is my friend," I explained.

"He will be disappointed."

I didn't have an answer for that.

"What do you have planned today?" I asked, changing the subject again and plaiting my hair into a French braid.

"I will hunt some meat for tonight's meal and for the feast in three days. Will you be comfortable in the village while I'm gone?"

He looked concerned.

"I'll survive," I joked.

"I hope so," Shiloh said. He looked shocked. It seems he didn't understand my humor.

He picked up his bow and arrows and left with a wave.

A hollow unresolved feeling still lingered within me. I liked Sunny as a friend. Now, I wondered about Chebona. Could there be something more between us once he had completed his ritual into manhood? Shiloh had made it clear Chebona hoped for more. As for me, I still needed to find myself. I couldn't see how our two different cultures could come together. Hopefully, I could put aside these thoughts and enjoy my day. I straightened my bedding and found some peppermint tooth powder and a chewing stick in my trunk. These pleasantries had been sorely lacking the past couple of days. Feeling much better, I got dressed and grabbed my notebook.

Outside the hut, several logs had been arranged as seats. I sat there, flicking through the now-familiar drawings. I saw Chebona's incomplete face staring back at me. I needed to finish this before I saw him again. I set about this task immediately, making it my top priority.

By now, his features were burned into my memory. All the adventures we shared made it easy to complete his picture. After an hour, I was happy with it. His smiling likeness looked back at me, displaying his youthful enthusiasm. I hoped he'd like it.

With that complete, I set off to explore the village. Everyone seemed busy with their own tasks. Several women were gathered around a large clay cooking pot. Savory smells drifted in my direction. These pots were scattered throughout the village. Families would come to eat from them throughout the day. The older women instructed the younger girls on how to prepare the meat and vegetables while the children ran about.

Another group was grinding limestone and mixing it with animal fat. They made a white paste that they tested on their bodies when finished. Red and black paint was also made using some sort of root and charcoal. From what I could gather, this was part of the preparations for the initiation ceremony. It was evident that only the chief and his family had any semblance of spoken English, so I made do with gestures and smiles.

The reliance on each other in this community melted my heart. There was no bickering, no hostilities, only people working together for the common good. Were they so dependent on each other for survival that they couldn't afford otherwise? I saw a stark contrast between life here and my time in Williamsburg. Had my own society become so complacent in our comforts that we had turned on each other? Had we failed to give to each other and only seen negative consequences as a result? I wasn't naive. I knew tribes warred against each other over territory, but I couldn't help think that my world would be better if we worked together like these people.

It made me realize that I wanted to contribute to the ceremony in some way. Shiloh was out hunting, and these women were making paint. What could I do instead of being a passive bystander?

What was I good at that could be helpful? I thought about the supplies we'd brought and remembered what Sunny had told me as we left the fort. Sugar—they didn't cook with anything sweet. Could I make something special with it for the celebrations?

As I was pondering this, an older woman beckoned me over. Two younger women were with her. One was stirring something in a large pot over the fire. As I got closer, I could see that it wasn't food they were cooking but garments that swirled about in the hot water. This is what Shiloh must have been referring to as the monthly wash. The other young woman took a flattened stick and removed the clothes, laying them on a large rock. Steam rose in the air. The old woman pointed to the pot, indicating that I should help. She handed me a stick, and I churned the animal skins in the thick liquid. By now, the clean clothes had cooled enough for the girls to beat them upon the rock. The excess water sprayed in a wide arc and fell as droplets over the ground. Once they were happy the clothing was clean, they hung it to dry over wooden racks. Here was my first lesson in the native camp. It felt surprisingly good to be able to beat the clothes out in this fashion. The slapping sound of the wet cloth on the rock was satisfying. And I had no doubt this is what made their clothing so smooth and supple.

Once we had finished, I bowed my head in thanks and made my

way to visit Winema at the chief's hut. An idea had formed in my mind as to how I could help. She would be able to tell me if my plan was viable. As I approached, several ladies sat outside, talking excitedly. The chief's children recognized me. They ran over and tugged on my arms. The twins were in the shade, and the older women were trying in vain to keep them on a large mat.

"Cards, cards," the children cried, shoving the pack in front of me.

"All right," I laughed.

Long guttural groans echoed from within the hut. That could only mean one thing. Aponi was in the throes of childbirth. How exciting for everyone in the village—soon another child would be added to their numbers. The next generation would continue the hopes and dreams of the current one. I waited outside, playing with the children, wanting to be there to hear the newborn's first cry. Winema came out eventually, looking tired.

"How is Aponi doing?" I asked.

She sighed, "The baby is upside down. It's going to be difficult."

"Is there anything I can do?" I asked.

She thought about it for a moment before replying, "Yes, come in. I could use some help."

Winema waved the children away, yelling after them.

The inside of the hut was dark and warm. A grassy smell filled the air. A pot of steeped nettles sat to one side, still steaming slightly. An elderly woman sat behind Aponi. Her wrinkled skin paid homage to the number of her years. Aponi was naked. She was down on her knees, holding onto two woven straps suspended from the roof. Large rivulets of sweat dripped down the side of her face. Her brow furrowed as another contraction overtook her. With her head bowed, she squinted her eyes shut and pushed, pulling down on the straps. I had already been outside the hut listening for most of the morning. I wondered how much more she could endure. I'd heard from other mothers in England that the first child was the most difficult. Then the more children you had, the easier and quicker the births would be. This didn't appear to be the case for her.

It was the first time I'd been present at a human birth, but these women were old hands. Winema instructed me to wipe Aponi's brow and give her some water after the contraction was over.

"The bottom wants to come out first," Winema said, explaining the problem to me as she pushed her fingers into Aponi's belly, feeling how the baby was oriented. "The child's knees are tucked up, making it hard for her to push the baby out."

"Is there some way we can get the legs down?" I asked, thinking of the foals I'd seen delivered at the Addington's estate. I'd been called on at times to help pull them out. I couldn't imagine how this could be done to a woman.

I wet the soft rag again in the bowl of water and wrung it out, leaving enough moisture on it to cool Aponi's face and neck. I slowly stroked her skin, squeezing the cloth as I did so. While she was content, I wet her arms and back. She smiled up at me weakly before her face turned into a grimace as another contraction seized her body. I stepped back. The two plaits which hung down either side of her face swung wildly as she rocked her head from side to side, groaning in agony.

Aponi cried out in her native tongue.

Winema answered her, "Be strong. The baby *will* come."

Before the next contraction hit, Winema knelt behind Aponi. She talked to her softly. To my surprise, Winema reached beneath Aponi's legs. She pushed her fingers up inside the pregnant woman, grasping at the unborn child. Aponi moaned and swung on the straps, gripping them for dear life. Winema was focused. The next few minutes were critical. Both Aponi and the child could die. Blood dripped onto the mat. Winema worked her fingers within the birth canal. Aponi grimaced.

"It's coming," Aponi grunted. Another contraction gripped her.

Winema removed her hand.

Aponi seemed to be losing her strength with each contraction. Winema was calm but brutal. She extended her fingers inside the poor pregnant woman again. Aponi cried out in pain.

"Got it," Winema said. "One leg is down. Getting the next one should be easier."

After another contraction passed, Winema managed to wriggle the other leg loose. Two tiny bluish wrinkled feet appeared beneath Aponi. Winema stroked the legs, gently tugging on them, wanting to help them on. The baby was almost out.

I encouraged Aponi, "When the next contraction comes, you need to push as much as possible. Your baby could come out on this push."

She looked at me and nodded.

Winema grabbed the two legs, and when the pains came again, she pulled on them. Aponi let out an almighty yell expelling all the breath from her lungs. A sudden *whoosh,* and the baby flopped onto the bloody mat. Winema cradled the head of the newborn child in her hands. The umbilical cord still wound its way inside. Aponi released her clasp on the straps and collapsed to the floor. She knelt there, shaking.

Winema took a cloth and wiped the baby's face removing the mucus and blood from around its nose and mouth. She turned the babe over so her hand was holding its chest. She looked worried. With a tender hand, she rubbed its back, alternating between circular motions and a light pat.

Winema whispered, "Come to me, young one."

I was nervous. The baby wasn't moving. Its limbs dangled helplessly. Aponi looked over her shoulder. Her forehead was creased with worry.

"Why does it not cry?" she asked.

Winema urged the baby, "*Bagid anaamo:* Breathe."

Turning it over again, she lay it on her lap, tilting its head up. She used her finger to open its mouth and scooped out a mixture of blood and saliva. Time stood still. All the women were quiet. Life had never seemed more precious or fragile to me. Winema took a deep breath and blew across the baby's face. A tiny cough broke the silence. I watched as the child's chest rose, and it took its first breath. Immediately, its arms and legs began moving on their own. The infant let out a piercing cry.

It was only then I realized I'd been holding my own breath.

Warriors

"It's done," I sighed. "You have a son."

Relief washed over Aponi's face. She was not the only one to feel relieved. Aponi turned toward the sound. I helped her sit comfortably on some furs so the baby could be placed in her lap. Aponi stroked his cheek, marveling at her new son.

She talked to him in her own language. Winema sat beside me, whispering a translation as Aponi spoke. *"You've had a hard time being born, my son. Let's hope your life will be easier."*

His little face looked up into his mother's eyes, and he answered her with a cry. It was the most joyful sound I'd ever heard. Aponi smiled.

"Your spirit is strong, little boy. What shall we call you?"

She thought for a moment.

"Normally, your father would give you a name, but today I think I have earned that right. Wynono would not deny me. What about Calian?"

I asked Winema, "What does that mean?"

She spoke softly, saying, "Warrior of life."

Calian nuzzled her breast. We looked at each other, smiling. There was no need for words. The old woman next to me started chanting, moving slowly to the rhythm of her own voice. We sat like this for several moments, watching the miracle of new life unfold. It was crazy to think we all started out this way.

Eventually, when the old woman stopped her chanting, I took my leave, glad of the cool air outside the hut. The day had rushed past faster than I realized. The sun was already low on the horizon, hurrying toward its resting place for the night. The women were gathered outside, awaiting the news.

I clapped my hands, acknowledging Aponi's effort.

"A boy," I announced.

When they didn't understand my English, I pointed to one of Winema's sons. They nodded and talked excitedly, happy for the chief. He now had four sons and three daughters. This was his first son with Aponi.

I dragged my feet toward the cooking pot near Shiloh's tent. It had been a long but eventful day. He was sitting on a log by the fire, scooping stew from a bowl set on his knee. One arm hung limply by his side.

"You're hurt," I exclaimed, forgetting my tiredness. I knelt beside him.

"I fell while hunting deer," he told me between mouthfuls.

I felt along his arm and up the shoulder, looking for swelling. He winced as I got closer to his neck.

Shiloh complained, "What are you doing? It already hurts without you poking me."

"I'm checking to see what type of injury you have. That way, I can figure out how to help you."

"I'm fine," Shiloh said, even though he wasn't. He pulled away from me.

I felt upset at being rejected. I was only trying to help him. Tears trickled down my cheeks. I wiped them away but not before he noticed.

"What's the matter?" he asked. He put down his bowl and gave me his full attention, which made me feel even worse.

Everything was the matter. After the tension of a difficult birth that almost cost a woman her life, I was confused with my feelings. I didn't know what had come over me. Shiloh's manner had been abrupt, which took me off-guard. At first, I thought he was being a typical male, stubborn and refusing help, but the look in his eyes was one of compassion.

"It's fine. I'm just a little emotional after seeing the birth of Wynono and Aponi's son."

"I am happy for them," he said before pausing and adding, "Wait, you were there in the hut?"

"She had a hard labor," I replied. "The baby came out feet first."

I wasn't sure if I was supposed to reveal that detail, but I was too tired to care.

He said, "It's a great honor to see the light of a new life."

"It is," I agreed.

"Have some stew," he offered me a bowlful.

The use of only one arm hampered his usual grace. He winced at each movement.

"You should see the deer. He's much worse than me," he said with pride.

"Shiloh," I said, wanting to convince him to let me help. "You don't have a broken bone, but you have pulled a muscle or tendon in your shoulder. Your arm should be immobilized with a sling so it can heal quicker."

"Is that painful?" he asked.

"No, it will reduce the pain."

He looked my way, saying, "You may do the sling."

After the meal, we went back to the hut, where I made a makeshift sling out of one of my petticoats. I tied a knot behind his neck.

"Once you put this on, it shouldn't come off for a few days."

He looked at the white triangle-shaped linen with disdain.

"You didn't say anything about looking silly. How am I supposed to bathe with this on?"

"You can take it off for bathing," I informed him.

"You'll need to help me."

Was he referring to the bathing or the sling?

I was sure Shiloh could adequately clean himself with one arm, but I agreed to go with him to the river as I much preferred his company to that of half the village during the morning wash. It'd be easy. I would manage it as I did with Chebona, but this time I would be prepared for the cold water so there would be no surprises.

The sling covered his bear paw tattoo entirely. A few stares were directed toward Shiloh and his bandaged arm as we walked past the cooking fires, heading to the river.

"The pain is much better," he conceded as we approached the chief's hut. Shiloh had wanted to congratulate Wynono in person. It wouldn't have been easy for him to see the new babe when he was trying to start a family of his own, but here, whenever something good happened, everyone was excited. Whether it was a birth, a kill from a hunt or a surprise haul of fish, people were happy in the village for the success of others.

Wynono slapped Shiloh on his back as he took in the sight of my makeshift sling. Shiloh winced, but I wasn't sure if that was from the pain or the embarrassment.

"It seems Koda has turned you into an English girl," he joked, seeing the lace edging on the sling.

Shiloh's countenance darkened, but he remained silent.

Winema welcomed us in and was lavish in her praise of my efforts during the afternoon.

Aponi and her new son were sleeping soundly. The ropes she had held on to had gone. The hut had returned to being a communal family center.

The chief said, "As you have given to me, helping my son be born,

Koda, so must I give to you."

I tried to assure him it wasn't necessary, saying, "It was my honor," but he already had gifts prepared. He hung a stunning shell necklace over my head. The beautiful piece of native jewelry had multiple strands hanging in various lengths. His generosity was evident as he also handed me a short blade knife adorned with a bone handle. Although the main shaft of the handle was smooth, the rounded end had an intricate carving of a horse head complete with a mane.

He said, "This is the blade that separated Calian from his mother. To cut the cord is a sacred act before *Ahone*. And now I give it to you as it is blessed and will protect you as it has protected us."

"Thank you," I said, accepting the knife with outstretched hands.

It's sheath hung from a strap that was intended for the waist, but it was quite short. I'd never liked belts around my waist. Now that I'd had a taste of freedom from corsets, I was loath to cinch it over my hips. Instead, I hung it over one shoulder, allowing the sheath to rest against the side of my ribs. I could wear it under my tunic throughout the day.

I thanked him again, feeling humbled by his thoughtfulness. "It was a privilege to see your son being born. I'm happy for you and your family."

He bowed.

With the feast coming up in a few days, I wanted to be sure I could get the ingredients I needed to cook something with the sugar and flour my father had sent. I asked Winema if they had access to milk in the village.

"We have goat's milk," she informed me.

That was perfect.

I asked, "If I can use some of the sugar, butter and flour that I brought, along with some eggs from your chickens, I can make pancakes for everyone. What about wild berries? Are there any of those left?"

Winona replied, saying, "Even though they have almost finished fruiting, the bushes still have many. I shall get the children to collect them tomorrow, if they can do so without eating them."

She smiled, watching them play a quiet game with stones in the firelight.

We bade our farewell and made our way down to the river's edge. The cool night air blew, causing tiny ripples on the water's surface. Clouds hid the moonlight, making it darker than the previous evening. I helped Shiloh with the knot of the sling, instructing him to try and keep the movement of his arm to a minimum.

"Can you untie my breechcloth?" he asked. He watched my movements, making me feel very self-conscious.

It fell to the earth, and he strode into the water. He was no more than a silhouette in the pale light.

I quickly undressed and slipped into the calm water on the river's edge. I ducked below the surface to keep the cool air from assaulting my skin. Foamy bubbles floated away from me as I rubbed the grit of the day away from my body with the soap.

Shiloh was content to float on his back and look up at the stars which peeked out from behind the clouds. He was silent in reflection. I wondered what I should say to him.

"What do you think of when you look at the stars?" I asked, disturbing his peace.

"I think of the story that our ancestors told. My father often recounted that there were six young brothers who were orphans in the first days. They lived by begging and wearing the clothes no one wanted. Nobody cared about them except for a pack of dogs in the camp. The boys would share their scraps with the dogs and sleep with them. They kept each other warm through the long, cold winter nights. The brothers loved those dogs and played with them every day. Too many people were unkind to the boys. The other children teased them because they didn't have fine buffalo robes like they did.

"The boys no longer wanted to be people. They decided they would flee the cruelty of the tribe. They considered becoming flowers, but the buffalo might eat them. Stones? No, stones could be broken. Water could be drunk, and trees could be cut and burned.

"They decided they wanted to be stars. Stars are always beautiful and always safe. When people look up at the stars, they're happy. The sun welcomed the boys. The moon called them her lost children.

"The sun looked on the people of the village with anger. He punished them with a drought for their wickedness. Meanwhile, the people heard the dogs howling at the sky because they missed the boys. Finally, the chief asked the sun for pity because the drought hurts all creatures, not just the tribe. Then the rains came."

He grinned, "We use the moon and stars in a practical way. They help us find the right time to plant and harvest our crops. The story of the dog lovers explains why dogs howl at the night sky, but it is more than a fable. It reminds us the sun and moon guide our lives."

I said, "In my world, people have made tools that help us see the stars more closely. If you put curved glass at either end of a tube, you get a telescope that allows you to see things in the distance."

Shiloh replied, "I have seen your sailors peer through these tubes."

"Yes," I said. "Those spy glasses work the same way, except telescopes are bigger and can see things much further away. When they look at the stars, they see that some are planets like our Earth."

I pointed, saying, "See that star? The red one? That's a planet called Mars. So far, they have discovered five other planets that travel around our sun. Our world is the third planet away from the sun, and Mars is the fourth."

Shiloh stood up, giving me an extended view of his naked body. I was more modest, remaining hidden beneath the dark water. Although it was only waist-deep, I could crouch with just my shoulders above the surface. He looked curious, peering into the night sky. "Do you think there could be people on these other worlds?"

"I don't know," I stammered.

I tried to look at the heavens to distract me from his muscular form.

"I know the temperature gets colder the further away from the sun you get. That red planet above us is far colder than here. Can you imagine

277

someone being able to live in those conditions?"

He shook his head. "I don't think so. It is hard enough in the winter for us to do so."

"Sit down. I'll wash your back," I said, trying to get at least some part of him underwater.

He complied.

As my hands glided over his skin, this didn't seem like such a good idea anymore. I felt too intimate. He cradled his injured arm in front of him. I undid the tie securing his hair and massaged some of my soap into his scalp. He stretched out, floating on the surface of the water with his eyes closed. He moved his head gently from side to side to wash away the soap. His feet settled on the river stones a few feet beneath him.

"Your touch is gentle and kind, like your name, Koda," he murmured.

From my vantage point, I could see the whole length of his naked body. He looked vulnerable, lying there with his hurt arm hugging his chest. His hair fanned out in the water, caressing my skin like a hundred tiny feathers. I knelt on the smooth, river stones behind him, held buoyant by the water. It was surprisingly comfortable as the stones would shift with my motion, cupping themselves around my knees.

I felt torn. Physically, Shiloh was the most impressive man I'd ever seen, but he was married, and I felt drawn to Chebona. Being there in the river with him, though, I was spellbound. The male form was all kinds of contradictions, I thought. Rigid, strong and muscular, and yet soft and vulnerable in other ways.

"Why did you come to our village with Chebona?" he asked, breaking my musings.

Even though I'd already told him about my work in the journal, I sensed he was asking about my intentions.

"Your brother was so excited for me to see his tribe," I said. "And I was curious. I like learning about other cultures. In my home, we don't live as you do. Our whole way of life is so different."

"Which life do you like better?"

"It is not as simple as that, Shiloh. Each has its good and not-so-good points."

"What is good and not-so-good?"

"Good is the sense of community in your village. Everyone helps each other and gets along. You may have heard about the conflicts in the colonies between the settlers and the army. In England, there are other conflicts over land and wars between countries. There are some people who are poor and don't have much. Your people don't have many possessions, but they seem to be happier. The not so good, is that you rely on the land to provide for you, if there's a hard winter or summer drought, it hurts your people more."

He said, "We also have conflicts between tribes over land, but we know that no-one owns the land. With the coming of the white man, there are things that are good and not-so-good, too."

"Like what?" I wanted to know.

"The good is metals and cloth and muskets. The not-so-good is your fire water. When you drink it, at first, you're happy, but then you can't talk or walk. After that, you feel sad and sick.

I smiled at the thought of Shiloh drinking. He was being totally honest.

He continued on a more serious note, "The Earth, though, provides for us just as it does for your people. There's no difference there."

"That's true," I said, keeping his face above the water as I massaged away the last of the soap from his scalp.

"I wish others could come here and experience what I have. Then they'd be better able to understand your way of life."

Shiloh said, "Most of your race wouldn't want to come here and learn from us. They think that it is only we who should learn your ways so we can improve. But you have had your eyes opened and know that isn't true. That is where you are different, Koda. So I ask you again, which is better?

Shiloh would be good at debating, I thought.

"I agree that a simpler life is best. It's easy to get lazy and caught

279

up in the comforts of modern life and the unnecessary dramas that come with that. However, it could be said that it is safer than living in the wilderness. Here you have dangerous animals."

Shiloh said, "Like the snake and the bear?"

I laughed, replying, "I was thinking of that deer."

He chuckled. "That was my own doing. I was too focused on trailing the deer to concentrate on my surroundings. Now, I have learned that lesson. There will always be more deer."

"Would you consider living here?" he asked.

"Think about what you ask of me," I replied, surprised by how forward he was, given I'd only been in the village for a day.

His question seemed out of place, but we began this conversation by talking about Chebona. My motivation for coming here was to learn more about this exotic country and to complete Mr. Miller's sketchbook. Although I liked Sunny from the very first time I saw him, I wasn't sure what would become of him as Chebona. I'm guessing Shiloh was probing on behalf of his brother, but I felt he was being presumptuous.

I asked him, "If you visited my town and were asked the same question, what would your answer be? It's not only a matter of lifestyle but the connections you've made. It's what you would be leaving behind that's important. A family and friends. People are why you should stay or leave a place, not belongings or the way of life."

"People come and go in our lives, too," he said.

Shiloh opened his eyes and saw that I had been looking down at his body in the dark water.

"Your hair is quite clean now," I said, perhaps a little too harshly. I was embarrassed and mad at myself for ruining the tender moment. I took it out on him, by saying, "You can do the rest yourself."

I rested the soap on his chest and put as much distance between the two of us as possible. He grabbed the bar before it sank into the darkness. I swam over to the bank, ready to make a swift exit.

"Turn around," I ordered him. " I want to get out."

By this time, he was standing by the edge of the river. The water reached over his thighs. With one hand, he washed his chest and then his waist. He focused on his groin, making me uncomfortable. The way he lingered there left me feeling it was intentional.

"No," he said.

"Shiloh, have you no respect? I can't have you see me naked."

He seemed angry. "Yet you were happy enough to stare at me while we talked."

Even though I was cold, heat flushed through my body. I wanted to turn away but somehow couldn't.

He said, "You've ordered me around enough today, Koda. I've had to wear your underclothes over my arm. Did you see the looks I got as we walked past the others? And the mockery from my elder brother? I did not feel like a man then. Now, I feel like a man."

He had not stopped soaping his manhood. He rubbed the shaft of his penis with slow, deliberate strokes. Was it my imagination, or was it getting larger?

"Why are you ashamed of your body and what it does?" he asked. "You can see me. I'm not ashamed."

I did not appreciate his defiance. It might be appropriate in his culture. Personally, I doubted that. Either way, he knew I wasn't a squaw. He knew damn well that Europeans valued modesty and discretion. Was he trying to provoke me? Or shock me? Or simply anger me and push me away?

"I'm not ashamed," I said. "You might be embarrassed wearing a sling made from woman's clothing, but that's your problem. You're the one who overreacted."

"Just as you are doing now."

I stayed in the shallows with only my head and shoulders above the water, saying, "I chose to be here. I choose who I want to be with. I choose when and where to take off my clothing. I'm ashamed of nothing this day other than caring about you."

Shiloh hung his head. He slipped back into the river and under the water. From what I could tell, he was accepting my point and conceding.

Was this his way of telling me he wouldn't watch me get out of the water naked? He drifted out into the channel of the river, keeping his back to me.

Shiloh was nothing like Chebona. How could he be tender and thought-provoking one moment and so stubborn the next? Not to mention he had no concern for the feelings of an innocent woman. Damn him!

I stormed onto the bank, grabbed my towel and rubbed my goose-bumped skin furiously to get dry and warm. From behind a tree, I got dressed. I was tempted to walk away and leave him, but I refused to be rude in response to his aggression, so I waited.

Shiloh stepped up out of the river and dried himself with his one good arm. I stood nearby in the moonlight and turned away as he struggled to dress with only one hand.

"I—I," he stuttered, picking up the sling and swallowing his pride. "I need your help."

"And I will help," I said, walking back to him with those few words. He was docile as I tied up the sling.

"Thank you, little one," he said, bowing his head and avoiding eye contact. "You're stronger than you look."

Although *little one* had originally been a term of derision, I sensed the meaning for him had changed now. He spoke with respect, acknowledging that I was helping him in ways he hadn't foreseen. Back when we first met by the river, he'd been dominant. He'd bested his brother and ridden with me on his horse. He saw my tiny stature as a point of weakness. Now, he seemed to offer me genuine admiration, but was it enough? There was no apology. Did he not to realize he'd offended me? Pride ruled his heart.

We walked back to the hut in silence.

He put fresh logs on the fire. The wood crackled. Warmth swirled within the hut. Already under my furs, I turned my back to him. I could almost feel his eyes burning through me.

After a heavy sigh, he went to sleep. It wasn't long before his breathing became slower.

How could he fall asleep so damn easily, as if without a care in the world? He was a married man. Regardless of culture, he should not have conducted himself like that before me, an unwed woman. I tossed and turned, willing my restless self to find slumber. Thank goodness the next few days would be busy with celebrations, and Shiloh's wife would be back from the women's hut.

After Chebona returned to the village, I needed him to take me back to the fort. Shiloh was too much for me. This was not what I'd come here for. I felt I had to put all this behind me. If I could have, I would have walked out of the village that night.

Festivities

A truce existed between Shiloh and me for the next few days. No more deep conversations were had. I kept our discussions focused on the day-to-day activities of the camp. I had no intention of bathing with him again.

The next morning we visited the chief to give him gifts. Everyone in the village brought something to represent how thankful they were that the chief's family was growing. Since I'd already given Wynono everything useful I had, Shiloh said we could give a gift as a household. We led a young black pony toward Wynono's hut. I stroked its soft mane, noticing how silky it felt under my fingers. Fond memories of my first filly stirred my thoughts back to my childhood in England. It had been a sweet little horse that I had called *Precious*. I was long overdue for a good fast ride.

Try as I might to distance myself, it wasn't long before we were talking in depth again.

"I wish I could give something of my own," I said to him.

"It's not the just pony I am giving him, but the opportunity to ride one day. And I will teach him as he grows older. There are many things you can give, that are not possessions. To give from your own soul is the richest gift."

"I'm not sure what else I can do for a newborn."

He was curious. "If he was born in England, what would he receive there?"

"Oh," I replied. "We have lords, which are like your chiefs, so he would have the right to farmland one day and inherit money from his father's estate."

Shiloh said, "For us, wealth means being able to ride well, hunt well, and bring up children well. Calian will need useful skills to serve him in life. Money and land are poor substitutes for skill."

"That it is," I said, agreeing with him. I'd never thought about it in that light before. As much as I despised Shiloh for what he did in the river, I couldn't help but admire his resolve. He was good at heart, albeit a little rough around the edges.

"What is it you English live for?" he asked. "What do you remember at the end of your lives?"

"I don't know," I said, not having considered this before. "I guess we all want to pass something on to our children."

"You should want to give them more than things," Shiloh said. "You should think about what satisfies you in life. That will be more important to your children than money."

He had a good point. What would I be able to teach my children one day? What could I teach Shiloh and his tribe here in America? They were far better at living in the wilderness than I would ever be.

Shiloh lifted the flap to Wynono's hut as we stepped onto the woven mats that covered the floor.

The chief welcomed us in and proudly displayed his new son on a pedestal of furs. He was wrapped in a colorful woven blanket. His small face peeked out from it. He had his eyes closed and was asleep, oblivious to the comings and goings around him.

Aponi was seated on a bundle of furs in the center of the hut. She was surrounded by an abundance of items that had already been presented. Large baskets of moss, tiny moccasins, cloaks, an intricate spear and a junior-sized bow and arrow set were just some of them. I gave a small smile when I saw the bright red ribbon I had given her when I first arrived plaited in her hair. She looked happy and proud to have given the chief another son. Her wrists were adorned with beaded bracelets that sat still in her lap.

"*Makadewa Nikkut*: Black One is outside," Shiloh said. "He will be a good pony for Calian. I will teach him to ride. When he can walk, I'll lead him around the camp. He'll grow to be a fine rider."

Wynono took his brother's hands in his. "Thank you, Shiloh. He could not have a better teacher. One day soon, I'm confident I will teach your son how to wrestle. For I wrestled a bear and still won." He touched his scar with pride.

Looking at the other children, I realized I did have something to give. Two of them had already shown interest in my sketches. I stepped forward and said to Wynono, "I would love to teach your children how to draw. Perhaps one day they can teach Calian."

"Thank you Koda. Your heart is true and pure. My children will do well to learn from you."

With the chief's blessing I assembled the four oldest children and had them bring over their paper and charcoal sticks. For the next hour, while other members of the tribe came and made their offerings, I taught the chief's children some basic drawing lessons. Aponi's youngest two daughters' attempts were no more than scribbles but at least by the end of it, they were holding the charcoal properly. Their grubby black fingerprints covered the paper. I added a few petals and made it look like a hodgepodge of rambling flowers. In the meantime, the girls used their blackened fingers to smear over each other's faces. It reminded me of the way I'd seen the women in the village testing out the paint they had made on their own bodies. Winema smiled at their antics.

The teenagers were more coachable. Kimi, her daughter, was particularly taken with the task. She easily grasped the shading technique and was able to produce a good picture of an old oak tree. Her younger brother, Tonshee, likewise showed some flair. He replicated a Spotted Bass and used the same technique to shadow the fish scales. I was delighted to see them try something new. They picked up the concept of fine arts quickly. The chief was pleased when he saw their efforts.

Wynono turned to me and said, "You learn the ways of the Powhatan and what is important quickly, Koda. As long as we have shelter, food and warmth, we can survive. But the ways in which we express the beauty around us make our lives have meaning."

I couldn't have agreed more.

The weather outside was clear and bright. Being inspired again to draw, I took my sketchbook with me to a few new locations around camp. I ventured a little further afield with the help of Tonshee. He had practically begged me to come along. Since most of the other villagers were busy preparing for the feast and ceremony, I was glad to have his company.

We went inland past an open section of plains where a heavily wooded area sprawled out before us. We were careful not to disturb the grasslands, knowing it was home to many animals that sheltered there. There were trees I had not seen before. I took a perfectly formed leaf and showed Tonshee how to do a rubbing. He told me it was from the Black Oak tree and placed the delicate, orange leaf on a flat stone. I used the edge of the charcoal stick to make its imprint on the page. Tonshee had brought his paper and charcoal and did the same. He thought it was a good way to draw by using the plant itself. He ran around collecting various-sized leaves and overlaid them to form a beautiful mosaic.

"Kimi will love leaf rubbings," he said. Then he asked me, "Why do the English want to know about the plants and animals here? Is it so they can take them and use them in their towns?"

I smiled. Even if the settlers did come to an understanding of the wildlife here, this simple way of life would be so foreign to them that few would see the benefits of living this way. Since being in the camp, I realized the amount of work it took to live like this constituted a full-time job.

I answered, "No, Tonshee, I'm not doing this for the English who have come to your country. They have their own way of living. Although, I'm hoping your use of plants for medicine can benefit our people, too. If your god made those plants, surely he would want all people to have good use of them. My friend, Dr. Taylor, lives in Williamsburg. He would love to know how these plants can help his patients."

"You're right," Tonshee said, flicking through the pages of my sketchbook. "The bounty of the land is for all. But why would they be interested in horned beetles?" He'd paused on the page I'd done of the beetle and its grubs. "Will they know about the grubs? Can we fool them into eating some?"

I laughed. "Not many English come and see the wonderful gifts that nature has given this great land. I want people from across the ocean to be able to look at the life that lives here. People there would be interested in seeing the different types of plants and animals that call this place home. It makes the world seem bigger somehow, knowing different creatures live in different places."

"I've only ever known this place." He sounded sad. "Because I'm the eldest son of the chief, I'll only know this place. Like the bog turtle, I will never leave where I have grown up, not like Chebona."

"Even so," I said, "Being the next chief, you'll have a great responsibility for your tribe. Who knows, in time, maybe even as chief, you can visit some of these places if you should so desire. When you have sons of your own, they can look after your people."

He smiled at this. "You mean when I am old and wrinkly and have not many teeth left? They'll say here comes the great Chief Tonshee! Look at him. He needs a stick to walk. How great will I be then?"

He may joke about it, but I thought he would be great because he'd have helped lead people and a new generation.

"Tonshee, your name shall be known across the sea. For every one that helps me with this book will be given credit. Your name will be written here, in the front, for all to see.

I pointed to the inside cover, where I'd left a blank page for such a reason.

I said, "Others will know that Tonshee helped Koda explain this land and its beauty."

He seemed to like that idea and his spirits lifted. He was proud that he would be going through the same ceremony as Chebona in a few years' time. He couldn't wait to be a man. It was a shame he was in such a hurry to grow up. Already he knew so many things about the natural world in which he lived. I was much older and an educated adult, and still, I didn't possess the knowledge he did. That was something to think about. My understanding was a bit broader, but being exposed to the world as your classroom had its advantages. We spent the next two days filling in my sketchbook along with my understanding. I was pleased with the progress I was making, but I still had dozens of blank pages to fill.

That night the long-awaited festivities began.

Earlier in the day, the village had learned that Shiloh and his hunting party had managed to kill a black bear, which was highly prized because of the danger it represented. If they were not careful, a bear could kill several men, especially if it had been wounded and angered. It was almost its own celebration. Once the kill was brought in, the women got to work quickly butchering it so it would be ready for the night's feast. Great slabs of delicious meat were roasted over open flames. The aroma wafted throughout the village, making my mouth water.

Just before dusk, everyone assembled together. I wore the beautiful shell necklace the chief had given me. If ever there was a special time to wear it, this would be it. I loved the way it hung down over my tunic, bouncing and jangling with each step I took.

Faint stars appeared overhead, watching us as we formed a large semi-circle around the fire. The unmarried women served the roasted meat on flat wooden boards. As I was Chebona's guest, I was excused from serving. I took my cues from those around me and skewered a large chunk of meat with my ornate bone-handle knife. Starting at one end of the line, the recipients would tear a chunk of meat off with their teeth and throw it onto the fire as an offering of thanks to *Ahone*. Once everyone had done this, we sat on large mats and feasted until our bellies could hold no more. I was seated next to Aponi. Her son was snuggled close to her breast. She leaned over to me.

"This is what Chebona wanted you to witness. Enjoy yourself. Not many who aren't Powhatan get to participate in such an event."

I nodded. I was thrilled, not knowing what lay ahead but being caught up in the moment all the same.

It was wonderful to see not only the children excited to be a part of the festivities, but the adults as well. All too often, the adults focused on the vital routines of day-to-day life. Here, they freely expressed their enjoyment of the meal with utter abandon. Their animated chatter and gestures were all building to the highlight of the evening: the first presentation of the boys going through their rites of initiation.

Chebona and the rest of the teenage boys were escorted into the village by the *kwiocosuk* or shaman. The priest was painted in black, while the boys and other dancers were in unique combinations of red, black, and white. Not one of them had a stitch of clothing on.

When I looked over at Shiloh and saw him smiling at me, I could almost hear him saying, "*Not ashamed.*" I had not been able to persuade him to wear the sling this evening. His earlier kill with the men had likely bolstered his confidence, although I noticed he did not get up to dance with the others. He held his arm close to his chest.

The sound of drums filled the night air. The constant beating drowned out the noise of people talking. Once the music started, it was as if human bodies had been taken over by a force that was bound to the rhythm of the drums. It started with the men and boys dancing in groups of four in a large circle led by their *weroance*: leader. They carried green boughs in their hands that added to the dance's dramatic movements. The shaman and a group of elite elders wore antlers on their heads. They positioned themselves in the middle of the circle of men and boys.

After the initial ceremonial dances were finished and the shaman had retired, the women got up and joined the men. Sticks and rattles were distributed to the audience. The instruments drowned out the natural noises of insects and frogs that tried in vain to compete.

Aponi handed me some sticks. I attempted to copy the rhythm of the others.

They struck the ground and hit sticks together. *Bang, thunk, thunk. Bang, bang, thunk.* Just when I thought I had mastered the rhythm, the drums would change beat, and a new rhythm would emerge. My attention was on the dancing. The dancers' movements were enchanting and surprisingly sensual. The women would bring their hips or buttocks close to the men, shaking them to the rhythm. At the same time, the men moved their hands in waves over the women's bodies without even a touch. Husbands and wives swapped partners on several occasions over the course of the evening. The young men, of course, would choose their favorite girl to partner with them. Often Chebona would look in my direction, and I would shake my head. As he was naked, I was not confident about being his partner. He even danced right in front of me, kicking up a little dirt as he shuffled with his feet, beckoning me to follow. As he danced with the other girls he made a pouty face, that caused me to smile. After each dance, his eyes came back to me. The open starry sky, smoldering fires and naked bodies were a world away from the polished dance floors, silks and satins of London's high society. I wanted to be with him but felt too self-conscious. It was just so different from how I was raised.

"Aponi, should I dance?" I asked, becoming more agitated as the evening wore on. I wanted to dance with Chebona but felt awkward. I didn't want the night to end before I had done so, but I also didn't want to stay on show for long. There was something about seeing him dance with the other girls that I didn't like. They smiled at him, encouraging him, and he smiled back.

"Dance, Koda," she said, "Chebona will be offended if you don't."

Being determined not to miss out the next time he looked over, I nodded in his direction.

Chebona came over and held his hands out to me. I didn't see his painted naked body any more. I saw him as a man I admired. I got up, but he didn't take my hands in his. Sensing my reluctance, he led me near the fire, where we were shielded by the others around us. He stood behind me. The pounding of the drums in my ears felt in time with the pounding of my heart and the sound of blood rushing through me.

He leaned in close to my ear and said, "Don't think. Just move with the beat."

So I did. I swayed my hips and lifted my arms, concentrating on the music. His hands glided around my body, not touching but oh, so very close. I could only see his fingers. My eyes followed where ever they led. Those hands swayed over my arms, around my waist, and over my necklace that rocked and bounced off his fingertips. All I could see were those strong, large hands. Clean and well-groomed nails held my attention as I imagined that he was touching me. His fingers hovered over my hips and down the front of my legs. It was hypnotic.

My breathing was labored, and the heat from the fire made me feel as though I was reaching fever pitch. I didn't see anyone else. I only saw Chebona. How long had we danced like that? I had no clue. His breathing was loud and heavy on my neck. When I turned my face over my shoulder, his face was next to mine. Our lips were there. Not a hair's breadth separated our mouths.

The smell of pine needles and freshly cut wood wafted from Chebona's breath. I hadn't seen him for several days, and now he was right here with me. We turned, entwined by the beat of the music. He shimmied close behind me. If I twisted and leaned back, I could kiss him. I wanted to feel his sweaty skin beneath my fingers. For a moment, I forgot about dancing, but I knew touching him would ruin the ceremony as contact was not allowed.

The music continued. His finger brushed a lock of my hair that had come loose. Chebona dropped his hand as if he had been burnt by something hot and came around to stand in front of me. He knelt down, leaning back and continued to move his hands inches away from my thighs. All the while looking up into my eyes. I forgot to dance. I just watched him. Watched his chest rise and fall with each movement. Watched his shoulders twist and flex as the shadows played on his skin. Watched him lean back, his stomach firm and taunt to show me his body. I looked back into his eyes. Desire was there. I felt it. Strong, primal, needy. I didn't know how to respond, so I didn't. Chebona tilted his head to the side, giving me a questioning look. When I just stood there, he got up and leaned in close.

"You've stopped dancing," he said.

"It doesn't feel like dancing anymore," I replied, shaking. The need welling up within me was great.

"I know," he agreed. "I would touch you if I could, but I'm not yet a man. Would you kiss me if you could?"

His words hung in the air between us.

"Right now, I can think of nothing else," I said, feeling torn by this strange, exotic custom.

Mercifully, the drums stopped. The dancing ended. The spell was broken, and reality had returned. The boys started following the shaman back to wherever they had magically appeared from at the start of the evening. Chebona looked at the backs of those departing and then over to me. I sensed he didn't want to leave. It was as if this moment was too important for him, but I understood he had to go.

Before he left, he said, "Do not forget me, Koda. I want to dance with you again tomorrow and the day after that."

How could I refuse him?

After the dance, Shiloh and I returned to the hut. He seemed aloof. I was sure he'd seen me dancing with his younger brother, but he didn't mention anything. As I lay down in the hut, I felt exhausted but happy. Something special had happened between me and Chebona. I couldn't deny it. If I were logical, I would put a stop to this whole thing. My head told me a future with Chebona would be difficult, but I wanted him. Could I see myself living here for the rest of my life? I felt sure he would not want to leave his people, and it would be cruel for me to expect him to do so. Perhaps some sort of compromise where we could spend summers here and the harsher winters back in town. Would he be content with that? My parents were another concern. They were liberal thinkers but would a union with a native be a step too far?

The hot coals from the fire in the hut cast a shimmering glow on the skins hanging from the wall. I threw off my furs in annoyance, flinging them away with a sigh.

Shiloh murmured, "Koda, you're as noisy and restless as a wild boar. What keeps you awake?"

Should I bare my soul to him? I was pretty sure he would take his brother's view on the matter. Regardless, it would be interesting to find out.

"You saw me, right? Dancing with Chebona?" I said, offering no further explanation.

"Ah," he replied, placing some dried wood on the fire. "And now you are thinking too much."

I stared up at the roof, making out the wooden poles that held the skins in place. The shadows from the flickering fire cast eerie patterns above me.

"I don't know what to do," I admitted.

"What do you want to do?"

"It's not as simple as that," I moaned.

My heart stirred at the memory of Chebona and me dancing together. It felt right, but there were so many obstacles.

"I'll ask you a question," he said. "What will make you happy?"

"It's not about what will make me happy?"

"Why not? Is your happiness not important?"

"Yes, but..." I replied, unable to finish the sentence.

"There are no buts, Koda. There's only you and your life."

"I guess."

"Will you be satisfied to go back to Williamsburg without my brother?"

Would I? That was a good question, it was hard to decide. I had come to rely on Chebona. I had feelings for him now that I could not deny. My silence prompted Shiloh further. "For if you won't have him, he will stay here."

A future without him hurt to think about. Sure, in time, maybe I could move on and forget him but did I want to? My heart already knew the answer.

"Go to sleep, little one. You'll know what to do. Don't torment yourself with problems. Let your heart be your guide. It will lead you on the right path."

I fell asleep and dreamed of figures dancing by the firelight.

Tonshee's leaf rubbing

Black Oak (with orange, yellow and brown Fall leaves)

Changes

When I woke early the next morning, I felt nervous about the evening ahead. It was the second night of the ceremony. I knew there would be more dancing. I didn't know what I wanted from Chebona, but I wanted something. If he selected me again, it would draw me closer to him emotionally. I tried to busy myself by taking Tonshee out of the camp while the sun was still low in the sky. Dawn's first rays stretched out through the foliage. Tonshee wasn't too thrilled about leaving so early and missing his breakfast. Once we were underway, he became more animated. We walked toward the river. My shoulder bag swung on my hip with a steady rhythm. The dirt on the trail was damp and cold, making the ground feel hard underfoot. Mist from our breath came out in puffs before us. I rubbed my hands together, and we quickened our pace to keep warm.

My young companion said, "At this hour, we should be able to find animals that usually sleep during the day."

We crept up through the thick grass by the river bank, watching a family of beavers as they busied themselves repairing their lodge. The dew still clung to the blades of grass, dampening our clothes. A fine, light fog hung low over the water. The smell of moist dirt was fresh and pleasant.

The beavers were fascinating to watch. Their industrious labors were in stark contrast to our stillness. They had plenty of material to choose from as leaves, twigs and sticks littered the river's edge. Every now and again, a leaf would escape and bob lazily downstream. I recorded details and drew my subjects, but my usual enthusiasm was lacking. Tonshee noticed my mellow mood.

"What distracts you? You've drawn the beaver tail too thin. It is much thicker and has overlapping tiles on it. The tailbone runs down the middle with a spongy sort of fat on both sides. It's good eating."

He was right. My drawing looked like an oversized rat.

I sighed.

"It's all right, Koda. Maybe you didn't notice, as its tail is very flat and mostly under water. They're interesting animals, huh? They don't hibernate but continue to eat and build through the winter."

"That's impressive," I replied. "I can't imagine how cold it will get out here, particularly once the water turns to ice."

Another thought occurred to me. "It must be hard to kill them once you've seen them living like this in the wild."

Tonshee replied, "An animal's life is a sacrifice we don't take for granted. All life is sacred, but for us to live, others must die. This is the way the great god *Ahone* designed it."

Still, I thought if I could live off plants and not hurt creatures like these, I probably would. It was much easier to see meat in a cooking pot, not knowing where it came from. I realized now why the natives place such importance on thanking their gods. It was because they appreciated all life.

Tonshee pointed out a water rat to me, swimming near the beavers, which was convenient as I could rename my first drawing. I took my time sketching the beaver's nest with its cumbersome logs. After a productive morning, our stomachs called us back to camp.

"You should eat with us," Tonshee said. "My father would like to see what you've done in your book. He'll be happy that his son and brother have been able to help you with it."

"I'd like that."

Tonshee smiled.

After we had eaten, I sat outside Wynono's hut. The twins played happily on a fur in front of me while their father studied my drawings with care. He turned the pages, interested in where Chebona had taken me when we drew some of the earlier sketches near Williamsburg. He came across the drawing of Shiloh with his bear paw tattoo and let out a sigh.

"Three years ago, I thought Shiloh would become chief."

I sat there stunned. This was the first time I'd seen Wynono vulnerable.

He continued, "I was attacked by a bear. Its claws were like knives. I thought I would meet my ancestors that day, but it was not to be. When I didn't come home that night, Shiloh and some of the men came looking for me. It was unwise to go out by myself, but I had wanted a bit of solitude."

He looked at me.

I nodded.

"It can't be easy being chief for all these people."

"I like it," he replied. "But sometimes I just want to be responsible for myself. That day I couldn't even do that properly."

"Surely, it wasn't your fault the bear attacked?" I said.

"There were signs on the forest floor. I should've been more careful. I'd stopped to rest and lit a fire. I'd caught some fish and roasted them on sticks. The smell carried on the breeze, and the bear came to investigate. All I remember is hearing the bushes crash around me. Before I could react, the bear had swiped me with his paw and thrown me into a tree. I crawled for hours, fearing it would hunt me down and finish me off, but it was the fish he wanted."

I winced as he showed me the scar running from his shoulder across his chest down to his stomach.

I said, "When we were coming here, Chebona caught two turkeys in the forest but only brought the carcasses back with him. He said he didn't want to attract any animals. He was thinking about bears. Now I know why."

Wynono answered, "There are many dangers where we live. I've told this story many times so others will not make that same mistake. My pride is not as important than the lives of my people. As chief, something good should come from my stupidity."

I admired his humility, although I thought he was being a little hard on himself. Living out here, there would always be risks.

Wynono continued, "When Shiloh found me bleeding by the riverbank, I wanted to give up. The pain was so bad. Honestly, death would have been a relief. But my brother was stubborn. He refused to leave me there, bringing me home. Of course, now I'm glad. Otherwise, my three youngest children would have never been born."

His twin boys lay on their stomachs on the rug, struggling to pull their legs up under themselves. They rocked back and forth. Their chubby fingers grabbed at the fur of the animal hide they were on. In no time at all, they would be crawling.

"Do you want to know something funny?" he asked.

"Sure."

"Do you know what happened to that bear?"

He kicked the black pelt beneath his feet. My eyes widened in surprise.

"No, really?" I said.

I couldn't believe the monster that had almost taken his life was now a rug his children were lying on.

"How can you be so sure it's the same bear?" I asked.

"The day after they brought me back to the village, Shiloh, Chebona, and a few others took it upon themselves to track down the bear. They traced it to a thicket near the river. Chebona wounded it with

300

an arrow through the heart."

"And that didn't kill it?" I asked, surprised by the notion.

"Bears are as strong as ten men. Even with an arrow in its chest, it didn't fall until dusk. Shiloh delivered the death blow, plunging his knife into its neck. When they cut off its head, there was still some of my flesh in its claws."

I was astonished by their courage and bravery. I could not imagine even my father hunting down such a fierce beast.

"Three claws," he said, pointing into the shadows at the edge of the fur. He tapped the three scars running over his body. Wynono was still holding my notebook open to the page where I'd drawn Shiloh. I shuddered at the realization I'd sketched Shiloh's tattoo with three claws.

"His tattoo! It's more than an animal print, isn't it?"

He nodded.

"It represents what he did for me, his brother."

I was astonished at the depth of their bonds. The love of their family was evident. There was nothing they wouldn't do for each other. I was beginning to see that their lives were intertwined in ways I'd never imagined.

He added, "And now my children play on this bear skin. It's a reminder for me that life can not be taken for granted. Just because you have something one day does not mean it will be there tomorrow. Every time I look at this hide, I thank the great god *Ahone* for saving my life. I didn't want this bear to die. It was only trying to survive and I was in the way. But if he would attack me, he would attack others. His death was not out of revenge but for the safety of the tribe."

"Thank you for sharing your story with me," I said, jotting down notes in my book.

This was a story I felt I needed to capture for those back in England. Few have understood the motivations of the natives in America, and I felt this helped explain their lives in more detail. I decided I'd sketch not only Wynono and his scar but also his children playing on the bearskin.

He was happy to let me draw them. By the time I was finished, the sun was high in the sky.

"I should get these two back to their mother so she can bathe them." He scooped them up, one under each arm and went back inside his tent.

I had just learned a profound life lesson from a real-life story - make the most of every moment.

That evening followed the same pattern as the previous night. First, there were offerings, then feasting and dancing. The time had finally arrived. My eyes searched for Chebona as soon as the boys entered the camp. He sought me out straight away and offered me the first dance—and every dance after that. If some of the other girls were hoping to dance with him, they would have been disappointed. Secretly I was pleased because it would have been hard for me to see him dance with someone else. This time I did not feel self-conscious. I let the rhythm take me where it led. My feet shuffled in the dirt. The short sharp movements in the dust formed imprints that changed as quickly as they were made. This night, Chebona faced me, looking into my eyes as we came under the music's spell once more. Under his gaze, I forgot all the reasons why I shouldn't be with him. All too soon, the drums ceased, and he was led away again.

On the third day, the camp was quiet. When I went for breakfast, no one was gathered around the cooking pot. The villagers stayed by their huts. Many women were painted from head to toe in black. Some of them were softly wailing, rocking backward and forward. It was so somber that I thought someone had died.

I took my cue and helped myself to some food from the communal pot and then returned to the hut.

When Shiloh woke up, I held out a bowl for him.

"What is going on today? The camp is different. Some of the older women are painted black."

"Those are the mothers of the boys who will become men today. They're mourning the loss of their sons. No one will do much work today. It's to be a day of reflection," he explained.

I smiled, "That explains why I'm up before you and getting you breakfast. Usually, it's the other way around."

Ever since that night in the river, Shiloh had gone out of his way to be kind and considerate. At first, he was brash with me, but since those early days, he'd been far more aware of my gentle upbringing. When he didn't bring me breakfast this morning, I suspected something was different, but I didn't realize he'd be mourning the loss of his young brother.

He'd made mistakes, but I was the one putting excess meaning into things when there was none. To be honest, I'd learned many things that I would've had no idea about if it wasn't for him. Some of them made me blush from head to toe. Life here was an education that I doubt many unmarried European ladies knew of before they went to the marriage bed. To these people, bathing naked, dancing naked or even wandering around their village with next to nothing on did not faze them in the slightest. I was determined it would not bother me either. As much as I wanted Shiloh to be considerate of my culture, I needed to take *his* culture into account as well.

"What shall we do today, then?" I asked him. "Can I still cook pancakes for the feast tonight? For the last few days, the children had been collecting berries."

"We still need to eat," he said. "I'll help you if you like."

True to his word, after breakfast, Shiloh set up a fire near our hut while I made several trips and collected all the necessary items.

This was going to be trickier than I'd thought. Controlling the temperature of the fire was the biggest issue. I decided to make a jam out of the berries and sugar. After that, I made the batter. Not being used to making portions for so many people, I started small. It reminded me of cooking on the ship with Abe. I suspected Mrs. DuPont would be proud of my efforts as well.

Once the jam was ready, I got one of the new flat-bottomed pans I'd brought with me and added some butter. Within seconds, the butter sizzled and turned from a creamy yellow to brown. The fire was too hot. I poked some of the larger logs to the side until I had a few embers glowing on the ash. I repeated my butter test. This time, it melted and bubbled away without burning.

Several of the children were interested in what I was doing. They'd snuck out of their huts. It must have been quite a sight and comical to watch as the first few pancakes didn't turn out well. Even though some of them were lumpy, the children were quite happy to eat them. My mistakes were their delight. I tried to caution them, wanting them to let them cool, but they didn't seem to mind.

I dished one up for Shiloh. He looked at the steaming mess on the plate with a polite but wary glare.

"I'll get it right soon enough," I said, trying to sound confident.

The next few pancakes were much better and even resembled a round, golden-colored disk.

Shiloh's nose bent down to get a whiff, and once it had cooled, he used his fingers to scoop some into his mouth.

"Put some berries with it, but be careful," I said. "They're still hot."

His eyes grew wide, and his eyebrows raised as he licked his fingers.

"They taste good."

I nodded. "Pancakes are one of my favorite treats. If we had cream, they'd be even better."

The children continued to hover like eagles soaring above the plain, looking for an easy meal. I had to shoo them away, telling them these were for the feast tonight. I think they understood my intent from my actions. This I replicated from watching their mothers when they cooked, but Shiloh translated anyway, calling after them in Powhatan.

All morning, I labored away, making enough for everyone to try some that night.

That afternoon, the six braves in the ceremony were led under the largest tree in the village. To my surprise, they were painted entirely in white, symbolizing their death as children and their rebirth as men. Even their hair was white. They lay in the grass without moving. They could've been corpses.

The ceremony began late in the afternoon. Shiloh and the rest of the male relatives stood in a ring around the braves and swayed from side to side. The hum of a low chant filled the air. No one was in a rush. The rest of the males in the tribe formed a gauntlet leading to the circle. Each man held a small tree branch, some were thin and wispy, others were as thick as my arm. Leaves moved in the evening breeze as the men held them above their heads. I wondered if the branches would be used as a canopy for the boys to go under.

The shaman entered the circle to retrieve a brave. Unlike the boys, his body was colorful, with strips of red, black and yellow paint covering his muscles. He had a buffalo skull for a crown, which sported fearsome-looking horns. One by one, he collected the braves. Together, they walked through the gauntlet, with the shaman shielding each brave from the blows of the short twigs and branches. I was horrified. I watched as Chebona was struck on the head and shoulders. At one point, he fell to his knees. I gasped. No sooner had he stumbled than he was up again, staring straight ahead, oblivious to everyone around him. The chanting was relentless. I wanted it to stop but was powerless to intervene.

Once Chebona cleared the gauntlet with the shaman, they returned again as did the beatings. It took almost an hour for this part of the ceremony to be completed for each brave. It was hard to watch. Most of them had cuts and scratches on their bodies. Trickles of blood oozed from their wounds, providing a stark contrast to the white paint. Once the braves were all back under the tree, the shaman cut thin branches from overhead. His sharp ax made quick work of the soft wood. He intertwined the twigs as makeshift crowns and placed one on each boy's head. Then he guided the braves to lay back down as if dead. The shaman paid no attention to the cuts and scrapes on his own body. However, the mothers put a ground salve of prairie goldenrod on their son's cuts. Although it looked like a weed, it was effective at stopping bleeding. As Chebona had no mother, Winema tended to her brother-in-law.

As I observed the sight before me, I thought about the differences between our two cultures. Back home, it was girls that were put on display for their coming of age. The two types of initiation were as far removed from each other as the distance between our two countries.

We feasted for the remainder of the afternoon. The boys, however, were still ritually dead, so they couldn't participate. I didn't blame them for taking a well-earned rest, and I hoped they'd get to eat in the forest tonight. My pancakes were well received by the villagers, with Winema wanting to know how they were made. At the end of the feast, the boys were whisked away to spend a final night in the wilderness. When they returned, they'd be considered men. I wondered how Chebona's time away had affected him.

As we walked back to the hut, I asked Shiloh, "How's your shoulder?"

"Much better."

He gave his shoulder a couple of cautious turns before entering the hut. Once inside, I stoked the fire, wanting to get warm.

A rustle at the hut's entrance heralded Shako's arrival back to her home, having finished her time at the women's lodge. I noticed she had a colorful bead necklace. She pulled it over her head before placing it around my neck.

"Thank you," I said, to which she nodded. "Did you make this for me?"

"I did."

"It's beautiful."

I was touched that she'd thought to make this for me during her confinement. Although she seemed to understand what I was saying, she couldn't speak much English.

Shiloh asked, "Could you draw Shako and me by the fire? Someday, if we ever have children, I'd like them to see us as a young couple."

For a moment, I saw a look of sadness on Shako's face. She was hurt by the reminder of the absence of children, but she quickly recovered with a smile. The night was early. Although the light wasn't good, I decided I would try for their sakes.

Shiloh sat upright on his furs. I had to reprimand him several times for fidgeting. I'd drawn a rough outline, wanting to capture his imposing upper physique, not just his facial features. Shako lay by his side and put her head on his lap. His hand rested on her long black hair.

My eyes darted back and forth between the page and my subjects. Every so often, I would study Shako.

"How did you two end up together?" It was a question I'd been dying to ask since I first rode into camp.

"Promised," she said, but I could barely make out her quiet voice. "You?" she asked in return.

"I'm not promised to anyone," I replied.

"Chebona?" she asked.

How could so much be said with one word?

"I don't know."

"Why not?"

By God, she was persistent. Shiloh was unusually silent. Did Shako imagine us as sisters?

"There is much to consider," I said, returning to my drawing.

She patted her chest close to her heart.

I nodded, understanding her meaning. What was there really to consider if you were led by your heart? Could I imagine myself living here like this with Chebona? Once again, I cautioned myself not to make any rash decisions. Why was everyone in such a rush?

"Can I see?" Shiloh asked as I put away my charcoal.

I laughed, "Usually, you have to wait until it's finished. I've only done the outline, so don't expect too much."

He looked at the page and gave a grunt. "It's just swirls and lines."

"Every piece of art has to start somewhere. Unless the basic proportions are sketched first, the end result won't turn out well. The light in here is too dark. If I continued, I'd strain my eyes."

He sounded surprised, "You can hurt your eyes with darkness?"

Shako replied, "Even our women don't make baskets at night. It can give you a pain in the head."

She patted the furs beside her, saying, "Shiloh."

After five days away from him, she was keen to make up for lost time. I put my sketching kit back in my bag and pulled out a towel. The act itself was suggestive that I was going to give them some privacy, but I added, "I'm going to bathe."

Normally, bathing took the best part of an hour, even at night.

"Do you need someone to go with you?" Shiloh asked.

I shook my head, looking at Shako as I replied, saying, "Your wife might have something to say about that."

He looked back and forth between us both, torn between his sense of duty to protect me and his desire to be with his wife. Shako might've had a hard time understanding this, but I admired him for his indecision. It showed his growth. When I thought about Shiloh previously, I considered him to have little feeling for the concerns of others. Now, I was starting to see how that had changed.

"Don't worry, I'll be all right," I assured him.

I took my things and left. As I walked away from the hut, I could hear laughter. I don't think they were laughing at me so much as rejoicing at being together again.

The moon and stars were unhindered by clouds—they were beacons lighting my path. I slipped off my clothing and hung them on a branch. The water was cold, but I didn't care. Although there was a steady current in the middle of the river, the water was flowing around the bend, forming a bathing hole where leaves would circle. I felt relief sinking into the depths of the water. I floated there, looking up at the stars. I felt as though the river was about to swallow me up, and I wouldn't need to return.

I rested in the water, reveling in the solitude. Bathing here, like this, was a simple freedom many Europeans didn't get to experience. You could immerse yourself here any time you liked. No one had to lug the water into your room. Granted, it wasn't as relaxing as a warm bath, but there was something refreshing about being able to clean yourself like this every day. Staying longer than I thought was necessary, I emerged from the water's frigid grip. I could stand it no more.

A streak of bright red on my towel, and the dull ache in my loins, told me all I needed to know about where I would spend my next few days.

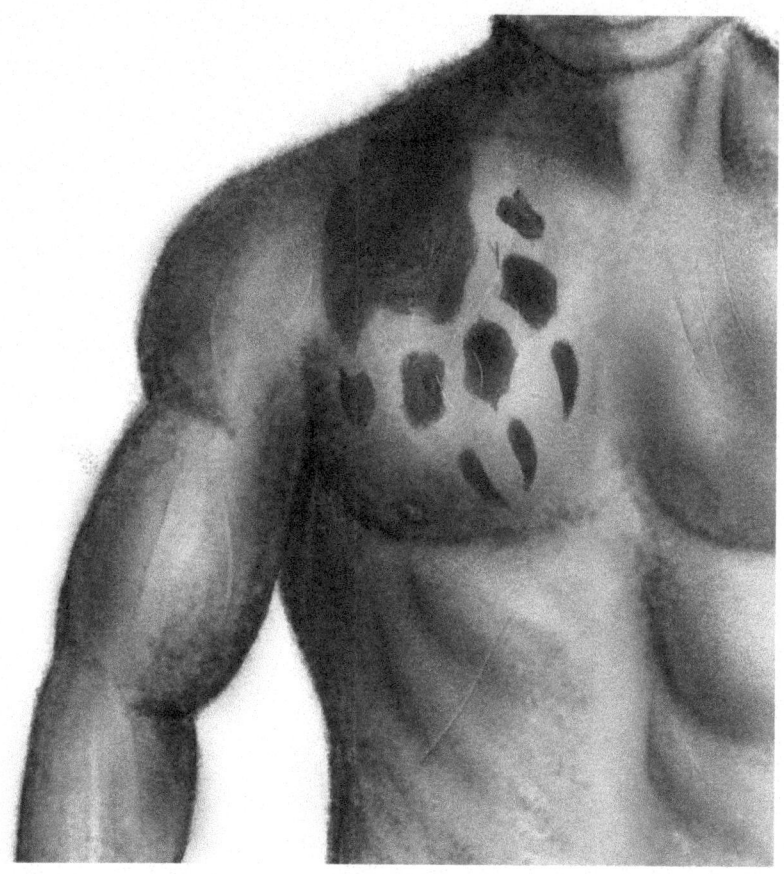

Shiloh's bear claw tattoo

Crenepo: Woman

By the time I returned to the hut and pulled open the skin cover, the fire had burned down to glowing coals. As it was quiet, I crept inside, thinking the others were asleep. Shako sat up and asked, "Is everything all right?"

Her question surprised me. She was far more perceptive than I realized.

I whispered, "I think it's my turn to go to the women's lodge."

She nodded.

"I'll take you there. Malia will care for you."

It was late when we walked through the camp to the outskirts of the village. I didn't know what I expected, but it was warm and inviting inside the women's hut. A fragrant pine smell permeated the air.

"Enjoy your time," Shako said, leaving me.

There were only two other women there, and they were already asleep when I entered.

Several piles of raised furs were laid out. Colorful woven blankets were folded at the end of each bed. I took the closest one by the fire to be comfortable after my long night swim. Slowly heat began to warm my limbs as I held my hands toward the coals. After a few minutes, I rose and fetched some wood from near the door. Two baskets were there. One was full of small pieces of buffalo hide, and the other of used skins already covered in blood. At least I knew what to do before morning came. I picked up a few pieces of wood and set them on the coals. Small crackles broke the silence. One of the girls rolled over to face the wall. I settled back on my bed, pulling the blanket up over me. I willed myself not to think about Chebona but instead wondered how Maggie's wedding preparations were going back in England.

The sound of a spoon scraping on the bottom of a bowl woke me, and I saw the two women peering shyly at me as they ate their breakfast. Both were about my age, and their long dark hair hung unbound down past their waists. I smiled and nodded. They pointed to their bowls and then indicated toward the door that I should serve myself from the pot outside.

The sun was low in the sky as I stepped out into the cool morning air. Clouds rolled overhead. Rain had fallen during the night, making the crunchy pine needles underfoot damp and soggy.

My thoughts returned to the last few days. I was glad I'd had the opportunity to see Chebona go through his initiation into manhood. Shako had missed the entire thing.

Not seeing or being able to talk to Chebona about the two of us made me feel uncertain. By the time I got back from the woman's hut, the dances we shared might seem like a dream. I wondered if he was thinking the same thing.

It looked like the cooking fire could go out at any moment. I spooned the cornmeal into my bowl. At least it was still warm.

During the morning, the women and I conversed, but not very well. Their English was limited, so we improvised with hand signals. I helped them make a new fire pit under the cover of the trees where the rain couldn't reach. When the women from the village brought the midday meal, it would stay hot and not be full of rainwater.

Back in the hut, Malia and Tala picked up the baskets they had been working on. Malia had a wide flat-bottomed version which I'd seen used for berry collecting. Due to its shallowness, this type of basket meant the fruit did not bruise. She'd not started this basket but had continued the work, as other women had done before her.

Tala wove a smaller, narrower version used for storage. Various unfinished baskets had been piled in one corner, along with the materials needed to make them. Sweet grass was used for the horizontal weave and the sturdier ash wood for the vertical columns. The rain outside drummed down on the roof as their nimble fingers moved quickly back and forth. They chattered between themselves, comfortable now with my presence.

Tala showed me how to start my own basket. The dried ash wood was fine but strong. A cross-like pattern had to be built from many fine strands to make a sturdy base. She wet the grass and twisted it under and over, teaching me how to make the weave consistent. I watched, fascinated. Handing it to me, I endeavored to copy her actions. Sometimes I lost track of the pattern, and she would look at me and smile with the long-suffering of a mother teaching her young daughter. Soon I was confident enough not to need any further instruction. However, my basket was not nearly as neat as theirs.

The rain slowed to a trickle over the next couple of hours. I hoped we could go outside soon as my fingers were sore and not used to working with stiff materials. As the morning wore on, perhaps Malia could sense my waning interest in basket weaving. She picked up the used basket of skins and wandered outside. The air was crisp and fresh. Together with Tala, she led me deeper into the woods.

Large drips of water fell from the leaves. They dropped on my head and snaked their way down my neck. Funny enough, it didn't bother me as much as it used to. We walked until we came to a rock cliff that formed a waterfall. To my surprise, there was a cave behind it. A pool was constantly replenished as a curtain of whitewater cascaded down from the top. A stream meandered from the pool through the forest to the swampy ground south of the village. It was the most beautiful waterfall I'd ever seen. Now, this is where the bathing should happen, I thought. The torrent of freshwater falling over the rocks shielded anyone that ventured into the cave from sight. A mist floated through the air giving it a magical feel.

Malia took the basket, filled it with water from the pool, and washed the hides on the rocks by the edge of the waterfall. Tala took off her clothes and climbed into the pool, laughing and dunking her head under the water. As soon as Malia was finished her task, she draped her dress over a branch and joined Tala. The two women beckoned for me to swim with them. Since there was no one else around, I pulled off my clothing and hung it next to Malia's. Before wading in, I looked around, unsure if our privacy would be interrupted at some point.

The pool was so much warmer than the river. As we were inland and surrounded by trees, the wind was absent. Bliss. We played in the water, splashing each other and putting our heads under the waterfall as it drenched our faces. I began to see the benefits of the women's hut.

After a while, the girls climbed into the cave at the base of the waterfall and crouched down. Channels of stone had been carved out, carrying the water and blood that fell from their bodies into the muddy earth below. I followed them. It was profoundly liberating sharing such a personal moment with these women. Even though they didn't speak English, we were all the same. True, my skin and hair might be a different color, but we were all women sharing this common bond. Previously, I had only ever looked at my courses with annoyance and discomfort, but here they seemed to welcome them as a source of life. For me, it was refreshing. Instead of sitting in a parlor back in England, sipping Chamomile tea and pretending nothing was happening, I was embracing the moment.

A voice called out over the thunderous sound of the waterfall, but

I couldn't discern whether it was male or female. Instinctively the hairs on the back of my neck stood up. The other girls paid no attention. I strained my eyes through the curtain of water pouring down in front of me, wondering who it could be. A splash in the pool announced another arrival.

Winema entered the cave a few minutes later, wringing her long hair and squatting down as we were. Her body bore the marks of carrying her children. There was no shame in that, only honor, and still, her body was ready to do more.

"Shako told me you were here," she said. "I'm so glad we could be together. I see you have met Tala and Malia."

I was surprised to see Winema here.

"Yes," I said. "They've been welcoming. They showed me how to make baskets. Although I'm not very good at it."

She laughed.

"I hope you aren't comparing yourself to these girls. They've been making baskets since they were children. Don't be too hard on yourself, Koda."

She was right.

"I'm happy to see you, Winema. But I didn't expect you to be here. Your boys are still babies."

She smiled, "It appears my body is ready for more children, although it could not keep up with the demand for milk from my boys. When your milk dries up, the body thinks you have weaned your young and makes it ready again. I was surprised. I didn't think I'd be visiting the red lodge for a while yet, but the goddess of the moon has called. The color of life flows from me."

"Is this pool only for women, right?" I asked.

"Yes, of course. The men are forbidden to come anywhere near here. Most tribes have these caves. It's like a sacred place where we can go in our time of strength."

Interesting that Shiloh referred to it that way, too.

"Because we bleed but do not get weaker," I said.

"Yes," she answered.

She seemed pleased that I understood their perception of this time for women.

"This is a wonderful place. I see why the women enjoy coming here." I said.

"For us, it's a welcome break from our routine. Our meals are made in camp and brought to us each day in pots. Our children are taken care of in the village, and all we need to do is look after ourselves and our bodies. When you're busy caring for the needs of your family, you don't always have the opportunity to do that. It's also a good chance to talk to each other about anything that may be troubling us."

I was amazed. "I didn't think anyone had any troubles here."

"When you live with others, there are always troubles. We sort them out here so things are in harmony when we are in the village."

There was a lot more going on here than I realized. Tala and Malia talked with Winema. They were excited about something, but I didn't understand their language. A smile crept across Winema's face.

She said, "The girls have been curious about you and Chebona. They saw you dancing together and want to know what it means. I have to admit I wondered about it, too."

They all sat there staring at me, waiting for my reply.

"I like him," I said. "How could I not?"

Winema relayed this to the girls. They squealed excitedly.

I held up my hand, trying to calm their enthusiasm.

I continued, "But it's not that simple. How do I know if this is right? I don't want to encourage his affection if this isn't going to work. In the village, life is easy, but I'm from another world. You choose your partner and stay here. But I'm not from here. I can't give up my whole life to live in the wilderness. I have family and friends that I can't leave behind. It would be the same if Chebona were to come back with me. We can't expect either of us to do that."

Winema nodded, "It is true what you say. You'll need to talk to Chebona to see what he thinks. It's too early to make a decision, but you can't blame us for getting excited. Chebona is well thought of here. There are a number of girls who have their hearts set on him. It's obvious, though, he only has eyes for you. That is the way of it here. Both parties have to be agreeable, or it doesn't happen."

I asked, "Does Malia or Tala have someone special?"

I couldn't remember them dancing with anyone in particular on the feast nights, although I had been somewhat distracted.

Winema relayed my question to the girls so they could answer for themselves while the chief's wife translated their responses.

Eventually, she said to me, "Tala has been promised to Hopi, one of the men going through the ceremony this year. She's hopeful they'll be married next year."

I smiled at Tala, happy for her.

"Malia is free to choose for herself. Her parents made no arrangements. She said she hasn't decided yet who it will be. She thinks the boys should make some effort to get to know her first. Several offers have been made, but she hasn't accepted them."

I liked Malia's way of looking at the situation. She was in no rush. Perhaps I should slow things down. That's what my head said, but my heart didn't agree.

When we left the cave, the clouds had cleared a little, but there was still a coolness to the air. We dressed quickly. Winema took what looked like several small sticks out of her bag and handed them to us.

"Here, chew on this. It will make you feel better."

The other girls already had some in their mouths.

"What is it?"

"Willow bark. It can help with the pain you may be feeling."

I put it between my teeth and nibbled. A strong bitter taste filled my mouth. As sharp as a lemon with none of the pleasant taste. I pulled a face.

"We're used to it," Winema laughed. "Even a little will be good for you if you can stand it."

I half-heartedly sucked on it as our moccasins picked their way over the pine cones that littered the forest floor.

"You must have many ways to help your people feel better. Our medicine is different, but I'd be interested to learn more about what you use to treat sickness."

"We use the plants found in this area. I'd be happy to show you, Koda. We have plenty of time to do that."

Doctor Taylor would be very happy, although he'd need to make this bark a lot more palatable before dispensing it to the townsfolk in Williamsburg.

I shook my head in an effort to rid the taste in my mouth.

Thankfully the rich aroma of a fresh stew greeted us as we arrived back at the hut. Tala laid the clean skins on a drying rack inside by the fire. The rest of us ladled the steaming food into bowls and joined her. After our bellies were full, I showed the girls how to do a French braid. They learned quickly and wanted to know more about the styles the English girls wore. No matter which culture women were from, they enjoyed looking beautiful. The two of them paraded around the hut each time a new style was mastered. I was reminded of the sleepovers I'd shared with Maggie growing up.

The next few days flew by. More women came while Tala and Malia left. Why had I ever thought this was going to be a bore?

One night we sat around the fire while Winema told us a story. She spoke Powhatan, then translated it for me.

"Long ago, before Mother Earth existed, the Creator sat alone in the darkness, thinking. With his thoughts, he formed Mother Earth. He covered the Earth with plants, trees, birds, animals and many crawling insects, but he was lonely."

We all sat enchanted by the sound of Winema's voice.

"From the soil of the Earth, he formed two companions, a man and a woman. Beside the man, he placed a bow and arrow. This was to show that the man was to be a provider of food and a protector for the woman. Beside the woman, he placed a birch basket filled with seeds.

"The basket and the seeds represented the natural resources given to them by the Creator. He also placed a leather scroll next to the woman. First, he blew life into the woman, and when she got up, she picked up the basket full of seeds but not the scroll. Her choice didn't mean that our people aren't educated, just that they chose a different way of learning. She learned from observing the world around her while being resourceful and careful.

"When the Creator blew life into the man, he picked up the bow and arrow and accepted his responsibility to provide food and protect the woman. Then the Creator said, '*Take care of Mother Earth, and she will take care of you. Don't become greedy. Take only what you need, and remember to give thanks before you do.*"

I marveled at the similarities to the Christian creation story.

Here in America, the Powhatans had a different way of learning. I'd grown up with books. If it had been me, I would've grabbed the scroll. Now, Native Americans were starting to learn from other cultures, like the French and the English. I thought about how eager Sunny had been to learn about lands he'd never seen. My books allowed him to learn without the need to experience their contents firsthand. He'd grown up in an isolated bubble of tribal life. Even his exposure in Williamsburg with my father was limited. He saw glimpses of European culture but didn't understand what life was like in England. Did that make it better or worse for him? I, too, had learned new things through my experiences in the village. I wondered if the European style of learning would change how the Native Americans viewed their own world. Would being here change me? It was then I realized it already had.

After she finished, I said, "Winema, your tribe has taught me many things. Your people have kept the Creator's pledge to take care of Mother Earth, and it has taken care of you. I fear greed in some of my countrymen is already changing your lifestyle by driving you further west."

I thought about colonial farmers who worked on the land, trying to get the most out of it. The same could be said for many industries: fishing, livestock, and forestry. They were beginning to echo what I'd seen in England.

The Powhatans ventured to new places to give the land rest enough to be replenished. This self-sufficient lifestyle was sustainable for them. With the ever-increasing European population, how long would it be before Mother Earth would refuse to take care of us unless we made more effort to help her? For we could not all live as the Powhatans did. We'd have to adapt if we wanted to be sure of our future.

"You've taught us too, Koda," she said. "Now we know how to make pancakes, braid as the French do and play cards."

That was a poor comparison, I thought, but I appreciated her kindness.

Later that night, Winema withdrew a wooden flute from a bag she had brought with her. She encouraged us to lie down, close our eyes and take deep breaths. Slowly, I'd breathe in and pause for a moment before breathing out. I'd only ever thought there was one way to breathe. How wrong I was. That I'd never thought about it before was a mystery to me. In the calm of the hut, listening to the peaceful melody of the flute playing in the background, I experienced a tranquility that was ethereal. My soul was still. The concerns I had about Chebona vanished from my mind. I was lost in the moment. Nothing was more important than my next breath. This was something special. As the evening came to a close, I desperately wanted to be able to experience that again. Now that my eyes had been opened to this reflective state of being, I decided I could do this before going to sleep each night. It wouldn't be the same without the sweet, musical notes that seem to hang in the air, but maybe by stilling my spirit, I could find that peace again.

For the next few days, we sang and played games. We did our hair, and when the sun emerged from the clouds, we warmed our naked bodies in the private courtyard at the rear of the hut. I felt the women were lucky to be able to do this each month. Only the excitement of impending childbirth would be a reason not to enjoy the women's hut.

Nemarough:
Man

Chebona was sitting next to his brother as I walked through the village, having finished my sojourn in the women's hut. I felt refreshed and invigorated by my time apart from the men. The two of them were chatting on the old log outside the hut. Carefree days had passed pleasantly with the women, and soon, it would be time to go back to Williamsburg. Being at the women's hut allowed me to refocus. There were a couple of things I wanted to accomplish before leaving. I needed to talk with Chebona about us, and I needed to focus on completing my drawings.

Was it just the ritual, or had Chebona changed? His physical appearance definitely had. One side of his head had been shaved, which gave him the fierce look of a warrior. His run through the gauntlet had left a long scratch on his cheek and bruises on his arms. Locking eyes with him, I expected to be welcomed with his friendly grin. I was disappointed when he looked at me with all seriousness.

Shiloh teased me. "Welcome back, Koda. Now that you've been to the woman's hut, you can tell us what happens there. Shako won't tell me anything at all."

"Well, you won't hear anything from me, either," I replied. "What I can say is that my time there was special. I'll remember it always."

As big and gruff as Shiloh seemed to be, he was a bit of a child at heart. I teased him, adding, "There are some things that should remain a secret. I feel like this is one of them. I wouldn't want to betray our sisterhood by sharing those details."

"Why won't you tell me?"

I laughed. "Why do you want to gossip about the women?"

He huffed as if the thought of doing that was beneath him.

If the ladies wanted to keep the secret of the woman's hut, I was happy to comply. In truth, it was an experience that couldn't be explained in mere words.

I walked past them and went inside the hut to retrieve my sketchbook. A fire smoldered in the pit. Sunlight streamed in through the opening in the roof. I turned to the back of the book and looked at the picture I'd made of Sunny when we'd first met. There was a stark contrast between the boy on the page and the man sitting outside now.

Shako came up behind me, carrying wood for the fire. She looked over my shoulder at the drawing.

"He's different. Yes?"

"Yes," I agreed.

How had that happened in the space of just a few days in the forest? Perhaps it was just as much a mystery as the goings on in the women's hut. I carefully pulled the page from the binding. Now I felt reluctant to give it to him.

"Go on," she urged. "He'll like that you've thought of him."

I nodded.

I walked slowly back outside and plopped down next to Chebona, saying, "I have a gift for you."

Sitting next to him, I felt self-conscious because of the unresolved tension between us. I held out the drawing, and he took it. He looked at the picture carefully.

"Thank you, Koda. I'll always remember my time in Williamsburg with fondness. It's well done."

Shiloh reminded me, "We've yet to finish the picture of Shako and me."

"Shako, come."

He called out to his wife, and she came obediently.

"The light is good now. Will you do some more?"

Shiloh took off his shirt and sat in a way that looked totally out of character. He had a faraway look in his eyes like he was thinking too hard. I had to laugh. Shako laughed as well.

"Sure," I replied. "But you need to sit like you were before, with Shako resting on your lap. Otherwise, I'll have to start again."

I went back to the hut and retrieved my drawing sticks. When I returned, the couple was in the right position. I sat next to Chebona, flipping to the page of the unfinished sketch and placed it on my lap. I could see Chebona's fringed leggings out of the corner of my eye. The leather bobbed and danced as his leg moved up and down impatiently. The silence between us drew out uncomfortably. There was so much unsaid, and I could tell that he was keen to talk to me. Neither of us would be content until we had spoken in private.

Now that I had the basic shapes mapped out on the paper, I could work on the next stage. It was distracting having Chebona there, but I was determined to give Shiloh and Shako my full concentration. I focused on their clothing. For me, drawing a portrait was like building a house: you couldn't move on to the next stage until the previous one was complete. The very last step was the detail. Small smile lines around the mouth, or in the case of Shako, the dimples on her cheeks. I was a long way from the finishing touches. I found it unnerving having Chebona scrutinize my every move.

As I sketched, he asked me, "Have you completed any more of your book while I was away?"

I was glad that he'd brought up that topic, as I wanted to spend time alone with him.

"Tonshee has been helping me, but I wondered if we could spend a few days looking for more examples in the wild."

"There are different types of plants and animals over the ridge," Shiloh said, pointing into the distance.

"Keep still," I replied. Shako looked at me in astonishment, shocked that I would speak to Shiloh without a sense of subservience, but I noted Shiloh didn't react. He accepted our relationship.

"I can spare a few days," Chebona answered. "But I need to get you back to your father. Winter will set in soon. Our tribe needs to travel to new grounds before the snow comes. I should be here to help them break down and set up a new camp."

I stilled my hands, unable to look at Chebona. The sketch of Shiloh and Shako stared back at me. The page was getting blurry as tears welled up in my eyes at the thought of leaving him. America was a vast land, far larger than England. Once the tribe moved on, it could be away for years.

"So you won't be wintering in town or at the fort?" I asked.

My voice sounded strained even to my own ears.

"Things have changed, Koda. I've changed. I need to be mindful of my people and our future now. I want a wife and a family. I can't do that away from the village."

So here was the crux of the issue, I thought. I'd wanted to take things slow. Was he trying to rush me? Or did he not see a future for us because it might take a long time to convince my family. It was hard to concentrate on drawing when we were dancing around these weighty matters. We needed to be alone. I felt uncomfortable discussing this in front of Shiloh and Shako. I would miss Chebona deeply if he left the region. What would my father do without his principal scout?

As if reading my mind, he said, "We have other boys that can do your father's bidding. It's beneath me now to work for him."

I snapped. "Is it beneath you to be my friend?"

Tears rolled down my cheeks as I stood. Feeling embarrassed, I turned away lest he saw them. The book fell to the ground. Shiloh got up and retrieved my journal, placing it on the log before he and Shako left us to continue our discussion in private.

"Please, talk to me," Chebona pleaded. I didn't know what to say.

Children chattered in the background and ran around between the huts playing a game with a hide-covered ball and sticks. The ball rolled over toward us, and Chebona kicked it back to them.

"I told you I would help you, Ally. And I will."

His use of my English name brought back the reality that we were from two separate worlds. He'd never fully be a part of mine. I'd taken for granted that he would always be there for me, not thinking about his responsibility to his tribe. That was selfish of me, but I still didn't like the fact that I might not have his company for much longer. What I'd thought of as friendship clearly was something more to me, and I'd only just now realized the depth of those feelings.

He came up behind me.

"I'll always be here for you."

Chebona wrapped his arms around my waist. I sank into his embrace. It felt good.

I said, "That will be difficult if you follow the tribe."

I could feel him smile as he rested his head against my hair.

"You've got the power to do something about that," he said softly.

"Just what exactly do you expect me to do?"

"Give us a chance."

"I want to," I admitted.

I leaned my head back onto his shoulder, and he held me tight.

"I know it's hard for you," he said. "We don't have to decide anything right now. Let's spend the next few days seeing if we can work out what a relationship between us would look like."

"I like the sound of that."

He turned me around and stared at my lips. "Will you let me kiss you? I've been wanting to do it for the longest time."

I nodded. My heart quickened at the thought of my first kiss.

He traced his finger over my bottom lip. My mouth opened slightly. His head bent down to mine, and I closed my eyes as his lips sought me out. Chebona was gentle at first, his mouth exploring mine. Tender, as if testing the pressure of our lips together. It was not enough for me. I wanted more.

I opened my mouth further and drew him in. The tip of his tongue touched mine, and then our tongues were stroking and moving together in unison. It felt wonderful. I wanted to be closer to him, but we were already pressed tightly together.

I grabbed his head, my fingertips softly scraping his scalp. His hands roamed over my hips and across my back, eventually coming up to my hair. He laced his fingers through my long locks, easing my head back to look at me. We were both breathing hard as he broke the kiss.

He smiled, "You taste even better than I imagined."

I blushed.

He leaned back in and caught my bottom lip between his teeth, sucking on it. That did all sorts of things to my insides.

The children were still playing and shouting behind us, but I barely heard them. Their ball bounced against my heel, and I pulled back, breaking the moment. Chebona grinned and picked up the ball. A couple of the youngsters were giggling, having seen us kiss. I could see the interruption was deliberate on their part.

Chebona threw the ball back to the kids, laughing and calling out to them in Powhatan.

"What did you say?" I asked.

"I asked them, *Are you having fun?*"

I chuckled at the attention we had drawn from them, saying, "Well,

I certainly was!"

Chebona smiled. "Do you want to go out west for a few days? There are bison on the plain. They're migrating south for winter. I think they'd look good in your book."

"Yes."

My head was still in the clouds. My body was still tingling from that kiss. And he wanted to talk about bison?

I'd shared something with Chebona that I hadn't with any other man. I felt vulnerable. He seemed to enjoy our kiss, although I wondered if I'd done it correctly. To me, it felt wonderful, and I couldn't wait to kiss him again. It was intimate. For me, it was totally foreign and new, but it felt natural.

"Come," he said, breaking my train of thought. "Let's get ready to leave."

"Today? I asked.

"Why not? As soon as you're ready. I'll get our supplies, but I won't be taking much. I suggest you do the same. It'll make the journey easier for the horses."

By mid-morning, we were ready to go. Shiloh lent us his two best horses. We left the camp the same way we'd come in. The children ran with us, waving us on until we reached the edge of the village. This time it was more emotional as I knew them all now. Their smiling faces and cheeky natures had touched my heart.

The day was still. The sun seemed to have little heat, competing with the brisk air around us. Chebona led the way as the trail by the river was too narrow to fit two horses abreast. It felt good to be riding again.

The gentle lope of the horse was calming to my soul. I was content to think about how the next few days would pass. The village had been wonderful, but there was no privacy there. Native American families ate together, bathed together, worked together and even slept together. All your business was their business. For the many benefits of tribal life, it could be stifling. I'd been so used to my independence and having my own room back home that leaving the village was refreshing. I inhaled the sweet air of the countryside, happy to be able to spend this time alone with Chebona.

Eventually, we headed inland through great vast open plains. The buffalo kept to themselves, eyeing our presence with caution. I sketched them moving in herds. The great thing about our adventure was that there was no rush and no real destination. There were no demands on our time. We had a general idea of where we were heading, but nature was nestled in every crevice and not in a specific place. Wherever was advantageous for life, there we would find it. Sometimes we walked, and sometimes we waited. At all times, we'd keep our eyes peeled for animals, plants or insects that I could document in my journal. It felt like the ultimate game of *hide and seek*. Once found, time was taken to draw and describe them in detail. By late afternoon, I had twelve new entries.

We decided to make camp by the river. Being mindful of our surroundings, the natural world abounded. This had a profound effect on my soul. Life was always trying to survive, but nature was harsh. Plants exploded into life to live for a moment and then withered away just as quickly. Others, like the mighty oak, stood proud, watching different creatures come and go. A living thing could be eating happily one moment and become another's meal the next. Death came to us all one way or another.

Chebona reminded me that we, too, needed to be on the lookout for danger.

"Even though it is beautiful here, it's wise not to let your guard down. Black bears live in the forest to the north. And there are three types of venomous snake. You already have the water moccasin in your journal. We'll look for the copperhead and timber rattlesnake. Hopefully, we'll find some juveniles for you to sketch. It'll be helpful for people to know not to catch them and risk dying in the process. There are easier ways of making a stew."

"Apart from the size of the snake, how do you know if it's fully grown?"

"On rattlesnakes, the number of segments on their tail gives you a good indication. If it has between eight to thirteen of them, it is probably fully grown. If you ever come across one, leave it alone. They can strike quickly before you even have time to react."

I certainly wouldn't be going out of my way to make the acquaintance of any snakes.

While Chebona caught fish for supper, I started the fire. This proved more difficult than usual as the wind had gained momentum throughout the afternoon. Sheltering the tender flames with my hands, I finally managed to get enough heat for the big bits of wood to catch. I'd not noticed a curious-looking turtle watching me. It ambled through the grass. Without warning, it snapped, striking fast for a creature I thought was sedentary.

"Ally, move back," Chebona said, hauling his net onto the bank and seeing me looking befuddled by this overly aggressive turtle.

"That's a snapping turtle. They have a painful bite. I've known people that have lost fingers because they got too close."

I scrambled onto a boulder out of harm's way. In America, even the most docile-looking animals were fierce. Forget about the bears and snakes, this turtle was scary. After a while, the turtle lost interest in me and headed back toward the river. Chebona gave him a wide berth.

While the fish was cooking, I sketched the turtle. I wanted to capture it on the page before its features faded from my memory. Its large beak-like nose looked more like that of a bird than a reptile, while its long tail was covered in spikes. Its head looked strangely detached from its body, being cradled in a pocket of thick skin that held it in place beneath its shell.

I tended to supper, while finishing the image. The smell of the fish made my stomach growl. Every minute or so, I had to stop sketching to turn our dinner so the skin wouldn't burn. Soon enough, the meal was ready, and we ate our fill while watching the sun descend to its resting place behind the mountains. The warm colors dominated the heavens. It was as though God himself had used a brush to paint the sky. It was beautiful.

Chebona retrieved a couple of blankets from his horse.

"We'll sleep by the fire."

He tossed some wild garlic into the coals, which surprised me.

"Why are you burning garlic?"

"The smell will keep snakes away," he replied. "As well as biting insects."

"Oh," I said. "We might need more of that. A lot more."

Chebona laughed. He stacked wood on the fire. As the garlic roasted it released a sweet smell. The only creatures I wanted in my vicinity were the horses.

Stars appeared overhead. Somewhere in the distance, a wolf howled. It reminded me of the story that Shiloh shared with me, and I wondered if the stars could hear them.

Sparks leaped up from the fire, but I shivered. Even wrapped in a blanket, the wind seemed to cut straight through me.

"Come here, Ally. We'll keep each other warm."

I snuggled my back into Chebona's chest. That felt so much better. With his warmth radiating through me, protecting me, I felt safe. For once, it felt normal and natural to be in the wilderness.

"Why didn't you call me by my native name?"

"You'll be leaving soon. If I call you by your English name, it helps me remember that all this is about to change."

I hung my head.

Chebona tucked a stray piece of hair behind my ear. His touch lingered on my neck. He drew random patterns on my back, slow and tender. The firelight flickered, and with it, my eyelids grew heavy.

"It was a good day," I said, stifling a yawn.

"It was," he said. "We've made many memories."

Chebona paused, and I sensed he wanted to say something more, so I stayed silent.

"I hope you've enjoyed your time with my people. I know it was a challenge for you to come here with me."

I sensed he was anxious and unsure about how I felt about the two of us. Was he prompting me for reassurance?

"Chebona, what are we going to do? I like it out here, just you and me. Life is simpler when it's just the two of us. Can't it be just the two of us?"

He turned me around gently to face him. His features looked soft in the warm light of the fire.

I rested my hand on his chest.

He looked down at my fingers and said, "I like it here alone with you, too."

Chebona cradled my face in his hands and used his fingers to trace the outline of my brow, my chin and finally, my lips. We lay down on the blankets by the fire. I leaned into him, resting my head on his shoulder. Our lips explored each other. He smelt of smoke and earth and man. He was tender and in no rush. At that moment, it was just the two of us taking comfort in one another.

"I don't think I'll ever feel for someone else like I feel for you," he said when we finally parted.

"I should hope not." I smiled.

"We'll figure this out, Ally. You're important to me. We'll take it one step at a time. As long as we agree and work together, I think we can have a future."

That was welcome news to my ears. I wouldn't be forced to choose between Williamsburg or the village, and neither would he.

"A compromise then," I said. "Perhaps living in both worlds. Do you think that's possible?"

"With you? Yes, I think so."

I put my arms around him and snuggled into his chest. The comforting sound of his heart was a steady rhythm, in time with his breathing. Chebona stroked my hair as I fell asleep.

Before I knew it, sunlight broke through the leaves. Birds called longingly to each other. I woke to the sound of splashing in the river. Chebona ducked under the water and came up again in a rush. I sat there watching him, wondering, what was he doing? Water dripped from his body. His chest heaved with the exertion of each plunge. I enjoyed seeing his muscles flex.

Finally, he emerged, holding a large crayfish in one hand. His smile showed me his foe had been elusive.

"A crawfish," he declared triumphantly.

This freshwater crayfish would've been a delicacy in any fine London establishment, and we were about to have it for breakfast in the wilderness! I clapped and cheered.

Chebona stepped up out of the water. To my surprise, he was naked. My heart raced. Although my instinctive reaction was to look away I couldn't. Now that his skin was free from paint, I saw him as a man. He held his prize above his head, its claws still snapping wildly. A thrill ran through me at the thought of having Chebona in my life. If I had stayed in England, I would never have witnessed such a sight. It brought a smile to my lips.

"Do you like what you see, my lady?" he joked, standing before me naked, holding the crawfish aloft but clearly not talking about his catch.

"I'm excited about what we will be eating, sir," I teased, replying in kind and talking to him as though he were an English gentleman.

"Is that all?"

I blushed.

Chebona got dressed while I cooked the crawfish on the hot coals. We spent the rest of the day walking along the river. We were part of nature being in the wilderness like this.

Chebona took me to a field of wildflowers. They were breathtaking. I only wished I had paints rather than charcoal so I could have caught their vibrant colors. I sketched insects, flowers and trees while Chebona lay in the sun. That afternoon, my eyes spent a little too long examining the muscles that defined his body, but I did manage to get some detailed drawings finished.

Yet another night passed as we enjoyed the spectacular majesty of the stars displayed above us.

Up until the third day, I'd gotten away without bathing, but I couldn't put it off any longer. I snuck down to the water's edge while Chebona still slept. The sun peeked above the horizon, filling the sky with dusky pink hues. All was still and quiet. Not even the birds had started their calls to one another yet.

I stepped into the cool water, not making a sound, trying not to wake him. It wasn't that I was embarrassed about him seeing my body. God knows I had seen his plenty of times and had become accustomed to its beauty, but bathing was still somewhat of a private affair for me. Perhaps this time, if he was awake when I finished, I would come out of the water without covering myself. The thought of him seeing me naked made me excited. I felt torn. On one hand, I was trying not to wake him. On the other, I was ready to splash around like he did yesterday.

I'd brought the last of my soap with me. Lathering every part of my body, I stood knee-deep in the water. I paid particular attention to the area between my legs and the bud under my fingers. It felt good to linger there. My lungs filled with fresh morning air as delight began to stir within me. Sensations began to build. Every fiber of my being felt alive and demanded more. I was so caught up in what I was doing, that I didn't notice Chebona walking up behind me. Small waves rippled past me, as he disturbed the water around me.

He whispered in my ear, "If you wanted pleasure, you only had to ask."

I flinched. I was mortified. Never in my life had I been more embarrassed. I couldn't turn around to face him. I couldn't speak.

"Ally, turn around."

I shook my head.

"Then give me the soap."

His voice was gentle. I handed it to him over my shoulder. Chebona began to rub my back, making long sweeping strokes down and around my buttocks. Ahhh, his slippery hands felt wonderful over my skin. I sighed, rolling my head back and losing myself in his touch. His fingernails scratched lightly down my back. Goosebumps rose on my skin.

Softly, he said, "Keep touching yourself."

I shouldn't, but I wanted to so badly. My loins throbbed with unfulfilled desire.

"Go on," he urged.

His hands concentrated on my bottom. His fingers slid between my legs, gliding over my groin.

Gone were all logical thoughts. My mind and body were concerned only with feeling.

His fingers teased me while his other hand sought my breast. My nipple hardened under his touch.

"Bend over a little."

I leaned forward, aching for more. His fingers slid into me. They moved in and out with a gentle rhythm.

Automatically, my hips moved to the beat of his fingers. Wave after rolling wave, the sensations took me to new heights. It felt so good. My breath came in fast gasps.

"Your body is so responsive, Ally."

His breath was warm on my neck.

I moaned, past all caring. With my hand at the front, I matched his speed and pace from behind.

His weight shifted, and I could feel his shaft pressing up against me. I wanted his fullness inside me. I turned and looked over my shoulder, longing for more.

"I will not take you," he said, reading my intent. "I want to. There is not a single thing I'd rather do. Me thrusting in you while you come tight around me. Your wetness all over me."

He squeezed my nipple. With his other hand, he thrust harder and faster.

"Come on my fingers, Ally."

I enjoyed the moment, thinking about what I was doing in plain sight of everything and anything. Birds soared through the sky. The water rippled over the rocks. A deer stood on the far shore watching us. The forest was coming to life. I felt as though I were a part of nature.

I didn't want it to end. His fingers and mine worked together, stroking, touching and moving as one. The moment between bliss and the peak overtook me, pleasure coursed through my body without mercy. His fingers slowed but did not stop, drawing out every second of my ecstasy. Standing there in the water, I shuddered with passion.

Slowly, he withdrew his fingers, lingering with his hand between my legs.

I straightened as he still cupped my breast. Holding me against him, I felt spent. My head lay back on his shoulder.

We stood like that, watching the sun come up.

I didn't need to think. I was content. The world continued on regardless. Dragonflies darted among the reeds by the bank. Fish swam at a leisurely distance. Birds winged their way across the brilliance of the morning sky. As I closed my eyes, I felt safe and loved.

At some point, though, I had to come back to reality.

My soap had gone floating down the river.

I laughed.

"What's so funny?"

"My soap is gone."

"It was worth it, was it not?" he asked.

"Yes, but now you have none."

"Are you offering to wash me," he chuckled.

"Is that what we call it?"

I could feel his hardness as I leaned against him.

"Turn around, Ally."

This time I did. He looked at every inch of my face as though he were breathing me in.

"Kiss me," he demanded.

"You're so bossy in the mornings," I smiled.

He pulled my hips to him, showing his urgency.

I touched his cheek, tracing my finger along his jawline.

Such a kind, handsome face. His lips parted. I rang my fingers over them. His tongue copied the motion of my fingers.

"I can taste you," he teased.

His member pressed against me.

Our mouths met with ravenous hunger. Something had changed between us. I could not get enough of this man. His mouth, his tongue—sweet Lord—his fingers as they played with my breasts.

My hands ran over his chest, swiping across his nipples. He gasped. I was pleased to see his response. His stomach muscles flexed as I ran my nails over them. Our mouths never parted. Our tongues danced with each other. Chebona guided my hand lower. His fullness throbbed in my fingers. He groaned. His hand covered mine as I caressed the length of his shaft. I rocked back and forth, rubbing him gently.

His breathing quickened. By this point, his mouth was no longer urgent on mine. Our lips brushed against each other, but neither of us could concentrate on kissing. It was enough to breathe. It was as if the effort to do more was too much.

His hand left mine, leaving me to satisfy him. Knowing that I could give him pleasure thrilled me. His hands settled on my hips, bringing me closer to him.

"Ally, your fingers..."

Chebona was so in the moment that he couldn't bring his sentence to a conclusion.

"Mmmm," was all I could say in reply. I was intent on seeing his enjoyment. I worked my hands faster and brought more pressure on his erection. He swayed in time with my hands, rocking his hips back and forth.

I felt the moment his frame tensed, and a shudder took him. His breaths came in ragged gasps. I knew then that he'd experienced his release. Feeling his shaft pulsate in my hand, I waited until his breathing returned to normal before pulling away. My hand was wet and sticky.

"It's my seed. You could bear a child if I came inside you."

"Oh," I said, and marveled at the idea.

"This is the best way to start the day," he grinned.

I couldn't have agreed more.

I looked around for the soap. It had floated into the reeds.

Going Home

The sun was high overhead as we returned to the village. I guided my horse along the track, his tail swished at a large fly that had been following us for the last few minutes. I patted his mane in an effort to reassure him that the pesky creature wouldn't be with us forever. He snorted at my attempt to placate him.

The day cast its warmth on us like a comforting blanket. I decided I'd never tire of the beauty of this countryside. There was a rugged harshness to the land underneath its natural beauty. In the distance, the mountains rose like sleeping blue giants. The green of the pine trees soothed the senses while the river to our left sparkled in the afternoon rays. No matter which way you looked, you couldn't help but be impressed with the Earth's splendor.

A lot had changed in the past three days. I looked at Chebona's strong figure leading the way and felt a wave of emotion wash over me. All I knew now was that I couldn't give this man up. It was a wonderful thing when someone wanted you as much as you wanted them. His willingness to do whatever it took for us to be together endeared my heart to him. What our future looked like, I wasn't sure. I had to go home before winter. It was expected of me. Back there, I would have to face my parents. My father liked Sunny but was that enough to get past the fact that he'd be asking for my hand? Father would talk to me before he gave his answer–of that, I was sure. Could I persuade him to consent to the marriage when I knew myself the many prejudices we would face?

The town had already shown its hostility toward Chebona, and that was when they knew him as Sunny. Now he looked like a fearsome Powhatan warrior. I wondered if they would misunderstand him even more. Besides, his heart was with his tribe. Even with a compromise, there would be challenges for us. There were many questions, but we were both content to live in the moment for now.

Falling in love was new and exciting for both of us. Neither one was prepared to cloud that with '*what ifs*'. Chebona didn't voice any concerns. Any doubts I had were shoved aside by the tenderness of his embrace. I locked them in the drawer in my mind. If life had taught me anything, it was that you could plan all you liked, but circumstances could change. Like a canoe in the rapids, you had to paddle hard to avoid rocks in the river. It was useless to torment ourselves with wondering. Right now, the priority was to get home safely. I had every confidence in my guide, who knew this land like it was his own. He was wary without being paranoid. He had a healthy respect for nature and his own abilities. I decided that was a very attractive quality.

Coming over the crest of the next hill, I saw the village and the plumes of smoke drifting skyward. As we rode back into camp, I realized I'd missed life here. It was a peaceful yet straightforward existence made rich by the connections of the people. I saw Malia standing by a cooking pot, waving to me. I waved back. Several other women were scraping the flesh from a buffalo hide stretched over a wooden frame. Their muscles worked tirelessly as they laid out strips of buffalo meat in the sun to dry.

We came to Shiloh's hut and Chebona helped me from my horse. He stole a kiss as he lowered me to the ground. His hands on my hips felt good.

"I see you've been studying more than plants and animals on your trip," Shiloh joked, slapping Chebona on the back.

I blushed.

"Looks like your plan worked well," Shiloh said to his brother.

I looked at Chebona, startled by that comment. He took my hand. It was a simple gesture. Words weren't needed. He was countering and contradicting Shiloh's remark with the tenderness of his touch. Once again, Shiloh was trying to provoke his younger brother.

"Well, we did have fun," I said, playing along with the brothers' banter.

"And I did enjoy myself in the river."

"In the river?" Shiloh asked. "That sounds like a good story."

He sat down on the log, wanting to hear all about our time away.

"Some things are meant to be private," I said, looking at Chebona, willing him not to tell.

"She's right, Shiloh. Come and help me with these horses. We're only staying the night. Tomorrow, we'll make for the fort."

He started undoing the strap that held the saddle in place.

"What are your plans then?" Shiloh wanted to know.

"We'll get to the fort and see Ally's family. I'll ask for their blessing for us to be together."

"What will you take as an offering for her?"

I interrupted Chebona before he could answer. "The English do things differently. In our culture, it's the woman's parents who offer a dowry or price to the man. Well, really, it's for both their futures."

Shiloh was confused. "How can this be?"

"I don't know a lot about it, but it's a tradition that the husband will take good care of his wife. If, for some reason, the marriage ends, the dowry will have to be repaid to the wife. Then she would have the means to be able to support herself."

"That won't happen in our case," Chebona insisted.

"Why would a man not take good care of his wife? Your wife is what makes life good."

The concept was foreign to him.

I said, "Not all men see it that way, Shiloh."

"Then they're fools."

Chebona began brushing down his horse, saying, "Ally, I'm not interested in taking anything from your father. All I want is you."

He looked at me tenderly.

My heart melted. "Let's just get back to Williamsburg. I'm sure the details will sort themselves out."

"Do you need me to travel with you?" Shiloh asked. "I have to help with the buffalo hunt before the snows come, but I could spare a few days."

"Perhaps as far as the river," Chebona replied. "From there, we should be safe."

"Then it is settled."

"Thank you, brother. I think we'll take just the two horses to the canoe. We'll leave most of Ally's things here. That way, we won't have to carry them back and forth."

He nodded.

I decided I would only take my satchel and sketchbook. Over the past three days, I'd gotten used to traveling this way, and I liked it.

That night we bade our farewells to Wynono and his family. We were cheered on by their good wishes. I was sure I'd be seeing them all again soon. I promised Shako I would continue working on the drawing of her and Shiloh and hoped that by the time I returned, I would have to add in a blossoming belly.

That night as we lay down to sleep, the wind howled outside the hut. Chebona wrapped his arms a little tighter around me. It took the longest time for me to fall asleep. It was silly to think the wild weather outside bode an ominous sign for our journey ahead.

The following day the winds hadn't stopped. Dust and leaves swirled around in every direction. Branches bent and heaved under the force of the wind. I tied my hat under my chin with extra care. Even so, the floppy brim rose and fell at the mercy of the weather.

"A sure sign winter is coming," Shiloh said as we readied the horses. He addressed Chebona, saying, "If you're planning on coming back, you can't stay too long at the fort."

Shiloh had consented and given his brother the larger horse so we could ride together. Sheltering behind Chebona, I pressed my cheek to his back as the horses trotted to the edge of the village. Many of the villagers had come to see us leave. They waved, squinting to keep the dust from their eyes. Their hopeful expressions tore at my heart. Tears streamed unbidden down my cheeks as I waved back. I couldn't put into words how this experience had changed me. The people here were the reason. They'd shown me the true meaning of the word friendship by including me in their lives. I'd come here with an idle curiosity to see how they lived, and I left with a deep respect for their culture. I was shaking, such were my emotions on leaving the village.

"Are you all right?" Chebona asked.

"Yes. It's hard leaving, isn't it?"

"Every time," he said.

We climbed the hill. The village looked small behind us. The wind whipped through the trees. We rode on without talking for a time. Even the birds were absent from the sky.

From in front of us, Shiloh called out, saying, "Koda, we're on your favorite trail."

What a wicked man, I thought, trying not to laugh. He was teasing me about our ride into the village. Little did he know I'd been reminded of the same thing while riding this trail. I'd changed and grown a lot since that day. I wasn't the naive young woman I once was.

I leaned forward with my head resting beside Chebona's shoulder and whispered, "It's beautiful here, especially with you."

"I think so, too," he answered.

I was impressed by Chebona's maturity not to be goaded by his brother. Shiloh might be the elder of the two, but Chebona carried

343

himself with dignity.

He tilted his head back, leaning into me. I squeezed him tight, enjoying the warmth of his body.

Shiloh looked back. He seemed surprised not to have elicited a response from either of us.

We reached the river late in the afternoon and decided to make camp for the night. The two brothers scouted the area. They talked between themselves when they returned, which had me worried.

"Did you find something concerning?" I asked.

"There are tracks, but they're not fresh," Chebona said.

"What sort of tracks?"

"*Shawnee.* Normally, they stay inland from us, but I found the feather of a falcon. It's worn as a symbol of strength by their braves."

Shiloh said, "Why did you tell her this? It's better that she doesn't know."

"Why would I want that?" I said. "I'd much rather know what's going on than be left ignorant."

"It serves no purpose," Shiloh said. "They've long gone, and there's no danger."

Chebona said, "I expect to reach the fort in two days, although this wind will carry us along faster. I'll paddle at night if I have to. After seeing this, I don't want to risk setting up camp with just the two of us."

"That's wise," Shiloh replied. "Let me hunt and get enough food for your journey. We'll cook it up tonight, and that way, you don't need to stop at all."

An hour later, Shiloh came back with three squirrels and a rabbit. He cut off the tails and threw them on the fire as an offering before we skinned and ate them.

"We give thanks, Great One, for your bounty and to you, my brothers, for your sacrifice that we may live. It's the way of this world."

I said, "I've never heard *you* say that, Chebona."

"I do it, Ally. Only not out loud."

Shiloh snorted. "How can the Great Spirit hear you if you don't say it aloud?"

"If he's the Great Spirit, he knows my thoughts. There's no need to make a show of them."

"What about your brothers then? These animals can't hear your thoughts."

"You're right. But they can't hear me after they're dead, either. That's why I say it before I kill them," Chebona explained.

"What if you miss and do not make the kill?"

"I don't miss." He grinned.

I laughed and teased him, saying, "Is that why you were splashing around madly while trying to catch that crawfish the other day?"

"What?" Shiloh asked, clearly wanting to hear more.

Chebona laughed, saying, "Yes. I'd already committed him to the Great Spirit. There was no way I was letting him get away."

"Oh, tell me more," Shiloh said.

I touched Chebona's shoulder gently, letting him know my teasing was in good spirits. "It was the funniest thing I'd ever seen."

Shiloh laughed, saying, "I shall try it your way, brother, but not with crawfish." He stroked the rabbit's fur, asking Chebona, "You still offer in the fire, though?"

"Of course."

I'd wondered why Chebona threw perfectly good food in the fire from time to time. Now it was all starting to make sense. I skinned and gutted the animals while the brothers bathed in front of me.

"You boys can have the squirrels," I said as they splashed around in the water. "I'm having the rabbit."

"You should eat both," Shiloh said. "It is not good to eat rabbit on its own."

"Really?" I replied, surprised by his comment.

"It leads to sickness."

"I've eaten rabbit in England, and it's been fine."

"But you would have eaten other meats and vegetables with it," he replied.

Chebona said, "Rabbit is good, but have too much and the body rejects it."

I wonder what Rhett would make of this sight. It was he that taught me to skin rabbits. I doubt he thought I would be doing it in front of two naked men swimming in a river.

What would my friends in England think when I told them I planned to marry a native? Would they think I'd lost my mind? I should write to them and include some of my sketches. I must stay positive and believe that I'll still be able to have contact with people back in England. If my parents didn't agree to our union, it would make it difficult to come back to the fort again. That would break my heart.

Soon the smell of roast squirrel and sizzling rabbit filled the air, and it lured the boys out of the water. After supper, Chebona and I lay under the blanket while Shiloh sharpened arrows on the far side of the fire. Owls called to each other as night descended. The stars looked beautiful. I knew they'd always been there back in England, but I'd never appreciated them as much as I had here. Every night promised the heralding of a new day to come.

It was nice to cuddle with Chebona in the flickering light of the fire. His hand moved from my back to my breast, circling my nipple. His other hand lifted my dress. I stilled his fingers. I didn't feel comfortable doing this in front of Shiloh.

"What's the matter?" he whispered. "You don't want to?"

"It's not that," I replied under my breath. "I don't want your brother as our audience."

He laughed quietly.

"I can't count the number of times I've been his audience."

"Really?"

Frogs called to each other. Cicadas sang in the dark, masking our conversation.

"When he and Shako first got married, I came for the wedding and had to stay with them. I hardly got any sleep."

"Still, that's not something I'm prepared to do. I don't want to make your brother feel awkward."

"He wouldn't be uncomfortable."

"*I* would be uncomfortable, Chebona."

He pulled me in closer, resting his hands around my waist. I was glad he'd respected my feelings. It would have been a step too far for me. Maybe I wasn't as liberal as the native women, but I had to remind myself that these experiences were still new. Could I be blamed for wanting to keep our time together private?

The fire crackled. One of the logs fell sideways, sending sparks flying into the night like newly formed stars. A thought occurred to me that I should have addressed earlier.

"Will I be your only wife?"

"Do you want me to have another one so quickly? It will make your work easier around camp, for sure. As a first wife, you'll be able to delegate chores and say when you want me to come to your bed."

I was horrified. "No, I don't want you to have another one at all. Ever."

My voice got louder. Shiloh looked up from his work, surely catching some of our muffled words, but he soon returned to his arrows.

We hadn't talked of love, but I knew Chebona cared for me and I for him. Was there a single point in time when anyone really knew they loved someone else? Was it written anywhere that I should confess my love as soon as I realized? My feelings were continuing to grow. Love could grow. The fact that we were planning our future together with everything else at stake was enough for me. I didn't feel like I needed a declaration to be able to do that. But the idea of sharing my husband with another woman was abhorrent to me. How did the native wives do it, I wondered? I wanted him to love me and me alone.

He chuckled.

"You're all the woman I will ever need, Ally. I knew that when I first met you."

"You did?"

"You know it to be true."

"I knew early on that you liked me but not from the first time you saw me. How could you be so certain? You didn't even know me. I might have been a horrible person. You were going on how I looked alone?"

On one level, I was teasing him. On the other, I really wanted to know what he thought of me back then.

He said, "I saw how you acted toward your family and then toward me. I saw how you cared for Tommy, a man who had just lost his leg at sea. At Mrs. Tinsdale's, you could've fled with me to safety, but you wouldn't leave your mother. I could see you had a pure soul, and that drew me to you."

I hadn't realized Chebona had been paying attention to such moments. I should've, though. He was attentive in every regard. That was one of the things I loved about him.

"And I thought you were cute," he said. "But I never thought we'd end up together."

I rolled over and kissed him.

"We'll have plenty of time to be intimate later," I assured him.

The following day the water on the river was choppy. Dark clouds loomed overhead, threatening to break into a storm. The wind was worse than yesterday, which I didn't think was possible. It swirled around and flexed everything it breathed on, like a toddler having a tantrum. Leaves fell from the trees.

Chebona spoke with Shiloh.

"Ally and I have talked about this and agreed. We're going to be wed. By this time tomorrow, we'll know if her parents will support a match. If they accept us, we'll stay at the fort and get married. We can winter there and come to you in the spring. Wynono has told me where you'll be, so we'll find you."

"And if they don't agree?" Shiloh asked.

"Then we'll return here in seven days."

Shiloh replied, "Just in case, I'll come back with the horses then. There's good hunting here, so it'll not be a wasted trip. You can wait in this area for me if it's safe."

"We're hoping for a favorable outcome."

Shiloh addressed me, saying, "I can't wait to see my little brother married. I hope that your family will welcome him and you can enjoy the winter with them."

"Thank you, Shiloh. That means a lot."

I hugged him.

"Be careful," he said to his brother, speaking over my head. "You have a lot to protect now."

"Don't I know it," Chebona replied, putting his arm around my waist. "We best be off."

I wondered if Chebona was at all nervous about what my parents would say.

I helped pull the canoe down to the water's edge. Its bottom scraped on the smooth pebbles that lined the bank. Small waves lapped at our feet. I removed my moccasins, not wanting to get them wet. Once the canoe was steady, I clambered in. Then Chebona climbed in behind me.

Shiloh waved from the shore, waiting till we were out of sight.

Sitting at the prow of the canoe, I had a magnificent view of the river. Even though the weather was turbulent, there was a rugged beauty to the land. Only two weeks had passed since I arrived, but already the countryside was descending into winter. I, too, had changed as a new season began in my life.

Chebona said, "I'll paddle for a few hours now, and you can take over in the afternoon. It's straightforward going this time. We've no belongings to weigh us down, and this wind will practically drive us along on its own."

He looked at me as I gazed down the river.

"Ally, you're happy, right? You're not too worried about your parents? I don't want you to have any doubts."

"I don't," I said.

"If it doesn't go well with your folks, I..."

"What?" I asked.

"I don't want you to have regrets later on. If you did, I wouldn't be able to stand it. I need to know you'll be satisfied with me, no matter what happens."

I turned back to look at him. The muscles in his shoulders and arms tensed as he drove the paddle in the water. A trickle of sweat ran down the side of his face. With this man, I felt safe.

I said, "My decision is made, Chebona. You make me happy, and I'm sure you'll do everything to keep it that way. I'll do the same for you. I hope our loved ones will see our bond and realize that's what I want. My parents might've had other expectations for me, but ultimately, they want to see me content. I'm trusting that this will be the case. Don't worry. I'm very persuasive, and if not, I'm sure they'll come around in time. What parent wouldn't want to see their only child again, no matter the reason?"

Chebona seemed pleased with my response, but I knew I'd need all those persuasive powers and then some once we reached the fort. I crouched down low in the canoe, feeling more exposed to the blustery conditions on the water.

"Get the blanket if you're cold," he said. "Will you sing a song for me this time? To help me paddle."

I chose a hymn called *The Pilgrim* because I felt it captured the spirit of both our lives. It seemed fitting. After all, we were all strangers and pilgrims on Earth.

My voice rang out clear and true.

Who would true valor see,
Let him come hither,
One here will constant be,
Come wind, come weather
There's no discouragement

Shall make him once relent
His first avowed intent
To be a pilgrim.

Whoso beset him round
With dismal stories,
Do but themselves confound,
His strength the more is,
No lion can him fright,
He'll with a giant fight,
But he will have a right,
To be a pilgrim.

No hobgoblin, nor foul fiend,
Can daunt his spirit,
He knows he at the end
Shall life inherit.
Then fancies fly away,
He'll fear not what men say,
He'll labor night and day,
To be a pilgrim.

Act IV

Through the Fire

On the River

Our canoe glided effortlessly through the water. It was almost as if the river itself was guiding us toward civilization. I took over paddling duties in the afternoon, so Chebona could get some sleep. I knew he'd be paddling through the night and needed to rest while he could. The current carried us on, which made the journey enjoyable.

As my paddle dipped in the water, I had plenty of time to think. The river opened up wide. The long silence played against my reasonings. I tried not to dwell on what the response would be to our announcement. Papa wouldn't try and force us apart, would he? Would he offer something to Chebona to give me up? The more I thought about it and the closer we got, the higher my anxiety rose. Instead, I diverted my thoughts to our future. It was fruitless continuing to ponder so many outcomes. Determination had me set my sights on one goal. We made a good team, I thought. We were stronger together than on our own. We would bring up a family with Native American and English heritage in this new land. Well, new to me anyway. Our children would benefit from both cultures and find a niche here. Perhaps we could even visit England for a time. Chebona would love that. When I felt my arms grow weary, I roused him from his sleep and swapped places with him in the canoe. With his muscular frame, he made the paddling look easy.

The sun dipped low on the horizon. The wind had eased. Leaves blew gently, falling from the trees as they prepared for winter. My eyelids grew heavy with the last rays of the sun. I closed them for a moment, tucking the blanket up under my chin.

I woke to Chebona's smooth, singing voice in the cool of the night. Stretching my cramped limbs, I figured I'd slumbered longer than I thought. Even though it wasn't yet dawn, the sky had begun to lighten.

Chebona looked tired. He said, "We'll arrive in an hour."

"Let's eat," I suggested.

I knew I'd welcome a hearty meal when we got to the fort, even from the army cook, but I was hungry now. Our dwindling supply of rabbit and squirrel was almost gone.

As the river widened, I was surprised not to see any other boats this close to civilization. Slowly, dawn broke, but the birds were unusually quiet. The sky was overcast and dreary.

Familiar landmarks came into view, and I knew we were close to our destination. An unnatural orange haze filled the sky. Smoke wafted up over the treetops. This wasn't right. A sickening dread lay in the pit of my stomach.

"Something's wrong," Chebona said.

I knew it, too.

Unanswered questions swirled around us as he quickened his pace, making short work of the remaining distance. He inhaled great gulps of air, willing his tired body to put in the extra effort. I fought to calm my own breathing. My mind went to the most dreadful places. All I could think of were my parents.

"What do you think it could be?"

"It is fire, no doubt. But it's not out of control, and it's not large enough to be the fort itself."

The current carried us on down the river. We rounded the bend, and the wooden ramparts of the fort came into view.

A bonfire burned on the grassy plain outside the fort. A slit trench had been dug, extending almost fifty yards. As we got closer, it became apparent this was no ordinary fire. It lit up the dark sky like a torch.

As we watched, several soldiers with bandanas over their mouths swung a body between them, throwing it onto the burning pile. The clothing caught fire. Smoldering arms and legs dangled in twisted heaps. It was a sight that would forever be ingrained in my memory. The shape of dead bodies made a mockery of life, for here burned someone's father or son. I looked toward the fort's large double doors and could make out a black sheet hanging there. The meaning was clear: *Plague.*

The stench of burnt flesh made me want to gag. I buried my head into Chebona's chest. He tightened his grip around me as we floated past the gruesome sight.

Several soldiers spotted our canoe. They shouted to us from the parapet. Even though we couldn't hear their words, their actions were clear enough. They were waving us on. Notwithstanding, there was no way I was leaving without knowing the state of my parents.

"Mama. Papa."

"Ally, we'll find out what's happened to them, but we can't go inside."

I nodded in agreement, unable to speak.

"We need to get upwind," Chebona said, paddling beyond both the fort and the fire.

He pulled the canoe up onto the bank. We walked slowly up the grassy slope with the wind at our backs. A guard called for us to halt at a distance of twenty yards.

"We are under quarantine for the pox."

"I need to speak with my father," I shouted in reply, "Colonel Singleton."

"Wait there," he informed me.

"Tell him his daughter is outside. He'll come to the wall, or he'll give you a message for me. Make haste, please."

The soldiers talked among themselves, and finally, one disappeared, hopefully to do my bidding. I felt confident that my parents were all right. All three of us had been inoculated for smallpox before we left England, although there were never any guarantees when it came to disease. Chebona, like everyone born here, was very much at risk. If he got sick and took the pox back to his village, it would be a disaster.

Rhett told me that the death rate from smallpox in the American colonies was one in three, but it was far worse for the natives. They seemed to have little or no natural resistance and there were records of Europeans arriving in villages ravaged by the disease to find not a single soul left alive. On our voyage over here, Dr. Taylor said he'd heard that nine out of ten natives exposed to the pox would die.

There was no way we could stay at the fort. Had the town been affected too?

After what seemed like an eternity, I noticed my father's figure walking along the gantry behind the main wall.

The sun had risen over the mountains. I shielded my eyes as I looked up to see Papa. His face was gaunt. All I wanted to do was hug him.

"I'm so sorry, Ally. I wanted to warn you, but I couldn't. I had no way to get news to you without endangering the Powhatans."

I shouted back, "That's fine, Papa. All I want to know is that you and Mama are well."

"We're both healthy, which is more than I can say for many of my soldiers. They've suffered heavy losses, as you can see. The town has an outbreak as well. We think a trader from the French territories may have infected the town first, then the pox spread here."

He turned his attention to Chebona.

"Sunny, I am afraid there is no avoiding it. Can Ally winter with your family? This is not a place I'd like my daughter to stay. Every day we deal with sickness and death."

Papa looked defeated. He was facing a foe that gave no quarter, one that would not surrender until it had done its worst. Now was not the time to talk of marriage when death was so evident all around us. My father was under stress, and shouting about our intentions wasn't going to help.

As an afterthought, my father added, "As long as that is all right with you, my dear? You've enjoyed your time there, I take it?"

"Yes, Papa. It's been wonderful."

I looked at Chebona and smiled.

"But don't you need help yourselves?" I asked. "You're looking worn out."

I had to offer. I felt rather than saw Chebona's body stiffen beside me.

"I have your mother," my father said. "God knows, that is enough. Even though you're inoculated, you could still catch this hideous disease. It's not worth the risk. And I wouldn't want you to witness the horror we see on a daily basis. For the most part, people are confined to their quarters to stop the spread. So whatever help you could give would be minimal. I know being cooped up here would drive you mad. At least with Sunny, you won't be stuck inside, even if it is freezing out there."

That he could humor me at a time like this gave me comfort.

"Sunny, I know that another mouth to feed in winter can be tough. As soon as it is safe to do so, we'll compensate you for your trouble."

"There's no need for that, sir, and it's no trouble. We'll come back in the spring when the weather will allow."

"Thank you, my boy. It's a relief knowing Ally is safe and being cared for."

He looked back at me.

"You fit right in, Biscuit. I hardly recognized you in your native dress. You've grown lean, and your skin is brown from being outdoors. Only your hair hidden under your mother's hat gave you away. I wish I could give you food before you leave, but that wouldn't be wise. If you like, you can stay in the shed by the river tonight. No one has been there. At least you'll have some shelter, and there may be a few supplies you can use."

Chebona and I looked at each other and came to the same conclusion. We wanted to get as far away from this place as we could. I wouldn't spend one moment here longer than necessary. I desperately wanted to see my mother, but I didn't want to make any demands of Papa.

"I can't wait to hug you and Mama when we return. You will tell her, won't you?"

That seemed like a long time under the circumstances.

"She'll be sorry not to have seen you, but I'll tell her. Stay safe."

I blew him a kiss, and he caught it like old times, pretending to snatch it out of the air with his gloved hand. I wondered what would have happened if we'd all stayed in England? I remember my father talking with Mama before he left, wondering if he should take one more commission or retire. How different things would've been if he hadn't come here. That one decision changed the course of our lives.

One last thing weighed on my mind.

"Any news from the town and Tommy?" I asked.

My father replied, "Initial reports were of the blacksmith and storekeeper taking ill. Apparently, the trader got his horse re-shoed and then went and got supplies. They took him to the doc's surgery, but by then, it was too late. All this happened a few days after you left. Since then, we haven't allowed anyone to go into town. But a few of my men had already been to the store and brought the bloody pox back with them. I'm sorry Ally, I've no idea about your friend. They were going to send word after it was under control, but we haven't heard from them yet. The best thing you can do is go back to the Powhatan village."

He was right.

I thought about my friends in town and hoped they were still healthy. Spring was a long way off. Waiting until then to hear from them would be torture.

Chebona whispered in my ear, "We should leave. We don't need anything. I'd rather head straight back. I can catch food further down the river, away from all this."

"Of course," I whispered in reply.

The chance that someone could've been in that shed without my father's knowledge was too great a threat. It wasn't worth considering staying anywhere near the fort.

I thought about my sketchbook in my satchel and the letters that I'd wanted to send back to England. For now, they would have to wait. Anyway, the ships wouldn't be taking anything back from here for a while.

My father watched as we paddled away. He walked to the end of the parapet and waved. I glanced at him one last time. In all my fretting over the past few days, I never considered this would be the outcome of our return to the fort. We were not able to find any of the answers we sought.

After the stormy weather yesterday, today was muted and sad. It was as if the dark clouds overhead were a reflection of our own somber mood. We continued for an hour or so upriver, each lost in our own thoughts. Although we were only a day or so away from the rendezvous on the tributary, it would be another six days before we were due to meet up with Shiloh. With the weather closing in, walking back to the village from there was not wise. The nights were starting to get a lot colder. We'd be forced to live off the land. That was an exciting adventure when we were documenting my journal, but now it was a case of survival. Was it the scene we had just witnessed that dampened my enthusiasm? Or was it that I didn't have an answer from my parents about Chebona?

However, more pressing matters required our immediate attention. We needed to find a suitable place to camp and hunt.

Our progress against the current was much slower than our approach to the fort. The sun was high in the sky and breaking through the clouds before Chebona slackened his pace. He seemed hesitant to pick a spot to stop, but he was clearly tired.

"What are you thinking?" I asked.

"I'm wondering, do we camp in the same spot we did when I first brought you to the village or choose somewhere else? I'm familiar with that territory, although I'm wary. It doesn't pay to camp in the same place too often."

I could see his point. "We've plenty of time before dark. Why don't we look for somewhere new, and if that doesn't work, we could go on to our original campsite."

"Yes, that will work."

Chebona steered us toward the river bank. The thick reeds slowed our approach.

"Up ahead is a clearing. We can put the canoe to shore there. How do you feel about trying to catch some fish while I scout the area?"

Being useful rather than sitting around waiting for Chebona to return appealed to me.

"I'll give it a go. I've fished before."

"I'll tie up the canoe and leave you some slack so you can drift out into the river. Then you can throw your net out from there."

"It'll be fun."

He said, "Fresh fish would be nice. Make sure you clean your catch in the current so the innards float down the river. We wouldn't want a bear stumbling across you while you're on your own."

Or anytime, I thought. The prospect of seeing a bear in the wild was the stuff of nightmares.

Chebona said, "Normally, I'd provide food, but it might be sometime before I get back. If you can catch some fish, at least we can eat something tonight. Wait till I come back before cooking it, though. Should something happen, you can always cut the rope and paddle into the middle of the river. You'll be safer there. If I don't come back before dark, you'll need to decide where you go. The fort or the village."

"Why do you say such things, Chebona? Now you're scaring me."

It was true. If something happened to him, how could I possibly leave him here? If I went back to the fort, I wouldn't know what happened to him until after winter. If I went to the village, Shiloh wouldn't be waiting for us at the tributary, so there'd be no horses. It was a long journey on foot to get help and, without Chebona, I'd probably get lost. I didn't want to think about either possibility.

"What about a third option? I come looking for you."

He sighed.

"That isn't the safest way. How would you cope if I wasn't able to? For that would be the only reason I wouldn't come back."

I stared at him.

"I'm being honest. Don't worry, Ally. In all probability, we'll be fine, but we need to talk about these things, just in case."

"Fine," I said, rather abruptly. I didn't provide him with an answer about what I might do. Was this our first argument as a couple? I knew I was being unreasonable, but it was only because I cared about him.

Chebona jumped across to the bank in one fluid movement. The canoe wobbled in the water beneath me. He secured the canoe to a large tree with a length of rope. Then he helped me cast the net into the water. Our hands brushed against each other as he showed me how to haul it back in again. I couldn't be mad at him. God forbid, what if something happened to him out there? I would never forgive myself if this was our last interaction. I took his hand and pulled him to me, kissing him passionately. I lost myself in the moment. We finally broke apart.

"Come back soon."

"I will," he smiled, joking with me as he said, "Make sure you catch a couple of fish. I'll be hungry for something other than you when I get back."

He took his bow and arrows, along with our empty waterskins and disappeared into the forest. Each minute he was gone seemed to drag on forever. My eyes scanned the woods, but all I saw were trees.

Every so often, I'd haul in the net to review my catch or lack of it. I knew I should try to cast it further out toward the channel. I left it sitting in the water longer a little while longer and practiced some deep breathing. Anything to calm me. When I was on my own, every sound seem magnified, every movement exaggerated. The wind in the trees, the splash of a fish jumping in the water and even the harsh call of a bird overhead set my nerves on edge. The net tugged and pulled a little. As I brought it to the surface, I grinned. I saw the telltale sign of several fish struggling to be free.

"Thank you for your sacrifice," I whispered to them.

Four beautiful silver-striped bass bounced against each other. I dragged the net in carefully and hauled it over into the bottom of the canoe. Then I looked away, not content to watch the life drain from them.

Taking my book out, I sketched my catch. Then I took my knife and filleted the fish just as Rhett had shown me.

Soon after, I heard footsteps approaching. My knife still in hand, I made ready to cut the rope should I need to.

A familiar voice called out from the long grass. "I hope you caught something?"

Hearing Chebona approach calmed my nerves, and relief washed over me as he came into view. He was a wonderful sight marching down the hill. My heart raced faster, just knowing he was near.

"So," I said, "are we eating here tonight?"

I held up the glistening white flesh of the fish.

"Yes, my lady. The forest is clear of any bear or human tracks. How about I cook since you've done all the hard work?"

"Sounds good to me."

He tugged on the rope, drawing the canoe closer to shore. Once he'd helped me out, he drew me to him. I relished being in the warmth of his embrace and lay my head on his shoulder. We stayed like that for a while, neither of us willing to part.

"We should get a fire started," he eventually said. "Before it gets cold."

I sighed. It was hard work living in the wilderness. There was always something to be done.

We collected the sticks we needed and started a fire. A rocky overhang sheltered us from behind, while an elevated position gave us a clear view of the water from both sides.

On his walk, Chebona had managed to find a freshwater spring. I gulped down the cool water. It soothed my parched throat. Who knew you could be so thankful for such simple pleasures? True to his word,

Chebona skewered the fish on sticks and hung them over the fire till they were done. Then he took a piece and threw it into the flames.

I said, "I thanked the gods when I cut off their heads and tails before I discarded them in the river."

He chuckled, "It doesn't work like that, Ally. For *Ahone* to receive it, it must go up with the smoke into heaven."

I didn't want to be cynical, but I thought that was a waste of perfectly good food. Still, there was plenty. The moist, tender flesh flaked off the bones as we picked at it.

I mumbled, "Mmmm, it's so good."

"Maybe I should get you to fish more often."

"You know I shot a deer in England."

"You didn't!"

"I really did, although I didn't like doing it."

I licked the fish juice from my fingers.

"You killed a deer on your own? I know you, Ally. You don't even like gutting rabbits. How did you manage to kill and dress a deer?"

"I had help."

I picked up a second skewer.

"Male help? I can't imagine a couple of English ladies doing a hunt before afternoon tea."

Even though he joked, I knew he was interested in who had taught me these things.

"Yes, a good friend of mine. Our neighbor, actually. We grew up together. His sister is my best friend back home."

"Huh, what else did he teach you?"

I looked at him. Was Chebona jealous? I decided to have some fun.

"He taught me how to fish, make traps, and other survival tricks. His family owns the shipping line we came to America on."

His face fell. "He's rich then?"

"Yes, and good-looking." I wiggled my stick in his direction, being

365

playful with him.

"He must care for you a lot to show you all these things."

"Probably. Do you want the last of the fish?"

He waved his hand dismissively.

"Do you know what else?" I asked with a sneaky little smile. I leaned into his chest.

"What?"

He sounded pitiful, but I loved him for it.

"He never kissed me."

"Oh." The sudden realization hit him. He smiled at me. "You mean like this?"

Chebona wrapped his arms around me and brought his mouth hard against mine. As if to prove a point, he ravished my mouth with his lips and tongue, leaving me breathless.

"I love you, Ally. I love everything about you."

I replied, "And one of the reasons I love you is that I know that. You leave me with no doubt about it."

For me, this was the key difference between the two men in my life. Rhett only ever left me with doubts. With Chebona, I had none. What I needed, what I longed for most, was commitment.

"Well, that was unexpected," he said. "I didn't think I could be jealous and excited at the same time."

We laughed then and there. Right in the middle of nowhere. We laughed so hard our sides hurt. When one of us would finish laughing, the other would snicker, and we'd start all over again. We lay on the ground, holding our stomachs.

After a while, Chebona said, "We didn't get to accomplish what we wanted at the fort."

I knew what he meant. Not being able to talk with my parents gave us no closure and didn't change our situation.

"I can't ask your father until spring. That's far too long to wait for you to be my wife."

I didn't want to wait that long either.

I said, "In both our cultures, it's expected you will ask for my hand, but circumstances have made that impossible. I'm of age and can take a husband of my own choosing. Even though it's not ideal, I choose you to be my husband. We'll talk to my family after we are married. It'll be a bit unconventional, but what other choice do we have."

I smiled at his handsome face in the firelight.

Chebona said, "This is one of many trials we may face in our lives. I'm glad that you chose me. I mean to be the best husband you could ask for. Now come here, and let us keep each other warm."

I snuggled under the blanket, cuddling him.

Trials

With morning came new hope. Although it was informal, I felt the commitment we had to each other was real. Outwardly, nothing had changed, but we had a definite direction in which we were heading. Returning to the village would allow us to move on with our relationship.

The riverbank where we camped opened out into a shallow, sheltered beach, which allowed the sun to warm the water. Bathing removed the smoke and grime that had invaded our pores while our clothes lay out in the sunshine to dry. We lounged on a large rock like lizards drawing in the radiant warmth. Sunrise cast a romantic glow on our lovemaking the last time we were together. Now we were in the stark light of day.

I traced my fingers over the thick lines of Chebona's tattoo. Beads of water were still drying on his skin.

"Did this hurt?"

"Yes," he said.

My fingers continue their exploration. His chest was smooth and hairless. I ran my fingernails over his taut muscles, hesitating near his nipples.

"Mmmm," he mumbled. "Don't stop."

With his eyes closed, I felt a little less self-conscious.

My hand moved lower to the ridges on his stomach. His muscles were like undulating hills and valleys.

I was feeling cheeky and said, "I feel like a pioneer exploring new territory. I like the scenery around here."

Looking up, I checked to see if his eyes were still closed.

Feeling bolder, my fingers splayed to the sparse hair on his groin and the base of his shaft. It moved and grew harder. Running down the length of him, I marveled at its design. Easing the fold of the skin back, the tip became clear. Shiny and delicate, I circled the rim, touching it gently with the tip of my fingernail.

He moaned. "Are we considered married now, do you think?"

"In our eyes, I suppose we are," I whispered.

"Good, because I want you so badly, I can't stand it. Once you're mine, there's no going back."

Truth be told, I wanted him, too. Since we'd first discovered each other, a hunger had grown inside me to have him completely, and now the thought was consuming me.

I looked up at his face. His gaze took my breath away.

"Sit on me."

I straddled him as he brought his knees up behind me.

"Lean back. It's my turn to do some exploring of my own."

His hands traced slow circles on the insides of my legs. His thumbs lightly touched between my thighs, folding back my lips to caress me more intimately. Desire rose and overtook me. I felt his hardness under my buttocks, and I strained against his fingers. He took his time with a slow rhythm building the sensations within me, making me wet and ready for him.

When I thought I could stand it no more, he lifted my hips and slowly brought me onto his hardened rod. He held me still until I was used to him.

"Ride me, Koda. You take the lead for our first time."

Bringing myself forward on my hands, I shifted my weight so our joined bodies rose and fell together. From my viewpoint, I could see him entering my warmth. He continued to rub my nub in tantalizing circles. His other hand was under my bottom, feeling where we joined. At first, I moved slowly, but I was intent on eagerly racing toward a destination. I hadn't thought it possible, but he glided effortlessly in and out of me. I enjoyed the control of lifting myself to his end and then returning again. Chebona groaned. Whether it was in frustration or pleasure, I didn't care. I focused on my own pleasure. He could come with me for the ride. Soon I heard myself crying out as I clenched around him, keeping him within me.

While I bounced along the last waves of pleasure, this undid him, and soon he was bucking his hips to meet mine. With his hands on my breasts, his thrusts took him to his limit and beyond.

I looked him in the eyes. My heart overflowed with emotion. I'd never felt more connected to another human being than at that moment.

"I'll enjoy doing that for a very long time," he said, echoing my sentiments exactly.

"Should we bathe again?" I asked.

"It may lessen the chance of my seed taking root," he answered.

"How do you know so much about this?" I teased.

The thought of carrying his child thrilled me, but was I ready for such a responsibility when we had to face so many other challenges? I wanted to be his and his alone for a while. I felt we had much exploring left to do, and children could be so demanding.

He said, "Living in a camp of women, you hear many things."

"What sort of things?" I asked.

"Timing is important. After you bleed, your body makes itself ready to receive a man's seed. Half a moon's cycle and you have a son. If we do it before then, you're likely to have a daughter, but only if we abstain until after the half-moon has come and gone. Eventually, my seed will pass from you if it hasn't taken hold, and you'll bleed again, ready for the next cycle."

"You make it all sound so unromantic."

"It's how life works," he responded.

To me, that sounded too prescriptive. If a child was born out of a union, I'd rather it was done with passion than forethought. I suppose it could be helpful if you had many daughters and wanted a son or vice versa.

We lay there until our stomachs started to grumble. Life among the Native Americans was a forever cycle of providing for our sustenance. I found myself daydreaming of an inn where we could choose between several meals and order what we desired without having to kill, gut and skin it. I was hungry. It would be at least an hour before we had anything ready to eat. Thinking about all the foods I'd missed lately didn't help either. Pies and custards. Even simple things like salt, sugar and spices. I hadn't realized how dependent I'd been on them.

"You have this faraway look in your eyes," he said, propping himself up on his elbow. "Are you thinking about how good I felt inside you?"

What a proud man he was. I didn't have the heart to disappoint him.

"As good as that was, I was thinking of how back in England, you can go to an eating establishment—a place where they will prepare your meal for you."

"What would you like, m'lady? I'm here to serve."

He was sweet.

"Anything quick and tasty will suffice," I replied.

"You rest and relax on the rock, and I will get you your heart's desire."

Who could pass up an opportunity like that?

I rolled over and enjoyed the sun's rays soaking into my skin. With my arms folded up under my head, I felt at peace.

I'd been with a man—properly been with a man—and I liked it. I knew some women who didn't. My Aunt Mary complained to my mother about her husband coming to her bed, insisting that she wanted to be left alone. Did people change over time? Surely, she didn't think like that when they were first married. I found it hard to imagine not wanting to be touched by someone who loved me.

I heard Chebona wading through the water but kept my eyes shut, refusing to be tempted to peek. I'd be surprised if we were eating anytime soon. About ten minutes later, I heard him shuffling the coals to rejuvenate our fire, which had already died down.

"We're ready," he announced soon after.

My nose twitched at a savory scent floating on the breeze. Lying there, I could smell rosemary and garlic, which surprised me as we hadn't traveled with any herbs. My mouth watered.

I sat up astonished. Chebona had managed to collect an abundance of freshwater shellfish from the river's muddy banks, and here they sat in the coals with their shells opened, glistening, ready to eat. A sprinkling of herbs had been scattered on the sizzling flesh.

He handed me my knife, and we both sat there naked, savoring the tender flesh.

This man had skills.

"Are you impressed?"

He grinned at me as though this was the most natural thing in the world.

"In many ways," I replied.

"What is in this?" I pointed to the green topping on the mussels.

"Wild garlic, sage and rosemary."

"Where did you find them?"

Chebona pointed to the grassy meadow behind us. All I saw was weeds, but he saw food and herbs. There was a lot I could learn from him.

Even though it was only an overnight trip to the tributary where we would meet Shiloh, he wouldn't be back in that area for at least another four or five days. I continued filling out my journal (when Chebona wasn't distracting me in other exciting ways, of course.)

We ventured a little further upriver and made a temporary hut out of branches. Our first home was crude, but I couldn't have been happier. We sought out experiences that reminded us that life was beautiful. Whether it was a morning stroll through the woods or tender words by the campfire, these simple pleasures made me glad for this life and my decision to be with Chebona. My husband—I could call him that now— had gone off to hunt early this morning, as I had mentioned that our seafood diet did not keep me full for long.

I sat in the grass by the river, enjoying the sun radiating through my doeskin dress. I was so engrossed in capturing the image of a beautiful black and white striped swallowtail butterfly in my notebook that I didn't notice the subtle footfall of another behind me.

When at last I glanced up, the first thing I saw was a pair of thighs in colorful fringed leggings. Not Chebona then, was my immediate thought. I was almost afraid to look higher. A red-painted face with a top knot of long bound hair stared back at me. As startling as this strange man's appearance was, it wasn't the most concerning thing about him. The knife he had tucked away, facing backward in his hand, commanded my immediate attention.

What should I do? Should I try to run or negotiate my way out of this situation? Either way, I was at a disadvantage. I was certain Chebona wouldn't be back in time to be of any assistance as he'd only been gone for an hour.

What did this man want from me? Was I to be a captive or a scalp? I had to believe that if he wanted me dead, I would have been so already. All these thoughts whirled around in my head. I made to get up, but before I could decide on any course of action, he had me in a vice-like grip with the knife at my throat. Struggling was futile, so I went limp in his arms, letting him bear my weight.

I recalled Rhett's advice about being captured. For all the bravado I'd shown back then in England about breaking his grip or kicking him in the groin, I felt completely out of my depth. I wasn't going to provoke this man. He dragged me toward the river where he had his canoe hidden in the reeds. I dug my heels into the soft earth, knowing Chebona would be able to see where my feet had been pulled through the undergrowth. I was making this difficult for this vicious native. Now that I knew he meant to take me away and not kill me, I needed to act fast. I had to leave some sort of clue.

As the man dragged me down the bank and into the water, I wrestled with him tearing some of the fringes off his leggings. They drifted like leaves onto the shoreline, their colors standing out against the mud. When we got to the canoe, he let go of me and took the paddle. He ordered me in, pointing with his finger. I looked at him and shook my head. The next thing I knew, the reeds beside me seemed to spin around. I'd been hit across the side of my head with the wooden handle.

A searing pain stabbed at my head, followed by a loud ringing in my ears. I was dazed. I lay there draped over the side of his canoe with my legs in the water as he took his knife to our canoe, rendering it useless. With each slash of his blade, I felt my heart sink a little further. If Chebona was going to find me, it would have to be on foot. My vision grew blurry, and then I knew nothing at all.

A throbbing ache and the midday sun stirred me back into reality. We were moving fast. I could tell by the rate at which he was paddling that we were heading upstream away from the fort. I lay on my stomach, head down and eyes lowered, not ready for him to realize that I'd woken. How would Chebona find me? Tears escaped my eyes and ran over the tip of my nose. Why? Why had this happened to me? When everything had been going so well, why had I been dealt this cruel blow? Chebona and I had become lax, surrounded by the euphoria of each other's company.

I should've gone with Chebona on his hunt. Why did we allow ourselves to get lulled into a false sense of confidence as if nothing could touch us? It was no good dwelling on the past. Where was this man taking me? Likely back to his camp. What would he do with me there? I didn't want to think about that.

Should I sit up and look at my surroundings? I might be able to recognize some landmarks in case I was able to escape. At the very least, I could try to reason with him. I knew a little of the Powhatan language. He knew I was not a native, so I probably was a bit of a novelty to him dressed in their clothing. My aching head made me aware of how he'd treated me on the riverbank when I refused to do what he said and I was afraid.

I had no idea how long I'd been unconscious. We could be miles away from Chebona by now. We were heading west toward the Powhatan village, but many tributaries branched off this river, and our village lay many miles from the first major one. I'm sure we would have passed that by now. Had we already taken another fork in the stream?

I sat up. My head complained. Blood dribbled down from a cut behind my ear and stained my doeskin dress. Back at the village, Wynono had given me a knife in a pouch. I'd taken to wearing it tucked under my arm, against my side. The strap was more comfortable to wear that way. It had gone unnoticed by my captor. What were my chances of pulling out the knife, stabbing him and jumping overboard? So far, my hands were not bound. I might not have an opportunity such as this again.

I peeked over the edge of the canoe. From the river's width, I could tell we had not turned off. That was good in one regard. If I could manage to get away, I'd follow the river back, but it might make it hard for any rescue if Chebona had searched along the tributaries. Did I expect him to rescue me? I had no doubt he would try. Yet, that would put him in danger. Would he enlist the help of Shiloh or others? There could be a great deal of loss if I were taken to another village and war erupted between the tribes.

I was at the front of the canoe. I swiveled, facing my captor at the rear. He raised the paddle once again as a warning. He resumed his hard strokes when he saw I didn't mean to escape.

I looked at him carefully, wanting to understand who he was and what motivated him. He was a warrior, for sure, or more accurately, a former warrior. He was much older than Wynono. Wrinkles had formed around his eyes and mouth. In certain areas, he still had an impressive physique, although muscle was hidden under fat like he'd been well-fed. Scars dominated his body, providing evidence of a battle-hardened veteran.

In my current state, I wouldn't be able to overwhelm him enough to inflict an incapacitating blow. The penalty for such a course of action didn't bear thinking about. Better to attack him when he was distracted or asleep. I hoped I would get my chance. The further we traveled, the longer and more dangerous it would be for me to return. I could try and steal the canoe. That would be my best option. Otherwise, he might track and catch up to me. Either that or I would have to kill him. Would I even be able to overpower this aged warrior? The thought of fighting him held no appeal for me, but there weren't any other options if it was to be him or me. If I escaped, I couldn't afford to have him find me again. These were all valid possibilities but was it safer just to tolerate whatever he had in mind?

At the bottom of the canoe, I noticed that there were two blankets and two saddle bags. Where was his companion? During the course of the afternoon, his strokes slowed. He was tiring. He pulled into the side of the river and kicked me, indicating I should get out. Thick grass lined the bank. My moccasins sank into the mud. He took a rope and tied my hands together in front of me, leaving a generous amount for a leash. The course material bit into the skin on my wrists. Even the slightest turn of my hands chaffed my flesh. I moaned. Perhaps my only chance of escape had gone, and I'd been a coward not to take it.

He secured the canoe to higher ground and relieved himself right in front of me. I turned away, disgusted. Once he finished, he pushed me toward a thick tree and tied the rope around it, affording me some access to move. My captor started a fire and left me alone, disappearing into the trees, presumably to find food.

I had a terrible thirst. Lying in the sun for most of the day with no liquid and a head wound made me dizzy. I used his time away to relieve myself. I was vulnerable here and weak. Hopefully, I wouldn't become dinner for some hungry animal before he returned.

Try as I might, I couldn't dislodge my knife with my hands bound.

I looked around the base of the tree for anything that could help me. There were some small rocks. I picked up one with a sharp edge and hid it in the grass beside me.

He returned with a headless, gutted turkey and threw it at my feet as if expecting me to start plucking.

"*Suckahanna.* Water," I stammered.

"*Powhatan?*" he bit back.

I nodded.

"*Non,*" he said, fingering my blond hair.

He spoke French.

"*L'eau,*" I said, repeating the need for water.

Thank heavens for Madame DuPont and her insistence on speaking French. Without that, right now, I'd be lost.

"*Tu es Francais?*"

He looked astonished that I could speak his language. If he thought I was French, he might rethink how he treated me.

"*L'eau,*" I said again, being stubborn and refusing to answer his question.

He handed me a buffalo skin that held a generous amount of water.

I drank greedily.

"*Assez,*" he said, insisting I had drunk enough and wrenching the pouch from me.

To my surprise, he had a tattoo of the French word *Liberté* on his forearm, meaning freedom. It wasn't large, but the letters were distinct. This Native American must have sided with the French during the Seven Year War, which had long since ended. From his dialect, it seemed he preferred French to English when dealing with Europeans. The French language must have immersed its way into his native culture as his tribe traded with the French interior. I was learning more and more about him as time went on.

"*Où m'emmenez-vous?*" I demanded, wanting to know where I was going to be taken.

Seeing that I had surprised him, I felt I could be bold.

He said, "*Maintenant, je vais vous emmener chez mon ami français. Il décidera quoi faire de toi.*"

To my relief, it seemed he was planning to take me to a French settlement rather than to his village.

"*Est-ce qu'on part demain?*" I asked, wanting to know how long we would be here. I had a feeling he wanted to wait for his partner.

"*Nous attendons que mon fils nous rejoigne.*"

I was right. We'd not be leaving without his son. I wondered if these were the two men who had left their tracks by the river.

I held my hands in front of me, and he undid my bonds. He didn't trust me completely, tying my feet together instead as I started preparing the bird for our meal.

As I pulled the feathers off the turkey, I imagined pulling the hairs out of his top knot. How dare he think he could take me wherever he liked just because he was stronger than me? What did the French want with an English lady? Did he mean to ransom me? Was I to become a slave? Or worse, a mistress? Was he intending to sell me to the highest bidder among the French traders? I shuddered at these thoughts.

By now, Chebona would be frantic with worry. He was probably blaming himself for leaving me alone. I hated to think about what he was going through. Not knowing what had happened to me would be the hardest pain to endure. I knew he would search for me.

I threw the plucked turkey in the direction of my captor, not caring how dirty it got as it rolled toward him on the ground. He eyed me and shook his head, taking it down to the river to clean it. I didn't want to look at him. I shuffled around to the far side of the tree, putting as much distance between us as I could.

Sitting there, I closed my eyes and took a few deep breaths. Even that could not calm my nerves. I knew he'd have to sleep at some point tonight. I'd have to outlast him or pretend to be asleep first. Then I would make my move. The thought of being caught while escaping made me nauseous. I held my hand on my stomach and willed my body to relax. I decided to get my knife out while I could before he tied my hands again. Smoke drifted from the fire, but I noticed it was quite light. He'd avoided using any damp wood to keep the smoke to a minimum. He must have known I wasn't alone and that there would be someone out looking for me. I peered around the tree trunk. He was tending the fowl over the fire, and his back was to me. I took the opportunity and hid my knife under a pile of leaves near the base of the tree.

Soon the smell of roasted meat began to permeate the air, making my mouth water. Footsteps heading in my direction had me open my eyes. The man tossed a turkey leg in front of me, sneering as it landed in the dirt. He was returning my favor from earlier. I refused to pick it up until he'd left. The one thing we had in common was our stubborn pride. The drumstick sat there on the ground staring at me. Already small black ants had started to devour it.

My captor settled back down by the fire and proceeded to eat the rest of the turkey. Taking large mouthfuls, he barely chewed before swallowing. I noticed he didn't offer any to the fire or to his gods. He was a brute. I wondered how people from the same culture could be so different. Then I remembered Montgomery. It wasn't a man's culture that made him brutish but the choices he made. Like Montgomery, this native had probably never stopped to consider that he could be in the wrong. Somehow, he justified his actions to himself, but how could this be anything other than greed and cruelty?

I snatched the leg from the ground, picked the ants off and dusted the dirt from the skin. I bit into the warm flesh. It was good. I sucked at the tender meat, depriving it of all its juices. Then when I could stand it no longer, I chewed it slowly, making it last. My stomach thanked me. I wouldn't say I was full, but at least now I was satisfied. I'd need my strength for what lay ahead, and who knew when my next meal would be?

Leaves rustled with the wind. Insects crawled over sticks on the ground around me. Birds landed on the river without a care. But me, I feared for my life.

My foe came over and kicked my legs to one side, wanting to see if anything lay hidden beneath them, but I'd kept the knife close to the tree.

He squatted down and tied my hands in front of me again. His breath stunk. He'd lost most of his teeth. I flinched as he pinched my cheeks. To him, it might have been playful. To me, it was repulsive. Then he returned to his fire and went to sleep shortly after the sun had set.

Soon, loud snores filled the night air. I reviewed my options again. Even though he said he planned to take me to the French, I couldn't be sure of the reception that might await me. There were too many unknowns for me to feel secure about anything. My best chance was to escape and return to our village. Back there, I would be protected. I felt certain Chebona wouldn't be where I was abducted from anyway. If I was lucky, I'd come across him on my way. I wanted to prevent the two men from meeting, for I was sure it would end in bloodshed. Even though Chebona had youth and speed on his side, I gathered my captor had plenty of tricks up his sleeve for winning in battle. I wasn't prepared for Chebona to take that risk.

A half-moon peeked out from behind the clouds, bright enough to light my way. The canoe was only a little out of the water. I decided to make my escape while it was easy to steal the canoe. Looking around the camp, I'd take his water pouch and the rope that had bound me. God, I hoped he was a heavy sleeper. He'd knocked back several large swigs from a metal container before he went to bed, which was a good sign. Earlier, he'd given me a drink of water from a skin pouch, so that flask probably contained some kind of liquor. Retrieving my knife from its resting place, I made quick work of the rope by pinning my knife between my knees and sawing back and forth with my arms.

Just as I was starting to loosen the ties from around my feet, I saw him roll over. I hid my knife under my thigh and held my breath. I sat there waiting until he lapsed back into a deep sleep.

Time seemed to pass incredibly slowly. I looked toward the heavens at the multitude of stars and wondered if Chebona was looking at the same sight. Perhaps he was trying to get to sleep, wanting to save his strength for another day of searching. If I was in his position, I'm pretty sure I wouldn't be able to sleep with so many tortured thoughts bouncing around in my head.

My kidnapper rolled over again, only this time it sounded as though he was getting to his feet rather than shifting his weight while he slept. I gathered up the loose strands of rope and curled them over my hands, hoping that if he approached me, he wouldn't see they were cut. Then I lay my head back on the tree trunk and closed my eyes. A shuffling sound alerted me to him walking around the camp. What was he doing? His footsteps came over toward me and halted inches away from my legs. I tried my best to slow my breathing, but being in such a vulnerable state, it was difficult to appear relaxed. My fervent hope was that in the darkness, he wouldn't be able to discern that the rope had been cut. I prayed I'd done a good enough job of making it look secure. Keeping my eyes closed was agony. I desperately wanted to open them and find out what he was up to. Eventually, he wandered off.

A steady stream of piss disturbed the leaves under a nearby tree. Maybe that's why he hadn't been able to get to sleep—his full bladder had prevented him from slipping back into slumber. I turned slightly and put my knees over the rope, showing him that I had registered his nearness. I knew that if I pretended to be asleep, he'd know I was faking it, so by rolling over, I was subtly showing my disdain. Would he check my bonds? I hoped not.

Sparks leaped into the sky as he threw another log into the burning embers. He settled back down with a sigh. I watched him with one eye barely open. Having tilted my head on my shoulder, I could still appear to be asleep. He rolled over, facing away from the fire. Still, I waited. This must be what a predator feels like before it attacks. It is patient, waiting for the opportunity to pounce. Except in my case, it was to flee.

I willed the forest into silence, afraid that the slightest noise would disturb him. I'd never paid particular attention to the night sounds before. Yes, they'd been mildly annoying, but tonight every rustle, splash and call of night creatures had me on edge. Was it my imagination, or was tonight particularly noisy?

After a while, his breathing became heavier, and a snorting sound escaped from his sleeping form. Have courage, I told myself. I took a long deep breath and stretched my legs out. I rolled up the rope and tied it over my shoulder. Picking up my knife, I got to my feet. At that exact moment, an owl decided to break the silence. A soft hoot carried on the wind. I was prepared to drop to the ground should he roll over but thankfully, he stayed still.

I tiptoed over to the fire and took his bag and waterskin. My eyes never left his body. As long as I could hear him breathing deeply, I reckoned I was safe.

My fingers tightened around the bone handle of my knife. For a moment, I considered plunging the blade deep into the side of his neck, but I doubted myself. Would I be able to strike a fatal blow? Could I? Uncertainty weighed on my mind. Fleeing seemed the best option.

I crept over to the canoe and placed his belongings inside. A fish jumped in the water ahead of me, and I froze. My knife was my security, and I was loathe to put it down. Instead, I bit onto the handle as I dragged the canoe into the water. The hide scraped softly on the loose stones. Surely he would hear that. I panicked. I had a sudden urge to jerk the canoe into the water and make a break for it, but I was too terrified.

Cool water swirled around my waist. My moccasins slipped on the rocks as I felt my way into the dark. Something brushed against the side of my leg. I forced myself not to cry out. A lump of dark fur moved through the water. What vile creature was that? It could have been a beaver or a water rat. I took one long last look at the otherwise quiet camp and hoped that I didn't come to regret leaving him there alive. The water was still. Until I was sure I was out of earshot, I willed the canoe on silently down the river. My feet pushed off the pebbles and rocks on the riverbed. Water lapped against my neck.

I dared not climb into the canoe for fear of any splashes waking my kidnapper. Instead, I allowed the current to carry me down the river, regardless of what nasty creatures swam around me. Once I reached the bend, I pulled the canoe in to the bank and climbed in.

All through the night, I paddled, imagining my adversary right behind me, running alongside the banks with his eyes searching for me. Watching and waiting. He would be mad as hell when he discovered I'd gone and taken his transport. I was taking no chances.

Alone

The dawn had broken on a new day and tinged the sky with brilliant orange. The sun's rays stretched out across the sky like fingers. My arms felt heavy, but I'd keep going and rest tonight. I was slower than that French-speaking bastard, so I guessed I still had plenty of paddling to do before I reached the turn-off for our village. I afforded myself the luxury of drinking a quarter of the water I'd stolen from him.

By this time, I was starving and feeling faint. Dried blood clung to my head. As if in answer to my prayers, I noticed a small fishing net lying at the far end of the canoe. If I put that behind the boat, I might catch some fish on my way, but I couldn't afford to stop. By mid-morning, I'd come to the tributary. The rest of the journey would need to be made on foot. I hauled in the rope and net, which had snared three decent-sized fish.

With no further use for the canoe, I thought about sinking it, to avoid revealing where I'd gone to shore. However, there was a better way. Chebona would be searching for me along the river. If I'd already passed him, we would have seen each other. If he hadn't reached this point yet, he would still be downriver. If I let the canoe drift downstream, it would tell Chebona I had escaped. He'd instinctively know the hostile native would never willingly abandon his canoe, so its presence could only mean I'd been able to evade my kidnapper. I was sure he'd understand I'd be heading for the tributary and then the village. Having made up my mind, I pushed the canoe back into the river and watched as it bobbed along with the current.

I made my way along the water's edge, following the tributary, not wanting to leave any signs my kidnapper might recognize. Chebona would know where I was going. My moccasins would be ruined, but at least they still provided protection. The water was cold. After a while, I couldn't feel my feet anymore. My toe caught on a submerged root and I tripped and fell, hitting my knee on a rock. The sharp, stabbing pain jolted me back to my state of peril. Deciding it was useless to carry around the fish, I gutted and skinned them in the water and chewed on the soft flesh. The net and rope jangled against my thigh as I walked. I didn't enjoy the taste of raw fish, but it would still provide energy. Even though a fire would be welcome, it wasn't a luxury I could afford. Who was I kidding? I didn't even have a flint to start one. I wasn't going to rub sticks together for hours.

Some rocks on the bank led back toward the path, and I used these to gain access to the main track. I hoped that the sun would dry my wet footprints long before anyone would see them.

My legs carried me until mid-afternoon. I was so tired. My blinks became progressively further apart. Once, I had marveled at the beauty of this place, safe and secure in Chebona's company. Now on my own, I saw the endless expanse of trees, the rugged rocks and the inhospitable wilderness. I stumbled again. It was dangerous for me to continue this way.

I decided to stop for the night. The area was heavily wooded with large trees. I didn't feel comfortable sleeping on the ground. At this point, snakes and bears were a far more likely danger than any human enemy. Climbing into one of the larger trees, I tied myself to the trunk above a high branch where neither animal nor man might reach me. With my back against the tree, I had an excellent view of the landscape below. Having a rope around my waist was uncomfortable, but it was better than falling. This wasn't the most luxurious of lodgings, but it was dry. I was so tired I went to sleep almost immediately.

It was dark when I woke. As I looked out across the land, I saw the tell-tale sign of a fire. Smoke tendrils wafted up into the blackened sky. Fear and dread took hold. What if my kidnapper had already managed to catch up to me? From the looks of it, there were several miles between us. The smoke was back toward the river. I was ahead of whoever that was, and I wanted to keep it that way.

But what if that was Chebona? In trying to evade whomever this was, would I be going further away from my love? Reason took over. The most logical course of action was to get back to the village and get help from Wynono and Shiloh. I didn't have long to wait for first light and set off as soon as I could see.

It was different traveling alone. My senses were heightened. Every sound demanded my attention in order to determine the level of threat. Chebona had been doing that for us while we were together, and I'd taken it for granted. We were all creatures of the Earth in a fight for survival. I kept up a steady pace, keeping to the track. I figured it would be at least another two days before I reached the village. Every step was another one closer to my destination. The day dragged on. I had almost run out of water. I wasn't too concerned, as dark clouds had been threatening all afternoon. That meant fresh water would soon fall from the sky. What I would need more than anything was shelter. Walking off the track, I covered my exit, beating the path behind me with a bit of brush. Once more, I made my way into the woods.

The wind picked up. Lightning rippled through the clouds. Thunder broke overhead. Sleeping in a tree wouldn't be possible tonight. I needed to find somewhere the rain couldn't reach me. Thankfully, I found two massive boulders that leaned toward each other with an overhang near the front. It was big enough for me to squeeze in. Unfortunately, it was already occupied by a snake with the same idea. Its rattle warned me that it had already staked out this territory.

The snake hissed. Its tongue flicked in and out. A flash of lightning and a clap of thunder heralded the imminent onslaught of a downpour. There must be easier places to hide from a storm than this.

I backed away slowly. Chebona's warning rang through my mind. Even when coiled, it was obvious the snake was large. This creature was dangerous, and it was cornered. The snake started to unwind. Its body moved like water running downhill. I put my hands out, showing it I meant no harm, but instead of calming the creature, this aggravated the situation.

The rattlesnake rose up and bared its fangs. I quickened my steps backward and unhooked the net from around my waist. If it struck, this would be my only form of protection. I realized that if the snake attacked, I wouldn't be able to respond quickly enough to defend myself. It would bite me before the net even left my hands. I had to act first. With my mind made up, I took the opportunity while I still had it and threw the net onto the snake.

My heart was in my throat as the net unfolded in the air. The snake lashed out, striking at me, but the net spread wide. The net fell, and I watched as the fine lines of string wrapped around its body. Twisting and turning, it tried to loosen itself from its bonds, but its motion only made it worse.

The more the snake struggled, the more tangled it became. Putting a healthy distance between us, I looked around. A large rock lay on the ground. Instinct rather than reason took over. I picked up the rock with both hands and brought it thundering down onto the snake's head. The rock crushed the side of its skull and rolled away. The animal was bloodied and stunned. Its body continued to twist and writhe. I grabbed the rock again and repeated the action. This time I heard a loud crack. The snake's mangled head lay pummeled into the dirt. Dark blood seeped into the soil.

"I'm sorry, my brother. Thank you for your sacrifice. You were advancing on me, and I had to defend myself. I have too much to live for to die right now."

The snake's body continued to wriggle. I needed to make sure it was dead. The only way to do that would be to cut off its head. I got out my knife. Still, I didn't want to get too close to a rattlesnake. Large drops of rain started to fall, splattering the dirt around me. Off to one side lay a broken branch. I placed it over the front of the snake and knelt on the branch, putting pressure on its body. Then I cut through its neck with a sawing motion. My knife caught on the tough bones of its spine. I was surprised by how difficult it was to sever the head. The rattling sound lessened but could still be heard. Even in death, with its head separated from its body, the snake was warning me of danger. Using a stick, I dragged the tangled mess of net and dead rattlesnake away from the front of the makeshift cave.

By this time, the heavens had opened and the rain was crashing down. I scooted in between the rocks. Trickles of water ran down the side of my neck. I held my knife out to clean the blade and then sheathed it again. What had I done? I could hardly believe it. I had killed something that could have killed me—just to be safe and dry. Was I mad or desperate? Probably a bit of both. There was a slight gap at the top of my shelter. Small rivulets of water ran down the inside of the rock, but being in here was better than being caught out in the storm. I angled the water pouch to catch some of the runoff.

Eating the snake held no appeal for me. I wasn't that hungry, having finished the remainder of my fish earlier that afternoon. I was cold, however, and I spent the next couple of hours rubbing my arms and legs, thinking about all the things I would have liked for warmth, such as a cup of Madame DuPont's hot chocolate. My mouth salivated at the thought. A hot bath would have been nice. I imagined the fragrant steamy bathwater swirling around me instead of the cold rain dripping on me. Even a piece of hot buttered toast with honey would be heaven right now.

Daylight slowly succumbed to twilight as night fell. The rain continued and brought with it the constant drum of nature. If my kidnapper was tracking me, the water would wash away any signs of my travels.

I wondered where the men searching for me were at this moment.

I hoped the old French tracker had become careless in his pursuit of me and had come to an untimely end. It was wishful thinking, but somehow, it made me feel better. Was Chebona safe? I worried that somewhere out there, the trader's son was stalking Chebona. Knowing there were two hostile natives pursuing us was unsettling.

Now that night had fallen, my eyelids finally closed.

Darkness was my blanket.

Timber Rattlesnake

Found

Rain poured throughout the night. The ground was sodden and muddy. As I made my way along the track in the early hours of the morning, my footprints could not be hidden. I had to hope it would be Chebona who found me, and not the French trader or his son. Time dragged. Even though I was edging ever closer to the village, my strength and resolve began to wane. The rope, long since discarded, had been thrown off to the side. I wanted this whole ordeal to be over. I pushed on for another hour with no change in the landscape.

A rustle in the trees caught my attention. I turned to one side. To my surprise, Chebona was waving at me with one hand while holding a finger to his lips to signal for me to be quiet.

Rejoicing and fear gripped me simultaneously, but joy won out. I wasn't alone anymore. Whatever we faced, we would face it together, and our odds for success had gone up significantly.

I raced over to him, and we embraced.

"I thought I'd lost you," he said. "I can't believe you're in my arms again."

His grip was tight, but I didn't mind.

I sobbed into his chest, breathing in the familiar scent of his clothes. "I'm so glad you found me."

"It wasn't difficult. I saw the canoe floating downstream. Was that a clue meant for me?"

I smiled. "I hoped it would be you who saw it first."

He grinned, "You also left a trail of fish bones."

I berated myself. I'd tried so hard to be careful.

I pressed my lips to his. Nothing had seemed so sweet. He swept my matted hair out of my eyes and looked down at me.

"Are you hurt?"

He noticed the dried blood on my head and the stains on my dress.

"I was hit on the head, but I'm all right now."

"Who did this to you?" There was anger in his voice.

I was on the verge of tears. "A French-speaking native. A trader. He'd painted his face red and had a top knot of long hair. He was battle-hardened and had many scars. After he kidnapped me, he waited for his son to join us upriver, but I managed to escape. I don't know if he meant to take me to the French or another trader, and I didn't intend to find out. I used my knife to cut the rope and escape while he was sleeping. Then I paddled his canoe overnight and came to the tributary. It's been awful. I've never felt scared and alone. I don't want to see him ever again."

He sighed. "That canoe had Shawnee markings, and I found colored tassels from his leggings on the riverbank, where you were taken."

"Yes, I wrenched them off deliberately so you could identify his tribe."

"Very clever."

He stroked my hair, holding me close to him. I relaxed.

"I'm glad you're back with me now," I sobbed. "I was worried I'd never see you again."

My joy was short-lived.

"We're being followed," he said.

A sinking feeling settled in the pit of my stomach.

"Do you think it's him?"

"I think it's the son. He probably saw the canoe as well. His tracks are light, suggesting that he's a youth and fleet of foot. Hopefully, he's at least an hour behind us. The tracks I saw by the river from his father were deeper, indicating he's heavier. I've not seen them since, suggesting he hasn't returned yet."

That brought me some comfort.

"Their tracks mirror the ones Shiloh and I found before we left for the fort. Those two have been in this area for some time."

That bit of information was worrying.

"The young man will be wondering what happened to his father. He won't give up until he finds him. We need to keep moving. The empty canoe will cause him doubt. The father would not let his canoe go down the river like that. The youth may be thinking something bad has befallen him."

"Why did the men separate?" I asked. "Surely, they would have stayed together and taken me with them?"

"They could've been watching us and waited until you were alone. They may have agreed to meet later once they knew I wasn't a threat."

"You mean the son would have tried to kill you?"

"The father could have been training his son for such a reason."

I shuddered.

"I suspect that was their plan," Chebona said, "but he didn't notice that I picked up his trail and was tracking him instead. Once I realized what was happening, I made my way back to our camp, only to find you gone."

"Do you think they're on their own or part of a tribe?"

"All men need allies out here, especially in winter. If they aren't associated with a tribe, they'll be working for French trappers. His persistence has shown me his intent. Why chase someone if you don't have a plan? I suspect they thought they could sell you for quite a price. Come, we need to keep moving."

I said, "Please tell me you recovered my journal from where I dropped it after the attack."

Just this morning, I'd been thinking about the time and effort spent putting it together. I hated to think it had somehow been lost or destroyed.

"I have it with me," he said, patting the leather bag slung over his shoulder. "Of course, I wouldn't have left without it. Let's go."

He handed me the bag. Like the canoes, the hide had been treated with oils to keep out moisture. I pulled back the cover and checked inside. Even with the heavy rain last night, the pages were still dry.

I breathed a sigh of relief before another thought hit me.

"Where are we going?"

"We'll return to the village. I'd like to keep the river at our backs. It will take longer, but it can offer us some protection. Besides, it'll be harder for anyone to track us that way.

"How much longer will it take?"

"An extra day, I should think."

My ordeal was far from over. On seeing Chebona again, I thought my nightmare had come to an end, but he'd shown me the danger hadn't yet passed. All I wanted was to go the quickest and easiest way, but that wasn't the best solution.

"What about Shiloh? We're due to meet him at the tributary."

"That's not an option now. It wouldn't make sense to head back in the opposite direction. We'd be going toward those following us."

"I wasn't suggesting we go back that way, but he'll be in danger, won't he?"

"I've no way to warn him, Ally. Shiloh is a seasoned warrior. He'll pick up on the subtlest of signs. And seeing another Powhatan on the trail may give them pause for thought. If there's one additional scout in the area, they may worry there are more."

The longer this ordeal dragged on, the less I liked it.

We went down to the riverbed. The murky brown water was not inviting. It swirled around like a stagnant soup. The rain had stirred up the mud on the bottom. A collection of leaves and debris floated on the surface.

Chebona turned to me and said, "I can't believe I haven't asked you this before, but can you swim?"

"Yes," I replied.

"Good, because it would be a lot harder if you didn't."

"You're not suggesting we swim across, are you?"

"There's no hiding the fact that our tracks come down to the water's edge. I want to make it look as though we crossed to the other side and traveled on from there. We'll walk in the shallows and cross back further down."

"Isn't that a waste of time? What makes you think he'll check the other side of the river?"

"Because that's what I'd do."

It was logical and wouldn't take long. If it worked, it could give us a big advantage as he'd have to spend quite some time searching the far bank to see where we came out of the water.

I hated the thought of getting wet and then walking for miles in damp clothing, but I wasn't going to argue.

I followed Chebona into the murky depths and swam behind him. He was fast. I was slow. The leather bag had been sealed with oil and floated. I pushed it ahead of me, keeping the opening above the waterline, not wanting to lose all my work. The current was surprisingly strong. After the recent rains, stormwater ran down into the streams and rivers. At one point, I tried to stand on the riverbed, but my feet couldn't touch the bottom. After almost five minutes, we reached the other side.

Chebona disturbed some rocks to make it look like we'd gone that way. He stepped up onto the bank, leaving footprints in the mud. I waited as he headed up the slope and into the forest to establish a trail. When he returned, I was surprised to see him walking backward. He did this so there was no indication he'd returned to the river. As soon as he was satisfied, we set off again.

"We need to move swiftly," he said, wading through the knee-deep water along the bank.

Chebona set a cracking pace. It was all I could do to keep up with him. We were in survival mode. We navigated the uneven surfaces in the water for what seemed like an eternity. I could feel my thighs starting to chafe as the wet leather rubbed against them. This route took a lot of mental focus. I didn't want to fall and slow us down.

My stomach growled loudly. My head started to pound from the physical toll my body was taking. I was not able to replace the energy I was expending. I voiced my displeasure.

"I haven't eaten since yesterday."

"You'll have to wait until tonight. We can't afford to stop now."

I drank some water from my pouch, trusting it would be enough to give me the strength I needed.

We continued for another hour, then crossed back to the opposite bank, wanting to pick up the trail to the village. Chebona led us across several boulders so we didn't leave muddy footprints on the shore, but the sun had moved on, leaving our wet trail visible on the rocks.

Stopping for a moment, I put my hands on my knees and took some deep breaths.

"Chebona, I need to rest or eat. I can't keep up this pace."

He looked over his shoulder and saw my weakened state.

"It'll be dark soon. Can you keep going for another hour?"

"No," I said, knowing I'd reached my limit.

He nodded.

"We'll stop soon, but I need to get to higher ground to find a good vantage point for the night. Just a little further. You can do it, Koda."

I loved how he called me Koda and not Ally. In my mind, Ally was fragile, while Koda was strong. I took heart from his words and determined to keep going. Within a few minutes, though, I found myself swaying. The landscape around me blurred. I took a few deep breaths and drew on all the reserves I had.

The late afternoon sunlight filtered through the trees leading up the ridge. The rays cast shadows along our path. It was all I could do to keep putting one foot in front of the other.

Along the way, Chebona stopped to gather several plants we could eat later. He picked dandelions, chicory and an edible yellow fungus that grew in large clusters on the side of the trees. He told me that, when cooked, these mushrooms had a dense, fleshy texture like chicken. He was trying to encourage me.

Near the top, we stopped. Chebona climbed and looked out from the canopy of the trees back the way we'd come.

After he dropped down into the pine needles on the ground, I asked, "What did you see?"

"Nothing."

"That's good, right?

"He wouldn't have started his fire yet. It's too early."

"Can we start ours? I'm cold and hungry."

He pulled me against him.

"I know."

Chebona rubbed my arms, saying, "I'd rather not. Starting a fire will give away our position if he's close."

I sighed.

"What we *can* do is keep each other warm and eat the plants. Then I'll go and check again after dark. If I still can't see anything, we'll light a small fire and cook the mushrooms."

At this point, I would've eaten anything. We sat under one of the big fir trees and munched on our greens. Their bitter, tangy taste wasn't unpleasant. My body was just glad I was feeding it.

How thankful I was for this competent man beside me. I didn't doubt that I was his top priority, even above himself. That knowledge made my heart overflow with feelings for him. He was thoughtful and caring, and I knew I was loved. Chebona faced life, even with all its dangers, with a calm, joyous spirit that engulfed me. He made me feel safe.

We gathered pine needles and sticks for a fire. He examined them carefully, throwing away half of the wood I'd collected because it was too green and would have produced too much smoke. I wasn't offended. I was glad he knew how to hide our fire.

Night fell. Sleep came quickly, wrapped in Chebona's embrace under the star-studded sky. Our small fire gave off a comforting warmth.

The following morning we proceeded back toward the river to pick up the trail. Chebona was still being careful to look for any sign of human company.

Having satisfied himself that we were free from danger, he suggested he go and find us some meat.

"Oh no, you don't. This time I'm coming with you. I'm not taking that chance again."

"Let's see who can spot an animal first," he said, challenging me.

"Mmm. I feel like wild turkey," I said, imagining a plucked bird roasting over a fire.

He teased me. "You can't always have what you want."

I was certain Chebona could wrangle a turkey from somewhere. Being fiercely competitive, I set about my task with relish, always keeping him in sight. We walked through waist-high grass toward a thicket. My eyes scanned the forest for any sign of movement in the bushes. I was so distracted in my pursuit of the elusive fowl that I didn't see Chebona slump to the ground.

"Ally, get down," he yelled, calling out in pain. I'd never heard his voice break like that before. He sounded like a wounded animal. And his use of my English name frightened me. Something was horribly wrong. I knew he was in trouble. I had to get to him.

I did as he commanded and turned toward his voice, dropping to my hands and knees in the long grass. I found him about fifteen feet away. To my horror, he had an arrow embedded in the left side of his back.

"Why did you come to me?" he whispered. "We need to separate, or we're making it too easy for him. He'll be here any moment. Quick, hide in the thicket."

His eyes darted about in concern. Pulling his knife from its sheath, he grimaced in pain, preparing to fight his attacker.

"Go," he mouthed angrily.

"No, whatever we face, we do so together. I'm not leaving you," I whispered.

He cursed, pulling me with him toward a boulder that could shield us.

Two more arrows endeavored to make their mark, but they narrowly missed, whizzing through the air. They bounced off the rocky outcrop and came to rest near our feet.

Chebona was breathing hard. Squeezing his eyes shut, he tried to block out the pain as he leaned forward. "These are Shawnee arrows. He found us."

He picked up the arrows and snapped the wooden shafts over his knee.

"Let's hope he doesn't have too many of these. Even so, the Shawnee are vicious fighters."

Again he winced in pain.

I wished there was something I could do for him.

Blood had started to spread in a slow circle on Chebona's leather shirt. Until we were out of danger, his wound would have to wait.

Chebona took one of his own arrows and placed it in his bow. Peering around the rock, he pulled back the bowstring and fired, muttering a curse as he did so. The arrow soared through the air, arcing as it disappeared into the woods.

"I can't see him. Damn, I can't believe he found us. I'm such a fool to have put you in danger."

"Don't talk nonsense," I said, putting my hand on his chest. "You can't predict his movements."

He looked around, trying to find a possible solution to our plight.

"If we can get down to the river, perhaps we can lose him," he said.

"Can you make it?"

"I think so. Go in front of me. Stay close to the trees. Brush up against the bark. That way, it'll be harder for his arrows to find their target."

That target being us, I thought.

"I'll follow. Promise me, though," he said through gritted teeth, "If I fall, leave me. I can't bear the thought of anything happening to you."

I didn't want to give him that promise.

"Ally, promise me."

Again, I was Ally in his eyes, not Koda. My heart sank. I nodded, if only to appease him and because every moment we delayed put us at a disadvantage.

We ran because our lives depended on it. I didn't look back. I knew that would only slow me down. If Chebona were struck again, he would fall, and I would hear him tumble through the brush. Regardless of what I'd promised him, I knew I would stop to help. There was no way I was leaving him to die alone.

Several more arrows sailed past in quick succession. They struck trees beside us, embedding themselves deep into the bark. Dead branches broke under our feet. Birds took flight. My heart felt as though it was about to beat right out of my chest. The leather satchel slung over my shoulder caught in one of the trees. In an instant, I felt myself yanked to one side and drawn to a halt. I shrugged clear of the bag, leaving it hanging on a branch as we rushed on down the hill. Chebona called out to me, telling me to keep going. Somehow we managed to reach the river's edge without being struck.

A loud war cry sounded out as the lone warrior descended on our position from behind. The guttural sound made the very hairs on my neck stand on end.

After all, we'd been through, this couldn't be our end, could it?

In the Wild

We stumbled into the water and swam out into the middle where the current was swift, carrying us back toward the main river. We were going the wrong way, but we had no choice. Blood ran from the arrow in Chebona's back, staining the water.

A dark figure moved through the fir trees lining the bank, blending in with the forest. This was no teenage boy. He was lean and tall. He ran along the riverbank, taunting us with his tomahawk. Red paint adorned his face, while a black band accentuated his menacing eyes. His long hair hung loose over his shoulders. On his headband, three feathers stood tall, symbolizing how many people he'd killed in combat. The tips had been removed, having been sliced on an angle. Shiloh had once told me, feathers like this symbolized how an enemy was killed. The clipped plumage showed us he'd slit his victim's throats. How could someone so young already be responsible for the deaths of three people? No doubt, his father was training him to be a fierce warrior like himself. The sight of him made my blood run cold. It was hard to see any way out of this.

We would have to come out of the water sooner or later, and he'd be there waiting.

The young warrior glared at us like a mountain lion stalking his prey. His fur coverings flapped behind him as he kept pace with our motion down the river.

Chebona took hold of a branch floating nearby. He beckoned for me to join him. I swam over and grabbed hold of the wood. The branch provided us with some cover. Another arrow fell short in front of us, splashing in the water. It seemed we were on the edge of his range.

We drifted into an S-bend on the river. Our side was shallow, allowing our feet to touch the smooth stones on the bottom of the river. The channel ran close to his side, leaving a gulf between us.

"Why doesn't he come into the river after us?"

"The water adds an unknown factor. In the river, the dominance of his power is limited. Even a weak man can drown another, and I don't think he's willing to take that chance with both of us. Better to wait until we come out, and we'll have to do that soon."

A cliff lay behind us with straggly bushes at its base. We could clamber up there, but there was no cover, and he'd be able to see where we were going.

Chebona said, "It may be that he's waiting for his father. It will be dark soon, and that will give us a chance to escape. Since the current has taken us downstream, we'll have to swim against it to exit behind him."

His voice sounded strained, and I wondered if he had the strength to do as he was suggesting.

I said, "When darkness falls, we can push the branch on down the river. He may think we're still using it for cover and not realize we've gone back upriver."

"Yes, yes," Chebona said, moving back toward the water's edge and sitting on a submerged boulder. He dragged the branch next to us, making it obvious we weren't finished with it just yet. I hoped the Shawnee would fall for our bluff later that night.

"Ally, there's something I need you to do."

"What? Anything."

He handed me his knife, saying, "I need you to cut the shaft of the arrow, but you must be careful. You cannot move the arrowhead around."

I looked at the thin stick protruding from his back. The cold seemed to have helped reduce the bleeding. Blood seeped from around the hole in his shirt.

"You must hold it still with one hand," he said. "Then carefully use a sawing motion to cut as close to the entry site as possible."

The arrow had penetrated his back muscle near the shoulder blade. Chebona hadn't found it hard to breathe, so I was sure it hadn't pierced his lung. That was good. It was difficult to tell what it was doing inside his body. There were major arteries leading to the arm. It didn't bear thinking about. I knew enough not to remove it. He'd have to stay like this until we got him back to camp. That way he wouldn't run the risk of the tip going in deeper, and further damage being done.

Pinching the arrow between my two fingers for stability, I cut the wooden shaft. Chebona grimaced. My knife made short work of the arrow. Before long, I held the severed end in my palm. Previously I'd thought the colorful feathers that adorned the native arrows were quite beautiful. Not anymore.

The sun sat low on the horizon. We were both starting to shiver. We needed the sanctuary the men of the village could provide. It didn't take a genius to know that a wounded man and a European woman were no match for our native foe on the far shore. We would have to outsmart him. How we'd do that was the tricky part. With the cliff behind us, our options were limited. If we headed in either direction, he'd be able to track us. We needed the cover of darkness.

The brave taunted us. At times, he would disappear back into the forest, leaving me worrying he was heading out of sight to cross the river. It soon became apparent, however, that he was fixing his arrows. He must have gathered those that missed us. He sat on the shore, muttering out loud as he secured loose arrowheads.

After speaking at length in Shawnee, which neither of us knew, he reverted to French, yelling out, "*Qu'avez-vous fait de mon père.?*"

"He's not happy," I said.

"You speak French?" Chebona asked, surprised I knew what the brave was saying.

"He's asking what I did to his father. He thinks I killed him."

Chebona said, "Don't respond. He's stalling, hoping his father is still out there somewhere."

"And he is," I said.

"But he doesn't know that for sure, and that works to our advantage."

"*Je t'aurai, femme. Je tuerai ton homme et te vendrai comme épouse.*"

I said, "He's bragging, saying he'll kill you and sell me."

"Don't be afraid, Ally. He's taunting us because that's all he can do. Once night has come, we'll make our move."

Darkness fell. Clouds covered the moon's light. It was difficult to spot the brave's outline in the darkness now, although I knew he was there. Night gave us an advantage. The odds were still heavily stacked in the brave's favor and each moment that passed increased those chances. But maybe we'd be able to evade him if we could make it to the far shore, without him detecting us.

Chebona waded into deeper water, making as though we were going to use the branch to continue downstream. He pushed it out into the channel as I slipped beneath the river and hid behind a boulder. Then he swam back and joined me. I didn't like getting cold and wet again, but I knew we needed to throw the enemy off our trail.

Chebona squeezed my arm and signaled that now was the time to swim upstream. The cliff loomed over us. If the foliage on our side of the bank was thicker, we could've taken to the shore, but it would've been too easy for the brave to spot our movements. We kept our arms and legs under the water to avoid making any unnecessary ripples. We struggled on together.

Chebona's strength was fading fast, so I went first. His one good arm clung to my waist while his other arm drifted limp behind him. He hung on to me, using only his legs to propel himself forward.

It was difficult pushing against the current with Chebona's weight dragging me back. I kicked my legs with every bit of strength I could muster. Even though I was breathing hard, I had to keep my mouth closed in case I swallowed any water. If I coughed or spluttered, it would give our location away. I felt like giving up and just going with the current. How easy would it be to keep drifting and die an easy death? Lulled into an endless sleep by the cold. If I gave up, I knew I'd slip effortlessly below the surface. Those thoughts flashed into my mind, but deep down, I knew we had to push on. Surviving was our goal and would be the sweetest victory over our foe in the end. Little by little, we edged our way in the opposite direction. My muscles began to cramp. I couldn't do this for much longer.

A patch of reeds lay ahead of us. I made my way toward them. The muscles in my arms were burning, but I persevered. The current wasn't as swift here on the curved edge of the river. I grabbed onto the grassy anchors with determination. I could feel the sandy bottom of the river beneath my feet. Stones helped my moccasins find some grip, and I used them to push forward. Behind me, Chebona tugged on my leggings. He pointed, indicating that we should cross the river.

"Don't fight the current," he whispered. "Let the river take you as we cross." He was pointing at the far shore but roughly a hundred yards behind us. "We should be able to make that embankment."

By this time, we were at least half a mile upriver. I hoped our ruse had worked and the brave had followed the branch down toward the main river. If it hadn't, we could be crossing right into his path. From his perspective, returning to the main river probably seemed like a good idea as he'd think we were returning to the English fort. He wouldn't know about the outbreak.

We glided across the river for several minutes, kicking softly at the water. More reeds lay up against the bank on this side, allowing us to shelter there. Chebona listened to the wind. I knew why. He was trying to understand if the brave lay on shore waiting for us. We snuck through the reeds and exited the river. Once we reached the narrow beach, we lay on our stomachs, praying our enemy wasn't just above us on the bank. It was a relief to be out of the water, but the cool night air assaulted my skin, making my teeth chatter. Putting my own pain aside, it was apparent that I would have to take the lead. Chebona lay prone, his face toward me. His eyes looked glassy and distant.

"Can you go on?" I whispered in his ear.

He nodded, but he didn't look convincing.

I also listened for any signs of the brave, but all I could hear were the usual night noises of the wild.

Where could we hide? We'd reached the trail back toward the village. Having been here before, I racked my brain to think of a good spot where we could rest for the night. It would need to be somewhere Chebona could easily get to in his weakened state, but one where the brave couldn't or wouldn't go. Did such a place even exist? I looked at Chebona, who was struggling to remain conscious. This was the first time I was fearful that he might not make it out of this alive. He could not die. I would not let him join his ancestors. Then I realized the solution.

The last time we were here, Shiloh pointed out the native burial ground. Would I be able to find it in the dark? We were out of options. I knew Native Americans were deeply superstitious. Even if the warrior didn't know about these sacred grounds, once he realized he was crossing the threshold, he'd retreat. Knowing it was forbidden, I had to pray that both the living and the dead would forgive us for trespassing. After all, we were trying not to enter the afterlife alongside these ancestors. We still had plenty of living left to do. They could hardly hold that against us, could they? I needed to make sure we'd be able to walk there within an hour or so.

"How close are we to the burial ground?"

He pointed upstream.

"Not far. It overlooks the horseshoe bend."

"I have an idea, but I don't think you're going to like it."

He looked at me with a blank stare.

"N—No," he whispered once the realization hit him.

"I can't think of anywhere else we can hide."

He pointed at a clearing on the hillside.

I shook my head. "He'll find us. It's too exposed."

"Forbidden," was all he managed to say.

"We may find somewhere close to it that will work."

That point of logic, at least, seemed agreeable to him, for he nodded.

I hauled Chebona's arm over my shoulder and led us past the grassy trail in the direction he'd indicated. Keeping to the safety of the trees, we hid in front of one, stopped for a bit, and then moved on to the next. Chebona's feet shuffled reluctantly, and his weight seemed to increase with each step. He was right. A little way upstream, the river curved. Changing direction, we started climbing uphill. This was even slower going. Chebona's body was extremely heavy to bear. I'd thought I'd already used all my strength swimming against the current, but from somewhere deep inside me, I found more. My breathing came in long gasps as we climbed even higher. Why did the dead need such a good view? It was wasted on them. With each step, I cursed them more. I heard rather than saw our destination.

A soft breeze rustled through the trees, along with another noise. Bones. Like a gruesome wind chime, long strings of small bones bumped together in an eerie jingle. They twisted and swirled in a macabre dance.

Smooth, round stones had been brought up from the river and meticulously placed around the perimeter of the sacred site. They guarded the precious remains. Tall trees and grasses grew in abandon, providing much-needed cover between the half-moon mounds. I looked at Chebona, but his eyes were closed, oblivious to our surroundings. I said a silent prayer for forgiveness. Whether it was to God or to his ancestors, I didn't much care. I gently lowered Chebona onto his side in between the mounds, which provided us with shelter from the wind. Still, it was bitterly cold, and our wet clothes clung to us like a second skin.

"Rest now, my love. We're safe," I whispered.

He barely acknowledged me, falling into what I hoped was a deep slumber. I examined his wound in the moonlight, which didn't look like it was bleeding. How long would the Shawnee brave continue to hunt us? At some point, he had to tire of the pursuit. Would he leave at first light if he couldn't find us? A more shocking thought came to mind. What if he came across our trail and tracked us to the burial ground? Would he come in after us or wait for us to perish from the cold? Let's get through tonight, I reminded myself. My priority was to get some rest, then I would be alert. One bad decision could spell disaster for us.

Closer to the edge of the stone circle were fresh mounds. Native Americans were often buried with some of their possessions. Numerous old pieces of pottery and jewelry were scattered around the area. I looked to see if there was anything I could scavenge.

Edging toward the outskirts on my hands and knees, I shuddered to think what was under this dirt. Some sections were too fresh for grass to have taken root, which meant the occupants had been recently placed there. My hand touched something soft, and I froze, worried that an animal may have uncovered a corpse. Soft fur ran through my fingers. Gently, I felt for the edge and realized this was a covering of four or five skins stitched together and draped over a fresh mound. In the darkness, I thanked God some kind relative had thought to put this covering over the grave.

These skins reminded me of the ones Nathan Tinsdale showed me back in Williamsburg. The beaver fur was soft and prized for being the warmest of pelts. Right now, I figured it was more useful to us than its recipient, who had long been cold in this earth. I dragged the covering back to Chebona. Using my knife, I cut his wet shirt and somehow managed to get it off by rolling him first one way and then the other.

We huddled beneath the pelts. Bit by bit, warmth crept back into my body. The soft grass on the ground provided a thick buffer against the earth below. Chebona stirred once more.

"Stay still, be quiet and do not roll over," I ordered.

I rubbed his limbs with my hands to create more heat.

"I'm sorry, Koda," he stammered from colorless lips.

"Why are you apologizing? None of this is your fault."

410

He was still concerned with my well-being.

"Shh, save your strength."

At least we had survived this day. I imagined myself by a roaring fire, but tonight even my imagination was not enough to comfort me. There was too much to worry about. I was exhausted. My eyelids became heavy, and the stars above me blurred.

A scurrying noise woke me and brought me back to the harsh reality of daybreak. It seemed a nearby squirrel wasn't used to having his peaceful habitat occupied by living humans. My ears strained for more unnatural sounds. I couldn't hear any.

Staring up into the tree from where the squirrel had scooted, I quietly thanked him. If I could get up into the branches, it would provide cover and let me see the trail Shiloh would be riding in on later today. God, I was hungry. Maybe that squirrel had some food it had been hoarding for winter. Now I was delusional, thinking of stealing food from a squirrel. I almost laughed at myself. I shook the waterskin I'd been carrying. It was half empty, like Chebona's. Luckily, we'd strapped these across our shoulders when we made our run for the river. My journal, though, was somewhere several miles away. I imagined it had fallen from the bag and was lying on the dirt with its pages blowing in the breeze. All my work was gone. As heartbreaking as it was to lose my sketches, they could be drawn again. Chebona, though, was irreplaceable.

Leaning over, I felt his forehead. He was warm to the touch but not feverish.

"Please tell me yesterday was a bad dream," he moaned, his eyes still shut.

"Hush, we aren't out of the woods yet," I warned him.

"Funny, I thought that was exactly where we were," he said softly.

"I'm glad you can still crack a joke. Promise me you won't be mad?"

His eyes flew open and took in the landscape around us.

"What have you done, Koda?" he whispered.

I was pleased he'd gone back to my native name, but I'd never seen him look so scared before. It seemed the dead put more fear into him than the living.

"I kept us alive."

"Koda, there are reasons people are forbidden to tread on this sacred ground. Many believe you will be cursed if you break these rules."

"Well, it's a good thing I'm not one of them. There weren't any other options—unless you wanted us to join their ranks?"

I waved my arm around, indicating the obvious.

"We may have just delayed the inevitable," he sighed.

Ungrateful man, I was simply trying to keep us alive.

"All of us die at some point, and I was damned if it was going to be us."

Tears fell in a steady stream down my cheeks as the gravity of the situation weighed heavily on my shoulders.

"It's all right," he said. "I'm not blaming you. I'm trying to understand, and I'm thankful for what you did."

He touched my hand, turning it over and bringing my palm to his lips. At least he was being reasonable. I had only been trying to protect him.

"I'm so thirsty," he said.

I held the water bag to his mouth.

"If I didn't have this stupid arrowhead in my back, we could fight him," he said after he had drunk his fill. "I feel helpless. I should be taking care of you."

"Oh, don't you give me all that male bravado. You *have* taken care of me, but things have changed, and now it's *my* turn. We are in a partnership, you know. That's how marriage works. Sometimes you help me, and other times I help you. I'm going to climb up that tree and see what I can discover. Will you be well enough here on your own?"

"I've little energy for anything else."

"I'll signal if I see Shiloh or the other native."

"Be careful."

The mighty oak had long been providing shelter for Chebona's ancestors. Its thick branches sufficiently carried my weight. I made sure I climbed on the side that was facing away from the river. I didn't want to give away my position to anyone looking from below. The past few days had taken a toll on me physically. I strained to pull myself skywards. My legs felt heavy, and my arms weak. Twigs and leaves brushed against me, scratching my skin, but my thoughts were more concerned with my balance than my comfort. By the time I was high enough, I was breathing heavily.

The valley below me stretched out for miles. I had to admit, this was a beautiful spot for the ancestors to inhabit. The fall colors were in stark contrast to the grey rocks that lined the banks of the waterways. The dark green of fir trees reached up and caressed the majestic blue of the heavens. My eyes scanned below me for any movement by the river.

Nothing.

Not even the thin tendrils of smoke from a fire could be seen. Had our enemy given up that easily? I doubted it.

Now it was a waiting game. We needed Shiloh. Would he notice the signs of the ambush and our escape?

Once he got to the tributary, he would, but how long would it take for him to backtrack and find us here?

I started to worry. I needed to get Chebona back to the village. The longer that arrow stayed embedded, the worse his outcome would be. If Shiloh hadn't arrived by nightfall, we needed to try and make our own way back.

Shawnee

For several hours, I rested my back against the tree and looked through the foliage for any sign of movement. Several creatures had been my companions during the morning. A bright red bird foraged in the grasses under a nearby tree. Every now and then, it would score a tasty grub from the underbrush and fly back to the safety of the branches to finish its meal. I was almost envious. The tap, tap of a woodpecker was annoying and yet somehow comforting at the same time. It was searching for food. Chebona and I had no such luxury. I took another mouthful of water and swished it around before swallowing. I'd been in the tree so long my bladder was ready to be relieved. I was contemplating going right there in the tree when a subtle movement startled my solitude.

Shiloh had climbed a tree a short distance away, further down the valley. How had I missed his arrival? God, it was good to see him. He motioned with his finger, pointing below. The Shawnee brave had crept into view and was searching the ground carefully. I'd missed both of them. I berated myself. What a lousy scout I'd make.

Shiloh shrugged his shoulders which I interpreted as '*Where was Chebona?*'

I made a slight motion of firing a bow and pointed to near my shoulder. His eyes went wide in shock. He pointed at the man below once more. I nodded. Then he disappeared behind the tree and vanished from sight. The brave looked in the direction of our hiding place, walking close to the edge of the burial ground.

Chebona was lying on his side against the trunk of the tree beneath me. Before I climbed up into the branches, I'd put a handful of stones in my tunic. This was an old Powhatan trick Chebona taught me while hunting by the river. Throwing stones could be used to signal other scouts or distract game. Now, I used it to get his attention without uttering a word. I dropped a small stone near his feet, and he immediately looked up. I motioned with my fingers, walking my right hand across my left palm, meaning I could see the brave hunting us. He got out his knife, and I shook my head, knowing he could be killed this time.

I could see Shiloh behind a tree not far from the brave. The determined expression on his face told me all I needed to know. Shiloh meant to kill him. I didn't know whether I liked having a bird's eye view or not. Still, the brave remained outside the sacred site, seemingly caught between seeking out his prey and respecting the traditions of the elders. He knew we were in here. I wondered if he felt pleased that he'd forced us to do something so abhorrent.

It was difficult to keep track of the man as he disappeared between bushes on the ground. At times, the twigs and leaves in front of me obscured my view. I craned my neck, desperate to spot him when suddenly we were staring at each other. The Shawnee brave looked up to where I stood high among the branches. He'd seen me. He took the bow off his shoulder and took an arrow from his quiver. A wide smile on his face betrayed the glee he was feeling. There was nowhere for me to go. I angled my foot to hide behind the trunk and turned side-on to give him a smaller target.

Before the brave could get an arrow away, Shiloh crept up behind him. What little noise there was from Shiloh's moccasins must have alerted the brave as he flinched when releasing the arrow. The thin shaft soared past mere inches from my arm.

Shiloh caught the brave off balance, and they both crashed heavily onto the dirt. He aimed to plunge his knife into his enemy's neck, but his opponent was quick. He rolled out from under Shiloh before he could stab him.

The two men faced off against each other, with the Shawnee warrior having dismissed his long-range weapon for his knife. They circled each other, waiting to see who would make the first move. Shiloh had lost the advantage of surprise without being able to inflict a wound. Now, they were more evenly matched. Shiloh was bigger and stronger, but his rival was younger and nimble It was Shiloh who attacked first, slashing at the air as he made a wide arc with his knife. The brave jumped back but not before Shiloh's blade tore across the front of his chest. It was not a deep wound, but it did serve to inflame the Shawnee's anger. Immediately he struck back, using his legs to wrestle Shiloh to the ground. They continued fighting, desperately trying to stay out of the way of each other's knives.

It was pointless for me to stay in the tree any longer. I could not just stand by and watch helplessly. When I looked down at Chebona's resting spot, he was no longer there. Carefully, I made my way down the branches, aware of the men's grunts and groans as each one strained to gain the upper hand.

I found Chebona staggering through the long grass toward the fight, bending over, holding his injured shoulder with his good hand. Although he had drawn his knife, the pain he was in meant he could only hold it with his limp hand. I ran on ahead of him to the rocky boundary of the burial ground, hesitant to leave the sanctuary it provided.

Shiloh was straddling his foe with his hands around his neck. Both of their knives had been flung to the ground. Blood and dust covered the men, and it was hard to tell who had been cut. I ran over and picked up the knives. They were slick with blood. The men paid no attention to me.

There was only ever going to be one outcome to this fight. Shiloh was going to win. He was bigger and stronger. His fingers were crushing the brave's windpipe. I almost felt sorry for the young man, but he'd brought this on himself. Shiloh had both knees up, pinning the brave's shoulders to the ground as he strangled him. The Shawnee warrior struggled, but his strength was fading, and he couldn't break free. What I didn't expect was for Shiloh to take so long to kill him. He was muttering something, locking eyes with the brave, allowing the Shawnee to continue breathing. What was he waiting for? Out of the corner of my eye, I saw Chebona cross the dusty track to reach the two men.

Chebona knelt down and placed his hand on the forehead of the Shawnee warrior. He rocked the young man's head back, exposing his throat. Shiloh released his grip on the brave's neck. The look in Chebona's eyes was not one I'd seen before, and it scared me. When it came to animals, Chebona killed them with respect. This was altogether different, primal and raw. No thanks was given for this sacrifice. Chebona used his knife to slit the throat of the one who had wounded him. He gave a satisfied howl as the Shawnee's blood spilled freely over the dirt. The warrior trembled as the last moments of his soul slipped away.

All three of us looked at each other, still taking in what had just happened. Shiloh wiped the blood from his hands on the dead brave's tunic.

"Are you all right?" I asked him.

"Yes, none of this is mine."

He put a hand on Chebona's thigh. "Let's get you home."

"Thank you, brother. I'm happy you came in time."

"I found signs where you were attacked. When I tracked toward the river, I came across your satchel in the trees. Inside were Koda's drawings. I knew you wouldn't have left them without good reason. That put me on guard."

My body started to shake uncontrollably, and not just from the cold. It was hard to believe the threat was over.

"Do you have horses nearby?" I asked Shiloh as I wrapped my arms around myself, trying to get warm.

"Yes, we should get going before this dead body attracts attention."

"You mean from his father?"

Shiloh looked confused by my question.

Chebona explained. "Koda was taken by a Shawnee French trader. She managed to escape, but he's still out there. This is his son. He tracked us from the river."

"Oh," Shiloh said. "I was thinking the blood will attract wolves or perhaps a bear looking for an easy meal, but if the father is still out there, we should go."

As we made our way back to the river, I refused to look behind me. I wanted to leave the memory of that sacred place as just that—a distant memory. Chebona and Shiloh talked in hushed voices as we picked our way through the trees. At one point, we stopped while Shiloh examined his brother's wound. He placed the back of his hand against his brother's forehead and frowned.

"What is it?" I wanted to know.

"Feel for yourself."

I copied Shiloh, touching Chebona's head. He was hot. Fever hot.

I looked at Shiloh.

"That arrowhead has to come out before we travel, doesn't it?" I asked.

He nodded.

"I can make it," Chebona argued.

"Yes, you could, but you'd be dead in a few days. Koda, talk some sense into your man."

"But the father," Chebona said.

I didn't mean to be dismissive of Chebona, but I understood Shiloh's concern. "Your brother is right. We need to care for you now, not later. It's better this way."

Shiloh said, "If the father comes, we will deal with him as with the son."

Once we reached the horses, Shiloh opened one of the saddle bags and pulled out my journal. "See, Koda. I would never leave this. I know how much it means to you."

"Thank you," I said, clutching the book to my chest. I felt as though I'd been reunited with a long-lost friend. I sat on a rock and flicked through the pages to see if any of them had been damaged or if moisture had caused the ink to run. A few of the pages had crumpled, but they could be straightened. Dirt had embedded itself in the top of the spine, but apart from that, my journal was fine.

"Can you start a fire?" Shiloh asked.

"Sure."

Chebona rested against a tree overlooking the river. The sound of water running over the rocks below him must have been soothing to his soul.

While I gathered kindling, Shiloh used his tomahawk to trim branches. He built a lean-to against a tree with low-hanging boughs. Even though his shelter was hastily constructed, it looked sturdy enough to protect us from a storm. The sky, though, was clear, leaving me wondering why he'd gone to such effort. Once the first sparks of my fire became flames, he said, "Now, we need to leave."

"What? Why?" I asked. "We should tend to Chebona. We've only just made camp."

"No, Koda. We've made a trap."

"Oh."

"We'll sit in the distance and watch the approaches," he said, placing a pot on the fire to boil water. "But we will not stay here."

"Do you have anything to eat?" I asked before we left the camp.

"Look in my saddle bag," he replied, dropping willow bark in the simmering water. "You'll find dried meat and cornbread in there."

Chebona and I ate our fill. How good it was not to have hunger pains gnawing at my stomach anymore.

Shiloh said to me, "Can you cut Chebona's shirt into strips to place over the wound? If you leave the sleeves, we can tie them around him to keep the bandage in place."

I looked at Chebona's sweaty blood-soaked shirt. "It's not very clean."

"I have some sage we can put over the wound. Don't worry, the deerskin won't touch his injury."

Once the pot had boiled, we made our way along the shore, sheltering in the lee of a cliff. I carried the pot while Shiloh beat the path behind us with a branch to clear our tracks. From where we were, it was roughly fifty yards back to the camp. Shiloh had deliberately set the camp on a grassy patch above the river. A steep bank led down to the water. The thick brush around us hid us from sight while allowing us to see if anyone crept into the makeshift camp.

"Chebona, go and sit in the river," Shiloh said. "The water there will cool you. I'll take the arrow out down there, so there's no sign of blood on the riverbank."

"Great. I can hardly wait," he replied, being sarcastic. "Don't get too much pleasure out of this, my brother."

"It'll be very satisfying," Shiloh answered, grinning.

Chebona's smile faded.

Shiloh added, "Not because it'll hurt you, my little brother, but because it'll help you."

"Hmmm..."

Chebona did as he was told and stepped down into the river. He sat on the pebbles in the shallows. Water lapped at his waist.

Shiloh held out his hand, helping me wade into the river behind Chebona. While still holding the handle, I rested the pot in the water, allowing the willow tea to cool. Shiloh washed his knife in the river, gently cleaning it in the slow-moving current.

"Chew on this," he said, fishing the soft willow bark out of the pot and placing it in Chebona's hand. I hated to think about the agony Chebona was about to endure.

Shiloh addressed me, saying, "As I work with the knife, gently pour the tea over the wound to wash the blood away. That will allow me to see what I'm doing."

Shiloh crouched behind his brother. The water flowed around them as they sat in the shallows. I couldn't look, but I felt compelled to. I didn't want to see my love in pain, but I had to keep a steady trickle of willow water running over Chebona's back. Shiloh needed to be able to see the arrowhead in the raw muscle.

"Did you get a look at the type of arrow he used?" Shiloh asked, taking Chebona by the shoulder.

"Yes, he fired off enough of them. They're not barbed if that's what you're asking?"

"Good. That'll make it easier to remove."

Shiloh made a small cut above the arrow shaft. Blood ran down Chebona's back. The red color seeped into the water around him. Peeling back the flesh, Shiloh used his knife to locate the stone tip. Chebona's knuckles turned white as he gripped his knees, holding them close to his chest. He took short shallow breaths to try and control the pain. Even so, he cried out several times. From the way he gritted his teeth, I knew he was trying not to make too much noise and attract attention, but the pain must have been unbearable. Eventually, Shiloh was able to remove the arrowhead.

"Got it!"

He threw the offending item into the depths, and it sank out of sight.

"Koda, hand me the sage."

"This is going to hurt the most, brother, but it is needful."

"Just get on with it," Chebona moaned. He grimaced, clenching his teeth as the wet sage was applied, followed by the makeshift bandage. Shiloh pressed his hand on the wound.

I wrapped the remnants of Chebona's shirt over his shoulder. Then I knelt down in front of him and took his hands in mine. He was pale. Beads of sweat clung to his forehead.

'That's one of the bravest things I've ever seen," I said.

It was true. The stamina of the Native American people was remarkable. Both Aponi's labor and Chebona's injury showed me a level

422

of resolve I didn't think possible. I wet my hands and caressed his face, wanting to cool him down. He opened his eyes and smiled at me weakly.

"I want to go home."

I squeezed his hand. "Me, too."

Shiloh said, "I'll prepare the horses. We leave now."

"Even though it's late afternoon?" Chebona asked, leaning on me as we climbed the bank.

"Especially because it's late afternoon," Shiloh said. "Our fire will act as a decoy for anyone following us, drawing them away from the hills and down to the river. But we'll head inland on the old track. We'll ride through the night and reach the village before dawn."

The sun sat low in the sky. Before long, it would dip below the mountains, casting shadows across the land. Then the cold dark of night would come. I couldn't wait to curl up in the warm, dry furs of a village hut.

Water dripped from our leggings. Chebona clutched at his shoulder, as I helped him sit on a fallen tree.

"Wait here," Shiloh said. "I'll gather the horses."

As he walked off along the path beside the river, I said, "Don't forget my journal."

I could see it sitting on a rock beside one of the saddlebags.

Shiloh turned back to me with a smile, saying, "I could never do that, Koda."

A gentle wind blew through the oak trees, rustling the leaves and causing them to fall like snowflakes. The yellows, oranges and reds made it seem as though the forest stretching along the riverbank was on fire.

Shiloh crept through the woods, crouching as he approached the makeshift camp. The two horses barely stirred. They stood with their heads bowed, waiting patiently for him. A thin trail of smoke drifted with the breeze, rising above the trees.

I expected Shiloh to fetch the horses and return to us immediately, but he didn't. He waited on the edge of the clearing, peering up into the hills, looking intently at the surrounding trees. He kept to the shadows. He stepped with care, sliding his feet through the undergrowth to avoid the crunch of dead leaves and broken twigs beneath his moccasins.

Down in the river, just below the camp, a fish jumped in the water. The splash caused him to turn and look at the reeds. In that instant, he had his knife drawn, ready to fight. Once he was satisfied there was no danger, he slipped his knife back into its sheath.

Rather than walk into the camp, he circled closer to where the horses stood. I watched as he stepped into their shadows, reaching out a hand and patting each horse as he crouched out of sight from the hill. He kept the river to his back.

Shiloh knelt down and grabbed my journal. Then he took the reins of his horse, turning it as he stood. He lifted the leather covering on the saddlebag, ready to slide my journal back inside, when an arrow shot out from the woods.

The motion caught my eye. A thin shaft streaked through the trees, catching the light of the sun as it shot out of the forest, flying true and flat as it soared toward Shiloh.

I wanted to shout. I wanted to scream and warn him, but it happened so quickly, far quicker than I could respond. I watched in shock as the arrow cleared the back of the horse, passing barely an inch above the saddle.

Shiloh had his back to me. The arrow struck him in the center of his chest. The sheer force of the impact caused him to keel backward. The journal flew from his hands, landing in the long grass. His body tumbled down the slope. He rolled end over end with his arms and legs flailing around. I saw his head strike a boulder as he landed in the river. Within seconds, his body slipped beneath the water. Reeds swayed around him. Blood ran with the current.

Chebona yelled, "Noooo!"

From the shadows, a dark face turned to look at us. The father ran with his bow in one hand and a tomahawk in the other. The thin fringes on his leggings swayed with his motion. Warpaint adorned his chest. Black stripes lined his face.

Chebona was up on his feet and staggering along the path with his knife in his hand, but he couldn't stand upright.

"*Pour mon fils!*" the old Shawnee warrior yelled, running toward us. "*Vous paierez pour la mort de mon fils!*"

Back when he kidnapped me, it was business. Following the death of his son, his anger had become personal. He sought revenge. He was shouting in French, lamenting his loss.

"*Mon fils. Mon fils unique!*"

That young man had been his only son.

"Chebona! No!" I yelled, rushing after him and wanting to get between them, but what could I do? I wasn't capable of bringing down an experienced Shawnee warrior by myself. I pulled my knife out, but it was designed for skinning game. The blade was short. It was no match for a tomahawk. Even Chebona's knife couldn't compare to the size and weight of the stone ax at the end of a wooden handle. Even a glancing blow would be enough to break bones.

The old man let out a bloodcurdling cry as he sprinted toward us.

I tried to pull Chebona back, but he wrestled free of my grip. He was enraged by the sudden death of his brother. The two of them met on the narrow track. The Shawnee warrior swung his tomahawk.

Although he must have been in excruciating pain, Chebona was light on his feet. He swayed, dodging the attack. The stone ax cut through the air barely an inch from his jaw. Before the warrior could raise his weapon a second time, Chebona had disarmed him with a swift kick to his wrist. The tomahawk tumbled down the edge of the bank and into the river.

While the man was recovering, Chebona struck with his knife. His blade cut into the old man's chest, drawing blood, but with his injured back, Chebona was unable to drive his knife deep. The Shawnee warrior knocked him into the rocks lining the path. His forehead struck an outcrop, and blood gushed down his face.

I screamed.

Chebona lay there dazed as the warrior loomed over him, ready to kill him.

"No," I yelled, stepping forward and raising my knife.

The old Shawnee man smiled at me and yet I could see anger burning in his eyes. I wasn't a threat. I was an annoyance, a pesky fly buzzing around his head. He'd kill Chebona and then deal with me. He ignored me. He lowered his guard as I stepped closer. He drew his knife. I was terrified, watching in horror as he grabbed Chebona by his hair. He wrenched Chebona's limp head back, exposing his neck. He meant for Chebona to die the same way as his son. As much as I willed Chebona to get up, I could see his eyes had rolled into the back of his head. The blow had knocked him unconscious. He would die without a fight.

I did the only thing I could. Some might think it cowardly to strike without warning. Some might call it unfair, but I couldn't stand there as my love died at the hands of this brute. Perhaps it was my upbringing in England, but back home, men would duel under strict rules. Here, though, there was no such honor.

I plunged my knife into the side of the warrior's exposed torso. The blade sunk in up to the hilt, cutting through his abdomen above his hip. He howled in agony. I staggered back with the bloody blade still in my hand, backing up toward the horses.

"*La pute!*" he said.

Calling me a bitch bought me time. My feet continued to shuffle along the dirt and rocks.

He left Chebona where he lay and turned toward me. The old man was in no rush. He seemed determined to make me pay for the pain I'd caused him, but it was he who'd kidnapped me. It was he and his son who attacked us.

I reached the clearing, still holding my pitifully small knife before me, looking for something else to use as a weapon. I considered grabbing the end of a burning branch from the fire, but he'd laugh at such a feeble attempt to ward him off. It was then I saw my journal. It was lying halfway down the embankment with an arrow sticking out of its leather cover. Shiloh was alive. He had to be. A glimmer of hope surged in my heart. My eyes scanned the reeds, looking for any sign of movement in the river.

Shiloh may have been hurt in the fall, but he hadn't been killed.

I squinted, looking deep into the old man's eyes, wanting to keep his attention fixed on me, hoping that somewhere out there, Shiloh would be creeping through the woods toward him.

The old man stepped into the clearing, saying, "*Il me fera plaisir de vous effacer de la Terre.*" He was bragging, announcing it would be a pleasure to erase me from the Earth.

I kept my eyes on him, saying, "No. That pleasure will be mine. It will be I that cleanses this Earth of you."

He laughed, but I didn't care. For me, this wasn't bravado, it was a distraction. Behind him, a dark figure loomed in the grass. Water dripped from wet leather. Blood ran from a gash on the side of Shiloh's head. He held his knife between his teeth. He meant to wrestle the Shawnee to the ground and disarm him.

Something alerted the old warrior to the danger behind him. Whether it was the soft squelch of moccasins or the changing shadows, he realized Shiloh was there. He wheeled around as Shiloh lunged at him. The two men struggled, crashing into me. I lost my footing. Together, the three of us slid down the bank into the river, tumbling as we fell. My head struck the ground hard before water splashed around me. Dazed, I shook my head to regain clarity. That was a mistake. Pain shot through my skull as my vision blurred.

I'd dropped my knife. Within seconds, it became apparent that all three of us had lost our knives in the fall. One of the knives lay halfway down the embankment, having caught on an exposed root. The other two had sunk into the depths of the river.

Reeds shook as the men fought in the shallows. I crouched, running my hands through the muddy water. My fingers skimmed across the rocks and pebbles, searching for my knife.

Shiloh went for the knife lying halfway up the bank. He scrambled out of the water but slipped back into the shallows. The warrior tried to grab Shiloh's slick, wet body but couldn't hold onto him. Shiloh lunged out of the river again, grabbing at the grass, wanting to get higher so he could get the blade, but the old Shawnee warrior was quick. He reached into the water and raised a rock high above him. In a swift motion, he brought it down on the side of Shiloh's head and dragged him back into the water, meaning to drown him. Shiloh pulled away, wanting to get out of his reach.

Mud swirled around them. The warrior swung at Shiloh, striking him on the jaw. Shiloh tried to fight him off, but the blood pouring from the cut on his head made it difficult to see. His motion was erratic. He was dazed. His arms flayed around. He was suffering under the weight of the blow to his head.

Standing knee-deep in the water, the Shawnee warrior yelled at him, "*Combattez-moi. Mourir dans la dignité, pas comme un chien.*"

Pride ruled this man's heart. He wanted Shiloh to rise up and fight him rather than taking an easy kill. My understanding of French might have been incomplete, but it seemed he wanted the honor of killing this Powhatan warrior in battle rather than killing him like a dog. I feared Shiloh would die if he continued to fight. As it was, his legs gave way and he slumped back into the water.

I had to do something. I challenged the old man to fight me by insulting him. "*Fais-moi face, bâtard!*"

Calling him a bastard aroused a sense of indignity in him. The Shawnee warrior turned to face me. Blood ran from the cut in his side. I had no weapon, no hope. All I could do was try to buy time for Shiloh to recover. Words can cut as deep as any knife, so I taunted the old man, blaming him for his son's death.

"*Vous avez tué votre fils. Pas moi. Pas mes amis. Vous. C'est ce que vous avez fait. Toi et ta stupidité.*"

It wasn't Chebona that killed his son. It was his own greed and stupidity. As I spoke, I kept my eyes on him, but my fingers continued searching the pebbles at the bottom of the muddy river. Shiloh groaned. He rolled over, struggling to get to his feet. He could see what was happening. He tried to step away from the bank, but his legs threatened to collapse beneath him.

The old man said, "*Vous allez mourir. La dernière chose que vous verrez, ce sont mes yeux. Et vous connaîtrez la terreur.*"

428

As long as he was telling me I was going to die, I was gaining more time to search for my knife. He was arrogant, standing in the water with his muscles flexing. He had bested two Powhatan braves and now had a woman cowering before him. My mocking had worked too well, for he came for me without mercy.

His fingers gripped my neck. I grabbed his wrists, wanting to wrench his hands away, but he was too strong. Murder filled his eyes. This was more than anger, more than hatred. There was a sense of satisfaction on his face. He was enjoying this.

He pushed my head beneath the water. I choked, unable to breathe.

I released my grip on his hands. My only hope lay with the knife. My fingers pushed at the rocks and pebbles on the bottom of the river, frantically trying to find the knife. He dragged me back up. Water washed over my face. I gasped for air, barely able to breathe. He smiled. He wanted to see me suffer. No sooner had I grabbed a breath than he plunged me back into the river again, squeezing my neck with his iron grip.

Pain washed over me. Darkness surrounded me. The veins in my neck throbbed. Then, there, beneath my fingers, lay a narrow piece of bone. Its smooth, worn surface had been honed by years of use before Wynono gifted it to me on my arrival in the Powhatan village. My fingers wrapped around the handle. I could feel the steel blade embedded in the sand.

The Shawnee warrior dragged me back out of the river again. Water streamed down my face, washing over my hair. In that instant, though, the hatred on his face faded. I don't think he knew quite what was going to happen, but he could see something had changed within me as I wasn't terrified of him anymore. My fear had been replaced with a surge of strength. He could see it in my eyes, of that I was sure. Even before my knife struck his neck, he knew he would die.

I swung my knife up over his shoulder, striking the side of his neck. A single blow punctured his skin. Blood sprayed from the wound. His grip on me eased. I fell away into the river. He staggered, grasping at his neck, unable to stem the flow of blood. As I got to my feet, I watched him collapse. He floated face down in the water, surrounded by a dark cloud of blood that pooled on the surface. His lifeless body drifted out into the current.

"Koda," a kind voice said. I turned and looked. Shiloh was standing knee-deep in the water with a knife in his hand. His shoulders were stooped. Blood ran down his neck and over his chest. Our eyes met, and he nodded out of respect.

Chebona staggered into view. He stood on the bank, holding onto a tree as he steadied himself.

I said, "I should have killed that French-speaking bastard before I fled from his camp."

My voice came out as a croak, and it hurt to talk.

I crumpled in the shallows. Shiloh came to me, kneeling down by my side.

"Are you all right?"

"Not really. My head is spinning. When I move, I feel like I'm going to be sick."

Tenderly, he reached over my shoulder and helped me stand. Together, we climbed the bank, pulling on roots to reach the clearing above. Chebona staggered over by the horses. He looked pale.

"We need to go," I said.

"You need to rest," Shiloh replied. "You can't ride just yet."

"But Chebona?" I managed to say, still feeling overwhelmed but concerned for his welfare.

"I'll send him ahead on a horse. He needs the shaman and the refuge of the healing hut. We'll follow once you're feeling better."

"No. We should all go together."

"We should, but he needs to go now, and you cannot ride."

I didn't have the strength to argue. I crawled into the sun and lay down on the warm grass, closing my eyes.

After some discussion, Shiloh helped his brother onto the horse. I sat up, resting my back against a tree. The world seemed to sway around me. It was all I could do not to vomit. As he left, Chebona held up his hand and waved to me. The rhythmic fall of his horse's hooves faded into the distance as I watched him leave. His body bent forward as he rode off down the trail. Blood was seeping from the wound on his head as well as his back. The sun set in front of him. I lamented that we hadn't been able to say our goodbyes properly.

Shiloh walked toward me, holding my journal. The arrow was still embedded in the thick leather cover. He wrenched the stone head out and tossed the arrow into the river. I was surprised to see him smile as he handed me the book.

"Koda, your sketches saved me. Everything happened so fast back there. A flicker between the trees alerted me, and my instinct took over. I turned with your book, holding it like a shield, and it spared my soul. Had I not lost my footing, I would've taken him."

I laughed and said, "Oh, no, he was mine for the taking."

He chuckled. "I guess he was."

My fingers ran over the jagged edges of the hole as I looked at the first few pages.

"Is it ruined?" he asked.

"It's perfect. Now it tells its own story."

Although I tried to hide it, my hands were still shaking. Little by little, normality returned. My head still ached but keeping my eyes closed helped me feel better. That was something I could do on the horse.

"I think I'm ready," I said to Shiloh, not wanting to fall too far behind Chebona.

"If you're sure, then I'll have you ride sidesaddle. That way, you can lean your head on my chest. If it is too much, little one, we can stop for a while."

"How will we make it back in the dark?" I asked.

"The trail to the village is simple enough. The horses know it well. I wouldn't have sent Chebona off on his own otherwise."

I nodded, which was a bad idea. A sharp pain ran across the side of my head.

Shiloh mounted the horse and held out his hand for me, helping me climb up in front of him. We sauntered off through the woods, following the trail in the moonlight.

"Your parents didn't approve of the match then," Shiloh said. "Is that why you came back?"

With everything else that had gone on recently, I'd forgotten what else had been happening.

"There was an outbreak of smallpox at the fort."

"No," he said. I felt him stiffen behind me. He spurred the horse on. What was he doing? Did he think we'd gone inside the fort to talk to my parents?

I complained, "Shiloh, slow down. We're not sick. We didn't get close enough to be infected. We'd be showing symptoms by now if we were because that was almost a week ago."

Mercifully he drew in the reins.

His voice softened as he spoke from the heart. "Whole villages have been wiped out by that disease. It's an enemy no one can see and kills even the strongest among us."

He started checking the skin on my arms for lesions.

"Shiloh, stop it."

I batted his hands away in frustration.

"Koda, you went into the cursed ground, and now all these things are happening."

"You're talking nonsense," I replied. "Firstly, the outbreak stemmed from a trader who came into town weeks ago. Then Chebona's injury came from the man hunting us before we went to the burial ground. That piece of land saved our lives. With your help, of course."

I'd totally forgotten to thank Shiloh. If it wasn't for him, we would be dead.

"I hope you're right, Koda. The will of the ancestors is strong. It is not to be ignored."

"You really believe the dead can affect the living?"

"There are things that can't be explained in this realm. The mind, body and spirit are interconnected, just as the spiritual world connects with the physical one."

"That may be true," I said, "but it doesn't mean that you can attribute it to the dead."

I leaned into him, signaling I was finished with this conversation. These beliefs had been ingrained in his culture for centuries. One conversation was not going to alter his opinion, but it might plant a seed of reason.

I looked forward to getting back to the village. Peace and quiet is what we needed to heal. Since Chebona and I were together now, maybe we could have a place of our own. That would be nice, but I knew I wasn't up to caring for Chebona by myself yet. He'd need constant attention throughout the night and possibly for many days after that.

The way back was slow and laborious. Within an hour, we'd caught up to Chebona.

I felt Shiloh take in a quick breath as we approached. Chebona was slumped over his horse's neck. The dumb animal had taken the opportunity to eat grass on the side of the path.

Shiloh shook my shoulder gently.

"Do you think you can go on alone, Koda? We only have a couple of miles to go."

"What?" I said sleepily. As I focused my eyes, I saw the object of his concern. Chebona was on the verge of falling from his saddle.

"Don't worry. He's still breathing."

My breath caught in my throat.

I cried out, "You must ride back with him as quickly as you can."

Without a moment to lose, Shiloh swung himself down off the horse and took the reins of Chebona's mare. He steadied his brother with one hand as he climbed up into the saddle and then rode off, beckoning for me to follow.

"Hold on, my love," I said.

I rode behind them as quickly as my body would allow.

Family

It was still dark as I rode into the village. The steady beating of a drum resounded like a heartbeat. At the far end of the camp, villagers congregated around the medicine man's hut. As I got closer, I could see it was the same Shaman that had initiated Chebona into manhood. He chanted a solemn song. The haunting wail of his voice scared me.

My mind was racing. Were these funeral rites? For all our efforts, I feared Shiloh and I had been too late to save my beloved. What would happen to me? Wintering with the Powhatan would be heartbreaking without Chebona by my side.

Smoke rose from the opening at the top of the hut. I hoped this was a good sign. Coming to a stop outside, I dismounted. Shiloh stood by the entrance, holding the leather flap open for me.

"He's in here."

A waft of willow bark welcomed me as I stepped into the darkened room. I grew accustomed to the scent after a few deep breaths. Winema was applying a poultice to the wound on Chebona's back. He slept on his

435

stomach. Apart from the occasional twitch of his hand, he didn't move.

"Come and lie down," Winema said. "You're injured. Let me put some warm bark on your head. It'll help with the pain."

She cleaned my head wound, applied some of the soft, sticky bark and wrapped my forehead with a cloth. Then she handed me a cup, saying, "Drink some honeysuckle tea. It will help you sleep so your body can heal."

"How is Chebona?" I asked.

"Time will tell. He's fighting the spirits now, but he's strong. He wants to live."

The smoke made my eyes water. I rubbed my eyelids with my fingertips. Winema noticed.

"Close your eyes," she said. "The sick usually sleep in here, so the scent doesn't bother them. We've gathered the willow bark from the eastern side of the tree and will smoke the hut for days if need be. All these things we can do to help his body, but whether it will be enough, I know not. If his fever breaks in the next few days, he should get better. This Basra root will help his wound. Whenever he wakes, we need to keep giving him this herbal tea. The rest will be up to the Great Spirit. I'll stay and look after you both. Rest now, Koda, and try not to worry."

I closed my eyes and cupped the tea between my hands, its warmth gave me comfort. Leaning down on the furs with my back against the wall, I sipped.

After a while, I opened my eyes again. I know Winema said I shouldn't, but I had to see Chebona, even if only faintly. I watched as Winema tended to him. Over time the chanting and pulsing beat of the drums caused my eyelids to grow heavy. My empty cup dropped onto the ground.

Sometime during the night, moaning woke me. Chebona tossed his head from side to side. My own head was feeling much better. Whatever was in that bark had worked wonders. I peeled the now cold strip from my head and leaned over to Chebona.

"I'm here, my love. All will be well."

I spoke this in part to convince myself. I felt his forehead and was surprised at its heat. He was burning up. Winema had fallen asleep, so I picked up the sponge and dipped it in the water beside him. I willed its coolness to do its work. Trickles of water flowed over him, and I dabbed at them.

"Koda," he mumbled weakly.

"Yes, shhh... Save your strength."

"Water."

I held a small bowl to his lips and dribbled the now-cool tea into his mouth. It was a slow process, but I was thankful he was taking it.

"It is too difficult," he complained.

"I know you don't get much like this," I said. "But just sip a little at a time."

"No, Koda. The fight. It's too difficult."

His confession surprised me.

"Don't you dare talk like that! You will not give up, do you hear me? We have so much more to do. Promise me you will fight this."

The desperation in my voice was scaring me.

He kept taking the fluid and reached for my hand.

"Good, one step at a time. I'll always be here. If it is getting too difficult, reach for me and I will pull you back to the living. I'll not give up on you, Chebona."

In the following days, he sought me out several times. Each time I would whisper in his ear and squeeze his hand, reeling him back from death's icy grip. I would talk about our life in the future. Our children and the home we would have. Painting a picture for him to reach toward.

On the fourth day, Chebona's fever broke, and I sobbed uncontrollably. He was still very weak, but I knew he was not on the edge of the cliff any longer. I could breathe again.

Over the past few days, Shiloh had built a hut for us, giving us somewhere we could call our own. Once Chebona had gained some strength, we moved him to our new lodgings. Each day I would rekindle the fire early.

How ironic it was that, just days ago, his life depended on keeping his body cool. Now he had lost so much weight that it was a constant struggle to keep him warm. He could only eat small amounts, and even then, more often than not, he would bring it up again. I held on to him at night and cradled him in my arms, thankful that he was still alive.

The camp had to move south before winter. This year it had been determined that the move would be short. With that in mind, the scouts had found a suitable site a couple of miles away, further down in the valley, where less snow would fall.

I was relieved. Moving Chebona would be hard enough as it was. Frantic preparations were made, with each household taking care of its own belongings. Wynono had given us all we needed inside our hut, and Shiloh insisted we share his cooking pot. There was no way Chebona was fit for hunting. I made him sit outside in the sun each day, wrapped warmly against the early winter chill. Sometimes I would take the net with me to the river to try and catch some fish, but it seemed even they were keen to move on to warmer places. Shako made healing soups and stews, and I was grateful for her labors.

On the day of the big move, all our worldly belongings sat on the back of a sleigh behind two horses. My ornate wooden chest had long since been broken up and used for firewood. It seemed an appropriate analogy for my old life passing away, allowing me to embrace the new one before me. Our bedding skins carried everything we owned wrapped within them. How easy it was to survive with so little. Over the past few weeks, I'd discovered what was truly important in life. As long as we had each other and we were safe, that was all that mattered.

The move to the new village site tired Chebona. He wasn't comfortable being back on a horse. As soon as we arrived, Shiloh helped with our hut, and I got him settled. He fell asleep almost immediately.

I longed for the day I would have my husband back. I knew it was selfish of me to want this so quickly. It was difficult caring for him like this when all I had ever known was his strength and happiness. Not only had the wound made his body weak, but now he was just a shell of the man I had once known. It was as if his whole identity had been affected when his strength diminished. In the healing hut, I would've given anything just to have him breathing. Now that I had been granted that wish, I would give anything to see his former glory return. Chebona didn't talk much during these days. I guess he felt he had nothing to contribute, but he didn't even ask after his nieces and nephews, who he adored. It was like he had visited death, and now living was too arduous for him.

I stood at our tent flap and watched the hustle and bustle of the village, wanting to be part of it all. We were still close enough to the river to hear the creatures that inhabited its waterways. Beavers felled saplings for their dams. Birds would land in the still bend of the river on their way south for the winter. Everywhere life was industrious, but I felt Chebona and I were standing still. Tears rolled down my cheeks. I quickly wiped them away once more, feeling guilty for my own self-pity. I decided that day to do something about changing our future.

"Do you want to come with me and collect specimens for my journal?"

I was hoping we could get back to our carefree days, but those hopes were dashed by his reply.

"Get Tonshee to help you. He'll be happy to do so."

I pleaded with him, "But I'd rather go with you."

"I'm not the one for that job."

He rolled over and faced the wall of our hut, indicating that our discussion was over.

Before winter set in, Tonshee and I gathered the medicinal bark, leaves and flowers I'd been learning about from Winema. It felt good to be productive. I pressed them and made notes on their importance. The women in the camp helped me make an extensive list of natural medicines to put in the book. My days were spent documenting these herbs and plants. I made another list for Dr. Taylor. I wondered when I'd see him or any of the townsfolk again.

Once again, I tried to snap Chebona out of his lethargy. I'd enjoyed my time with Tonshee and wondered if his uncle might find the same sense of relief with this young, enthusiastic boy.

The next day, I spoke to Chebona, saying, "I thought I might bring Tonshee here to play cards with you. The men have brought in a buffalo. I need to help the women prepare it."

My aim was two-fold. Since I could not snap Chebona out of his gloomy state, I thought his eldest nephew might be a welcome distraction. I desperately needed to escape the confines of our lodgings.

Chebona snapped at me, saying, "Are you sick of your husband already, then?"

I know I shouldn't have said it, but I felt humiliated by his stubborn attitude toward me, so I replied, "We're not married yet."

He reacted to that with, "You don't really want me anyway, do you?"

"Of course, I do," I said, trying to soften the argument.

"I'm not the same as I once was, Koda."

"Neither am I," I replied. "We've both been hurt, but we don't have to stay this way."

"You don't understand me. You can't understand."

"You really are trying to push me away, aren't you?"

"I don't blame you. I'm no man like this."

It broke my heart to hear him talking in this manner.

"Look, Chebona, I don't expect you to be better already, and neither should you, but you must make some effort."

"I can't."

"I think you can. Start small. Spend time with others. Talk with them. Remember why life is worth living. Stop thinking about all the things you can't do, and focus on doing something new each day. After a while, you won't have to try at all."

He hung his head. I could see he was struggling. Deep down, he wanted to change, but it was difficult for him. I reached out and took his hand, saying, "I want my husband back."

I bent over him, put my hands on either side of his face and kissed him gently on the forehead.

"Please," I whispered.

"I'll try," he responded.

I kissed his lips, tenderly at first and then with more vigor. He did not return my enthusiasm. My heart ached.

"You promised you would try," I said.

"You ask too much."

"I'll be back later. Be nice to Tonshee. He'll be confused if he sees his uncle like this."

I lifted the tent flap. The cold wind stung my face, but it didn't hurt as much as the pain in my soul. The first snow had begun to fall.

A month passed, and my thoughts, as they so often did, turned to my family and friends. By now, the quarantine on the pox should have lifted for both the fort and Williamsburg. I knew Papa would be busy with his troops, while Mama would be helping where she could. I hoped my parents weren't worried about me. I longed to get a message to them, but that would have to wait. How were the townsfolk faring? It was hard not having any news from them. Anything could have happened, and I'd be none the wiser.

Chebona had been making more of an effort of late and now visited others in the camp. Sometimes I would even hear his laughter, particularly in Shiloh's hut, and when I did, I wouldn't enter for fear of interrupting them.

By now, it was far too cold to bathe in the river. Although some of the tribe did jump in and out quickly, that wasn't my idea of fun. I much preferred to warm some water in a pot and clean myself with a cloth. Taking clothes off in winter wasn't worth the effort, except to bask in the warmth of the fire. I was surprised that the men continued to hunt. I guess the snow made it easier for them to pull large kills behind the horses on the sleds.

I knew how much it hurt Chebona not to be a part of these expeditions. I tried to distract him with tales of my home back in England.

"You'll return there one day?" he asked.

"Not without you. We'll go together. Although I'm sure you'll not enjoy crossing the Atlantic."

"Why do you say so? I love the water. It would be like a dream to be surrounded by the ocean and not able to see land."

I dared not mention the storms that so often took lives. "If you're lucky, you'll see a whale—a great sea beast, as large as many buffalo, which spouts water through a hole on the top of its head."

"I should like to catch that fish. It could feed us for many moons."

I laughed. "It's not a fish but a mammal that gives birth to live young and suckles its babies with milk."

"You lie."

"No, it's true, I swear," I grinned.

Slowly, Chebona was coming back to me, giving me hope that the days ahead would be brighter.

A loud commotion outside our home brought our attention back to reality. Coming out of the hut, we saw Wynono leading a group of braves. Five deer carcasses were tied to the sleds behind their horses. This was a good kill. For the past week, we'd gone without fresh meat. The dried stores we had, although plentiful, would not sustain us through winter. Women, young and old, danced around the men celebrating their good fortune. Several cutting stations were set up by the women eager to butcher the meat and get it into the pot for dinner. We cooked inside the huts now as it was too cold to stay outside for long. This meant that our home had the delicious smell of food all day. We were both putting on weight, but in Chebona's case, I was happy.

I put on an apron and stepped out into the cold. My warm breath swirled around me in clouds, fanning my face. The tiny droplets were content to hang in the air. I rubbed my hands together. It was not good having numb fingers when dealing with a sharp knife.

Our hut was set next to Wynono's lodge. After the attack, he wanted to keep an eye on his little brother. He was good to us, often bringing over a warm drink or stopping by to tell us about the goings on in the village.

After Tonshee started coming to our hut, the chief's other children also began visiting. There was something about the young ones' company that didn't let any of us stay too serious for long. Their zest for life encouraged Chebona to become their fun-loving uncle once more.

I shared the cutting station with Winema at the rear of the camp. The knives made a satisfying sound while blood dripped vivid red on the snow beneath our feet.

Aponi had her infant son strapped to her breast in a roll of leather called a papoose. His little head was covered in furs to keep him warm.

"Isn't it easier to work without him on you?" I asked as I drew my blade between the skin and flesh of the buck's hind leg.

"You wouldn't say that if you had children." Aponi smiled. "Don't you know it's worse if you put them down? All they do is cry, wanting to be next to their mother."

Winema looked at me knowingly. "Speaking of that, Koda, I haven't seen you at the women's hut for a while. Nearly two moons have passed since the last time we were there together. Of course, it's understandable since you were still caring for Chebona."

Winema was right. I hadn't noticed I'd missed my last two cycles. My time and attention had been focused solely on my husband. Hope surged in my breast, and I smiled, knowing how much this would mean to him. In summer, I could be a mother. My parents had no idea I was even married. Well, technically, I wasn't in the eyes of the church or even our village. Chebona hadn't been well enough to have a ceremony, and no one had pressed him about it, knowing it was more important that he recover. Polite society might think this was inappropriate, but their approval meant nothing to me. Marriage was more than a formality. Marriage was the exchanging of vows before those you trusted, making the commitment that you would spend the rest of your lives together. We hadn't had the chance to make those vows yet, but I knew we would.

The idea that a tiny life was forming inside me was quite remarkable.

"Koda, are you all right?" Aponi asked.

"She has realized she's been granted a wonderful gift," Winema answered. "You must go and tell Chebona. Tonight, we'll have more to celebrate than the killing of these deer."

"I can hardly believe it," I said.

I washed my knife and put it in its sheath.

"Do you think there could be some mistake? I might just be stressed. I've heard that happens to women sometimes. I'd hate to tell Chebona only to find out I wasn't with child at all. To get his hopes up if it was not true would crush him."

I knew I was babbling, but this was important to me.

Winema came over and probed my stomach.

"You've put on weight."

"Maybe that's from overeating."

"Or maybe you are eating for two."

She put one hand on my breast and squeezed gently.

"Oww, what are you doing, Winema?"

"They are tender, yes?"

"Yes."

"All the signs are there, Koda. Go and find your man. This is a joyful time for you both. Celebrate and be happy in your good fortune."

I found Chebona with his brothers in Wynono's hut. Thick smoke swirled as they sat, passing the pipe amongst themselves.

Wynono looked surprised to see me.

"Is everything all right?" Chebona asked, seeing the blood on my apron. I hadn't thought to take it off before I came in. Usually, a woman would clean herself before entering a hut.

"Yes, I'm fine. Can I speak with you outside?"

Chebona got up and came over, bringing two furs with him. Concern was written all over his handsome face. We stepped out into the bitter cold. I took off my apron and draped it over a log. Chebona wrapped a fur around my shoulders. He shivered beneath his cloak. Not wanting to keep him outside for long, I asked, "Are you well?"

"I think I should be asking you that. You're starting to scare me. What happened?"

I took a deep breath.

"I mean, are you well enough to commit yourself to me?"

He took my hands in his with regret in his eyes. "What? I'm sorry, Koda, I've not been acting like the man you deserve these past few weeks."

"It's not that. I believe I'm going to have a child, and I need to know that you're willing to marry me. I thought it didn't matter, but I realized while walking over here that it does. It's what I want."

His eyes went wide. "You're with child?" He held his hand near my stomach. He looked shocked. "But we've not known each other since before my accident."

"I know. But I hadn't been paying attention to my cycles. It was only when Winema mentioned that I'd not been to the women's hut that I stopped and thought about why. I'm pregnant, Chebona. You're going to be a father."

He stood silent. A large grin lit up his face.

"You haven't answered my question," I said.

"I'm just so happy. What was the question again?"

I laughed, saying, "We have promised ourselves to one another but not before anyone else. I think it is only right for the sake of our child that we do so."

Chebona said, "If you're asking me to marry you, of course, I will. However, I am ashamed we didn't do this sooner. When do you want it to be? Tonight? After all, we have enough food for a celebration."

He pulled me into his arms and kissed me. The earthy taste of tobacco was still on his tongue. His lips were soft and full. His hands pulled me to him. His mouth was hungry. I moaned into him.

"I have missed you," he said, tearing himself away. "You were right in front of me the whole time, and I couldn't see it for my own self-pity."

"Shhh, all is well. You took some time to heal. Healing takes place in the mind too, not just the body."

"You sound like a wise old native."

I hit him playfully on the chest. "Hey, not so much of the old, if you don't mind."

"Come," he said. "We must share our news with my brothers and make preparations."

"You really want to do this tonight?" I asked.

"Why not live in the moment, my love? It makes life exciting, does it not?"

I had to agree it did.

Commitment

Winema fastened a cloak of ornate feathers over my shoulders. Although I was familiar with the browns and blacks of outer feathers, having used them as quills with ink, I'd never thought of feathers as a fabric before. I hadn't known how soft and warm the white inner vanes were with their fluffy, wispy ends. The feathers there were as soft as down, while the layers looked majestic. It was as though I were ready to take flight.

Under the cloak, I wore a bright red smock covering my deerskin leggings. Brilliant beadwork adorned the bodice. Once I was joined to Chebona, I would shed the cloak, revealing the vibrant colors beneath.

Winema said, "This is what I wore when the chief and I were joined."

"It's beautiful."

"Are you sure you understand the vows we discussed?"

I nodded. I'd been rehearsing them in my mind as I got ready.

Thank goodness, Chebona would take the lead, and I would only need to repeat his words for the most part. I told myself if I didn't get it word-perfect, the heart of it was all that mattered.

A large fire had been started that afternoon and diligently tended until it blazed against the frozen ground. The tribe was in the mood for a celebration. Snowflakes fell from the darkened sky, but they were breezy, adding an air of mystique to the occasion. They shone like stars in the firelight. The smell of sage filled the air.

Amidst my happiness, sadness wove its way in. My family had no idea any of this was happening. I wished Mama and Papa were here with me. I stood a little straighter, smoothing the fine feathers under my fingers. My new native family was waiting for me outside.

I wondered if Maggie and Charles were married yet. Their wedding should have happened by now. How ironic that our unions would be so different. As young girls, we'd planned and talked about this day countless times. Walking down the aisle on the arms of our fathers, resplendent in pleated white satin, it would be the greatest day of our lives. In England, my dress would have been supported by a wide pannier, giving me an air of elegance, but that couldn't compare to the regal feeling of thousands of fine feathers that formed my cloak. Back there, my beau would wait for me at the end of the aisle in his finest jacket, waistcoat and breeches. The church would've been filled with flowers while musicians played sweet melodies, but out here, the wilderness was our chapel.

"It's time," Winema said.

She led me to the fire where Wynono stood, looking every bit the chief, being resplendent in his feathered headdress and ornate leather clothing. The rest of the tribe was gathered in a half-circle behind me.

Chebona emerged from his hut, and my heart soared. He had on new deerskin fringed leggings and a beaded vest. Over his shoulders hung a grey wolf cloak that reached to the ground. This man had risked it all for me many times, proving his love. In the end, all that mattered was the person standing beside me. All my doubts vanished. Here was where I wanted to be. Standing there in the snow, this is how I wanted to be joined to my man. I had come to know, love and respect him over the past few months. We'd been through so much in our short time together. I felt like I had already known Chebona for a lifetime. We'd faced the trials of life together and had overcome them.

Our church was nature, and our priest was a leader of people from a proud and loyal family. There may not have been bells ringing out over the English countryside, but the crackle of burning wood was every bit as harmonious as a church organ. We were surrounded by those who would freely give anything to see us succeed. I couldn't have asked for more than that.

Wynono first washed my hands, then Chebona's, signifying our cleansing before the Great Spirit. The chief's voice rang out loud and clear.

"Now you will feel no rain,
for each of you will be shelter for each other.
Now you will feel no cold,
for each of you will be warmth for each other.
Now there is no loneliness,
for each of you will be companion to the other.
Now you are two bodies,
but there is only one life before you.
Enter into the days of your life together with thankfulness,
and may your days be good and long upon the Earth."

After Wynono finished, Chebona took a few steps to his left. He was shuffling around the fire while reciting his vows, as designated by Powhatan tradition. He spoke the first of our seven vows to each other.

"O, my beloved,
our love has become firm by your walking together with me.
Together we will share the responsibilities of the lodge, food and

449

children.

May the Creator bless noble children to share.

May they live long."

Once he'd finished, I took a step toward him, following his lead, and recited my first vow.

"This is my commitment to you, my husband.

Together we will share responsibility of the home, food and children.

I shall share the responsibilities for the welfare of the family and the children."

He took another couple of steps away from me, moving around the vast fire.

"O, my beloved,

now you have walked the second step.

May the Creator bless you.

I will love you and you alone as my wife.

I will fill your heart with strength and courage.

This is my commitment and my pledge to you.

May Ahone protect the lodge and the children."

I closed the gap between us once more, bringing us back together. I loved the way our vows mirrored each other in a kind of call/response.

"My husband,

at all times, I shall fill your heart with courage and strength.

In your happiness, I shall rejoice.

May God bless you and our honorable lodge."

I couldn't take my eyes off Chebona. The light of the fire radiated off his face, making the cold of winter seem like a summer's day.

"O, my beloved,
now since you have walked three steps with me,
our wealth and prosperity will grow.
May Ahone bless us.
May we educate our children,
and may they live long."

Slowly, the two of us made our way around the fire.

"My husband,
I love you with single-minded devotion.
I will treat all other men as my brothers.
My devotion to you is pure, and you are my joy.
This is my pledge and commitment to you."

The women of the tribe shed tears watching us, which only served to strengthen my love for them.

"O, my beloved,
it is a great blessing that you have walked four steps with me.
May the Creator bless you.
You have brought favor and sacredness to my life."

Emotion welled up within me. My voice broke as I spoke.

"O, my husband,
in all acts of righteousness,
in material prosperity,
in every form of enjoyment,
I shall participate,
and I will always be with you."

I think I missed some of the words in that vow. I'm sure it was longer. Chebona smiled at me. He knew, but he didn't care. Such was our love.

"O, my beloved,
now you have walked five steps with me.
May the Creator bless and make us prosperous."

I was thankful that some of the vows were succinct.

"O, my husband,
I will share both in your joys and sorrows.
Your love will make me very happy."

By this time, Chebona had circled around the fire and was almost back in front of Wynono. Wood crackled. A branch within the fire collapsed, causing sparks to rise up into the heavens.

"O, my beloved,
by walking six steps with me,
you have filled my heart with happiness.
May I fill your heart with great joy and peace, time and time
again.

May the Creator bless you."

I stepped closer to Chebona again. It was all I could do not to reach out and take his hand, but we hadn't completed our vows yet.

"My husband,
the Creator blesses you.
May I fill your heart with great joy and peace.
I promise I will always be with you."

Chebona took the final step, and we were nearly back in front of Wynono.

"O, my beloved,
as you have walked the seven steps with me,
our love and friendship has become inseparable and firm.
We have experienced spiritual union in Ahone.
Now you have become completely mine.
I offer my total self to you.
May our marriage last forever."

I felt my heart racing.

"My husband,
by the laws of our Creator,
and the spirits of our honorable ancestors,
I have become your wife.
Whatever promises I gave you,
I have spoken them with a pure heart.
All the spirits are witnesses to this fact.

I shall love you forever."

I took his hand in mine. Wynono closed with a prayer.

"God in heaven above,
please protect the ones we love.
We honor all you created,
as we pledge our hearts and lives together.
We honor Mother Earth
and ask for this marriage to be abundant
and grow strong through the seasons.
Uniting our tribes and our peoples as one."

Drums began beating in a steady rhythm, concluding the ceremony.

Chebona grabbed both of my hands and led me to our hut. A fire crackled in the middle of the floor. The pit was surrounded by rocks to catch any sparks. Beyond them lay fur skins, soft and lavish.

"Aren't we staying for the celebrations?"

"First, I want to be with my wife. I thought you might like that, too."

I smiled, glad to have my husband's attention back.

Inside, our lodge was clean, warm and cozy. I'd had plenty of time on my hands over the last month to make our new hut comfortable, but for now, there was only one thing on our minds.

Chebona unfastened my feather cloak and gently folded it along with his fur robe. I worked my shirt over my head and undid my leggings.

He gazed at me with appreciation, admiring my body in the flickering light.

"I missed you," he whispered, pulling me to him.

He undid the ribbons in my hair, letting it fall in soft waves around my shoulders. He ran his fingers through my long locks and held them up to his face.

"I love everything about you, my wife."

I assured him, "The feeling is mutual. But you know what I love the most?"

He whispered close to my ear. "Tell me."

"Your soul. It's beautiful, pure and honest. There's not another person in this world who's as wonderful as you. I can't believe we are now one."

He looked up at the roof of our hut as if talking to the gods. "What have I done to deserve such a woman?"

I brought his head back down to my lips. "You've been yourself."

I kissed him then. Slow and passionate, with all the feeling that I had inside.

When we parted, we were breathless.

I laughed. "You have too many clothes on and have me at a disadvantage."

I helped lift his shirt over his head. His wound still pained him to move, but it was healing well, and there was no sign of infection. He'd have a scar on his back, but he would wear it with honor, knowing he had killed the man who had given it to him. He fumbled with his leggings, his desire evident as they fell to the floor. I marveled at his form. He'd lost some weight, which made his muscles appear even more defined.

"What will you do with me, my love?"

I could think of a few things, but I let my actions speak for me. I led him to the pile of furs that made up our bed and indicated that he should lie there.

Leaning over him, my mouth explored his body, and my hands followed. His hair smelt of sage and smoke, a wonderfully heady combination. His hands roamed my body. His fingers drew tiny patterns over me. The firelight cast shadows over his exposed skin, begging to be explored. First, his chest and stomach, then lower around his loins.

"Koda," he groaned.

I looked up. His shaft grew stiff in my hands. I kissed it. My mouth toyed with the pulsating tip. My tongue slid over the smooth skin with ease. He tensed as my mouth closed over him, pushing his hips to meet me. Such power I had over this man, and I gloried in it. It felt more intimate to me like this than when he was inside me. Here I could control his joy without being distracted by my own.

I rocked back and forth, I moved my lips while my hands fondled his sack.

Drums continued to beat outside while my mouth kept time.

His breathing came in ragged gasps, and I pulled away before he came. I wanted him inside me now.

I lay back on the pelts and drew his head to my breasts. He sucked my soft skin. His tongue fluttered over my nipples. His fingers circled my bud, making me wet and ready to receive him. When I thought I could stand it no longer, he bade me to turn around and entered me from behind while he stroked my back. The pounding in my loins, the pounding of my heart and the pounding of the drums seemed to work in unison as we delighted in each other. Sounds so primal but so sensual swirled around us. I noticed our silhouettes cast on the wall of the hut. With all my senses overwhelmed, I cried out, unable to contain my ecstasy any longer. In the final moments of my release, I heard him call out my name.

"Koooooda."

Hearing him call out my name with such passion, melted my heart.

Slowly we came back down to Earth. We lay there spent, my head resting on his chest. Chebona played with my hair, curling it in his fingers.

After a few minutes, he said, "I suppose we should return to our celebration."

"If it weren't for the food, I would gladly stay here forever."

"Ah, yes, you must keep my son strong and healthy."

"What makes you so sure it will be a son?" I asked teasing him.

"Wait and see. I'm sure of it."

$\mathscr{L}etters$

That winter was cold and harsh, but our love kept us warm. The days were short, with long nights. One evening, Shiloh rushed to our hut and called for us to come outside.

"What is it?" Chebona said, clambering to get his feet in his thick leather moccasins as I wrapped myself in a pelt and stepped out into the snow behind him.

"The spirits smile at us. They smile on you and Koda."

I was confused, I didn't know what he meant. Shiloh's wife, Shako, stood behind him, pointing north over the hills. High in the sky, curtains of light descended upon the mountains. I stood there with my mouth open. I'd never seen anything so beautiful. Chebona wrapped his arms around my shoulders and held me close as we watched the lights dance before us. Glowing green ribbons wound their way through the sky.

"What is that?" I asked.

Chebona said, "It is the great spirit, Nanabozho. Each winter, he ventures to the north and signals with fire, letting us know that although he has departed our lands, he has not forgotten us. Seeing this is a good sign for our marriage. It's a blessing."

When we returned to our hut, I sat by the fire and drew sketches of the night sky in my journal, noting not just the shapes but the way they moved as if they were alive. I wondered if this had been observed by English naturalists, as I'd never seen or heard of these northern lights before.

As the days grew longer, shoots began to appear on the trees. New life sprouted around us, once again proving its ability to overcome adversity. Fresh grass and tiny wildflowers littered the once-barren spaces pushing up through the ground. Birds and animals scurried around in an endless search for food for their new offspring, and I emerged from my hut significantly rounder than before. None of my clothes fit now. Winema gave me her pregnancy clothes.

"You'll have your baby before I need them again," she said. She was still hopeful that she and the chief could increase their family.

Chebona had returned to full strength and vigor. Our nights were a testament to that. Married life agreed with me very well. I had no complaints at all. Only one unresolved issue kept invading my thoughts.

We'd talked about visiting my parents. Chebona would not risk us all returning to them, such was his concern for me and our unborn child. After much deliberation, I agreed to write a note explaining our situation, which he would relay, along with gifts for my parents. He was going to deliver these in person, accompanied by two other braves. One was the father of a young man who, like Chebona, was a scout at the fort. Knowing that smallpox had broken out, he was keen to learn of his son's welfare. The father must have been deeply worried. Being a parent, it seemed, held its own troubles. I hoped for his sake that the boy had avoided the curse of this disease.

After our last experience visiting the fort, I had to agree with Chebona. We didn't know the state of things there. Besides, in my condition, it would be a slow and tedious journey. If it was still not possible to have contact with those in the fort, at least a note could be left announcing our marriage. I didn't fancy turning up on their doorstep with a baby. That might be too much of a surprise. I'd rather ease my parents into my decision. Turning up in person would be a huge shock.

The men in the village spent their days divided between hunting and preparing the fields for planting. As soon as one area was ready, the women would come behind them and plant the crops. Once all the fields were seeded, Chebona would go to the fort. Every person was needed to ensure the success of the crops and the continuation of life in the village. From the doorway of our hut, I could see my husband turning over the soil in the next field. It was good to see him using his arms easily once more. He'd come home at night exhausted but happy.

I'd become quite proficient at making herbal medicines. Not being content just to document them in my journal, I spent many hours collecting plants and making concoctions, all under the wise tutorage of Winema, of course. Some I found worked better than others, although we had to be careful with the amount of each plant we used and the dose given. I erred on the side of caution, not wanting to make someone sicker than they already were. It was a skill that their culture had honed for centuries. One recent infusion of the narrow-leaved purple coneflower proved beneficial to Chebona for relieving the stiffness in his shoulder. I combined it with bear fat to soothe his aching muscles after a long day in the fields. It gave me pleasure to rub this over his body.

Everyone, including pregnant women, were expected to take part on planting days. Sweat dripped into my eyes, and I wiped my brow with my hands. Straightening my back, I looked at the small mounds of earth that housed the squash seeds. Row upon row dotted the fields, reminding me of a very methodical rabbit. Bending over like this was uncomfortable. Now and again, the baby would move, adjusting its position. Across from me, Shako worked on her row of beans in silence. Shiloh, who had recently returned from a hunt, walked between the rows offering us water. The cool liquid felt good. After I'd quenched my thirst, I poured some over my head. Shako looked at me. Disapproval evident in her eyes.

"Is she all right?" I asked Shiloh as I handed the scoop back to him.

He spoke softly so she wouldn't hear his reply. "She is unhappy. How can a sick man give a woman a child while a strong one cannot? It doesn't make sense to her."

Shako held out her hand for water, snatching it from him. There was no easy solution for them, and I was reminded that even in such a simple existence, there was heartache and sorrow. That was life. It had good times and bad, and no one was immune from either, no matter what we did or didn't do.

By evening, I was so tired I didn't have the energy to write that all-important letter to my parents. During the day, I would think about the things I wanted to include. Many thoughts buzzed around my head, like the insects that annoyed us as we were planting.

Finally, the weather gave me the opportunity to write. A spring rain swept through the village for two days making planting impossible. Of course, the men still hunted and fished as our need for food never diminished. I pulled out Papa's gift. The ornate box that housed the ink and quills stared back at me.

After several drafts, I was finally satisfied with my letter.

Dear Papa and Mama,

I hope this message finds you well and that the disease in both the town and fort has abated.

How hard it has been these past few months being separated from your loving presence. I've found great consolation in my Powhatan family, for they have accepted me as one of their own.

You may be wondering why I haven't come with Sunny back to the fort. It is for a joyous reason. You are soon to be grandparents! Sunny and I were married last winter. That was why we traveled to the fort previously—to talk to you about this. Unforeseen circumstances prevailed against us with the outbreak of the pox. Be happy for me, for I am happy beyond words. I am well, and the babe is growing quickly inside me. It is due to be delivered in the sixth week of summer.

This is not perhaps the life you would've chosen for me, but it is the one I've chosen for myself. I hope you'll be glad for us both. Sunny and I are determined to spend time uniting our two cultures and would like your blessing. He has brought gifts for you. These come at a significant cost to him and his family, so please accept them graciously. As soon as it is safe for me to travel, I'll come and see you again.

I look forward to receiving your reply.

Your loving daughter,

Ally

They would be shocked. Of that, there was no doubt. I just hoped they would treat Chebona well, for it would make things difficult if they didn't. Could they see beyond their initial reaction to the love we shared? If they could, this would work.

I wrote to Maggie and Rhett as well.

Dear Maggie,

Oh, how I miss you! I'm sure you've written, but I haven't been at the fort due to an outbreak of smallpox, so I have not received any letters from home. I can only imagine how you would have recounted your marriage in your letters. I hope married life is all you hoped it would be. You must think me a terrible friend, for I know this is only the second letter I've written, but circumstances prevented me from corresponding. I am well, but my father had me stay away from the fort for safety's sake. And I have news of my own. I hope you are sitting down, for I fear you may faint if you aren't.

My life has been full speed ahead since I set foot on the ship bound for America. I've been living with a Powhatan native tribe for the past few months. During this time, I've come to know and love one of the men from their village. I imagine your hand has come up to cover your mouth in shock by now. I am married and expecting a child in the summer. Chebona is a wonderful man, and if you ever meet him, which I hope you will, you'll find this to be true for yourself. I am happy, and although my life is quite different from English life, I am content and could not ask for more. I am writing to Rhett now, so I ask that you not discuss this with him until he has read his letter from me. I want to be the one to tell him.

463

I know your wish had always been for us to be sisters, and we often talked about our families joining. I'd thought of that too, but our heart dictates its course in the end, and some plans don't always work out. Please know that our bond will always be of the utmost importance to me, no matter the circumstance.

I look forward to our two families meeting each other as soon as possible.

Your loving friend always,

Ally.

Rhett's letter was the hardest one to compose.

Dear Rhett,

I'm so sorry I was not able to write sooner. You wouldn't believe all the things that have happened to me since arriving in America. At the beginning of last winter, an outbreak of smallpox devastated the town and the fort. Thankfully, our family had been inoculated against this awful disease in England. There have been mob uprisings, kidnappings and native attacks. I cannot begin to thank you enough for all you taught me before I left. If it hadn't been for you, I wouldn't have been prepared for what was to come. I certainly wouldn't be here today to write about it to you. I don't mean to paint a horrible picture of my time in America, for it hasn't all been bad. I love my life here.

You'll notice I've sent you a journal depicting the native flora and fauna of the region where I've been living. Originally, Mr. Albert Miller was on the voyage with us. He was a young botanist who planned to document life in the Americas. Unfortunately, he died during the crossing, and I thought it a good idea to take up his endeavor myself with the help of a local tribe. Could you pass this on to Mr. Miller's father in the hope that he may find comfort in the fact that his son's mission was not in vain? As you can see, the address is written on the inside cover of the journal along with a dedication to Mr. Miller. My hope is that this may be published one day.

On a more personal note, I have some other news, and I hope you won't think ill of me. During my time here, I have wintered at the Powhatan camp and have come to love and respect the young man who helped me work on the journal.

Chebona and I married a few months ago. We are expecting a child this summer. I know you'll be shocked and may be shaking your head at me, thinking I've rushed into this, but I am happy. I hope you will be pleased for me. Life doesn't always turn out as we expect it might.

Give my love to your father and mother. I hope they are well. Until we see each other again, take care of yourself.

Ally

I didn't need to address our relationship, or lack thereof, in Rhett's letter. We'd made no promises to each other except to write. There were no declarations of feelings, only words that would never be said now. It seemed wrong to mention what could have been when there wasn't hope of it becoming a reality.

In my correspondence, I made sure to include a letter to Tommy and Millie. I hoped they were well. The tavern wouldn't have had any customers while smallpox ran its course. It wasn't only people's health that was at stake but their livelihoods as well. I was sure the town would rally around its community and help where needed. At least, I hoped so.

By the following week, the fields were finally finished and the tribe celebrated with a feast. When I first came to America, I expected the natives to be primitive and simple, eating only the most meager of meals. What I found was a culinary delight that would have impressed even Madame DuPont. Although we only ate game as a protein, it was enhanced with herbs that delighted the palate. Winema and Shako had tutored me in the art of balancing flavors. Wild garlic and sage were my favorites, and tonight's communal meal was beyond anything I'd ever tasted as they combined wild turkey with deer and field mushrooms. The rich abundance and variety of foods in America excited me. I determined my next book would be about them.

As the evening wore on, the realization that Chebona was leaving for the fort tomorrow sunk in. After our run-in with the Shawnee, I was nervous about him traveling back to Williamsburg. As we lay by the fire, he gently traced the curves of my bulging stomach with his fingers. The baby stirred within me.

"He is strong and eager to be in this world. Are you sure the dates are right? You seem bigger than five cycles?"

"It can't be earlier than that," I said. Although, I had wondered the same thing myself.

"Please be patient with my family, Chebona. This will be a shock for them. Imagine we had a daughter, and you sent her to the English camp. And she returned with a husband. How would you feel?"

"I know what you say, Koda. I'm expecting them to be angry with me for a time. This wasn't the task your father asked of me. I promise not to take it to heart. This world is changing, and the people within it. We'll not be the first, nor the last, to face such challenges."

"How long will you stay?" I asked.

"That's hard to answer. Many circumstances are unknown. If I can't get into the fort, I'll leave your letter and the gifts. Depending on what has happened to Karuk's son, I'll likely be gone for five days, maybe longer, but I don't want to be away from you for too long."

He pulled me closer to him, and I breathed in his familiar scent.

"Maybe it's too risky to stay at the fort," I said.

Worry started to invade my thoughts.

"I'll be careful," he said.

He kissed the top of my head.

"It pleases me you're still concerned about your husband's welfare," he chuckled. "I need to sleep now, my beautiful wife, or I'll be too tired to ride tomorrow. Things will work out as the Great Spirit intends."

I wondered exactly how much influence the Great Spirit had on the ways of humanity. I couldn't fault Chebona and his family for their sincerity and passion, but I wasn't convinced providence alone ruled our lives. I hoped Chebona was right, but I wondered what the future would hold.

The babe inside me twisted and rolled in a pattern that seemed impossible. It was active tonight, keeping me from my own slumber. I put my hand on my stomach and gently caressed the skin, hoping to calm it down. Taking some deep breaths, my breathing slowed, and little by little, the tiny life inside me found its own comfortable place.

As Chebona lay there on the furs, gently snoring, I watched the fire. By this time, it was smoldering but still throwing out warmth from its glowing coals. Occasionally, a burnt log would fall from its resting place. Flames would rise along with sparks. Seconds later, the fire would die back down. I found the flickering light soothing.

My letters and my journal lay by the door of the hut, neatly bound with twine, ready to be sent to Williamsburg and then on across the ocean. I could see the indentation from where the arrow had pierced my leather-bound sketchbook. There was nothing I could do about that scar. And even if there had been, I didn't know that I wanted it to be repaired. That scar saved a life. I hoped those that viewed my work would understand all it took to get this information to them. I was proud of my efforts and everyone that had helped me along the way. I remembered how my longing for adventure drove me to these shores. My life had changed in ways I couldn't have imagined back in England. So far, I'd lived through plenty of adventures, and I was sure there were more to come.

As my eyes became heavy, I basked in the warmth of the flames.

Thinking about my old home in Cambridge, I realized fire was a luxury I could walk away from. Here in the American wilderness, though, the fires that warmed our huts were life. Without them, we'd perish. Fire had come to surround me. It was raw and crackled with heat, bursting with energy. My passion for Sunny was ignited as we danced in front of the fire during his initiation. I'd been married in front of a bonfire that fought off the cold, bitter night.

For me, fire was a metaphor for life. All I could do was light my own flame. The course the fire would take was impossible to predict. In England, we tamed fire in a hearth. Here in the village, we surrounded it with rocks. But like me, fire longed to be free. With all I'd been through since those lazy days in the English countryside, I'd journeyed through the fire and out the other side. I had no regrets about the life I'd lived. As the fire continued to burn within my soul, I looked forward to all that lay ahead.

The End

Purple Coneflower (Echinacea)

Afterword

Writing *1770: Through the Fire* has been an adventure. I feel like I've been on a journey along with Ally. Perhaps one not so laced with danger or excitement but one of self-discovery. I'm an avid reader, but I'd never dreamed I could write a book. If it wasn't for my husband showing me it could be done, I wouldn't have attempted to write a novel. My interest started with editing his science fiction works and morphed from there.

The advent of Covid-19 had me give up my day job, and I found myself with spare time. Walks in the forest with Peter helped flesh out the direction of all our stories, although he wrote several novels to my one. I owe him a massive shout-out, and thanks for the time he's spent with me on this project.

Another huge thank you to my dear friend Geri, an English teacher who was my first beta reader and provided many helpful insights into grammar. Also, thank you to fellow writer Kat Fieler who took time out of her writing schedule to review this book for me. John Stephens, David Jaffe, LuAnn Miller and Karen Woodcock have all helped refine this work, and I thank them for stepping outside their usual genre. The illustrations in this novel were drawn by my talented daughter, Sarah Cawdron.

My appreciation for authors has increased a hundredfold. Writing is the easy part. The difficult part comes in the endless revising to get it to the point you're happy with the result. To quote Margaret Atwood, *"The waste paper basket is your friend,"* or, in my case, the delete key. To say I've put my heart and soul into this endeavor would be an understatement. Three years on and I can finally say I'm proud of my efforts. Absolute perfection belongs to God alone, so I hope you can forgive me for any oversights that may be found. Please know it was not for lack of trying.

Writing this debut novel came from my long-held interest in peoples and cultures long past. How they lived is fascinating. Their way of life was different from ours, but their emotions and feelings are something we can all relate to.

Neil Gaiman says authors write naked, and while reviewing this novel, my husband and I had a good chuckle at several points where my life has been laid bare in these pages. At one point, I use the word *palaver* to describe the commotion at Mrs. Tindale's house. This was a quiet nod to my late father, who seemed to use this obscure word at every opportunity. Were he here, he'd be happy to know the word *palaver* lives on.

I'm thankful and excited to inform you that *1770: Through the Fire* is part of the **Lunar Codex**. Dr. Samuel Peralta has headed up this initiative which stores the work of 30,000 artists from 137 different countries in three lunar probes. These time capsules are designed to last anywhere from five hundred thousand to a million years on the surface of the Moon, so Ally's story will live on amongst the stars.

With any work of historical fiction, you want the details to be accurate, which led me down another path of discovery that was most enjoyable. Now and again, I learned interesting little snippets of information. For example, the phrase *"I'll eat my hat"* refers to when sailors would hide their tobacco in their hat lining. When they ran out of tobacco, they'd chew on the lining of their hats instead. I had to incorporate that into a discussion with Tommy on the ship. I even watched a video on olden-day amputations so I wouldn't embarrass myself by writing something inaccurate. **Jon Townsend's YouTube videos** on 18th-century Colonial life were invaluable in getting my brain in the right headspace for this endeavor. Masterclasses with several prominent authors also helped encourage and inspire me. I have to give a brief nod to Jane Austin, in Ally's story, who lived in Southampton and often walked among the spa gardens with their views across the river. She, of course, is one of my favorite authors.

If you're curious about the kind of foods eaten in the 1770s, I've included the recipe for the pound cake cooked by Mrs. Tinsdale and shared between Ally, Tommy and Sunny.

INGREDIENTS

1 lb sugar (2 cups)

1 lb butter at room temperature.

1 lb flour, sifted with salt (four cups before sifting)

1 dozen eggs

1/4 teaspoon salt

1/4 cup fresh lemon juice

1 tablespoon fresh lemon rind, grated

DIRECTIONS
- Preheat oven 325 degrees Fahrenheit.
- In a mixing bowl, add cream, butter and sugar.

- Add one egg at a time, beating it well.
- Gradually add sifted flour, 1/2 cup at a time, until it is all blended.
- Add lemon juice and lemon rind, and blend.
- Pour into a buttered/floured tube pan.
- Bake 1hr 15mins to 1hr 30mins until a toothpick in center comes out clean.

I hope you felt immersed in the Powhatan camp, as most of these details are factually correct. Yes, they even had a **women's hut**. I did background research into their traditional stories, customs, terms and initiation rights, including **the wedding ceremony**. The age we live in makes it easy to access this information. The various songs I wove into this novel are all actual songs from before that era.

I enjoyed writing Ally's story, a journey from an innocent girl to a woman who could take care of herself, although she needed help at times—and isn't it like that for all of us?

Originally this book had plenty more material that I wanted to include, but once I reached halfway, I realized there'd have to be a sequel. So the lives of Ally, Chebona, Shiloh and Rhett will live on in my next novel, titled *1776: Hearts on Fire*. With what I've learned along the way, it won't take as long to finish.

My hope for you as a reader is that you found yourself lost in the reality of another time and culture. If you did, be sure to leave a review online.

You can find me online at

https://www.instagram.com/fcawdron/

https://www.buymeacoffee.com/fionacawdron/email-newsletter

Fiona Cawdron
Brisbane, Australia

Made in USA - North Chelmsford, MA
1375887_9798386634896
07.10.2023 0950